D1116838

THE LITERARY HERITAGE OF THE ARABS

The

LITERARY
HERITAGE
of the ARABS

AN ANTHOLOGY

Edited by Suheil Bushrui & James M. Malarkey

In collaboration with C. Bayan Bruss

SAQI

First published 2012 by Saqi Books
Copyright © Suheil Bushrui and James Malarkey 2012
ISBN 978-0-86356-824-4

*Every effort was made to obtain the necessary permissions with reference to copyright material.
The publishers apologise if inadvertently any sources remain unacknowledged and will be happy
to correct this in future editions. Due to exorbitant fees for permissions from some publishers, the
editors have regrettably not been able to include some poems from a few celebrated poets.*

*All rights reserved. No part of this book may be reproduced or transmitted in any form or by any
means, electronic or mechanical, including photocopying, recording or by any information storage
and retrieval system, without permission in writing from the publisher.*

*This book is sold subject to the condition that it shall not, by way of trade or otherwise, be lent,
re-sold, hired out, or otherwise circulated without the publisher's prior consent in any form of
binding or cover other than that in which it is published and without a similar condition including
this condition being imposed on the subsequent purchaser.*

A full CIP record for this book is available from the British Library.
A full CIP record for this book is available from the Library of Congress.

Printed and bound by CPI Group (UK) Ltd, Croydon, CR0 4YY

SAQI

26 Westbourne Grove, London W2 5RH
www.saqibooks.com

892.709
L776

For Abdul Rahman Muhammad Moumena
In grateful recollection of his generous support and inspiration1

CONTENTS

INTRODUCTION

The Importance of Arabic Literature

In their Introduction to *The Arab World: Forty Years of Change*, American anthropologists Elizabeth and Robert Fernea remark that "the people of the Middle East still remain as distant from the American public as they were nearly a half a century ago," when the authors underwent their first fieldwork experience in southern Iraq. Nowadays, media and film may convey more images of Arabs, yet, as the Ferneas comment, "The very nearness of the television images, presented without explanation or background, accentuates the differences between 'us' and 'them'; they dress differently, look different, and seem to worship a different god."[1] This was in 1997. Since then, benefiting from increased media resources and the intensification of electronic communication, it is easy to presume that the public is now far better served and informed. In fact, unlike the years prior to 9/11, scarcely a day goes by when the public does not hear in the news terms such as "Arabs, Muslims, Iraqis, and Palestinians", not to mention "Saudis", "Egyptians," "Lebanese," "Jordanians" and "Syrians" and, sometimes, "Gulf Arabs" or "Tunisians," "Libyans" and "Algerians". Far more is also heard about Arab immigrants in Europe and America – most often in terms of problems they pose instead of gifts they bring.

There may now be more press reports and books about the Arab world than ever before, but in spite of this sheer volume, scarcely any of the news speaks well of this region or its people, which, in effect, is mostly known for its turmoil and troubles. Until very recently the content of typical coverage was almost entirely about several unending issues: brutal violence – of which Arabs are either perpetrators or victims; political negotiations – virtually always leading to nowhere; excerpts from speeches by Arab leaders – either taken too seriously or dismissed too readily; or the latest reports on the price of oil and the spread of arms. These patterns served to deepen the contours of an entirely negative image of the Arab: not merely as different, alien, mysterious, much less beguiling (as perceived in earlier times); but now as treacherous, dangerous, incorrigible, and tiresome.[2] The series of political uprisings in 2011, celebrated by some as the "Arab Spring" or the "New Arab Renaissance" has surely raised hopes, even generated as much admiration as fear in the outside world. Yet the net result – at this time of writing – is an image of an Arab world seething

i

with protests and bloodshed, contention and instability, with democracy and prosperity always around the corner and the question of Western interests always inextricably linked.

Thus, there is every reason to suppose that, in spite of the exciting news, the public today possesses no deeper knowledge of Arabs than before; perhaps less. If anything, the general public may have acquired only an illusion of greater insight and understanding due to the continual coverage of volatile events and the crisp summations of our self-assured pundits. Aside from recognizing that serious problems do persist in that part of the world, we are obliged to question how well current media coverage actually can reveal the full complexity of reality. Pertaining to this anthology, how might an acquaintance with Arabic literature help the reader enter the far more nuanced heart of Arab experience and aspiration? Scholars have long known that if students, workers and citizens want to get beyond stereotypes, there are two essential pathways that have been tested and proven over time. Each path involves displacement, receptivity and sustained engagement.

The first way is the oldest: the path of travel, encounter, making acquaintances, seeing the landscapes and taking stock of how people live their lives – including what they live for, what they fear as well as what they want and need. One must inhabit their world with a disinterested frame of mind to comprehend the rationale behind customs and beliefs that may at first appear alien and feel awkward. This path of learning requires continual involvement in daily life as well as assiduous study of language, culture, religion and history. With patience and persistence, the rewards are usually mutual enrichment and friendship as well as improved means for discussing conflicting viewpoints and interests.

Early Muslims had become aware of these benefits of travel as the empire expanded and contact with other cultures increased. Cartographers, geographers and historians such as al-Masudi (known as the "Herodotus of the Arabs") al-Bakri, al-Idrisi, Ibn Batuta and Leo Africanus left vivid and valuable accounts of their journeys from Africa to Asia. By the 17th century Christian and Muslim Arabs were venturing to Europe, preceding, in effect, the stream of travellers who would soon move in the reverse direction as Europe was expanding to the East during the 19th century.[3] Some of these European pioneers of travel writing and ethnography include Richard Burton, Freya Stark, Gertrude Bell, Charles Doughty, T. E. Lawrence, Carleton Coon and Wilfred Thesiger.

The works of these authors still merit re-reading for their infectious curiosity, vivid portrayals and accurate renditions of life and talk during generations past.

They eagerly sought to master the language and to accurately depict the culture. They often expressed respect and admiration for the Arabs, particularly for their physical hardiness, expansive hospitality, nobility of bearing and devotion to honour. Having spent months, if not years, on the ground among Arabs, they were able to skirt stereotypes while conveying the uniqueness of individuals and settings. The convulsive events from the Ottoman Empire through the two World Wars have profoundly reshaped the Middle East and affected how its inhabitants see the world. Yet, the most faithful echo of the many dilemmas, struggles and dislocations of the Arabs over this past century is found in their literature as well as in their private conversations.

Indeed, the second proven path towards understanding the Arabs involves the study of this remarkable literature. Poetry, novels, short stories and plays written in Arabic offer a window, as with other literate civilizations, to what many Arabs across the ages have held to be sacred, admirable, noteworthy or scandalous. Few civilizations have invested the word with as much potency and virtue as have the Arabs. A well-known hadith has it that "underneath the throne of God lie treasures the keys to which are the tongues of poets". According to Abu Tammam "without high virtues by poetry laid down / No glorious deed by man can be achieved". Folk tradition as well warns that "for truly the excellence of man resides in two very small parts: the heart and the tongue."[4] Arabic literature offers glimpses of other times and worlds, occasions for reflection on social change and recognition of the perennial values that permeated the spirit of Arab civilization at its height.

Scholars who pioneered the study of Arabic language in the West fashioned translations of the Holy Qur'an, poetry, philosophy and prose narratives beginning with *The Thousand and One Nights* (commonly known as *The Arabian Nights*) that are still consulted today. Although translation is a particularly demanding art – especially when traversing two unrelated languages – it is through its painstaking artistry that Arabic literature reveals the deepest thoughts, imaginings and longings of a people otherwise remote from the English-speaking world. The range of Arabic works in translation offers incontrovertible proof of the multi-faceted nature of Arab culture, its sheer inventiveness and its unmistakable resonance with universal themes found in many literatures, Eastern and Western. In reading sound translations of Arabic literature, the outsider enters into companionship with those writers from times near and far who will enrich the experience of the reader and elevate the receptive soul. Indeed, it is through this intersubjective process that cracks inevitably appear in the wall between "Us" and "Them". We discover that we can achieve, despite differences of word and sect, a deeper understanding.

Richard Burton, R. A. Nicholson, Arthur J. Arberry, Ameen Rihani and Franz Rosenthal are just a few of that first wave of Western translators who brought Arabic literature into awareness in the English-speaking world. Many others of talent have followed in their footsteps including a generation of Arabs who have mastered the English language. Doubtless the West will come to know the Arabs better if we study these distinguished renditions of Arabic literature. As students familiarize themselves with this literature they quickly come to recognize that beneath the exotic veneer, and across the lines that divide, we share many common values and aspirations. Our awareness that many of these earlier and accurate translations are no longer in print was a factor in prompting us to issue a volume that draws from their best work along with that of more recent scholars who have helped expand the availability of Arabic sources in the West.

Our anthology of Arabic literature reveals a world of thought and feeling largely unseen and unheard in the English-speaking world. We include a wide-ranging selection across virtually all genres of poetry and prose, including works by Christian and Jewish authors who formed an integral part of the culture of the Arab world. These selections will appeal to the student of culture and history as well as to the general reader who seeks acquaintance with gems of Arab thought and expression from classical times to the present.

We hope that readers of this literary heritage will not only come to share our enthusiasm for its noble literature but also come away with an enlarged sense of both the unique genius of Arab civilization and its impact across the ages. And, yes, we confess our additional hope that some curious readers will find themselves initiating personal encounters with Arabs in their own communities and ultimately travelling in these ancient lands to discover for themselves the culture of the Middle East in its current transition. Whichever be the first sally into the extensive reaches of Arab literature we pray that the reader will have a far longer journey, continuously enlightening and invigorating. In the words of Robert Browning: "since Arab lore / Holds the stars' secret – take one trouble more / And master it!"[5]

Principles of Selection with Notes on Translation and Transliteration

The problems of producing an anthology on Arabic literature are those that face an anthologiser of any great literary tradition. To the perennial quandary of what to include and what to omit should be added the matter of available

and effective translations as well as the criterion of introducing what in many cases will be a new culture to a wide audience with the aim to provide, however imperfectly, a taste of the range and depth of the literature in question. We stand by our own choices; yet readers may wish to consult other anthologies which overlap to a degree but differ in scope and emphasis.[6]

Choosing from the extant corpus of belles-lettres in the Arabic language poses problems peculiar to this field including questions of classification concerned with the larger issue of Arab identity and more specifically with Arab lineage, language, history and culture. Anthologisers have not infrequently evaded such issues by taking as their baseline pre-Islamic Arabic poetry and the Qur'an then tracing out the various literatures which these earlier sources have inspired – in the diverse languages of the Islamic world such as Arabic, Persian, Turkish and Urdu. Such an approach certainly underlines the pre-eminence of Arabic as the language of the Islamic revelation. However, by its multiple focus, this delimitation sacrifices not only the distinctive qualities of Arabic culture but also obscures the perspective of growth, flowering, decay and rebirth of one of the world's greatest literatures.

It should be stressed that this anthology is the very first representative sample of *all* Arabic literature, ancient and modern, in English translation. Most of the principal works and authors have been tackled by at least one gifted translator. By this criterion, a number of items in this collection virtually select themselves. Each item was originally translated either because the translator was fascinated by the subject or for ulterior motives. In both cases the interest of the English-speaking world in Arab culture was the most significant factor and it is perhaps true to say that outside Europe no other culture has so fascinated the English mind.

Every item included that has been taken from another source has been reproduced intact (with individual spelling, orthography, etc.) apart from certain academic footnotes that were felt to be unnecessary in this context. We make no apologies for omitting anything that others may deem essential to include – no anthology can claim to be perfect – and the omissions we have made were all carefully considered. Furthermore, the anthology is inspired not by any racial, nationalistic or religious consideration but by the universal spirit and noble values that lie at the heart of Arabic literature and Arab civilization.

Translating Arabic into English is a notoriously difficult exercise with the gulf between the two languages being as wide as the difference between the climates and geographies of the two areas where English and Arabic developed. Some translators have succeeded in conveying the meaning of Arabic texts by neglecting the aspects of form, rhyme and meter; others are academically

worthy at the expense of literary style. Few have combined both merits to produce definitive renderings.

Some Arab writers, especially those who employ highly complex imagery, such as the "Arab Shakespeare", al-Mutanabbi, have clearly been less well served by translators. Nevertheless, there have been a few creditable attempts such as those given here. It is hoped that future attempts will be more successful. The Holy Qur'an itself is, of course, practically untranslatable into any other language. The English reader must at best either content himself with a literary but distorted version, which would be certainly unacceptable to Muslims, or accept a more workman-like effort, which conveys the literal meaning and inner spirit of the original. The translation represented here comes into the latter category, and is acknowledged by Muslims to be one of the most acceptable English versions so far produced.

The variety of translators represented in this anthology necessarily involves a variety of methods and styles yet may perhaps be regarded as a cross-section of the best English versions of Arabic literature currently available. Excellence is still rare in translation but at least we have come a long way from the infantile "imitations" by the Victorian writer J. D. Carlyle and others. Certainly the best results have been obtained by those translators who are not steeped in the culture and the language of the Arabs but express themselves fluently and lyrically in English.

In this anthology, therefore, the aim is not necessarily to select the best translations but to encompass as wide a spectrum as possible, showing the variety of different approaches and styles of translation over a period of some four hundred years from the 17th century to the present day.

Transliteration of Arabic names and terms has yet to be completely standardized and inevitably varies from one individual to another. The translations reproduced here bear witness to this, and one even has 17th century English spelling. However, certain preferences are noticeably prevalent today: "Qur'an" in place of the traditional English spelling of "Koran", for example. Names of Arab writers have been spelt in such a way as to evoke in the reader something close to the actual name in Arabic; this should surely be the criterion for all transliteration. Poems which have no titles in the original are titled by the first line of the poem and listed as such in the Table of Contents.

Finally, it must be emphasized that poetry is the outstanding element of Arab culture, perhaps its national art. Its conventions (as in pre-Islamic times) have continued to be very strict especially with regard to subject matter and sequence and until very recently the rhyme was expected to be the same throughout even the longest poems. This extraordinary fact alone is

an indication of the richness of the language and indeed the Classical Arabic tongue is surely one of the most outstanding and creative of inventions in the early history of the human race. The potential for continual rhyming combined with an exceptionally refined grammar makes it almost impossible to translate without sacrificing some nuances or departing radically from the style of the original. Therefore, we would be remiss not to encourage our readers to, sooner or later, find their way to the original sources in the Arabic language.

To then clarify what we regard as "Arabic Literature", we shall now go on to review its scope, subject matter and major themes in the context of formative historical and cultural developments.

Who are the Arabs?

In the 10th century AD (4th century AH) the prose writer al-Tawhidi, a shrewd judge of character with a keen sense of humour, placed the following remarks into the mouth of Ibn al-Muqaffa in *Kitab al-Imta 'wa'l Mu'anasa* (The Book of Enjoyment and Good Company):

The Arabs did not have a proper condition to follow as a pattern nor a Book to guide them. They are people of a poor land, deserted from mankind; everyone among them, in his loneliness, has need of his thought, his contemplation, and his mind. They knew their livelihood came from the plants of the earth, so they marked each of them and attributed to each its type, and they knew the benefit that was in the fresh plant and the dry plant, and their growth cycles, and which were suitable for sheep and camels. Then they contemplated time and its succession and rendered it as spring, summer, mid-summer and winter. They knew that their drink was from the heavens, so they invented for them constellations. And they were aware of the changing of time, so they made for it divisions of the year. They needed to spread out on the earth, so they made of the heavenly stars guides for the sections of the earth and its regions, and followed the land by means of them. And they made among themselves something which would prevent them from doing evil and which would make them serious of the beautiful, by which they would avoid baseness and which would spur them on to excellent qualities, even to the extent that a member of their nation, though he be in any remote spot of the earth, describes these excellent qualities, not omitting a thing from his description and he is immoderate in the censure of evil acts and condemns them at length. They do not discourse except in

discussion which encourages good deeds, the preservation of the neighbor, the giving away of goods, and the setting up of commendable acts. Every one of them achieves that by his mind and deduces it by his native intelligence and his thought, without learning or becoming well mannered; instead, his natural disposition is well bred and his mind is perceptive. This is why is said they are the most intelligent nation, because of the soundness of natural endowment, correctness of thought, and acuteness of understanding.

Though non-Arabs may be inclined to a less generous appraisal, most will agree that the term "Arab" has acquired such a variety of meanings and connotations that its true definition has become blurred and needs restating.

The Arabs, in common with a number of other ethnic groups, including Hebrews, Babylonians and Phoenicians, trace their lineage back to Noah's son Shem. These groups are therefore collectively known as "Semites". Long before the rise of Islam, Arabia was the name given to the Arabian Peninsula. The people who lived there were called Arabs to distinguish them from Persians, Indians, Turks and Chinese. However, some Arab tribes had already established a foothold in regions beyond the Arabian Peninsula: the Kings of Hira in Iraq, the Ghassanids of Huran (the Syrian Desert) and the Taghlibites in Damascus. The Arabs also had contact with the people of Palmyra and Petra.

The coming to power of the Ummayads saw a period of considerable expansion and conquest (see *Arab History* section below). The hybrid Arabs from outside the Arabian Peninsula assimilated several foreign cultures. However, they assumed superiority over what they termed "A'ajem" (one whose tongue is not Arabic) and married only their own kind, remaining aloof as a ruling class. In the 'Abbasid era, these class-barriers were dismantled; the A'ajem became Arabised and many married into Arab families. Despite the supremacy of the Caliphate and the predominance of Arab culture in all conquered territories, the "Shu'ubyyah" movement gradually gained ground especially among those of non-Arab descent. This movement extolled the influence of non-Arabs on Arab achievement and challenged the presumed superiority of Arab contributions to Islamic civilization.

By the end of the 12th century AD and the demise of the Caliphate in Baghdad, Arab lands had come under the rule of Turkish and Persian families belonging to a variety of Muslim sects. The word "Arab" had now begun to be used only to describe Bedouin tribes of Arab origin. For example, in *The Thousand and One Nights*, published in the 14th century Egyptian edition, the term is used to designate Bedouins who lived by raiding and pillaging.

During the Ottoman period (1517–1918) the Turks enjoyed absolute

ascendancy and for four hundred years the Arabs were treated as second-class citizens in their own homelands. This was followed by a short period of French and British mandates which eventually gave way to independence for several Arab countries. Finally, a League of Arab Nations was born, emphasizing the links that bind all Arabs: geographical proximity, economic and cultural inter-dependence, and a shared culture and history including the unique common heritage aptly summed up by the poet Abu Tammam:

> Blood relationship we may lack,
> But literature is our adopted father.

In recent decades nationalistic feeling has spread in varying degrees throughout the newly emancipated countries and newly formed states. Once again the word "Arab" has acquired a different meaning. It no longer refers only to the Bedu or nomadic tribes of Arab origin living in the desert nor exclusively to their descendants of pure Arab origin. The term today defines anyone who lives in an Arab country, speaks the Arabic language, possesses an Arab culture and shares in the common heritage of the Arab nations. The diverse dimensions of Arab identity today may be divided into three main areas: the Arab intellectual heritage, a modern Western heritage and a heritage of varying social ideologies. In other words, the Arabs of today are of mixed blood, interests and ideas, having evolved and integrated with other peoples and cultures.

Arab History

Long before the remarkable growth of Arabic civilization, Arabia itself had been divided into North and South since the earliest recorded times. The people of the North all led primitive, nomadic lives while their southern counterparts in Arabia Felix (Yemen) enjoyed the same kind of opulence that characterized the ancient Greek and Roman civilizations. The two sharply contrasting parts of the Peninsula were separated by an ill-defined but vast stretch of virgin desert. This colossal gap between them was reflected in their respective languages; unlike the North, where the recognizable precursor of Classical Arabic, the language of the Qur'an, was spoken, the Sabaeans of the South had their own dialect of "Himyarite" which subsequently fell into permanent disuse.

These two parts of Arabia experienced an extraordinary reversal of fortunes in the first millennium AD. While the South experienced a steady decline into disorder and backwardness, eventually capitulating to the Abyssinian invaders

half a century before the birth of the Prophet Muhammad, the primitive Northerners increasingly began to show a profound sensitivity. The selection of pre-Islamic poetry, entitled *Mufaddaliyat*, collected by al-Dabbi after the advent of Islam, bears eloquent testimony to this. From the North emerged the man who was to exert the greatest possible influence not only on Arabs but also on the world at large.

In the 6th and early 7th centuries, Arab society was predominantly tribal, like its Northern European and American counterparts; the heroic ideal was embodied in an oral poetry, the purpose of which was to celebrate the bravery of the clan and its chief. The Arabs call this pre-Islamic period the Jahiliyya, or "days of ignorance"; in Europe, during the so-called Dark Ages, civilization was kept alive by Celtic monks living in monasteries on the north-western extremities of the continent. Slowly, the polytheistic tribes were Christianized. The process can be discerned in Anglo-Saxon literature where the old heroic ideals were progressively adapted and put to Christian use. With the Arabs, the move from polytheism to belief in one God involved a complete metamorphosis, not just a change of address. R. W. Southern has compared Islamic civilization of the late 10th century with that of the West during the same period and concluded that the latter was inferior in terms of both its cultural knowledge and material development. The West was predominantly agrarian, feudal and monastic; the Islamic world was urban, its civilization formed around wealthy courts and linked together by superior lines of communication.[7]

The Prophet Muhammad, of whose early life we know very little indeed, was born around the year 570 AD in Mecca and evidently embarked upon his mission towards the beginning of the 7th century AD. Hitherto his fellow Meccans had practised a very rudimentary form of religion and worshipped a variety of deities. He now enjoined them to worship one God alone, and preached to them from his divine revelations. These are called the "Qur'an" ("recitation" or "discourse"). After twelve years of teaching the word of God in the face of severe contempt and persecution, the Prophet was forced to flee to nearby Medina in 622 AD. Almost immediately the new religion of Islam established itself and within a remarkably short space of time allegiance became widespread. During the decade that followed, which is the first decade of the Islamic calendar, the whole of Arabia was converted to Islam under the inspired and undisputed leadership of the Prophet Muhammad, the "Messenger of God".

The Prophet died in 632 AD at the age of sixty-two and was succeeded by a series of his companions who took the title of Caliph (Khalifah), which means successor. The first of these was Abū Bakr aṣ-Ṣiddīq (632–634 AD), the Prophet's father-in-law, followed by ʿUmar ibn al-Khattāb (634–644 AD),

'Uthmān ibn 'Affān (644–656 AD) and 'Alī ibn Abī Ṭālib (656–661 AD) in turn. The rule of the "Orthodox Caliphate" lasted for twenty-nine years, during which time Persia and Syria were conquered by the Arabs. The new empire, however, was all but torn apart by civil war as both Uthman and Ali were brutally murdered, and the Caliphate passed to the Ummayad family of Damascus in 661 AD. The followers of Ali eventually would initiate a new Islamic "denomination" or sect that become known as Shi'a Islam.

The Ummayad Dynasty (661–750 AD) was distinguished mainly by the achievements of its armies which extended the frontiers of the empire as far as Transoxania and parts of India and Spain. At home there was an increasing tendency to adhere to aristocratic principles; the ruling class paid only lip service to religion and had scant regard for culture. Nevertheless, a number of "sciences" prospered, especially those concerned with elucidation of the Holy Qur'an: theology, history, law and grammar. The growth of free thought was accompanied by restlessness which manifested itself in open dissension and, in 750 AD, the Shi'ite and Persian Muslims joined forces under the leadership of the 'Abbasids to overthrow and all but exterminate the Umayyad.

Thus the great 'Abbasid dynasty (750–1258 AD) was established. It flourished for almost five hundred years, including that splendid period known as the "Golden Age" of Islamic culture. The 'Abbasid capital was built at Baghdad and the prevailing influence in the Muslim world became Persian. Among the early Caliphs of this period was the celebrated Harun al-Rashid from 786 to 809 AD. There was a steady decline after the death of al-Rashid with power becoming increasingly dispersed in the provinces, and the Caliphate acting as little more than a figurehead. However, the Arabs were indisputably involved in shaping a leading empire of the world comprising the whole of Western Asia and North Africa and parts of Europe (Spain, Sicily and Malta) – notably, the fabled Andalusia – while profiting from lucrative trade relations with Islamic countries from Iran through India.

By the middle of the 13th century AD, corruption and decadence had reached such proportions that the Caliphate retained none of its original dignity and power. The 'Abbasids were duly unseated by ruthless hordes of Mongol invaders in 1258 AD. From that time onwards the Arab empire ceased to be a unit of any kind and the age was characterized by successive wars. The chief protagonists were the Mamluks of Egypt and the Mongols who laid waste to almost all of Western Asia. In Spain, however, Arab culture continued to prosper independently for another two centuries. Meanwhile the Crusades (1097–1293 AD), begun as a Christian campaign to wrest back the Holy Land from Muslim occupation, brought the first direct contact between East and

the West though this conflict diminished soon after the Mongol invasion. This calm paved the way for improved East-West relations.

What had been less of an Arab and more of a Muslim empire was now divided into four separate empires, each of which established itself within a few years of the others. The Safavid kingdom of Persia, founded in 1502 AD, was closely followed by the Mogul empire of India in 1525 AD. In Central Asia, the Uzbeks (after centuries of Arab and Mongol rule) became the dominant tribe of their region; in advance of these, the Ottoman Turks had risen to take Constantinople in 1453 AD and went on to establish their ascendancy in Egypt, Syria and Arabia – the very heart of the Arab world. Thereafter Arabic culture became submerged by a tidal wave of Turkish culture to the extent that even the Arabic language was dropped from official use.

The Ottoman Empire lasted for four centuries; a period looked upon by Arabs as a "slough of despond". Its administrators failed to learn the lessons of history and fell into increasingly corrupt and tyrannical ways which largely contributed to their downfall. At the end of the First World War, repercussions were felt by all nations irrespective of their involvement or non-involvement in the hostilities, Ottoman rule was overthrown, and the colonial gap was filled by England and France. The foundations were laid for increased European involvement and influence and ultimately for the emergence of the Arab world of today.[8]

Arabic Literature

There is perhaps no other literature so closely allied to the history of its people as is that of the Arabs. The monotony of nomadic life, the rise of Islam, the Arab conquests, the imperial luxury of early 'Abbasids, the interaction and cross fertilization with other civilizations (notably in Spain), the decline and overthrow of the Caliphate, the period of cultural stagnation, the reactions and inspirations owing to the colonial encounter, and the eventual reawakening of the Arab world to form the vibrant independent states of today – these are all faithfully reflected in Arabic literature, the ups and downs of which parallel the fortunes of the Arabs themselves.

In al-Nadim's *Fihrist*, written in 988 AD, the author catalogues all known books in Arabic on the subjects of philology, history, poetry, theology, law, philosophy, science, magic, foreign religions, fables and alchemy. This remarkable work, in the words of H. A. R. Gibb:

reveals to us how enormous was the output of Arabic literature in the first three centuries of Islam, and how very little has come down to us. Of many authors we possess only small fragments, and the great majority would otherwise have been completely unknown to us even by name.[9]

Comparison could be made here with the corpus of Old English literature dating from the same time as the greatest period of Arab culture and also incomplete. But, as suggested above, the West was culturally inferior to the Muslim world during these centuries and the loss of a part of its literature is not as significant. We would need to turn to the 16[th] and 17[th] centuries of Western literature and contemplate the effect of being without the majority of works produced in the Renaissance in order to appreciate how posterity's careless abandon can result in a more random selection than any anthologist's.

A purist would rightly insist that Arab literature *per se* – that is, in Arabic and by pure-blooded Arabs – is confined to those centuries immediately before and after the Islamic dispensation. From the so-called "Golden Age" onwards, following the astonishingly far-reaching Arab conquests, there were increasing exchanges of influence and intermingling with other cultures. Literary Arabic became obsolescent after the rise of the Ottoman Empire and it was largely owing to the determination of the small core who kept the language alive (especially in Egypt) that Arabic literature enjoyed a powerful renaissance in the late 19[th] century.

The Holy Book of Islam has of course held – and continues to hold – primacy of place in Arabic literature. The Qur'an contains several verses referring to the "Arabic Qur'an" and several branches of Arabic writing stemmed from the need to elucidate it. Even the pre-Islamic qasidas gain their pre-eminence in part due to the philological value they bring to this process, particularly since some Qur'anic suras (chapters), notably the early Meccan ones, are phrased in a similar way to them. Nowhere else, perhaps, is the symbiosis between religion and literature so clear-cut as in the culture of the Arabs. For Westerners accustomed to reading the Bible in a variety of translations, this has proven hard to appreciate, even though the influence of the Jewish and Christian scriptures upon the literatures of Europe is challenged only by Classical models. Hellenic, as well as Persian and Indian influences are also discerned in Arabic works, but these cannot be compared to the Qur'an's role as both exemplar and inspiration.

The most essential point about Arabic literature is that it stems directly from the Holy Qur'an – pre-Islamic poetry notwithstanding. Apart from some 1[st] century AD graffiti (which hardly counts as literature), we have no evidence

of writings in Arabic before the time of the Prophet Muhammad. Illiteracy was widespread and the select few who could read or write learned these arts from teachers outside Arabia. This was, however, no bar to a fundamental appreciation of poetry among the Bedouin nomads. Many individual tribes preserved an oral tradition by the use of rawis, who earned a living purely by memorizing and reciting poetry:

> Among the pre-Islamic Arabs, words in themselves seem to have retained something of their ancient and magical power; the man who, by skilful ordering of vivid imagery in taut, rightly nuanced phrases could play upon the emotions of his hearers, was not merely lauded as an artist but venerated as the protector and guarantor of the honour of the tribe and a potent weapon against its enemies.[10]

The predominant, indeed almost the sole form of poem, was the qasida, a complex type of ode which made constant use of rhyme, the purpose of which was to convey in rich imagery the evocative experience of tribal life. These qasidas were written down in the 8[th] and 9[th] centuries AD; scholars of the time realized the importance of preserving the old poetry both for its own merit as the begetter of the developing poetic tradition and for its inestimable value in shedding light on the language of the Holy Qur'an. Some of the suras – particularly the early Meccan ones – are phrased in a manner not unlike the pre-Islamic qasidas rather than the standard form of high-minded expression in Arabic.

As the earliest examples we have of Arabic poetry – the authenticity of the majority having been conclusively established – these odes are especially remarkable for their refinement, one might almost say "perfection". The themes themselves are simple, desert ones portraying the purely observable. There are no devices such as simile but frequent use of personification and direct association. It is the manner in which these themes are treated and the form in which they appear that reveal a long-established prior tradition:

> The technical complexities of the earliest known poems are so highly developed that one can assume poets had been composing and reciting their verses for several centuries previously. Form and style do not spring forth fully armed without generations or even centuries of growth.[11]

The finest poems of this period appear in collections made after the rise of Islam. Especially worthy of mention are the *Mufaddaliyat* (compiled by the

philologist, al-Mufaddal), the *Hamasa* of Abu Tammam (emulated, if not matched, by the *Hamasa* of his pupil, al-Buhturi), the *Kitab al-Aghani* of 'Abu'l Faraj al-Isfahani, and, above all, the *Mu'allaqat*. The last-named collection is made up of seven exquisite odes by as many poets (though another three are sometimes added to make ten in all). These odes, which constitute the most precious literary heritage of pre-Islamic Arabia, were composed by Imru al-Qais, Tarafa, 'Amr ibn Khultum, Harith, 'Antara, Zuhair and Labid. These poems and others by their contemporaries form the authentic voice of pre-Islamic life or the Jahiliyya (Days of Ignorance).

> In the poetry of the sixth century we hear the Arabic language as it was spoken throughout the length and breadth of Arabia.[12]

In addition to the abundance of poetry, some prose-tales were also passed on through the rawis, but whereas all the poets' names are known, the prose belongs in its entirety to the realm of folk tradition. As such, it is of little interest as literature although as early as the 8th century AD folktales from elsewhere were translated into Arabic and given literary form which greatly enhanced their value in the eyes of the scholars (see below, *Kalila wa Dimna*).

The period immediately preceding the coming of the Prophet Muhammad saw increasing dissatisfaction – particularly among thinking men – with the Bedouin way of life and its attendant superstitions. Small wonder, therefore, that poetry went entirely out of favour when new religious ideals supplanted the inherited values. The practice of writing poetry came virtually to a standstill as converts flocked to the Prophet in their thousands to hear the divine revelation. After his death in 632 AD it became necessary to preserve in written form what had been divinely revealed to the Prophet and which was regarded by believers as the Word of Almighty God. The result was the Holy Qur'an.

The first suras of the Qur'an were collected in 633 AD and these were written down with immense care to ensure that the Divine Word would be reproduced undiluted and unadulterated. Many of them – and more especially the later chapters – must have seemed highly obscure and esoteric to early scholars. Even today, much of the intricate imagery needs detailed explanatory annotation. Several branches of Arabic literature stemmed from the need to elucidate the Qur'an including grammar and lexicography. The Arabic language itself became the sacred language of Islam. The significance of this is hard to appreciate in the predominantly Christian Western world since the Bible is read almost exclusively in modern translation – most impressively in the English rendering known as the King James Version.

Arabic thus became the widespread language it remains to this day (despite the intervening age of depression), its influence moving hand in hand with that of the new religion during the first three centuries of Islam.

The sudden decline of poetry during the Age of the Prophet meant that literary activity was effectively confined to religious writings by the time of his death. Of the very few other works that have come down to us from the period, there is only one poem of any importance: an ode by Ka'b bin Zuhair, son of one of the poets of the *Mu'allaqat*. This is dedicated to the Prophet himself and describes the beginnings of Islam which makes it a valuable historical document. Despite the fact that early Muslims came to view poetry as "irreligious", their descendants drew little distinction between religious and secular matters, literary or otherwise, and looked upon everything as a sacred reflection of the will of God.

During the period of the Orthodox Caliphate (632–661 AD), which saw the first steps towards the foundation of a great new empire extending far beyond the borders of Arabia, literature largely conformed to the habits developed in the last years of the Prophet's life. Activity centred on the writing down of the Holy Qur'an, the authorized recitation of which dated from 646 AD. In the new provinces of Syria and Persia the conquerors and the indigenous population rapidly coalesced and loan words began to creep into Classical Arabic. In Arabia itself the growth of urban communities and the accompanying influx of foreigners brought with it an almost equal threat to the language; but the classicists and philologists waged a determined campaign to counter this trend. Their success was due above all to the publication of the Qur'an as the unimpeachable source of divine teachings, written – as it was revealed – in Arabic.

When the Caliphate passed to the Umayyad of Damascus, the shift of geographical focus brought with it a host of new attitudes and practices – not least in the field of literature. Poetry once again became fashionable and for the first time it was written down as it was being composed. Storytellers and poets thus merged into the new phenomenon of the court poet. Poetry lost its desert flavour (which was almost meaningless to urban dwellers) and was instead tailored to meet the requirements of the court as it had previously been tailored to the needs of the poet's tribe. Poems of rivalry persisted, though these were considerably more sophisticated than those of the pre-Islamic period. The main thrust, however, was directed into panegyrics singing the praises of the Caliph or other such figures and reflecting the growing affluence and imperial splendour of the age. The sweeping aside of the old desert principles nevertheless had its disadvantages and complications as well.

The passions of the Umayyad age were multiple and conflicting, and the poets shared in the general psychological instability and conflict of principles and parties.[13]

There was a tendency to nostalgia among the growing populations in the diaspora but in many ways the new status quo rendered the old ideals irrelevant and untenable.

Still, in literary terms the future lay with those who were not afraid of innovation and the most interesting literary development in this period was the independent love-poem, the ghazal, which was more direct in diction and simpler in theme than the old qasida. The poet Jamil (c. 660–701 AD) is credited with its invention, but it was Umar ibn Abi Rabia (644–719 AD) who brought its simple, conversational style to near-perfection. Among their contemporaries the most important poets were al-Akhtal, a Christian (c. 640–710 AD), and the protagonists in Arabic literature's most celebrated long-standing feud, al-Farazdaq and Jarir (both d. 728 AD).

As for the Arabic tongue, it had (in the eyes of the purists) suffered inevitable adulteration as the area of its use had expanded from the desert to embrace the towns and cities of the great Arab empire and as it came to be spoken by many subject peoples. This kind of purism could be – and was – extended to the discussion of literature. Arabic poetry, it was argued, had been fixed for all time in its pre-Islamic mould; the qasida was the highest form in which it could be composed and pure Bedouin diction alone constituted the language in which it might be expressed. Traditionalism like this may have lost out along with racial snobbery at the passing of the Ummayads but as an attitude of mind it retained its sway in times to come.

It was the succeeding generation, coinciding with the last years of the Ummayads and their overthrow, which saw the first known writing of Arabic prose. The secretary to the last Umayyad Caliphs, Abd al-Hamid al-Katib (d. 750 AD), pioneered the art of letter writing, and his disciple Ibn al-Mucaila (d. 757 AD) produced the first Arabic version, *Kalila and Dimna*. This translation – far more literary than the original Sanskrit fables of Bidpai on which it is based – became the model for all ensuing Arabic prose styles and became known as "al sahl al-mumtani" (a style which is ingeniously simple yet almost impossible to emulate).

The foundations had now been laid for the "Golden Age", which was heralded by the new 'Abbasid rulers from their magnificent capital at Baghdad. After an initial period of adjusting to the change which sent far fewer shockwaves through the empire than had the beginning of the city, whose international

trade had begun to flourish, education became all-important as Muslims grew eager to learn the recently evolved sciences. There was a burgeoning of literature, and Classical Arabic achieved its final stage of development during the two centuries that followed.

Apart from its basic conventionality, the chief characteristics of Arabic poetry were by now radically different from those associated with it in pre-Islamic times; the pagan elements had been almost entirely discarded in favour of more original poetry bearing both Persian and Hellenistic influences. With the important discovery of a cheap way to manufacture paper, prose writing also became solidly established as a literary medium. Meanwhile the development of all aspects of Islam – encouraged if not actively pursued by the 'Abbasid rulers – saw the creation of the two Sahihs (collections of Islamic tradition) known as Hadith (the authenticated accounts of the words and deeds of the Prophet Muhammad), which are second only to the Qur'an in historical importance for Muslims. These were later supplemented by another four Sahihs, to make six in all. The finest and most reliable biography of the Prophet was written at this time by Ibn Ishaq (d. 768 AD) which incorporated verse as well as prose to achieve a strikingly original literary form. It is in the subsequent revision of Ibn Hisham (d. 833 AD), however, that the book has come down to us.

The most popular poetic form of the period was the courtly ghazal – a more refined and artificial version of its Umayyad forerunner – employing dazzlingly virtuosic use of words. Once again its supposed creator, Ibn al-Ahnaf (d. 808 AD), was not a poet of the first order. All poets of the period certainly owed much to the pioneering work of Bashshar ibn Burd (715–783 AD) whose strong individuality set the tone for the verse of the 'Abbasid period. However, expediency and sycophancy began to creep in as poets strove to please their masters and thereby to ensure that their own bellies would continue to be filled:

> The patronage accorded by the 'Abbasid caliphs, viziers, and governors to poets, whom they employed as encomiasts [eulogists], not only made the panegyric [madih] an especially favourite form of poetical composition but led poets to prostitute their art, and resulted in that false glitter and empty bombast often said to be characteristic of Arabic poetry.[14]

The epitome of such excess – yet without doubt one of the greatest of all Arab poets – was Abu Nuwas (c. 747–810 AD), the dissolute boon companion of Hārūn al-Rashīd and a passionate extoller of the twin glories of love and wine.

His dubious philosophy was offset by the pious and deeply felt poetry of his contemporary Aby'l 'Atahiya (748–826 AD), which became the standard for Arabic religious poetry in the centuries that followed.

Another factor that was having a detrimental effect on literature at this time – and on poetry in particular – was the ever-growing ascendancy of philology with its pedantic insistence on convention and formalization. However, this did not prevent the emergence of some of Arabic literature's most outstanding individual writers. Foremost among these was the poet al-Mutanabbi (915–965 AD), a peerless composer of exotic and intricate verse, often referred to as the "Arab Shakespeare". Another very significant figure was Abu'l 'Ala al-Ma'arri (973–1058 AD), a blind poet and sage whose free-thinking verse questions the absolutism of any religious tradition. Al-Hamadhani (969–1008 AD) introduced a completely new form of literature called the maqama (lit. "assembly") in which poetry and prose alternate to achieve a dramatic effect. This form, which is the single most individual feature of Arabic literature, was subsequently perfected by al-Hariri (1054–1122 AD), whose racy muqamat are among the most highly esteemed works in the Arabic language.

Scientific and philosophical writings also flourished under the 'Abbasids and one of the earliest important figures was Zakariya al-Razi (864–925 AD). A century later Ibn Sina (980–1037 AD) – known to the West as "Avicenna" – wrote what became standard works on medicine and philosophy. His contemporary al-Biruni (973–1051 AD) was equally influential in the field of science, especially astronomy. Historical writing was also well served by al-Tabari (839–924 AD) and the more philosophical al-Mas'udi (d. 956 AD).

In the 2nd century of Islam, a movement inclined to mysticism made an unobtrusive appearance. The group of ascetics who brought it into being were called "Sufis" and the earliest known Sufi writer was the poetess Rabia al-'Adawiya (d. 801 AD) from Basra. It was in Persia that the movement flowered and indeed the bulk of Sufi literature came to be written in the Persian language. Its importance to Arabic literature became most apparent in the Renaissance in the late 19th century, the Sufi influence being discernible in many of the finest Arabic writings of that time and even up to the present day.

The later part of the 'Abbasid period is known as the "Silver Age" of Arabic literature and the most notable figure apart from al-Harrir is the great religious and philosophical writer, al-Ghazzali (1059–1111 AD). Despite his controversial propagation of Sufi mysticism as a complement to orthodox theology, he remains the most widely read author of religious writings in Islam. He was particularly severe in his castigation of other philosophers. After his death a leading Andalusian writer, Ibn Rushd (Averroes) (1126–1198 AD), sprang vigorously

to the defence of pure philosophy in direct contradiction to al-Ghazzali. A variety of factors – the sway of non-Arabic speaking rulers uninterested in the patronage of poets and writers in Arabic, the stranglehold of the philologists and legalistic-minded theologians, and the emergence of Persian literature – all combined to serve notice of the termination of Medieval Arabic culture.

By the 11[th] century the focus of cultural activity among Arabs had shifted to Spain where a parallel development had taken place during the "Golden Age" centered on Baghdad. Andalusia (as the Arabs called it) provided a sure strong-hold for the Arab empire in Europe. The Arabs remained masters of most of the Spanish mainland from the Umayyad invasion of 711 AD until their defeat and expulsion in 1492 AD. Despite being regarded with some contempt by their Near Eastern counterparts, the Arabs of Andalusia produced a glorious civilization of their own. It was not until the 11[th] century AD that their unique achievements became fully established; but Andalusian culture influenced European civilization to an extent that has yet to be fully appreciated.

Andalusian poetry is distinguished mainly by its emphasis on the beauties of nature, employing a floral delicacy as opposed to the geometric formality of the East. Two new forms of poetry were introduced by the Andalusians: the zajal and the muwashshah, both strophic verse-forms reminiscent of the ballad. The finest exponent of the latter was Ibn Zaydun (1003–1070 AD) and other leading poets included the "Troubadour", Ibn Quzzman (c. 1090–1095 AD). The rise to power of the latter was greatly instrumental in establishing literature as a central feature of Andalusian culture.

Prose writing also prospered in Andalusia. One of the foremost Arab travel writers, Ibn Jubayr (1145–1217 AD), came from Valencia. The most eminent of all Andalusian literary figures, however, is Ibn Hazm (994–1064 AD), whose *Tawq al-Hamama* (The Dove's Neck-Ring) is a remarkably perceptive account of the psychology of love and lovers. He was also a noted theologian with progressive ideas about the oneness of religion and the unity underlying all religious faith.

While literature continued to find expression in all its forms in Andalusia, the later period was dominated by the mystics Ibn Arabi (1165–1240 AD) and Ibnu'l Farid (1181–1235 AD) as well as (in the century after their deaths) the versatile Ibn al-Khatib (1313–1375 AD). The Mongol invasion of 1258, however, was the beginning of a barren period in the history of Arabic literature. Classical Arabic gave way to a low colloquial form of the language, which diverged to the extent that today the two basic forms of Arabic have very little in common. The Mamluks of Egypt (who made Cairo the capital of the Arab world from the 13[th] century AD onwards) had scarcely more interest in literature than the Mongols

(who nevertheless proceeded to adopt the religion of the vanquished). Indeed only one poet of any significance, al-Busiri (1212–1296 AD), emerged under their ascendancy.

In other parts of the Arab East poetry faded altogether, and historical and geographical writings came to the forefront of literature. Ibn Khallikan (1211–1282 AD) produced one of the finest biographical dictionaries ever compiled. Meanwhile in the Maghrib, the Arab name for the conquered lands to the west in North Africa (from whence derives the term, "Moor"), two further illustrious figures were to appear before the eclipse of Arab domination: Ibn Battuta (1304–1377 AD), a traveller–geographer from Tangiers, and the historiographer Ibn Khaldun (1332–1406 AD) of Tunis. The latter is still regarded as a historian–philosopher of the greatest significance whose approach to history and style of writing remain unique in world literature.

It was approximately at this time that two of the great legendary works of Arabic literature were given their final form. *The Romance of Antar*, probably written by more than one author around the time of the Crusades, is an idealization of the virtues of chivalry and other deeply held Bedouin principles. It has one of the seven poets of the *Mu'allaqat* as its hero – though the depiction appears to be far from accurate – and is the first literary indication in over six centuries of Islam of a yearning for the old desert life. More celebrated still is *The Thousand and One Nights*, which for the vast majority of Europeans represents the sum total of their knowledge of Arabic literature. It first appeared in Arabic by this full title during the Mamluk dynasty in Egypt. Not a singular work of a specific author, it is, rather, the culmination of an evolving collection of highly suspenseful and colourful stories originating from many cultures of the Middle East and South Asia. Woven together through a clever system of embedded literary frames, these tales are spun by the beautiful Scheherazade to entertain the Caliph night after night in hopes of achieving a stay of execution. The humorous turns and fantastical motifs resemble later collections of folk-tales such as *The Decameron* and *The Canterbury Tales*, which at the time, as now, appealed more to common folk and less to common decency. Though *The Thousand and One Nights* are regarded by many Arabs as vulgar and lacking in literary merit, selections continue to be cleansed and abridged to the delight of children who grow up with these kinds of images of the Arab East.

The ascendancy of the Ottomans coincided with a period in which Arabic literature was almost totally lost from view. The Holy Qur'an remained almost the sole official publication in Arabic and business was conducted in Turkish. However, the Turkish language never had the kind of influence exerted by the Arabic language centuries earlier. So when the time came for Arabic literature

and other forms of Arab culture to be resuscitated in the 19th century, long neglect proved no obstacle.

It was Napoleon's invasion of Egypt in 1798 that provided the impetus for the Arab Renaissance. This significant event brought a stultified world suddenly up to date and breathed the air of Western Civilization into the virtual corpse of the Ottoman-dominated Near East. Anti-feudal movements and liberation organisations began to rise up in earnest thereafter as the decrepitude of the Ottoman Empire was laid bare for all to see. One man who was instrumental in encouraging this awareness and urging drastic remedies was Abdul-Rahman al-Kawakibi (1849–1903). Before him was al-Tahtawi, who was the first to be influenced by Western culture. Al-Kawakibi was a fervent Arab nationalist, a fearless denouncer of tyranny and a true champion of orthodox religion. The best example of his writings is his symposium on the destiny of Islam, *Umm al-Qura* (Mother of Communities).

European influence became increasingly evident at this time. It is not surprising that many of the pioneering figures of the literary renaissance came from Lebanon, traditionally the crossroad between East and West. Beirut was the focus of scholarly activity and attempts were made to revive the classical models such as maqama. Perhaps the most telling contribution to the modern movement was that made by Lebanese immigrant (Mahjar) writers in America, especially for the new ground they broke in the art of the prose poem and the essay. The three main figures, who also wrote significant works in English, were Christians with a strong disposition towards reconciliation with Islam: Gibran Kahlil Gibran (1883–1931), Ameen Rihani (1876–1940) and Mikhail Naimy (1889–1988). These three have continued to exercise a powerful influence on Arab writers up to the present day.

In the Muslim world, the Renaissance first flowered in Egypt, which produced a poet and dramatist in Ahmad Shawqi (1868–1932). As a poet he was matched – possibly even bettered – by his contemporaries Hafiz Ibrahim (1871–1932) and Khalil Mutran (1872–1949). Early attempts at the novel in Arabic were made by Jirji Zaidan (1861–1914) and this form has since found an outstanding exponent in Naguib Mahfouz (1911–2006). Special types of novel-writing have also been introduced to Arabic literature during the 20th century, the most important and original of these being *al-Ayyam* (The Days), an autobiographical novel written in 1926 by Taha Hussein (1889–1973). Prose drama meanwhile developed in the hands of Tewfiq al-Hakim (1898–1986) and the Arabic short story – especially that with a comic flavor – was successfully introduced by Mahmud Taymur (1894–1974).

Since the Second World War a number of different literary movements have

sprung up all over the Arab world as well as among the diaspora communities of both South and North America and other parts of the world. No longer can Arabic literature be considered homogenous as it was in the centuries following the Islamic dispensation; nor has it the "borrowed" flavour of the period following the Arab conquests up to the present. Rather, it is the sum of the national literatures of the various Arab countries, all of which have their own distinctive characteristics. Nevertheless, there is an awareness of common identity among Arabs and nowhere is this more strongly reflected than in their poetry.

One of the recent trends has been towards the development of free verse led by the Iraqi poets Badr Shakr al-Sayyab, Abd al-Wahhab al-Bayati and Nazik al-Malaika. Some of the Palestinian poets such as Mahmud Darwish have produced verse that powerfully expresses the anguish of homelessness. The European influence, meanwhile, continues; the works of Garcia Lorca, Sartre and T. S. Eliot (especially *The Wasteland*) find many an echo in post-war Arab literature. The spectacular blossoming of Arab women writers during this period, such as Salma al-Jayyusi, May Rihani and Fudwa Tuqan, have opened new vistas of expression and insight. The Left is also increasingly finding a voice causing the dividing line between literature and political writing to become more and more blurred. Despite this, the result is far from negative, for the poetry and prose of today's Arab world is as strong and vibrant as it was in the Golden Age.[15]

Indeed, at this very moment, nearly unparalleled in ferment and experimentation, we anticipate that literary developments ahead will become more diverse in form, more global in influence and more open to interpretation.

NOTES

1. Elizabeth and Robert Fernea, *The Arab World: Forty Years of Change*, Garden City, New York, Anchor Books, 1997.

2. See Norman Daniel, *Islam and the West: The Making of an Image*, Oxford, One World Press, 1997 (1960); Jack Shaheen, *The Reel Bad Arabs: How Hollywood Vilifies a People*, New York, Olive Branch Press, 2001; Mohamed Nimer, *Islamophobia and anti-Americanism: causes and remedies*, Beltsville, Maryland, Amana publications, 2007; and Peter Gottschalk and Gabriel Greenberg, *Islamophobia: Making Muslims the Enemy*, New York, Rowman & Littlefield, 2008.

3. See, for example, Ross Dunn, *The Adventures of Ibn Batuta*, Berkeley, University of California Press, 1986; Paul Lunde and Caroline Stone, *Meadows of Gold: the Abbasids by Mas'udi*, New York, Kegan Paul, 1989; Dale F. Eickelman and James Piscatori, *Muslim Travellers: Pilgrimmage, Migration, and the Religious Imagination*, Berkeley, University of California Press, 1990; Nazik Saba Yared, *Arab Travellers & Western Civilization*, London, Saqi Books, 2nd edition, 2010; and Nabil Matar, *In the Lands of the Christians: Arabic Travel Writing in the 17th Century*, London, Routledge, 2002.

4. Suheil Bushrui, *The Wisdom of the Arabs*, Oxford, Oneworld Publications, 2002.

5. Robert Browning, *Sordello*, London, J. M. Dent and Company, 1902.

6. Other anthologies differ by exclusive emphasis on classical or modern Arabic literature, on either poetry or drama, or on women writers, e.g.: Khuri, Monah and Hamid Algar, *An Anthology of Modern Arabic Poetry*, Berkeley, University of California Press, 1984; Mahmoud Manzalaoui, *Arabic Writing Today; The Drama*, Cairo, ARCE, 1977; Salma Khadra Jayyusi and Roger Allen, *Modern Arabic Drama: An Anthology*, Bloomington, Indiana University Press, 1995; Salma Khadra Jayyusi, *Short Arabic Plays: An Anthology*, Northampton, Interlink Books, 2003; Robert Irwin, *The Penguin Anthology of Classical Arabic Literature*, London, Penguin Books, 2006; Kamal Boullata, *Women of the Fertile Crescent: Modern Poetry by Arab Women*, Boulder, Lynne Rienner, 1994; Arthur J. Arberry, *Modern Arabic Poetry: An Anthology with English Verse Translations*, Cambridge, Cambridge University Press, 1967 [original edition, 1950]; Abdallah al-Udhari, *Modern Poetry of the Arab World*, Harmondsworth, UK, Penguin Books, 1986; John Asfour, *When the Words Burn: An Anthology of Modern Arabic Poetry 1945–1987*, Dunvegan, Ontario, Cormorant Books, original edition 1988, revised edition 1992; Desmond O'Grady, *Ten Modern Arab Poets: Selected Version*, Dublin, Dedalus Press, 1992; Nathalie Handal, *The Poetry of Arab Women: A Contemporary Anthology*, Northampton, MA, Interlink Books, 2001; Denys Johnson-Davies, *The Anchor Book of Modern Arabic Fiction*, New York, Anchor Books, 2nd edition, 2006; Paul Starkey, *Modern Arabic Literature*, Washington DC, Georgetown University Press, 2006; David Tresilian, *A Brief Introduction to Modern Arabic Literature*, London, Saqi Books, 2008; *Cambridge Modern Arabic Literature*, edited by M. M. Badawi, Cambridge, Cambridge University Press, 2006. Wider in scope are various anthologies spanning the Islamic world (e.g., R. A. Nicholson, *Translations of Eastern Poetry and Prose*, Cambridge, Cambridge University Press, 1922; James Kritzeck, *Anthology of Islamic Literature*, New York, Pelican Books, 1984. However, of necessity these anthologies leave out many important Arabic works including those of Christian and Jewish Arabs. Two other collections may be mentioned that are similar to ours in scope: Pierre Cachia, *Arabic Literature – An Overview (Culture and Civilisation in the Middle East)*, New York, Routledge Curzon, 2002 and Robert Irwin, *Night and Horses and the Desert: An Anthology of Classical Arabic Literature*, Woodstock, New York, Overlook Press, 2000. Despite inevitable overlap, the above works differ considerably

from the present collection concerning the choice of material and the quality of the translations.

7. R. W. Southern, *Western Views of Islam in the Middle Ages*, Cambridge, MA, Harvard University Press, 1962, chapter 1.

8. For much greater historical depth and detail the reader should turn to Albert Hourani, *A History of the Arab Peoples*, Cambridge, MA, Harvard University Press, 1991.

9. H.A.R. Gibb, *Arabic Literature*, Oxford, Oxford University Press, 1963, pp. 87–88.

10. H.A.R. Gibb, *Arabic Literature*, Oxford, Oxford University Press, 1926, reprinted in 1974, p. 29.

11. Omar Pound, *Arabic and Persian Poems*, Cambridge, Fulcrum Press, 1970, p. 11.

12. R. A. Nicholson, *The Literary History of the Arabs*, Cambridge, Cambridge University Press, 1930, reprinted in 1979, p. xxii.

13. H.A.R. Gibb, *op.cit*, p. 43.

14. Phillip K. Hitti, *History of the Arabs*, London, Macmillan, 1937, reprinted in 1970, p. 407.

15. For a more in depth survey of the history of Arabic literature, see: Roger Allen, *An Introduction to Arabic Literature*, Cambridge, Cambridge University Press, 2000.

Part I

THE PRE-ISLAMIC PERIOD
(Jahiliyya)

The Mu'allaqat

Stay!—let us weep at the remembrance of our beloved, *at the sight of* the station *where her tent was* raised, by the edge of yon bending sands between Dahul and Haumel,

"Tudam and Mikra; a *station*, the marks of which are not wholly effaced, though the south wind and the north have woven the twisted sand."

Thus I spoke, when my companions stopped their coursers by my side, and said: "Perish not through dispair: only be patient."

"A profusion of tears," *answered I,* "is my sole relief; but what avails it to shed them over the remains of a deserted mansion?"

"Thy condition," *they replied,* "is not more painful than when thou leftest Howaira, before thy present passion, and her neighbor Rebaba *on the hills of Masel.*"

"*Yes,*" *I rejoined,* "when those two damsels departed, musk was diffused from their robes, as the eastern gale sheds the scent of the clove-gillyflowers:

"Then gushed the tears from my eyes, through excess of regret, and flowed down my neck, till my sword-belt was drenched in the stream."

"Yet hast thou passed many days in sweet converse with the fair: but none so sweet as the day which thou spentest by *the pool of* Daratjuljul."

On that day I killed my camel, to give the virgins a feast; and, oh how strange was it that they should carry his trappings and furniture!

The damsels continued till evening helping one another to the roasted flesh, and to the delicate fat, like the fringe of white silk finely woven.

On that happy day I entered the carriage, the carriage of Onaiza, who said: "Wo to thee! Thou wilt compel me to travel on foot."

She added (while the vehicle was bent aside with our weight), "O Amriolkais, descend, or my beast also will be killed!"

I answered: "Proceed, and loosen his rein; nor withhold from me the fruits of thy love, which again and again may be tasted with rapture.

"Many a fair one like thee—though not, *like thee*, a virgin—have I visited by night; and many a lovely mother have I diverted from the care of her yearling infant, adorned with amulets:

"When the suckling behind her cried, she turned round to him with half her body; but half of it, pressed beneath my embrace, was not turned from me."

Delightful, too, was the day when Fatima first rejected me on the summit of yon sand-hill, and took an oath, which she declared inviolable.

"O Fatima!" said I, "away with so much coyness; and if thou hadst resolved to abandon me, yet at last relent!

"If indeed my disposition and manners are unpleasing to thee, rend at once the mantle of my heart, that it may be detached from thy love.

"Art thou so haughty, because my passion for thee destroys me; and because whatever thou commandest my heart performs?

"*Thou weepest;* yet thy tears flow merely to wound my heart with the shafts of thine eyes—my heart, already broken to pieces and agonizing."

Besides thee, with many a spotless virgin, whose tent had not yet been frequented, have I held soft dalliance at perfect leisure.

To visit one of them, I passed the guards of her bower, and a hostile tribe, who would have been eager to proclaim my death.

It was the hour when the Pleiads appeared in the firmament, like the folds of a silken sash variously decked with gems.

I approached: she stood *expecting me* by the curtain; and, *as if she was preparing* for sleep, had put off all her vesture but her night-dress.

She said: "By Him who created me," and gave me her lovely hand, "I am unable to refuse thee; for I perceive that the blindness of thy passion is not to be removed."

Then I rose with her; and as we walked she drew over our footsteps the train of her pictured robe.

Soon as we had passed the habitations of her tribe, and come to the bosom of the vale, surrounded with hillocks of spiry sand,

I gently drew her towards me by her curled locks, and she softly inclined to my embrace; – her waist was gracefully slender, but sweetly swelled the part encircled with ornaments of gold.

Delicate was her shape; fair her skin; and her body well proportioned: her bosom was as smooth as a mirror,

Or, like the pure egg of an ostrich, of a yellowish tint blended with white, and nourished by a stream of wholesome water not yet disturbed.

She turned aside, and displayed her soft cheek: she gave a timid glance with languishing eyes, like those of a roe in *the groves of* Wegera looking tenderly at her young.

Her neck was like that of a milk-white hind, but, when she raised it, exceeded not the justest symmetry; nor was the neck of my beloved so unadorned.

Her long coal-black hair decorated her back, thick and diffused, like bunches of dates clustering on the palm-tree.

Her locks were elegantly turned above her head; and the riband which bound them was lost in her tresses, part braided, part disheveled.

She discovered a waist taper as a well-twisted cord; and a leg both as white and as smooth as the stem of a young palm, or a fresh reed, bending over the rivulet.

When she sleeps at noon, her bed is besprinkled with musk: she puts on her robe of undress, but leaves the apron *to her handmaids*.

She dispenses gifts with small, delicate fingers, sweetly glowing at their tips, like the white and crimson worm of Dabia, or dentrifices made of esel-wood.

The brightness of her face illumines the veil of night, like the evening taper of a recluse hermit.

Or a girl like her, a girl of a moderate height, between those who wear a frock and those who wear a gown, the most bashful man must look with an enamoured eye.

The blind passions of men for common objects of affection are soon dispersed; but from the love of thee my heart cannot be released.

O how oft have I rejected the admonitions of a morose adviser, vehement in censuring my passion for thee; nor have I been moved by his reproaches!

Often has the night drawn her skirts around me, like the billows of the ocean, to make trial of my fortitude in a variety of cares;

And I said to her, when she seemed to extend her sides, to drag on her unwieldy length, and to advance slowly with her breast:

"Dispel thy gloom, O tedious night! That the morn may rise; although my sorrows are such, that the morning-light will not give more comfort than thy shades.

"O hideous night! – a night in which the stars are prevented from rising, as if they were bound to a solid cliff with strong cables!"

Often, too, have I risen at early dawn, while the birds were yet in their nests, and mounted a hunter with smooth short hair, of a full height, and so fleet as to make captive the beasts of the forest;

Ready in turning, quick in pursuing, bold in advancing, firm in backing; and performing the whole with the strength and swiftness of a vast rock which a torrent has pushed from its lofty base;

A bright bay steed, from whose polished back the trappings slide, as drops of rain glide hastily down the slippery marble.

Even in his weakest state he seems to boil while he runs; and the sound which he makes in his rage is like that of a bubbling cauldron.

When other horses that swim through the air are languid and kick the dust, he rushes on like a flood, and strikes the hard earth with a firm hoof.

He makes the light youth slide from his seat, and violently shakes the skirts of a heavier and more stubborn rider;

Rapid as the pierced wood in the hands of a playful child, which he whirls quickly round with a well-fastened cord.

He has the loins of an antelope, and the thighs of an ostrich; he trots like a wolf, and gallops like a young fox.

Firm are his haunches; and when his hinder parts are turned towards you, he fills the space between his legs with a long thick tail, which touches not the ground and inclines not to either side.

His back, when he stands in his stall, resembles the smooth stone on which perfumes are mixed for a bride, or the seeds of coloquintenda are bruised.

The blood of the swift game, which remains on his neck, is like the crimson juice of hinna on gray flowing locks.

He bears us speedily to a herd of wild cattle, in which the heifers are fair as the virgins in black trailing robes, who dance round *the idol* Dewaar:

They turn their backs, and appear like the variegated shells of Yemen on the neck of a youth distinguished in his tribe for a multitude of noble kinsmen.

He soon brings us up to the foremost of the beasts, and leaves the rest far behind; nor has the herd time to disperse itself.

He runs from wild bulls to wild heifers, and overpowers them in a single heat, without being bathed, or even moistened with sweat.

Then the busy cook dresses the game, roasting part, baking part on hot stones, and quickly boiling the rest in a vessel of iron.

In the evening we depart; and when the beholder's eye ascends to the head of my hunter, and then descends to his feet, it is unable at once to take in all his beauties.

His trappings and girths are still upon him: he stands erect before me, not yet loosed for pasture.

O friend, seest thou the lightning, whose flashes resemble the quick glance of two hands, amid clouds raised above clouds?

The fire of it gleams like the lamps of a hermit, when the oil poured on them shakes the cord by which they are suspended.

I sit gazing at it, while my companions stand between Daaridge and Odhaib; but far distant is the cloud on which my eyes are fixed.

Its right side seems to pour its rain on *the hills of* Katan, and its left on the *mountains of* Sitaar and Yadbul.

It continues to discharge its waters over Cotaifa till the rushing torrent lays prostrate the groves of canahbel-trees.

It passes over *mount* Kenaan, which it deluges in its course, and forces the wild goats to descend from every cliff.

On *mount* Taima it leaves not one trunk of a palm tree, nor a single edifice, which is not built with well-cemented stone.

Mount Tebeir stands in the heights of the flood, like a venerable chief wrapped in a striped mantle.

The summit of Mogaimir, covered with the rubbish which the torrent has rolled down, looks in the morning like the top of a spindle encircled with wool.

The cloud unloads its freight on the desert of Ghabeit, like a merchant of Yemen alighting with his bales of rich apparel.

The small birds of the valley warble at day break, as if they had taken their early draught of generous wine mixed with spice.

The beasts of the wood, drowned in the floods of night, float, like roots of wild onions, at the distant edge of the lake.

Translated by Sir William Jones[1]

ODE OF LABID

Gone are they the lost camps, light flittings, long sojournings in Miná, in Gháula, Rijám left how desolate.

Lost are they. Rayyán lies lorn with its white torrent beds, scored in lines like writings left by the flood water.

Tent-floors smooth, forsaken, bare of all that dwelt in them, years how long, the war-months, months too of peace-pleasures.

Spots made sweet with Spring-rains fresh-spilled from the Zodiac, showers from clouds down-shaken, wind-wracks and thunder-clouds;

Clouds how wild of night-time, clouds of the dawn darkening, clouds of the red sunset, – all speak the name of her.

Here, in green thorn-thickets, does bring forth how fearlessly; here the ostrich-troops come, here too the antelopes.

Wild cows, with their wild calf-sucklings, standing over them, while their weanlings wander wide in the bare valleys.

Clean-swept lie their hearth-stones, white as a new manuscript writ with texts fresh-graven, penned by the cataracts,

Scored with lines and circles, limned with rings and blazonings, as one paints a maid's cheek point-lined in indigo.

All amazed I stood there. How should I make questionings? Dumb the rocks around me, silent the precipice.

Voices lost, where these dwelt who at dawn abandoning tent and thorn-bush fencing fled to the wilderness.

Now thy sad heart acheth, grieveth loud remembering girls how closely howdahed, awned with what canopies.

Every howdah curtained, lined with gauze embroideries, figured with festoons hung red from the pole of it.

Trooped they there the maid-folk, wild white cows of Túdiha, ay, or does of Wújra, long-necked, or their fawns with them,

Fled as the mirage flees, fills the vale of Bíshata, fills the tree-clad wádies, íthel and rock-mazes.

What of her, Nowára, thy lost love, who fled from thee, every heart-link
 sundered, close loop and free fetter!
Hers the Mórra camp-fires lit how far in Fáïda, in Hejáz what marches! How
 shalt thou win to her?
Eastward move they marching, to Muhájjer wandering camped in Tái, in
 Férda, ay in Rukhám of it.

Southward on to Yémen, to Sowéyk their sojournings, to Wahéf el Kahri, ay,
 and Tilkhám of it.
Man, have done! Forget her, – one too far to comfort thee! Who would his
 love garner first let him sunder it.
Shed the love that fails thee. Strong be thou, and break with her. Keep thy
 gifts for friendship, freed from thy wilderment.
Mount thee on thy nága. Travel-trained and hard she is, low her back with
 leanness, lessened with hump of her;
Shrunk her sides and wasted, jaded with long journeyings, spare as her hide
 shoe-straps frayed by her road-faring.
Light she to her halter, to thy hand that guideth her, as a red cloud
 southwards loosed from its rain-burden.
Nay a fair wild-ass she; at her side the white-flanked one, he the scarred ass-
 stallion, bitten and struck for her.
Climbed they two the hill-top, he the bite-scarred ass-tyrant her new mood
 resenting, being in foal to him.
On the crags high posted watched he from Thálabut all the plain to guard
 her, ambushes laid for her.
Six months of Jumáda wandered have they waterless, browsing the moist
 herbage, he her high sentinel.
Till returned their thirsting, need of the far water clefts, all their will to win
 there speeding them waterwards.
What though with heels wounded, still the hot wind driveth them, as a
 furnace burning, fire-scorched the breath of it.
In their trail a dust-cloud, like a smoke it wavereth, like a fire new-lighted,
 kindling the flame of it,
Flame fanned by the North-wind, green wood mixed with dry fuel, smoke
 aloft high curling. So is the dust of them.
He, when her pace slackened, pushed her still in front of him. Nay, she might
 not falter, tyrant he urged her on,
Till they reached the streamlet, plunged and slaked their thirst in it, a spring
 welling over, crest-high the reeds of it;

All its banks a cane-brake, thick with stems o'ershadowing; bent are some,
 some standing, night-deep the shade of them.

Say is this her likeness? Or a wild cow wolf-raided of her sweet calf loitering,
 she is the van of them.
She, the short-nosed, missed it. Lows she now unendingly, roams the rocks,
 the sand-drifts, mourning and bellowing,
Lows in rage beholding that white shape, the limbs of it, dragged by the grey
 wolf-cubs, – who shall their hunger stay?
Theirs the chance to seize it, hers the short forgetfulness. Death is no mean
 archer. Mark how his arrows hit.
Stopped she then at night-fall, while the rain in long furrows scored the bush-
 grown hill-slopes, ceaseless the drip of it,
Dripped on her dark back-line, poured abroad abundantly: not a star the
 heaven showed, cloud-hung the pall of it;
One tree all her shelter, standing broad-branched, separate at the sand-hills'
 edge-line, steep-set the sides of them.
She, the white cow, shone there through the dark night luminous, like a pearl
 of deep-seas, freed from the string of it.
Thus till morn, till day-dawn folded back night's canopy; then she fled
 bewildered, sliding the feet of her,
Fled through the rain lakelets, to the pool of Suwáyada, all a seven nights'
 fasting twinned with the days of them,
Till despaired she wholly, till her udder milk-stricken shrank, so full to feed
 him suckling or weaning him.
Voices now she hears near, human tones, they startle her, though to her eye
 naught is: Man! He, the bane of her!
Seeketh a safe issue, the forenoon through listening, now in front, behind
 now, fearing her enemy.
And they failed, the archers. Loosed they then to deal with her fine-trained
 hounds, the lop-eared, slender the sides of them.
These outran her lightly. Turned she swift her horns on them, like twin spears
 of Sámhar, sharp-set the points of them.
Well she knew her danger, knew if her fence failed with them hers must be the
 red death. Hence her wrath's strategy.
And she slew Kasábi, foremost hound of all of them, stretched the brach in
 blood there, ay, and Sukhám of them.
Thus is she, my nága. When at noon the plains quiver and the hills dance sun-
 steeped, cloaked in the heat-tremors,

Ride I and my deeds do, nor forbear from wantoning, lest the fools should
 shame me, blame me the fault-finders.

Do not thou misprize me, thou Nowára. One am I binder of all love-knots,
 ay, and love's surrender;
One who when love fails him, wails not long but flies from it; one whom one
 alone holds, hard death the hinderer.
What dost thou of mirth know, glorious nights, ah, how many—cold nor
 heat might mar them—spent in good company?
Came I thus discoursing to his sign, the wine-seller's drank at the flag-
 hoisting, drank till the wine grew dear,
Bidding up each full skin, – black with age the brand of it, pouring forth the
 tarred jars, breaking the seals of them;
Pure deep draughts of morning, while she played, the sweet singer fingering
 the lute-strings, showing her skill to me.
Ere the cock had crowed once, a first cup was quaffed by me: ere slow man
 had stretched him, gone was the second cup.
On what dawns sharp-winded clothed have I the cold with it, dawns that held
 the North-wind reined in the hands of them.
Well have I my tribe served, brought them aid and armament, slept, my mare's
 reins round me, night-long their sentinel;
Ridden forth at day-dawn, climbed the high-heaped sand-ridges hard by the
 foe's marches, dun-red the slopes of them;
Watched till the red sun dipped hand-like in obscurity, till the night lay
 curtained, shrouding our weaknesses;
And I came down riding, my mare's neck held loftily as a palm fruit-laden, –
 woe to the gatherer!
Swift was she, an ostrich; galloped she how wrathfully, from her sides the
 sweat streamed, lightening the ribs of her;
Strained on her saddle; dripped with wet the neck of her, the white foam-
 flakes wreathing, edging the girth of her;
Thrusteth her neck forward, shaketh her reins galloping; flieth as the doves fly
 bound for the water-springs.

At the King's Court strangers thronged from what far provinces, each athirst
 for bounty, fearing indignity.
Stiff-necked they as lions in their hate, the pride of them, came with stubborn
 proud feet, Jinns of the wilderness.

Stopped I their vain boastings, took no ill-tongued words from them, let
 them not take licence. What were their chiefs to me?

I was provided camels for their slaughtering, I who their shares portioned,
 drawing the lots for them.

Every mouth I feasted. Barren mount and milch-camel slew I for all daily. All
 shared the meat of them.

Far guest and near neighbour, every man rose satisfied, full as in Tebála, fed as
 in green valleys.

Ay, the poor my tent filled, thin poor souls like sick-camels, nágas at a tomb
 tied, bare-backed, no shirt on them.

Loud the winter winds howled; piled we high the meat-dishes; flowed the
 streams of fatness, feeding the fatherless.

Thus the tribes were trysted; nor failed we the provident to name one, a wise
 man, fair-tongued, as judge for them,

One who the spoil portioned, gave to each his just measure, spake to all
 unfearing, gave or refused to give,

A just judge, a tribe-sheykh, wise, fair-worded, bountiful, sweet of face to all
 men, feared by the warriors.

Noble we; our fathers wielded power bequeathed to them, dealt law to the
 nations, each tribe its lawgiver.

All our lineage faultless, no light words our promises; not for us the vain
 thoughts, passions of common men.

Thou fool foe, take warning, whatso the Lord portioneth hold it a gift
 granted, dealt thee in equity.

Loyalty our gift was, faith unstained our heritage; these fair things He gave us,
 He the distributor.

For for us a mansion built He, brave the height of it lodged therein our old
 men, ay, and the youths of us,

All that bore our burdens, all in our tribe's sore sorrow, all that were our
 horsemen, all our high councillors.

Like the Spring are these men, joy to them that wait on them, to the weak, the
 widows, towers in adversity.

Thus our kin stands faith-firm, purged of tribe-malingerers. Woe be to all false
 friends! Woe to the envious!

Translated by Lady Anne Blunt and Wilfried S. Blunt[2]

Ka'b Bin Zuhair

SU'ÁD IS GONE

Su'ád is gone, and to-day my heart is love-sick, in thrall to her, unrequited,
 bound with chains;

And Su'ád, when she came forth on the morn of departure, was but as a
 gazelle with bright black downcast eyes.

When she smiles, she lays bare a shining row of side-teeth that seems to have
 been bathed once and twice in (fragrant) wine—

Wine mixed with pure cold water from a pebbly hollow where the north-
 wind blows, in a bend of the valley,

From which the winds drive away every speck of dust, and it brims over with
 white-foamed torrents fed by showers gushing from a cloud of morn.

Oh, what a rare mistress were she, if only she were true to her promise and
 would hearken to good advice!

But hers is a love in whose blood are mingled paining and lying and
 faithlessness and inconstancy.

She is not stable in her affection—even as ghouls change the hues of their
 garments—

And she does not hold to her plighted word otherwise than as sieves hold
 water.

The promises of 'Urkúb were a parable of her, and his promises were naught
 but vanity.

I hope and expect that women will ever be ready to keep their word; but
 never, methinks, are they ready.

Let not the wishes she inspired and the promises she made beguile thee: lo,
 these wishes and dreams are a delusion.

In the evening Su'ád came to a land whither none is brought save by camels
 that are excellent and noble and fleet.

To bring him there, he wants a stout she-camel which, though fatigued, loses
 not her wonted speed and pace;

One that largely bedews the bone behind her ear when she sweats, one that
 sets herself to cross a trackless unknown wilderness;

Scanning the high grounds with eyes keen as those of a solitary white oryx,
 when stony levels and sand-hills are kindled (by the sun);

Big in the neck, fleshy in the hock, surpassing in her make the other daughters
 of the sire;

Thick-necked, full-cheeked, robust, male-like, her flanks wide, her front (tall) as a milestone;

Whose tortoise-shell skin is not pierced at last even by a lean (hungry) tick on the outside of her back;

A hardy beast whose brother is her sire by a noble dam, and her sire's brother is her dam's brother; a long-necked one and nimble.

The *kurád* crawls over her: then her smooth breast and flanks cause it to slip off.

Onager-like is she; her side slabbed with firm flesh, her elbow-joint far removed from the ribs;

Her nose aquiline; in her generous ears are signs of breeding plain for the expert to see, and in her cheeks smoothness.

Her muzzle juts out from her eyes and throat, as though it were a pick-axe.

She lets a tail like a leafless palm-branch with small tufts of hair hang down over a sharp-edged (unrounded) udder from which its teats do not take away (milk) little by little.

Though she be not trying, she races along on light slender feet that skim the ground as they fall,

With tawny hock-tendons—feet that leave the gravel scattered and are not shod so that they should be kept safe from blackness of the heaped stones.

The swift movement of her forelegs, when she sweats and the mirage enfolds the hills—

On a day when the chameleon basks in some high spot until its exposed part is baked as in fire,

And, the grey cicalas having begun to hop on the gravel, the camel-driver bids his companions take the siesta—

Resembles the beating of hand on hand by a bereaved grey-haired woman who rises to lament and is answered by those who have lost many a child,

One wailing shrilly, her arms weak, who had no understanding when news was brought of the death of her unwedded son:

She tears her breast with her hands, while her tunic is rent in pieces from her collar-bones.

The fools walk on both sides of my camel, saying, "Verily, O grandson of Abú Sulmá, thou art as good as slain";

And every friend of whom I was hopeful said, "I will not help thee out: I am too busy to mind thee."

I said, "Let me go my way, may ye have no father! For whatever the Merciful hath decreed shall be done.

Every son of woman, long though his safety be, one day is borne upon a gibbous bier."

I was told that the Messenger of Allah threatened me (with death), but with
 the Messenger of Allah I have hope of finding pardon.

Gently! Mayst thou be guided by Him who gave thee the gift of the Qur'an,
 wherein are warnings and a plain setting-out (of the matter).

Do not punish me, when I have not sinned, on account of what is said by the
 informers, even should the (false) sayings about me be many.

Ay, I stand in such a place that if an elephant stood there, seeing (what I see)
 and hearing what I hear,

The sides of his neck would be shaken with terror—if there be no forgiveness
 from the Messenger of Allah.

I did not cease to cross the desert, plunging betimes into the darkness when
 the mantle of Night is fallen,

Till I laid my right hand, not to withdraw it, in the hand of the avenger whose
 word is the word of truth.

For indeed he is more feared by me when I speak to him—and they told me I
 should be asked of my lineage—

Than a lion of a jungle, one whose lair is amidst dense thickets in the lowland
 of 'Aththar;

He goes in the morning to feed two cubs, whose victual is human flesh rolled
 in the dust and torn to pieces;

When he springs on his adversary, 'tis against his law that he should leave the
 adversary ere he is broken;

From him the asses of the broad dale flee in affright, and men do not walk in
 his wadi,

Albeit ever in his wadi is a trusty fere, his armour and hard-worn raiment
 smeared with blood—ready to be devoured.

Truly the Messenger is a light whence illumination is sought—a drawn Indian
 sword, one of the swords of Allah,

Amongst a band of Kuraish, whose spokesman said when they professed
 Islam in the valley of Mecca, "Depart ye!"

They departed, but no weaklings were they or shieldless in battle or without
 weapons and courage;

They march like splendid camels and defend themselves with blows when the
 short black men take to flight;

Warriors with noses high and straight, clad for the fray in mail-coats of
 David's weaving,

Bright, ample, with pierced rings strung together like the rings of the *kaf'á*.

They are not exultant if their spears overtake an enemy or apt to despair if
 they be themselves overtaken.

The spear-thrust falls not but on their throats: for them there is no shrinking
 from the ponds of death.

Translated by R. A. Nicholson[3]

al-Aswad Bin Yafur

ODE FROM THE MUFADDALIYAT

The care-free sleeps, but I feel no sleep come nigh to mine eyes:
 Care is my fellow, at hand always to pillow my head.
It is not sickness, 'tis Care that thus wasted my frame:
Care fills my vision, and grips my fainting heart with its pain.
A heavy burthen it is, whereso I venture my steps,
 There rises ever in face a barrier not to be passed;
No way lies open to me between Iraq and Murād—
 Not even where the wide torrent stretches broadly its bed.
Yea, surely well do I know, and need no lesson from thee,
 The path I travel was traced for those who bear forth the dead.
Death and Destruction have climbed atop of cliffs where I wend,
 And watch my shape as I totter (though the narrowing pass);
No wealth of mine, whether old or newly got, shall redeem
 The pledge they hold of me—nought but life itself shall avail.
What can I hope, when Muḥarriq's house have gone to decay
 And left their palaces void? What better, after Iyād?—
The folk who dwelt in Khawarnaq and Bāriq and as-Sadīr,
 And the high-pinnacled castle that stood beside Sindād—
A land which Ka'b son of Māmah chose and Abū Du'ād
 To be the place where their fathers' stock should prosper and grow.
Now sweep the winds over all their dwellings: empty they lie,
 As though their lords had been set a time and no more to be.
Yea, once they lived there a life most ample in wealth and delight
 Beneath the shade of a kingdom stable, not to be moved.
They settled after in Anqirah, and there by their stead
 Flowed down Euphrates, new come to plain from mountain and hill.
Lo! How luxurious living and all the ways of delight
 Decline one day to decay, and pass therefrom into nought!

And if thou seekest examples, look at Gharf and his house:
 In them shalt thou, if it list thee, many find to thy hand.
What hope for us after Zaid whose kin were lost for a maid,
 Scattered and banished and slain, for all their goodly array?
They chose the broad open land because of strength that they had,
 And best of helpers were they beyond all bountiful hands.

If now thou seest me a wreck, worn out and diminished of sight,
 And all my limbs without strength to bear my body along,
And I am deaf to the calls of love and lightness of youth,
 And follow wisdom in meekness, my steps easy to guide—
Time was I went every night, hair combed, to sellers of wine,
 And squandered lightly my wealth, compliant, easy of mood.
Yea, once I played, and enjoyed the sweetest flavour of youth,
 My wine the first of the grape, mingled with purest of rain—
Wine brought from one with a twang in his speech, and rings in his ears,
 A belt girt round him: he brought it forth for good silver coin.
A boy deals it to our guests, girt up, two pearls in his ears,
 His fingers ruddy, as though stained deep with mulberry juice,
And women white like the moon or statues stately to see,
 That softly carry around great cups filled full with the wine—
White women, dainty, that shoot the hearts of men (with their eyes),
 Fair as a nest full of ostrich eggs betwixt rock and sand.
Kind words they speak, and their limbs are soft and smooth to the touch,
 Their faces bright, and their hearts to lovers gentle and mild.
Low speech they murmur, in tones that bear no secrets abroad:
 They gain their ends without toil, and need no shouting to win.

Yea, oft at dawn would I ride afar in dangerous meads—
 Dark grasses clothing the runnels, joyful sight for the herds;
Thereon the clouds of the night had loosed their burthens, and clumps
 Of ṣafrā, juicy and fresh, and zubbād, thickened the grass,
In Jaww and al-Amarāt, around Mughāmir's sides,
 And Ḍārij, and Qaṣīmah, choicest land for the chase:
My mount a steed, ever prompt to yield the whole of its speed
 To ride the wildings to bay, a racer not to be beat;
The lonely bull that exults in fleetness he courses down
 By running skilful in turns, now swift, now slackened as meet.

And oft have I followed after friends departing, my beast
 A stout she-camel, well-knit, that yields not calves nor milk,
Strong as a wild-ass: the Spring has filled the chinks of her frame—
 Smooth now the surface, whereon no tick can find room to lodge.

All these—it boots not to tell of things so utterly gone:
 Time's work is nought but to turn all lovely things to decay!

Translated by C. J. Lyall[4]

al-Khansa

LAMENT FOR MY BROTHER

What have we done to you, death
that you treat us so,
with always another catch
one day a warrior
the next a head of state;
charmed by the loyal
you choose the best.
Iniquitous, unequalling death
I would not complain
if you were just
but you take the worthy
leaving fools for us.

Fifty years among us
upholding rights
annulling wrongs,
impatient death
could you not wait
 a little longer.
He still would be here
and mine, a brother
without a flaw. Peace
be upon him and Spring

rains water his tomb
 but
could you not wait
 a little longer
 a little longer,
you came too soon.

Translated by Omar Pound[5]

al-Tirrimah

IN THE HEART OF THE DESERT

A foolish man rides here
with my saddle
and on my camel.

Translated by Omar Pound[6]

Jamil

OH, THAT YOUTH'S FLOWER ANEW MIGHT LIFT ITS HEAD

Oh, that youth's flower anew might lift its head
And return to us, Buthaina, the time that fled!
And oh, might we bide again as we used to be
When thy folk dwelt nigh and grudged what thou gavest me!

Shall I ever meet Buthaina alone again,
Each of us full of love as a cloud of rain?
Fast in her net was I when a lad, and till
This day my love is growing and waxing still.
I have spent my lifetime waiting for her to speak,
And the bloom of youth is faded from off my cheek;

But I will not suffer that she my suit deny,
My love remains undying, tho' all things die.

Translated by R. A. Nicholson[7]

Katari of Mazin

TO HIS OWN SOUL

I said to her when she fled in amaze and breathless
 before the array of battle—Why dost thou tremble?
Yea, if but a day of life thou shouldst beg with weeping
 beyond what thy doom appoints, thou wouldst not gain it.
Be still then, and face the onset of death, high-hearted,
 for none upon earth shall win to abide forever.
No raiment of praise the cloak of old age and weakness:
 none such for the coward who bows like a reed in a tempest.
The pathway of death is set for all men to travel:
 the crier of death proclaims through the earth his empire.
Who dies not when young and sound dies old and weary,
 cut off in his length of days from all love and kindness;
And what for a man is left of delight in living,
 past use, flung away, a worthless worn-out chattel?

Translated by C. J. Lyall[8]

'Umar Ibn Abi Rabi'ah

BLAME ME NO MORE, O COMRADES!

Blame me no more, O comrades! but to-day
quietly with me beside the howdahs stay.
Blame not my love for Zaynab, for to her
And hers my heart is pledged a prisoner.
Ah, can I ever think of how we met

Once at al-Khayf, and feel no fond regret?
My song of other women was but jest.
She reigns alone, eclipsing all the rest
Hers is my love sincere, 'tis she the flame
Of passion kindles—so, a truce to blame!

Translated by R. A. Nicholson[9]

Part II

THE ISLAMIC AGE

The Holy Qur'an

Revealed at Mecca

In the name of God, The Most Gracious, The Dispenser of Grace:

All praise is due to God alone, the Sustainer of all the worlds, (1)
The Most Gracious, the Dispenser of Grace, (2)
Lord of the Day of Judgment! (3)
Thee alone do we worship; and unto Thee alone do we turn for aid. (4)
Guide us the straight way. (5)
The way of those upon whom Thou hast bestowed Thy blessings, (6)
Not of those who have been condemned [by Thee], nor of those who go astray! (7)

SURAH XIX: MARY

Revealed at Mecca

In the name of God, The Most Gracious, The Dispenser of Grace:

Kaf. Ha. Ya. 'Ayd Sad. (1)
AN ACCOUNT of the grace which thy Sustainer bestowed upon His servant Zachariah: (2) When he called out to his Sustainer in the secrecy of his heart, (3) he prayed: "O my Sustainer! Feeble have become my bones, and my head glistens with grey hair. But never yet, O my Lord, has my prayer unto Thee remained unanswered." (4) "Now, behold, I am afraid of [what] my kinsfolk [will do] after I am gone, for my wife has always been barren. Bestow, then, upon me, out of Thy grace, the gift of a successor (5) who will be my heir as well as an heir [to the dignity] of the House of Jacob; and make him, O my Sustainer, well-pleasing to Thee!" (6) [Thereupon the angels called out unto him: "O Zachariah! We bring thee the glad tiding of [the birth of] a son whose name shall be John." [And God says,] "Never have We given this name to anyone before him." (7) [Zachariah] exclaimed: "O my Sustainer! How can I have a son when my wife has always been barren and I have become utterly

infirm through old age?" (8) Answered [the angel]: "Thus, it is"; [but] thy Sustainer says, "This is easy for Me – even as I have created thee aforetime out of nothing." (9) [Zachariah] prayed: "O my Sustainer! Appoint a sign for me!" Said [the angel]: "Thy sign shall be that for full three nights [and days] thou wilt not speak unto men." (10) Thereupon he came out of the sanctuary unto his people and signified to them [by gestures]: "Extol His limitless glory by day and by night!" (11) [And when the son was born and grew up, he was told,] "O John! Hold fast unto the divine writ with [all thy] strength!" – for We granted him wisdom "while he was yet a little boy, (12) as well as, by Our grace, [the gift of] compassion and purity; and he was [always] conscious of Us (13) and full of piety towards his parents; and never was he haughty or rebellious." (14) Hence, [God's] peace was upon him on the day when he was born, and on the day of his death, and will be [upon him] on the day when he shall be raised to life [again]. (15)

AND CALL to mind, through this divine writ, Mary. Lo! She withdrew from her family to an eastern place (16) and kept herself in seclusion from them, whereupon We sent unto her Our angel of revelation, who appeared to her in the shape of a well-made human being. (17)
She exclaimed: "Verily, I seek refuge from thee with the Most Gracious! [Approach me not] if thou art conscious of Him!" (18)
[The angel] answered: "I am but a messenger of thy Sustainer, [who says,] 'I shall bestow upon thee the gift of a son endowed with purity.'" (19) Said she: "How can I have a son when no man has ever touched me? – for, never have I been a loose woman!" (20)
[The angel] answered: "Thus it is; [but] thy Sustainer says, 'This is easy for Me; and [thou shalt have a son,] so that We might make him a symbol unto mankind and an act of grace from US.' And it was a thing decreed [by God]: (21) and in time she conceived him, and then she withdrew with him to a far-off place. (22) And [when] the throes of childbirth drove her to the trunk of a palm-tree, she exclaimed: "Oh, would that I had died ere this, and had become a thing forgotten, utterly forgotten!" (23) Thereupon [a voice] called out to her from beneath that [palm-tree]: "Grieve not! Thy Sustainer has provided a rivu-let [running] beneath thee; (24) and shake the trunk of the palm-tree towards thee: it will drop fresh, ripe dates upon thee. (25)
Eat, then, and drink, and let thine eye be gladdened! And if thou shouldst see any human being, convey this unto him: 'Behold, abstinence from speech have I vowed unto the Most Gracious; hence, I may not speak today to any mortal.'" (26) And in time she returned to her people, carrying the child with her. They

said: "O Mary! Thou hast indeed done an amazing thing! (27) sister of Aaron!
Thy father was not a wicked man, nor was thy mother a loose woman!" (28)
Thereupon she pointed to him. They exclaimed: "How can we talk to one who
[as yet] is a little boy in the cradle?" (29) [But] he said: "Behold, I am a servant
of God. He has vouchsafed unto me revelation and made me a prophet, (30)
and made me blessed wherever I may be; and He has enjoined upon me prayer
and charity as long as I live, (31) and [has endowed me with] piety towards my
mother; and He has not made me haughty or bereft of grace. (32) Hence, peace
was upon me on the day when I was born, and [will be upon me] on the day of
my death, and on the day when I shall be raised to life [again]!" (33)

SUCH WAS, in the words of truth, Jesus the son of Mary, about whose nature
they so deeply disagree. (34) It is not conceivable that God should have taken
unto Himself a son: limitless is He in His glory! When He wills a thing to be,
He but says unto it "Be" – and it is! (35)
And [thus it was that Jesus always said]: "Verily, God is my Sustainer as well
as your Sustainer; so worship [none but] Him: this [alone] is a straight way."
(36) And yet, the sects [that follow the Bible] are at variance among themselves
[about the nature of Jesus. Woe, then, unto all who deny the truth when that
awesome Day will appear! (37) How well will they hear and see [the truth]
on the Day when they come before Us! Today, however, these evildoers are
obviously lost in error: (38) hence, warn them of [the coming of] the Day of
Regrets, when everything will have been decided – for as yet they are heedless,
and they do not believe [in it]. (39) Behold, We alone shall remain after the
earth and all who live on it have passed away, and (when) unto Us all will have
been brought back. (40)

AND CALL to mind, through this divine writ, Abraham. Behold, he was a
man of truth, [already] a prophet (41) when he spoke [thus] unto his father:
"O my father! Why dost thou worship something that neither hears nor sees
and can be of no avail whatever to thee?" (42) "O my father! Behold, there has
indeed come to me [a ray] of knowledge such as has never yet come unto thee:
follow me, then; I shall guide thee onto a perfect way." (43) "O my father! Do
not worship Satan – for, verily, Satan is a rebel against the Most Gracious!"
(44) "O my father! I dread lest a chastisement from the Most Gracious befall
thee, and then thou wilt become [aware of having been] close unto Satan!"
(45) He answered: "Dost thou dislike my gods, O Abraham? Indeed, if thou
desist not, I shall most certainly cause thee to be stoned to death! Now begone
from me for good!" (46) [Abraham] replied: "Peace be upon thee! I shall ask

my Sustainer to forgive thee: for, behold, He has always been kind unto me. (47) But I shall withdraw from you all and from whatever you invoke instead of God, and shall invoke my Sustainer [alone]: it may well be that my prayer [for thee] will not remain unanswered by my Sustainer." (48) And after he had withdrawn from them and from all that they were worshipping instead of God, We bestowed upon him Isaac and Jacob, and made each of them a prophet; (49) and We bestowed upon them [manifold] gifts out of Our grace, and granted them a lofty power to convey the truth [unto others]. (50)

AND CALL to mind, through this divine writ, Moses. Behold, he was a chosen one, and was an apostle [of God], a prophet. (51) And [remember how] We called upon him from the right-hand slope of Mount Sinai and drew him near [unto Us] in mystic communion, (52) and [how], out of Our grace, We granted unto him his brother Aaron, to be a prophet [by his side]. (53)

AND CALL to mind, through this divine writ, Ishmael. Behold, he was always true to his promise, and was an apostle [of God], a prophet, (54) who used to enjoin upon his people prayer and charity, and found favour in his Sustainer's sight. (55)

AND CALL to mind, through this divine writ, Idris. Behold, he was a man of truth, a prophet, (56) whom We exalted onto a lofty station. (57)

THESE WERE some of the prophets upon whom God bestowed His blessings – [prophets] of the seed of Adam and of those whom We caused to be borne [in the ark] with Noah, and of the seed of Abraham and Israel and [all of them were] among those whom We had guided and elected; [and] whenever the messages of the Most Gracious were conveyed unto them, they would fall down [before Him], prostrating themselves and weeping. (58) Yet they were succeeded by generations [of people] who lost all [thought of] prayer and followed [but] their own lusts; and these will, in time, meet with utter disillusion. (59)

Excepted, however, shall be those who repent and attain to faith and do righteous deeds: for it is they who will enter paradise and will not be wronged in any way: (60) [theirs will be the] gardens of perpetual bliss which the Most Gracious has promised unto His servants, in a realm which is beyond the reach of human perception: [and,] verily, His promise is ever sure of fulfilment! (61) No empty talk will they hear there – nothing but [tidings of] inner soundness and peace; and there will they have their sustenance by day and by night: (62)

this is the paradise which We grant as a heritage unto such of Our servants as are conscious of Us. (63)

AND [the angels say]: "We do not descend [with revelation], again and again, other than by thy Sustainer's command: unto Him belongs all that lies open before us and all that is hidden – from us and all that is in-between. And never does thy Sustainer forget [anything] – (64) the Sustainer of the heavens and the earth and all that is between them! Worship, then, Him alone, and remain steadfast in His worship! Dost thou know any whose name is worthy to be mentioned side by side with His?" (65)

WITH ALL THIS, man [often] says, "What! Once I am dead, shall I again be brought forth alive?" (66) But does man not bear in mind that We have created him aforetime out of nothing? (67) And so, by thy Sustainer, [on Judgment Day] We shall most certainly bring them forth together with the satanic forces [which impelled them in life] and then We shall most certainly gather them, on their knees, around hell; (68) and thereupon We shall, indeed, draw forth from every group [of sinners] the ones that had been most determined in their disdainful rebellion against the Most Gracious: (69) for, indeed, We know best as to which of them is most deserving of the fires of hell. (70) And every one of you will come within sight of it: this is, with thy Sustainer, a decree that must be fulfilled. (71) And once again: We shall save [from hell] those who have been conscious of Us; but We shall leave in it the evildoers, on their knees. (72)

AS IT IS, whenever Our messages are conveyed to them in all their clarity, those who are bent on denying the truth are wont to say unto those who have attained to faith: "Which of the two kinds of man is in a stronger position and superior as a community?" (73) And yet, how many a generation have We destroyed before their time – [people] who surpassed them in material power and in outward show! (74) Say: "As for him who lives in error, may the Most Gracious lengthen the span of his life!" [And let them say whatever they say until the time when they behold that [doom] of which they were forewarned – whether it be suffering [in this world] or [at the coming of] the Last Hour: for then they will understand which [of the two kinds of man] was worse in station and weaker in resources! (75) And God endows those who avail themselves of [His] guidance with an ever-deeper consciousness of the right way; and good deeds, the fruit whereof endures forever, are, in thy Sustainer's sight, of far greater merit [than any worldly goods], and yield far better returns. (76) And hast thou ever considered [the kind of man] who is bent on denying the truth

of Our messages and says, "I will surely be given wealth and children"? (77) Has he, perchance, attained to a realm which is beyond the reach of a created being's perception? Or has he concluded a covenant with the Most Gracious? (78) Nay! We shall record what he says, and We shall lengthen the length of his suffering [in the hereafter], (79) and divest him of all that he is [now] speaking of: for [on Judgment Day] he will appear before Us in a lonely state. (80) For [such as] these have taken to worshipping deities other than God, hoping that they would be a [source of] strength for them. (81) But nay! [On Judgment Day] these [very objects of adoration] will disavow the worship that was paid to them, and will turn against those [who had worshipped them]! (82)

ART THOU NOT aware that We have let loose all [manner of] satanic forces upon those who deny the truth – [forces] that impel them [towards sin] with strong impulsion? (83) Hence, be not in haste [to call down God's punishment] upon them: for We but number the number of their days. (84) On the Day when We shall gather the Godconscious unto [Us,] the Most Gracious, as honoured guests, (85) and drive those who were lost in sin unto hell as a thirsty herd is driven to a well – (86) [on that Day] none will have [the benefit of] intercession unless he has [in his lifetime] entered into a bond with the Most Gracious. (87) As it is, some assert, "The Most Gracious has taken unto Himself a son"! (88) Indeed, [by this assertion] you have brought forth something monstrous, (89) whereat the heavens might well-nigh be rent into fragments, and the earth be split asunder, and the mountains fall down in ruins! (90) That men, should ascribe a son to the Most Gracious, (91) although it is inconceivable that the Most Gracious should take unto Himself a son! (92) Not one of all [the beings] that are in the heavens or on earth appears before the Most Gracious other than as a servant: (93) indeed, He has full cognizance of them, and has numbered them with [unfailing] numbering; (94) and every one of them will appear before Him on Resurrection Day in a lonely state. (95)

VERILY, those who attain to faith and do righteous deeds will the Most Gracious endow with love: (96) and only to this end have We made this [divine writ] easy to understand, in thine own tongue, [O Prophet,] so that thou might convey thereby a glad tiding to the God-conscious, and warn thereby those who are given to [futile] contention: (97) for, how many a generation have We destroyed before their time – [and] canst thou perceive any one of them [now], or hear any whisper of them? (98)

SURAH LIX: EXILE

Revealed in Medina

In the name of God, The Most Gracious, The Dispenser of Grace:

ALL THAT IS in the heavens and all that is on earth extols God's limitless glory: for He alone is almighty, truly wise. (1) He it is who turned out of their homes, at the time of [their] first gathering [for war], such of the followers of earlier revelation as were bent on denying the truth. You did not think [O believers] that they would depart [without resistance] – just as they thought that their strongholds would protect them against God: but God came upon them in a manner which they had not expected, and cast terror into their hearts; [and thus] they destroyed their homes by their own hands as well as the hands of the believers. Learn a lesson, then, O you who are endowed with insight! (2) And had it not been for God's having ordained banishment for them, He would indeed have imposed [yet greater] suffering on them in this world: still, in the life to come there awaits them suffering through fire: (3) this, because they cut themselves off from God and His Apostle: and as for him who cuts himself off from God and His Apostle – verily, God is severe in retribution! (4) Whatever [of their] palm trees you may have cut down, [O believers,] or left standing on their roots, was [done] by God's leave, and in order that He might confound the iniquitous. (5) Yet [remember:] whatever [spoils taken] from the enemy God has turned over to His Apostle, you did not have to spur horse or riding-camel for its sake: but God gives His apostles mastery over whomever He wills – for God has the power to will anything. (6) Whatever [spoils taken] from the people of those villages God has turned over to His Apostle – [all of it] belongs to God and the Apostle, and the near of kin [of deceased believers], and the orphans, and the needy, and the wayfarer, so that it may not be [a benefit] going round and round among such of you as may [already] be rich. Hence, accept [willingly] whatever the Apostle* gives you [thereof], and refrain from [demanding] anything that he withholds from you; and remain conscious of God: for, verily, God is severe in retribution. (7) [Thus, part of such war-gains shall be given] to the poor among those who have forsaken the domain of evil: those who have been driven from their homelands and their possessions, seeking favour with God and [His] goodly acceptance, and who aid [the cause of] God and His Apostle: it is they, they who are true to their word! (8) And [it shall be offered, too, unto the poor from among] those who, before them, had their

abode in this realm and in faith – [those] who love all that come to them in search of refuge, and who harbour in their hearts no grudge for whatever the others may have been given, but rather give them preference over themselves, even though poverty be their own lot: for, such as from their own covetousness are saved – it is they, they that shall attain to a happy state! (9) And so, they who come after them pray: "O our Sustainer! Forgive us our sins, as well as those of our brethren who preceded us in faith, and let not our hearts entertain any unworthy thoughts or feelings against [any of] those who have attained to faith. O our Sustainer! Verily, Thou art compassionate, a dispenser of grace!" (10)

ART THOU NOT aware of how those who would always dissemble [their real feelings] speak to their truth-denying brethren from among the followers of earlier revelation: "If you are driven away, we shall most certainly go forth with you, and shall never pay heed to anyone against you; and if war is waged against you, we shall most certainly come to your succour." But God bears witness that they are most flagrantly lying: (11) [for] if those [to whom they have pledged themselves] are indeed driven away, they will not go forth with them; and if war is waged against them, they will not come to their succour; and even if they [try to] succour them, they will most certainly turn their backs [in flight], and in the end will [themselves] find no succour. (12) Nay, [O believers,] you arouse in their bosoms a fear more intense than [even their fear of] God: this, because they are people who fail to grasp the truth. (13) Never will they fight you, [even] in unison, otherwise than from within fortified strongholds or from behind walls. Severe is their warlike discord among themselves: thou wouldst think that they are united, whereas [in fact] their hearts are at odds [with one another]: this, because they are people who will not use their reason. (14) [To both kinds of your enemies, O believers, is bound to happen] the like of [what happened to] those who, a short while before them, had to taste the evil that came from their own doings, with [yet more] grievous suffering awaiting them [in the life to come]: (15) the like of [what happens] when Satan says unto man, "Deny the truth!" – but as soon as [man] has denied the truth, [Satan] says, "Behold, I am not responsible for thee: behold, I fear God, the Sustainer of all the worlds!" (16) And so, they who come after them pray: "O our Sustainer! Forgive us our sins, as well as those of our brethren who preceded us in faith, and let not our hearts entertain any unworthy thoughts or feelings against [any of] those who have attained to faith. O our Sustainer! Verily, Thou art compassionate, a dispenser of grace!" Thus, in the end, both [the deniers of the truth and the

hypocrites] will find themselves in the fire, therein to abide: for such is the recompense of evildoers. (17)

O YOU who have attained to faith! Remain conscious of God; and let every human being look to what he sends ahead for the morrow! And [once again]: Remain conscious of God, for God is fully aware of all that you do; (18) and be not like those who are oblivious of God, and whom He therefore causes to be oblivious of [what is good for] their own selves: [for] it is they, they who are truly depraved! (19) Not equal are those who are destined for the fire and those who are destined for paradise: those who are destined for paradise – it is they, they [alone] who shall triumph [on Judgment Day]! (20)

HAD WE bestowed this Qur'an from on high upon a mountain, thou wouldst indeed see it humbling itself, breaking asunder for awe of God. And [all] such parables We propound unto men, so that they might [learn to] think. (21)

GOD IS HE save whom there is no deity: the One who knows all that is beyond the reach of a created being's perception, as well as all that can be witnessed by a creature's senses or mind: He, the Most Gracious, the Dispenser of Grace. (22) God is He save whom there is no deity: the Sovereign Supreme, the Holy, the One with whom all salvation rests, the Giver of Faith, the One who determines what is true and false, the Almighty, the One who subdues wrong and restores right, the One to whom all greatness belongs! Utterly remote is God, in His limitless glory, from anything to which men may ascribe a share in His divinity! (23) He is God, the Creator, the Maker who shapes all forms and appearances! His [alone] are the attributes of perfection. All that is in the heavens and on earth extols His limitless glory: for He alone is almighty, truly wise! (24)

SURAH LXXXIX: THE DAWN

Revealed at Mecca

In the name of God, The Most Gracious, The Dispenser of Grace:

CONSIDER the daybreak (1) and the ten nights! (2) Consider the multiple and the One! (3) Consider the night as it runs its course! (4) Considering all this – could there be, to anyone endowed with reason, a [more] solemn evidence of the truth? (5)

ART THOU NOT aware of how thy Sustainer has dealt with [the tribe of] 'Ad, (6) [the people of] Iram the many-pillared, (7) the like of whom has never been reared in all the land? – (8) and with [the tribe of] Thamud, who hollowed out rocks in the valley? – (9) and with Pharaoh of the [many] tent-poles? (10) [It was they] who transgressed all bounds of equity all over their lands, (11) and brought about great corruption therein: (12) and therefore thy Sustainer let loose upon them a scourge of suffering: (13) for, verily, thy Sustainer is ever on the watch! (14)

BUT AS FOR man, whenever his Sustainer tries him by His generosity and by letting him enjoy a life of ease, he says, "My Sustainer has been [justly] generous towards me"; (15) whereas, whenever He tries him by straightening his means of livelihood, he says, "My Sustainer has disgraced me!" (16) But nay, nay, [O men, consider all that you do and fail to do:] you are not generous towards the orphan, (17) and you do not urge one another to feed the needy, (18) and you devour the inheritance [of others] with devouring greed, (19) and you love wealth with boundless love! (20) Nay, but [how will you fare on Judgment Day,] when the earth is crushed with crushing upon crushing, (21) and [the majesty of] thy Sustainer stands revealed, as well as [the true nature of] the angels; rank upon rank? (22) And on that Day hell will be brought [within sight]; on that Day man will remember [all that he did and failed to do]: but what will that remembrance avail him? (23) He will say, "Oh, would that I had provided beforehand for my life [to come]!" (24) For, none can make suffer as He will make suffer [the sinners] on that Day, (25) and none can bind with bonds like His. (26) [But unto the righteous God will say,] "O thou human being that hast attained to inner peace! (27) Return thou unto thy Sustainer, well-pleased [and] pleasing [Him]: (28) enter, then, together with My [other true] servants – (29) yea, enter thou My paradise!" (30)

Translated by Muhammad Asad[1]

Hadith

SELECTED SAYINGS

— To seek learning is a sacred duty incumbent on every Muslim man or woman.
— No-one can be considered a believer until he desires for his brother what he desires for himself.
— God wills that whosoever among you wishes to undertake any task must be conscious of the obligation to perfect it.
— Your blood, your possessions, your wives are inviolable.
— Faith is indeed in giving and seeking advice.
— He who preaches prejudice is not one of our number.
— Woman is but man's full-sister.
— A man's conduct is a measure of his faith.
— Beneath the throne of God lie treasures the keys to which are the tongue of the poets.

Translated by S. B. Bushrui[2]

— Actions are but by intention and every man shall have but that which he intended. Thus he whose migration was for Allah and His Messenger, his migration was for Allah and His Messenger, and he whose migration was to achieve some worldly benefit or to take some woman in marriage, his migration was for that which he migrated.
— Islam has been built on five [pillars]: testifying that there is no god but Allah and that Muhammad is the Messenger of Allah, performing the prayers, paying the *zakat*, making the pilgrimage to the House, and fasting in Ramadān.
— Verily the creation of each one of you is brought together in his mother's belly for forty days in the form of seed, then he is a clot of blood for a like period, then a morsel of flesh for a like period, then there is sent to him the angel who blows the breath of life into him and who is commanded about four matters: to write down his means of livelihood, his life span, his actions, and whether happy or unhappy. By Allah, other than Whom there is no god, verily one of you behaves like the people of Paradise until there is but an arm's length between him and it, and that which has been

written overtakes him and so he behaves like the people of Hell-fire and thus he enters it: and one of you behaves like the people of Hell-fire until there is but an arm's length between him and it, and that which has been written overtakes him and so he behaves like the people of Paradise and thus he enters it.

— That which is lawful is plain and that which is unlawful is plain and between the two of them are doubtful matters about which not many people know. Thus he who avoids doubtful matters clears himself in regard to his religion and his honour, but he who falls into doubtful matters falls into that which is unlawful, like the shepherd who pastures around a sanctuary, all but grazing therein. Truly every king has a sanctuary, and truly Allah's sanctuary is his prohibitions. Truly in the body there is a morsel of flesh which, if it be whole, all the body is whole, and which, if it be diseased, all of it is diseased. Truly it is the heart.

— What I have forbidden to you, avoid; what I have ordered for you [to do], do as much of it as you can. It was only their excessive questioning and their disagreeing with their Prophets that destroyed those who were before you.

— The blood of a Muslim may not be legally spilt other than in one of three [instances]: the married person who commits adultery; a life for a life; and one who forsakes his religion and abandons the community.

— Allah the Almighty is good and accepts only that which is good. Allah has commanded the Faithful to do that which he commanded the Messengers, and the Almighty has said: *"Oh ye Messengers! Eat of the good things, and do right."* And Allah the Almighty has said: *"Oh ye who believe! Eat of the good things wherewith We have provided you."* Then he mentioned [the case of] a man who, having journeyed far, is dishevelled and dusty and who spreads out his hands to the sky [saying]: O Lord! O Lord! – While his food is unlawful, his drink unlawful, his clothing unlawful, and he is nourished unlawfully, so how can he be answered!

— Leave that which makes you doubt for that which does not make you doubt.

— Let him who believes in Allah and the Last Day either speak good or keep silent, and let him who believes in Allah and the Last Day be generous to his neighbour, and let him who believes in Allah and the Last Day be generous to his guest.

— I have been ordered to fight against people until they testify that there is no god but Allah and that Muhammad is the Messenger of Allah and until they perform the prayers and pay the *zakāt*, and if they do so they will have

gained protection from me for their lives and property, unless [they do acts that are punishable] in accordance with Islam, and their reckoning with Islam, and their reckoning will be with Allah the Almighty.

— Verily Allah has prescribed proficiency in all things. Thus, if you kill, kill well; and if you slaughter, slaughter well. Let each one of you sharpen his blade and let him spare suffering to the animal he slaughters.

— Fear Allah wherever you are, and follow up a bad deed with a good one and it will wipe it out, and behave well towards people.

— Be mindful of Allah, and Allah will protect you. Be mindful of Allah, and you will find Him in front of you. If you ask, ask of Allah; if you seek help, seek help of Allah. Know that if the Nation were to gather together to benefit you with anything, it would benefit you only with something that Allah had already prescribed for you, and that if they gather together to harm you with anything, they would harm you only with something Allah had already prescribed for you. The pens have been lifted and the pages have dried.

Translated by Ezzedin Ibrahim and Denys Johnson-Davies[3]

Shaybani's Siyar

THE ISLAMIC LAW OF NATIONS

Muhammad b. al-Ḥasan said that Abū Yūsuf said: I asked Abū Ḥanīfa [his opinion] concerning the spoil taken by Muslims from unbelievers in the territory of war, and how they should divide it, whether its division should take place in the territory of war or in the territory of Islam after they have taken it there. Also what would he assign to the horse-rider and the foot-warrior, and whether he would give preference to certain kinds of horses over others? How would he divide up one-fifth [share]? Would the slaves be entitled to any share of the spoil? Would the women be entitled to any share of the spoil? What would be the status of the territory conquered by Muslims; would it be regarded as household property [to be divided as spoil among the warriors] or not?

Abū Ḥanīfa replied: If the Muslims captured any spoil, it should never be divided in the territory of war because they would not have yet taken it to a place of security. Its security would be achieved after they take it to the dār al-Islām. But if they ever divided it in the territory of war, it would be

permissible, although it would be commendable if they divided it after they have taken it to the dār al-Islām. So also held Abū Yūsuf and Muḥammad [b. al-Ḥasan]. However, Abū Yūsuf held that if the Imām could not find transport to carry it [to the dār al-Islām] he may divide in the dār al-ḥarb.

Abū Ḥanīfa held that the slave is not entitled to a share of the spoil, but if he participated in the fighting he would be entitled to compensation, not to a share. He held the same opinion concerning women and mukātabs. Abū Yūsuf and Muḥammad [b. al-Ḥasan] held similar opinions.

Abū Ḥanīfa held that the volunteer who joins an army and the warrior whose name [is registered] in the dīwān [of the permanent army] receive equal [shares]. But [Muslim] merchants who enter [the enemy territory] in pursuit of their trade and find themselves in the Muslim army would not be entitled to anything of the spoil.

Abū Ḥanīfa held that the horse is entitled to one share and the foot-warrior to one share because, he said, he would disapprove of rating the animal higher than an individual Muslim. But Abū Yūsuf and Muḥammad [b. al-Ḥasan] held that the horse should be given two shares and the foot-warrior one on the strength of the ḥadīth and the sunna.

Abū Ḥanīfa held that two or more horses [i.e., owned by one warrior] would not be entitled to more [than the share of one horse] because, he said, if two horses were to be given [two separate] shares, then three horses or more should be given, too. So also held Muḥammad [b. al-Ḥasan] but Abū Yūsuf held that he was in favor of giving [separate] shares to two horses, but not to more.

Abū Ḥanīfa held that a thoroughbred horse, a hybrid, and a jade would be entitled to equal shares, making no distinction between one and the other on the strength of God's command in His Book [the Qur'an], in which no preference is given [to the horse] over other [riding animals]. So also held Abū Yūsuf and Muḥammad [b. al-Ḥasan].

Abū Ḥanīfa held that if the Imām conquered a territory of the unbelievers he would have the choice to do whatever appeared to be more advantageous and acceptable to the Muslims. If he decides to take out the land and property the one-fifth [state share] and divide the four-fifths among the warriors who captured it, he may do so. The one-fifth would be [then] divided into three parts: one for the poor, one for the orphans, and one for the wayfarer. But, Abū Ḥanīfa said, if the Imām decides to immobilize the land and leave it to its people as Dhimmīs who would be obliged to pay for themselves and their land [the poll tax and] the kharāj, as [the Caliph] 'Umar b. al-Khaṭṭāb had decreed for the Sawād [territory], he may do so.

Abū Yūsuf said: I asked Abū Ḥanīfa [his opinion] concerning men who

would be called to take part in an expedition and those who do not take part but instead would contribute (i.e., pay scutage) to those who take the field.

[Abū Ḥanīfa] replied: If the Muslims were short in spoil or fay', no harm is there if they help each other. But if the Muslims had sufficient fay', I would disapprove of giving it.

I said: I asked Abū Ḥanīfa [his opinion] about [the Muslim] who takes an animal from the fay' for a ride or wears a garment, whether he disapproves of that and prohibits it.

He replied: If [the Muslim] were wounded and was afraid of its [effect] on his life, it would be all right to take the animal for a ride or use clothing, if he were in need of them.

I said: I asked [Abū Ḥanīfa his opinion] about the man who takes weapons from the fay' to fight with them.

[He replied]: It would be objectionable for him [to do so].

I asked: If he were in need of them?

[He replied]: No harm then if he were in need and could not find any other [weapons].

I asked: If an enemy shoots [the Muslim] with an arrow and the latter shot it back to him or snatched a sword from the hand of the enemy and struck them with it, do you think that there would be any harm in that?

He replied: There is no harm in it.

I asked: If a man hamstrung his own animal and, fearful of an enemy [attacking] him, found an animal belonging to the enemy on which he rode and returned to his people, do you think that there would be any harm in that?

He replied: No harm in it, if he were frightened, or hungry, or in need [of the animal], or [was afraid] of treachery.

I said: I asked [Abū Ḥanīfa his opinion] about the killing of women and children and very old men chronically ill and incapable of fighting?

[He replied: He said] he would prohibit [such killing] and he disapproved of it.

I asked: If [a Muslim] captures a prisoner of war, would it be lawful to kill him or should he be brought to the Imām?

He replied: Whatever he did would be all right. Abū Yūsuf and Muḥammad [b. al-Ḥasan] held that he should do whatever he deems good or advantageous to the Muslims.

I said: I asked [Abū Ḥanīfa his opinion] about the corpse of an enemy killed by the Muslims, whether [it would be all right] to sell it to the unbelievers.

He replied: No harm in doing so in the dār al-ḥarb, i.e., outside the army camp of the Muslims. Do you not think that it is lawful for the Muslims to take

away the property [of the enemy]? So, if such [property] were taken in lieu of their corpses, it would be all right. However, Abū Yūsuf disapproved of such [an act] and prohibited it. He held that it is unlawful for the Muslims to sell corpses, to transact with interest, to sell wine or swine, whether to the inhabitants of the territory of war or others.

I said: I asked [Abū Ḥanīfa his opinion] about an army if it attacks the territory of war and takes spoil and thereafter another Muslim army which had not taken part in the fighting would join it before the spoil is taken to the dār al-Islām and before it is divided up.

He replied: [The second army] would be entitled to participate in the spoil, because the first had not yet taken it to a place of security and was still in the dār al-ḥarb.

[I said]: I asked [Abū Ḥanīfa his opinion] about the commander of an army who attacks the territory of war, whether he has the right to promise primes before the taking of spoil by saying, "He who captures anything may have for himself such-and-such [a portion of it]."

[He replied: As to that, I would say "yes"] but as to offering primes after the spoil has already been captured, he [the commander] should not do it.

[I said:] I asked [Abū Ḥanīfa his opinion] whether there is any harm for the Muslims in seeking the assistance of unbelievers [in a war] against the inhabitants of the territory of war and whether they would be entitled to any [regular] share of the [captured] spoil.

He replied: There is no harm in seeking their assistance, provided the command is in the hands of the Muslims, but if the command were in the hands of the unbelievers, the Muslims should not participate in the fighting along with unbelievers, unless they were fearful of their safety—[in such a case it would be all right to fight with them] in self-defence. But [if the unbelievers participate with the Muslims] they would not be entitled to any share, save to compensation.

I said: I asked [Abū Ḥanīfa his opinion] about the prisoner of war, whether he would be killed, released on ransom, or divided [as spoil]?

He replied: He should not be released on ransom; he should be killed or taken as fay'. The Imām can make a choice and do whatever he deems advantageous to the Muslims.

[I said:] I asked [Abū Ḥanīfa]: Would it be lawful to exchange Muslim prisoners for prisoners of the unbelievers?

He replied: There is no harm in it, but I disapprove of ransoming prisoners of the unbelievers with property.

I said: I asked [Abū Ḥanīfa his opinion] about men who take spoil

consisting of camels, horses and sheep and are unable to drive them or about any of the animals belonging to the Muslims that resist being driven.

He replied: I disapprove of hamstringing or mutilating them, but there is no harm in slaughtering them and burning them so that the enemy would not get any benefit of them.

Abū Ḥanīfa said: If the unbelievers captured a slave or a riding animal or clothing [from the Muslims] and the Muslims recaptured [any of] them as spoil and the owner found it before the spoil was divided, he may take it without paying anything [as a right of postliminium], but if he found it after the spoil was divided he may take it by paying its value, unless it were gold or silver or anything to be weighed or measured; then, Abū Ḥanīfa added, the owner would not have to take it if he found it after the spoil was divided, for he would have to take something by paying as much in weight or measure.

Abū Ḥanīfa said: If a slave ran away to the enemy and was taken [by one of them] and thereafter was recaptured by the Muslims, his master may take him back without paying anything, whether before or after the spoil was divided, because the runaway slave is unlike the prisoner of war or the property captured and taken to a place of security.

Abū Ḥanīfa said: If a riding animal escaped [to the territory of war] and was captured [by the unbelievers], and thereafter recaptured by the Muslims, the owner may take it back without paying anything if he found it before the spoil was divided, but he must pay its value if he found it after the spoil was divided. Thus the runaway slave is treated differently from the riding animal which ran away.

However, Abū Yūsuf and Muḥammad [b. al-Ḥasan] held that these cases should be treated alike if [the unbelievers] captured them in their territory, regardless whether [the captive] were a runaway slave, and expelled person, or a prisoner of war. If the owner found him before the spoil is divided, he may take him without paying anything; if he found him after the division, he must pay its value. Abū Ḥanīfa held that if an unbeliever entered the dār al-Islām under an amān along with the said slave and sold him there, nobody would have the right to claim ownership [of the slave], according to the opinion of all [the jurists], except in the case of the runaway slave, whose master, according to Abū Ḥanīfa, has the right to take him wherever he may find him without paying anything.

Abū Ḥanīfa said: If a Muslim slave is captured by the unbelievers and a Muslim purchases this slave from them, his master has the right to take him back by paying his value, if he so wishes. But if he did not take him back and the unbelievers recaptured him and [the slave] was purchased by another man,

Abū Ḥanīfa held that [the first] owner would have no right to take him back until purchased by the second owner who takes him back by paying the price of the second sale; thereafter the first owner takes him back on payment of both prices. Abū Yūsuf and Muḥammad [b. al-Ḥasan] held the same opinion.

Yūsuf and Muḥammad [b. al-Ḥasan] said: If a slave girl became blind in the hand of the purchaser or suffered a defect and her [first] master wanted to take her back, deducting from her price a portion equivalent to the [value of the] defect, it would not be lawful for him to do so. He should either take her by paying the full price or leave her. This is also the opinion of Abū Ḥanīfa, as far as Abū Yūsuf knows. Do you not think that if a man sold a slave to another and the slave became blind while in the possession of the vendor, the purchaser would be told that he can take the slave by paying the full price or leave him?

If a man cuts off the hand of the slave girl and her master collects the arsh [damages] and the [first] owner from whom the unbelievers had captured the slave girl wanted to take her back and demanded to deduct from her price a portion equal [to the value of the defect], it would not be lawful for him to do so; if he wants to take her back, he has either to pay the full price or leave her. [For] do you think that if [the owner], in whose hand was the slave girl, caused the loss of her eye, he can deduct anything from her price? If this [case] were like any other sale transaction, deduction from the price [equivalent to the value of the defect] would be lawful. If it were also like the shuf'a [*jus retractum*] sale, deduction from the price would be lawful. And [also] like the purchase [of a house], if part of it is destroyed, a portion of the price equal [to the value of that part] would be deducted from the price to be paid by the pre-empting purchaser.

Do you not think that if [the person] who has purchased [the slave girl] from the enemy had intercourse with her, nothing would be deducted from her price and the [first] owner could take her back [only] by paying the full [price], and the intercourse would be lawful? If she gave birth to a child and the owner in whose hand was [the child] set him free and the [first] owner took the slave girl back by paying the full price, nothing would be deducted from her price. If the child were killed and an arsh were paid [to the owner], the [first] owner could [still] take the mother by paying the full price or could leave her.

If [the mother] gave birth to a child and the mother were set free [by the owner] and the first owner wanted the child, he should either pay the full price [of the mother] or leave him. Such a purchase is neither like [an ordinary] sale or the shuf'a sale, for [in this situation] the man [the first owner] has a priority right of purchasing the thing by paying the [full] price in the condition in

which it is found, regardless of changes over which he had no control, and he must pay the full price [if he wishes to take it back].

If the price could proportionately be divided between the mother and the arsh [paid] for the injury of the child, or if it could be divided between the mother and the defect caused to her, then the price could be proportionately divided between her and the defect caused to her when [for instance] she is blinded by her possessor. Similarly, one could divide the price between her and the nuptial gift due to her, if her possessor had intercourse with her, provided he has to pay damages to her, not being the owner of her entire person, [and] if any accident takes place, the price would be diminished proportionately. If such were the case it would not be lawful [for the owner] to set her free. Do you not think that the pre-empting purchaser (shāfi') would be entitled to purchase a house by the shuf'a from the vendor and annul the payment of price on the part of the [frustrated] purchaser? But if the owner of the slave girl set her free, his manumission would be lawful, and if he sold her, his sale would be lawful; if the [first] owner wishes to take her back, he would have to pay the price offered by the second purchaser. But if she were given as a gift [to another man], the first owner would be entitled to take her back by paying her value to the person to whom she was given as a gift. Such [a transfer] at any rate is neither like [an ordinary] sale nor the shuf'a sale. Do you not think that if a man sold a slave woman, it would not be lawful for him to resell her or set her free or give her as a gift after his first sale [to another man] is achieved, while the latter [owner] would have the right to sell her or give her as a gift, and if he had intercourse with her, the intercourse would be lawful, and if she gave birth to a child, would become an umm walad for him? But if the vendor had intercourse with her [after selling her], the intercourse would be unlawful, and if she gave birth to a child for him, she would not become an umm walad for him, in case the purchaser wanted to take her as well as her child. Thus, such [a transaction] would be neither like a shuf'a, nor a sale, nor a gift.

If a man gave a [female] servant as a gift to another man and her value increased by him, he who gave her as a gift has no right to take her back. If a man gave a gift to a member of his near of kin who is unlawful to him [in marriage] and [the beneficiary] obtained possession, he who gave the gift has no right to take it back. If the female slave were captured by the unbelievers [and sold to the near of kin], the [first] owner would have the right to take her back from the near of kin or any other, whether her worth has increased or not—together with her children—but the person who gave her as a gift would not have the right to take the child if the child were born when she was in the

possession of the receiver of the gift.

If a mukātaba were mortgaged with a man and was [thereafter] captured by the unbelievers as a prisoner from Muslim hands and purchased by another man from them [the unbelievers], the [original] owner would not have the right to take her back until the man in whose hand she was mortgaged would pay her price and from whom the owner would take her by paying the debt and the price. Such [a transaction] is neither like a sale, nor gift, nor shuf'a.

If a man sold a slave woman but, before the purchaser obtained possession and paid the price, the inhabitants of the territory of war captured her and another man purchased her [from them], the [first] purchaser would not have the right to claim her until the original vendor had recovered her from the one who had purchased her from the enemy by paying her price. If he obtains her on paying the price, then the [first] purchaser would have the right to take her by paying the original price with which he had purchased her and the other price which the [original] owner had paid to redeem her.

If a slave, liable both to a debt and a tort, were captured by the unbelievers and purchased [later by a Muslim] from them, the latter would be liable for the debt [of the slave] but not for the tort. If the [original] owner took him back by paying the price, he would be liable for [both] the debt and the tort. If [the slave] returned to the first owner, he would be liable to the tort and the debt; if he did not return to the first owner, the tort would be waived, but he would remain liable for the debt. [For] do you not think that if a slave in debt were sold by his master, but not if he were set free? [And] do you not think that the debt for which a slave was mortgaged would be disregarded until [the original mortgagee] takes [the mortgaged slave] back on paying [the purchaser] the price and thus receives his mortgage, and thereafter the original owner could redeem him by paying the debt?

If the inhabitants of the territory of war captured a male or female slave or any property from the Muslims and thereafter became Muslims while still in possession of these objects, then the slave would become their property, [so much so] that the [original] owner would not have the right to take him back; if the slave were in debt, [the new owner] would remain liable for debt; if he were liable to a tort, [the new owner] would not be liable for it. If the [captured] property were a mortgage, it would not revert to the charge of mortgage, and the debt for which [the property] was given in mortgage would be waived, if the value of the [mortgaged property] were equal to the debt.

If a free man were captured by the inhabitants of the territory of war and those people while in possession [of the free man] became Muslims, the free man would remain free and would never become a slave. The same would hold

true in the case of the mudabbar, the umm walad, and the mukātab, who revert to their original status and do not become slaves [of the captor]. This applies to any property which is not lawful to be sold and which the people of the territory of war capture—those people would not have the right to own it if they capture it.

If a free man asked another man to purchase [him from the unbelievers] he would remain a free man and the merchant who purchased him would have the right to recuperate from him [i.e., the prisoner] the price [paid to the enemy]. Likewise, if a mukātaba, an umm walad, and a mudabbar [were made prisoners and purchased at their demand from the enemy], the purchaser will have the right to recuperate from [the mukātaba, etc.] the price paid [to the enemy] after these [mukātaba, etc.] obtain their freedom.

If a free man asked another to purchase for him a named free man [a prisoner in the hands of the enemy] from the dār al-ḥarb and if the other purchased him, the free man who has been purchased would not have to pay the price at all, but the commanded person has the right [to recuperate the price] from the man who gave the order, provided he had guaranteed the price, or had said, "Purchase [him] for me." On the other hand, if he said: "Purchase him for yourself and consider it a charity," he would not be liable [to reimbursing].

If a man purchased a slave from the unbelievers [in the dār al-ḥarb], who had captured him from the Muslims, and the [new] purchaser mortgaged him, and if the original [Muslims] owner arrived later, he would not have the right to redeem [the slave] until he paid the debt [for which the slave was mortgaged] and separated the different charges. Thereafter, [the original Muslim] owner can recuperate him on payment of the price [paid to the enemy]. If the owner wanted to pay the debt to the mortgagee and also the price, and if [the mortgagee] voluntarily renounced the debt, he might do that; but the [original] owner would not constrain him to redeem until he takes him back with payment of the debt.

If [the slave] were hired [while in the hands of the purchaser], the hiring would be permissible and the [original] owner may take back [the slave] and cancel the hiring for the remaining period [if he wishes to do so]. The hiring is different from the amount of mortgage. For do you not think that the hiring is a divisible thing, if it is made for a number [of days, for instance]? The present case is likewise [divisible]. But God knows best!

Translated by Majid Khadduri[4]

Part III

THE UMMAYAD DYNASTY

al-Akhtal

YOUTH DEPARTED BUT OFTEN I ENJOYED IT

Youth departed but often I enjoyed it
 With beauties and drinking the red
I drank the wine in their shop
 And played with the singers chaste games
I am protected by an armor whose ardor is
 Like a camel scab guarded by the sword
He runs to me with his armor and weapons
 He walks with his arms like listing camel
I came early to the wine seller with a friend
 His reproachers howled the howl of dogs
A joyous one, pleasure kissed him as if
 His breast was touched with gilded sheen
Wearing kings' garments, eyes of fawns
 In every view are pleased with him
They look from behind veils as he appears
 A look of camels at the fine stallion
Dewy cups when they are drunk, his promises
 Are not tricky like unfruitful lightning
And when glasses go round at the drinking
 He has no excessive frowns
The swords came early and late to them
 They left Hawazin like a broken horn
They left your uncle of Gana holding
 A broken cup like a fox hole
They left Banu Tamim's remnant following
 The Banu Thabin like straggling asses
They met the rings of Banu Sulaim, and
 They cursed and the scars did not leave
And I knew that when they were ringed
 In every angry nose was a sign of shame
Horses run with armored men as if they were
 Thicket lions of the knights of Taglib.

Translated by Arthur Wormhoudt[1]

al-Farazdaq

LET ALL WEEP FOR AL-HAJJÁJ

Let all weep for al-Hajjáj, who weep for Faith or one
That sold unto God his life in guarding the Moslem land;
And him let the orphans weep whose mother, with arms begrimed,
From Fortune in wasting years of famine hath naught left o'er.
For ne'er since Mohammed died have eyes flowed for any man
Like him or beheld his peer, excepting the Caliphs' selves;
Nor ever the like of him was laid for the earth to bear,
Nor written a name like his in letters announcing death:
So firm to beat back and rout the demon of Mutiny
When War shows her grinning teeth—a she-camel scabbed and old.
Nay, never I saw a day of heavier grief and woe
And fuller of hands raised up to wipe the o'erflowing eyes
Than that morn when al-Hajjáj was carried upon his bier,
Who many a burden used to shoulder and win safe through.
When news of his death was brought, the woman that oft let stray
Her flocks in the wilderness would fain keep them close in fold,
And cried to her slaves, "Fetch home the cattle and tether them,
For he that was wont erstwhile to shepherd our flocks is dead."
Ay, dead, he that shepherded the Faith for believing men
And smote with his Indian blade the head of its adversary.
And would they had been cut off, the hands that interred the son
Of Yúsuf, what time they cast the earth o'er the covering stones!
But how could ye as ye gazed—and he in his winding-sheet—
At last lay him down betwixt the sides of a hollow grave?
For did not ye know 'twas he, whom there ye were burying,
That ruled in his master's name the frontiers of empire far?
He healed with his Mashrafite good sword the corrupted Faith,
And rancorous hates that breed dissensions he purged away.
No money prevailed on him to alter the just decree:
His sentence a rope, whereof not loose were the strands or weak,
But woven from left to right, for firmness, and then made fast
In knots twisted well and tied securely behind the neck.
The army that stood beyond the River, the tribes called up,
O hearing the death of him, their captain, with one voice cried,

"Unhappy are we: alas, the Strength of our host is dead,
Whereby every heart in hour of peril was braced again."
Yet surely, if al-Hajjáj is dead, Abu'l-'Ás's race
Of generous hawk-like chiefs are living and have not died;
And never there failed Marwán a proud scion of his House,
A man perfect as the moon at full and without eclipse,
Who filled with his glory's light the region of al-'Irák,
And no one his vengeance feared except for his own ill deed.

Translated by R. A. Nicholson[2]

Jarir

AL-FARAZDAQ VISITED THE FOLK OF HIJAZ

al-Farazdaq visited the folk of Hijaz
 Did not enjoy them, was not praised
You shamed your folk at the Ka'ba's wall
 And among the Baqi'ain and evergreen
We found Farazdaq at the two fairs
 Filthy outside and in witness
The bright son of 'Abd al-'Aziz forbade you
 By your worth to reject the mosque
You compared yourself as sharper than Thamud
 They said: You strayed and were unguided
They were weak when punishment settled
 Three nights at the rendezvous
You likened yourself to the ass penis
 Filthy smith and tinkerer
We found Jubair the father of Galib
 A distant relative of Ma'bad
Don't you work the bellows of Malik but
 Where is Suhail in respect to Farqad
Worst of colts is Ibn ass penis
 And you meet Qufaira at the fort
al-Farazdaq's root is the worst of roots
 Filth dirt, a pale spark

Jubair commanded Galib with an order
 From a zealous blood relative
He said: Hold to the twist of the tongs
 And scrape the drill with file
And Ji'thin, Minqar came down on her
 Like the return of Falji's hard hoof
She is drowsy by length of being knelt on
 As one watches the toothless charmer
Didn't you revenge the daughter of the smiths
 And leave her grieving at the crushing?
Did you not revenge the loosening of the belt
 And breaking the anklets and bracelets?
You started to track their trail at morning
 With the gait of a quick curl-tail dog
You found the Banu Minqar weakened with
 A weapon of your strange murder
Nawar says: You disgraced the smiths
 Would that Farazdaq had not been born!
She said: You were at Dhu Haumal and Rimah
 Would you had not been present
al-Farazdaq conquered the two small dogs
 And was equal to the black fever
So patch up for your ancestor his bellows
 Repair your goods so you aren't ruined
Bring up the anvil and bring the hammer
 Broaden the base for your bellows
I joined al Ba'ith to one with the cross
 To the smith with a strong rope
And they were joined when the race was hot
 To a high one at the far goal
He cut off their breath in the running
 By turning reins and he was not wearied
We are men who love trustworthiness
 Cautious of tales of martyrdom
We don't take support for a neighbor's bond
 Without swords nor wrap up in a cloak
You fixed your support against a betrayal
 At Jaishan and the sword was not sheathed
When you supported yourself, you the meanest,

You sat apart on the ass of an ignoble man
Far from the folk who protected al Zubair
 But as for Zubair may he not be far
You blamed horsemen on the day of Gabit
 And days of Bishr Banu Marthad
And day of Balqa O Smithsons we witnessed
 The jousting and you witnessed not
They came early to Abjar and the Haufazan
 In a swift drinking though driven off
And the day of two Bahir they pursued us
 Theirs the hooftracks in the middle
We put the swords in the skulls of kings
 And we cured the pride of the chiefs.

Translated by Arthur Wormhoudt[3]

Abd al-Hamid al-Katib

THE ART OF SECRETARYSHIP

And now: May God guard you who practice the craft of secretaryship, and may He keep you and give you success and guidance. There are prophets and messengers and highly honored kings. After them come different kinds of men, all of them made by God. They are of different kinds, even if they are all alike in fact. God occupied them with different kinds of crafts and various sorts of businesses, so that they might be able to make a living and earn their sustenance. He gave to you, assembled secretaries, the great opportunity to be men of education and gentlemen, to have knowledge and (good) judgment. You bring out whatever is good in the caliphate and straighten out its affairs. Through your advice, God improves the government for the benefit of human beings and makes their countries civilized. The ruler cannot dispense with you. You alone make him a competent ruler. Your position with regard to rulers is that (you are) the ears through which they hear, the eyes through which they see, the tongues through which they speak, and the hands through which they touch. May God give you, therefore, enjoyment of the excellent craft with which He has distinguished you, and may He not deprive you of the great favors that He has shown unto you.

No craftsman needs more than you to combine all praiseworthy good traits and all memorable and highly regarded excellent qualities, O secretaries, if you aspire to fit the description given of you in this letter. The secretary needs on his own account, and his master, who trusts him with his important affairs, expects him, to be mild where mildness is needed, to be understanding where judgment is needed, to be enterprising where enterprise is needed, to be hesitant where hesitation is needed. He must prefer modesty, justice, and fairness. He must keep secrets. He must be faithful in difficult circumstances. he must know (beforehand) about the calamities that may come. He must be able to put things in their proper places and misfortunes into their proper categories. He must have studied every branch of learning and know it well, and if he does not know it well, he must at least have acquired an adequate amount of it. By virtue of his natural intelligence, good education, and outstanding experience, he must know what is going to happen to him before it happens, and he must know the result of his actions before action starts. He must make the proper preparations for everything, and he must set up everything in its proper, customary form.

Therefore, assembled secretaries, vie with each other to acquire the different kinds of education and to gain an understanding of religious matters. Start with knowledge of the Book of God and religious duties. Then, study the Arabic language, as that will give you a cultivated form of speech. Then, learn to write well, as that will be an ornament to your letters. Transmit poetry and acquaint yourselves with the rare expressions and ideas that poems contain. Acquaint yourselves also with both Arab and non-Arab political events, and with the tales of (both groups) and the biographies describing them, as that will be helpful to you in your endeavors. Do not neglect to study accounting, for it is the mainstay of the land tax register. Detest prejudices with all your heart, lofty ones as well as low ones, and all idle and contemptible things, for they bring humility [sic] and are the ruin of secretaryship. Do not let your craft be a low one. Guard against backbiting and calumny and the actions of stupid people. Beware of haughtiness, foolishness, and pride, for they mean acquiring hostility without (even the excuse of) hatred. Love each other in God in your craft. Advise your colleagues to practice it in a way befitting your virtuous, fair, and gifted predecessors.

If times go hard for one of you, be kind to him and console him, until everything be well with him again. Should old age make one of you unable to get around and pursue his livelihood and meet his friends, visit him and honor him and consult him, and profit from his outstanding experience and mature knowledge. Every one of you should be more concerned for his assistants, who

may be useful when needed, than for his own children or brothers. Should some praise come (to one of you) in the course of his work, he should ascribe the merit to his colleague; any blame he should bear all by himself. He should beware of mistakes and slips and of being annoyed when conditions change. For you, assembled secretaries, are more prompt to be blamed than a woman, and blame is more detrimental to you than to them. You know that every one of you has a master, one who gives from his own as much as can be expected, and (every one of you) has the obligation to repay him, since he deserves it, with fidelity, gratefulness, tolerance, patience, good counsel, discretion, and active interest in his affairs, and to show (his good intentions) by his actions whenever his master needs him and his resources. Be conscious of (your obligations)—God give you success—in good and bad circumstances, in privation as in munificence and kindness, in happiness as in misfortune. Any member of this noble craft who has all these qualities has good qualities indeed.

If any one of you be appointed to an office, or if some matter that concerns God's children be turned over to one of you, he should think of God and choose obedience to Him. He should be kind to the weak and fair to those who have been wronged. All creatures are God's children. He loves most those who are kindest to His children. Furthermore, he should judge with justice, he should honor the noble (descendants of Muḥammad), augment the booty (gained in wars against infidels), and bring civilization to the country. He should be friendly to the subjects, and refrain from harming them. He should be humble and mild in his office. He should be kind in milking his land tax and calling in outstanding claims.

You should explore the character of him with whom you associate. When his good and bad sides are known, you will be able to help him to do the good things that agree with him, and be able to contrive to keep him from the bad things he desires. You must be able to do that in the subtlest and best manner. You know that a person who is in charge of an animal and understands his job, endeavors to know the character of the animal. If it is inclined to gallop, he takes precautions with the hind legs. If it is ungovernable, he does not goad it when he is riding it. If it is inclined to kick, he takes precautions with its forelegs. If he fears that it will shy, he takes precautions with its head. If it is restive, he gently subdues its desire to go where it wants to go. If it still continues, he pulls it slightly to the side, then has its halter loosened. This description of how to take care of an animal contains good points for those who want to lead human beings and deal with them, serve them, and have intimate contact with them. The secretary, with his excellent education, his noble craft, his subtlety, his frequent dealings with people who confer with him and discuss things with

him and learn from him or fear his severity, needs to be kind to his associates, to flatter them, and to supply their wants, even more than the person in charge of an animal which cannot answer, does not know what is right, does not understand what is said to it, and goes only where its master who rides upon it makes it go. Be kind – God show mercy unto you – when you look after things. Use as much reflection and thought as possible. God permitting, you will thus escape harshness, annoyance, and rudeness on the part of your associates. They will be in agreement with you, and you will have their friendship and protection, if God wills.

None of you should have too sumptuous an office or go beyond the proper limits in his dress, his mount, his food, his drink, his house, his servants, or in the other things pertaining to his station, for, despite the nobility of the craft by which God has distinguished you, you are servants who are not permitted to fall short in their service. You are caretakers whom one does not permit to be wasteful or spendthrift. Try to preserve your modesty by planned moderation in all things I have mentioned and told you. Beware of the wastefulness of prodigality and the bad results of luxury. They engender poverty and bring about humiliation. People who (are prodigal and live in luxury) are put to shame, especially if they be secretaries and men of education.

Things repeat themselves. One thing contains the clue to another. Let yourselves be guided in your future undertakings by your previous experience. Then, choose the method of doing things that is most definite, most accurate, and that promises the best result. You should know that there is something that defeats accomplishment, namely, talking about things. The person who does it is prevented from using his knowledge and ability to think. Therefore, everyone of you, while he is in his office, should endeavor to talk no more than is sufficient; he should be concise in the matters he brings up and in the answers he gives; and he should give thought to all the arguments he advances. His work will profit from that. It will prevent too much preoccupation with other things. He should implore God to grant him success and to support him with His guidance, for he must fear making mistakes that might hurt his body and (cast doubt upon) his intelligence and education. When any one of you says or thinks that the high quality and efficiency of his work is obviously the result of his own cleverness and knowledge of how to do things, he provokes God. God will let him depend upon himself alone, and then he will find that he is not adequate to his task. This is no secret to those who reflect.

None of you should say that he has a better understanding of affairs, or knows better how to handle difficult matters, than other members of his craft, than those who serve together with him. Of two persons, discerning people

consider him the more intelligent who throws off conceit and thinks his col-leagues more intelligent and more skillful than he. But at any rate, both parties should acknowledge the excellence of God's favors. No one should let him-self be deceived by his own opinions and consider himself free from mistakes. Nor should he strive to outdo his friends, equals, colleagues, or his family. Everybody must give praise to God, in humility in the face of His greatness, in meekness in the face of His might, and in fulfillment of the command to speak God's favors.

In this letter of mine, let me refer to the old proverb: "He who accepts good advice is successful." This is the essence of this letter and the best that is said in it, after the references to God it contains. Therefore, I have placed it at the end, and I close the letter with it. May God take care of us and of you, assembled students and secretaries, in the same way He takes care of those whom, as He knows in His prescience, He will make happy and guide aright. He can do it. It is in His hand.

Farewell, and God's mercy and blessings upon you.

Translated by Franz Rosenthal[4]

Ibn al-Muqaffa

THE RABBIT AND THE ELEPHANT

Over one of the lands of the elephants the years had grown weary, and it became barren and its waters failed. Its springs sank, and its plants and trees withered and cracked. A fierce thirst afflicted the elephants, and they com-plained to their king.

The king dispatched his messengers and scouts to every region to search for water. And some came home and reported discovery of a certain place where a fountain bubbled up called the Fountain of the Moon and the water was plen-tiful. So the king and his company made their way to drink at the fountain, and the whole herd followed.

Now the fountain was in the land of the rabbits, and when the elephants came these were trampled in their burrows, and many perished. Then the rab-bits gathered round their king and spoke to him of the harm the elephants were doing; and he asked for opinions and counsel. At this a rabbit called Firouz, whose learning and wisdom the king knew of old, stepped forward; and she

said, "If the king wills, let him send me to the elephants accompanied by one he trusts to see and hear all that passes and report it to him." To which the king replied, "We trust you, and we approve your offer. Go forth to the elephants, conveying to them, in my name, what you wish. And remember that the judgment and wisdom, the mildness and courtesy of the messenger, convey the character of him from whom the message comes. Be mild, generous, patient and politic. Hearts are softened by the courteous messenger, but hardened by the coarse."

On a moony night the rabbit started, and came to the elephants; but hated to approach them for fear that even unintentionally they might trample her under their feet. But she ascended a high mountain, and shouted to the king of the elephants, and said, "The moon has sent me to you; and the messenger should not be blamed for the words he carries, if even they are uncivil." "What is the message?" said the elephant-king. She said, "The moon tells you that when a creature knows his strength over the weak and takes pride in his superiority and swaggers about it, he may find his strength is bane. Now the moon has observed that you know your strength over creeping things, and are swollen with it, and that you have resorted to the fountain which bears his name, and have drunk from the waters and troubled them. Therefore he dispatched me to you. And I give you warning that if you persist in your conduct, your sight will be darkened and your life destroyed. If you doubt my message, come to the fountain this hour, and the moon will meet you there."

The king of the elephants marveled at the speech, and went to the fountain with Firouz the messenger, and looked in the pool and saw the moon gleaming. Then Firouz said to him: "Dip your trunk into the pool and draw water to wash your face, and kneel to the moon." So the elephant lowered his trunk into the pool, and at once the water rippled. And the elephant believed that the moon shuddered. "Why did the moon shudder?" he said. "Can he be angry with me for putting my trunk in the water?" The rabbit Firouz said, "Yes." Then the elephant knelt down again, and did penance to the moon for his sins, and undertook that neither he nor any of his herd should repeat the misdeeds done in that place.

Translated by Herbert Howarth and Ibrahim Shakrullah[5]

Ibn Ishaq

THE PROPHET'S MISSION

When Muhammad the apostle of God reached the age of forty God sent him in compassion to mankind, as 'an evangelist to all men'. Now God had made a covenant with every prophet whom he had sent before him that he should believe in him, testify to his truth and help him against his adversaries, and he required of them that they should transmit that to everyone who believed in them, and they carried out their obligations in that respect. God said to Muhammad, "When God made a covenant with the prophets (He said) this is the scripture and wisdom which I have given you, afterwards an apostle will come confirming what you know that you may believe in him and help him." He said, "Do you accept this and take up my burden?" i.e., the burden of my agreement which I have laid upon you. They said, "We accept it." He answered, "Then bear witness and I am a witness with you." Thus God made a covenant with all the prophets that they should testify to this truth and help him against his adversaries and they transmitted that obligation to those who believed in them among the two monotheistic religions.

One whom I do not suspect told me from Sa'īd b. Abū 'Arūba from Qatāda bn Di'āma al-Sadūsi from Abū'l-Jald: "The Furqān came down on the 14th night of Ramaḍān. Others say, No, but on the 17th; and in support of this they appeal to God's word: "And what we sent down to our servant on the day of al-Furqān, the day the two companies met" which was the meeting of the apostle and the polytheists at Badr, and that took place on the morning of Ramaḍān 17th.

al-Zuhrī related from 'Urwa b. Zubayr that 'Ā'isha told him that when Allah desired to honour Muhammad and have mercy on His servants by means of him, the first sign of prophethood vouchsafed to the apostle was true visions, resembling the brightness of daybreak, which were shown to him in his sleep. And Allah, she said, made him love solitude so that he liked nothing better than to be alone.

'Abdu'l-Malik b. 'Ubaydullah b. Abū Sufyān b. al-'Alā' b. Jāriya the Thaqafite who had a retentive memory related to me from a certain scholar that the apostle at the time when Allah willed to bestow His grace upon him and endow him with prophethood would go forth for his affair and journey far afield until he reached the glens of Mecca and the beds of its valleys where no house was in sight and not a stone or a tree that he passed by but would say, "Peace unto thee, O apostle of Allah." And the apostle would turn to his right and left

and look behind him and he would see naught but trees and stones. Thus he stayed seeing and hearing so long as it pleased that he should stay. Then Gabriel came to him with the gift of God's grace whilst he was on Ḥirā' every year for a month to practice *taḥannuth* as was the custom of Quraysh in heathen days. *Taḥannuth* is religious devotion.

Abū Ṭālib said:

> By Thaur and him who made Thābir firm in its place
> And by those going up to ascend Ḥirā' and coming down

Wahb b. Kaisān told me that 'Ubayd said to him: Every year during that month the apostle would pray in seclusion and give food to the poor that came to him. And when he completed the month and returned from his seclusion, first of all before entering his house he would go to the Ka'ba and walk round it seven times or as often as it pleased God; then he would go back to his house until in the year when God sent him, in the month of Ramaḍān in which God willed concerning him what He willed of His grace, the apostle set forth to Ḥirā' as was his wont, and his family with him. When it was the night on which God honoured him with his mission and showed mercy on His servants thereby, Gabriel brought him the command of God. "He came to me," said the apostle of God, "while I was asleep, with a coverlet of brocade whereon was some writing, and said, 'Read!' I said, 'What shall I read?' He pressed me with it so tightly that I thought it was death; then he let me go and said, 'Read!' I said, 'What shall I read?' He pressed me with it again so that I thought it was death; then he let me go and said, 'Read!' I said, 'What shall I read?' He pressed me with it the third time so that I thought it was death and said, 'Read!' I said, 'What then shall I read?'—and this I said only to deliver myself from him, lest he should do the same to me again. He said:

> 'Read in the name of thy Lord who created,
> Who created man of blood coagulated.
> Read! Thy Lord is the most beneficent,
> Who taught by the pen,
> Taught that which they knew not unto men.'

So I read it, and he departed from me. And I awoke from my sleep, and it was as though these words were written on my heart. Now none of God's creatures was more hateful to me than an (ecstatic) poet or a man possessed: I could not even look at them. I thought, Woe is me poet or possessed—Never shall

Quraysh say this of me! I will go to the top of the mountain and throw myself down that I may kill myself and gain rest. So I went forth to do so and then when I was midway on the mountain, I heard a voice from heaven saying, "O Muhammad! thou art the apostle of God and I am Gabriel." I raised my head towards heaven to see (who was speaking), and lo, Gabriel in the form of a man with feet astride the horizon, saying, "O Muhammad! thou art the apostle of God and I am Gabriel." I stood gazing at him, and that turned me from my purpose moving neither forward nor backward; then I began to turn my face away from him, but towards whatever region of the sky I looked, I saw him as before. And I continued standing there, neither advancing nor turning back, until Khadīja sent her messengers in search of me and they gained the high ground above Mecca and returned to her while I was standing in the same place, then he parted from me and I from him, returning to my family. And I came to Khadīja and sat by her thigh and drew close to her. She said, "O Abū'l-Qāsim, where hast thou been? By God, I sent my messengers in search of thee, and they reached the high ground above Mecca and returned to me." I said to her, "Woe is me poet or possessed." She said, "I take refuge in God from that O Abū'l-Qāsim. God would not treat you thus since he knows your truthfulness, your great trustworthiness, your fine character, and your kindness. This cannot be, my dear. Perhaps you did see something." "Yes, I did," I said. Then I told her of what I had seen; and she said, "Rejoice, O son of my uncle, and be of a good heart. Verily, by Him in whose hand is Khadīja's soul, I have hope that thou wilt be the prophet of this people." Then she rose and gathered her garments about her and set for to her cousin Waraqa b. Naufal b. Asad b. 'Abdu'l-Uzzā b. Quṣayy, who had become a Christian and read the scriptures and learned from those that follow the Torah and the Gospel. And when she related to him what the apostle of God told her he had seen and heard, Waraqa cried, "Holy! Holy! Verily by Him in whose hand is Waraqa's soul, if thou hast spoken to me the truth, O Khadīja, there hath come unto him the greatest Nāmūs (meaning Gabriel) who came to Moses aforetime, and lo, he is the prophet of his people. Bid him be of good heart." So Khadīja returned to the apostle of God and told him what Waraqa had said, and that calmed his fears somewhat. And when the apostle of God had finished his period of seclusions and returned (to Mecca), in the first place he performed the circumambulation of the Ka'ba, as was his wont. While he was doing it, Waraqa met him and said, "O son of my brother, tell me what thou hast seen and heard." The apostle told him, and Waraqa said, "Surely, by Him in whose hand is Waraqa's soul, thou art the prophet of this people. There hath come unto thee the greatest Nāmūs, who came unto Moses. Thou wilt be called a liar, and they will use thee despitefully and cast thee out

and fight against thee. Verily, if I live to see that day, I will help God in such wise as He knoweth." Then he brought his head near to him and kissed his forehead; and the apostle went to his own house. Waraqa's words added to his confidence and lightened his anxiety.

Ismā'īl b. Abū Ḥakīm, a freedman of the family of al-Zubayr, told me on Khadīja's authority that she said to the apostle of God, "O son of my uncle, are you able to tell me about your visitant, when he comes to you?" He replied that he could, and she asked him to tell her when he came. So when Gabriel came to him, as he was wont, the apostle said to Khadīja, "This is Gabriel who has just come to me." "Get up, O son of my uncle," she said, "and sit by my left thigh." The apostle did so, and she said, "Can you see him?" "Yes," he said. She said, "Then turn round and sit on my right thigh." He did so, and she said, "Can you see him?" When he said that he could she asked him to move and sit in her lap. When he had done this she again asked if he could see him, and when he said yes, she disclosed her form and cast aside her veil while the apostle was sitting in her lap. Then she said, "Can you see him?" And he replied, "No." She said, "O son of my uncle, rejoice and be of good heart, by God he is an angel and not a satan."

I told 'Abdullah b. Ḥasan this story and he said, "I heard my mother Fāṭima, daughter of Ḥusayn, talking about this tradition from Khadīja, but as I heard it she made the apostle of God come inside her shift, and thereupon Gabriel departed, and she said to the apostle of God, 'Thee verily is an angel and not a satan.'"

Translated by Alfred Guillaume[6]

Bashshar Ibn Burd

WILL NO EMISSARY BE FOUND

Will no emissary be found to speak in my name to all Arabs,
To those who live and to those who rest beneath the earth,
To tell them that I am a man of most noble origin.
My grandfather was Khusraw, my father Sasan. With these do I share my fame.
And were I to enumerate my ancestors, it would be proved that my
 grandfather was a king.
The kingly crown has descended to me.
Behold this valorous man—he either sitteth among his retinue, while people
 creep towards him on their knees,
Or he goeth, adorned with sparkling gems, into the council.
A noble, clothed in royal furs, he is surrounded by courtiers.
His servants bring him viands on golden dishes.
My father never drank that beverage of mingled camel and ewe's milk which
 they [the Bedouins] drink from small wine-skins
Never did he gather the bitter fruit of the colocynth, nor bite them with his
 teeth from hunger.
Never did he approach the prickly bushes to shake the berries from them.
Never did we roast lizards that flick their tails.
Never did I catch lizards on the parched earth and devour them greedily.
My father never warmed himself, seated before a camp fire with legs spread
 wide apart.
Nay! Nor did my father ever ride on a camel's hump!
In very truth, we have been kings for many generations.

Translated by Hilda Kasanina[7]

Part IV

THE ABBASID DYNASTY

Rabia al-Adawiya

O MY JOY AND MY DESIRE AND MY REFUGE

O my Joy and my Desire and my Refuge,
My Friend and my Sustainer and my Goal,
Thou art my Intimate, and longing for Thee sustains me,
Were it not for Thee, O my Life and my Friend,
How I should have been distraught over the spaces of the earth,
How many favours have been bestowed, and how much hast Thou given me.
Of gifts and grace and assistance,
Thy love is now my desire and my bliss,
And has been revealed to the eye of my heart that was athirst,
I have none beside Thee, Who dost make the desert blossom,
Thou art my joy, firmly established within me,
If Thou art satisfied with me, then
O Desire of my heart, my happiness has appeared.

Translated by Margaret Smith[1]

Ibn al-Ahnaf

LOVE

Dear love
'tis less than I have vowed
but let me gather in
and bring all love from earth and sea and sky;

then
let us to its equaling
that love,
when death has ravished us,
encase our shroud.

Translated by Omar Pound[2]

Abu Nuwas

FOUR THINGS

Four things banish grief and care,
Four sweet things incline
Body and soul and eyne
To enjoy, if they be there:
Water, wine,
Gardens bright and faces fair.

THOU SCOLDER OF GRAPE AND ME

Thou scolder of grape and me,
I ne'er shall win thy smile.
Because against thee I rebel
'Tis churlish to revile.

Ah, breathe no more the name of wine
Until thou cease to blame,
For fear that thy foul tongue should smirch
Its fair and lovely name!

Come, pour it out, ye gentle boys,
A vintage ten years old,
That seems as though 'twere in the cup
A lake of liquid gold

And when the water mingles there,
To fancy's eye are set
Pearls over shining pearls close strung
As in a carcanet.

Translated by R. A. Nicholson[3]

THE GREAT OFFENCE

She seemed so bored,
I wanted to embrace her by surprise;
But then the scalding waters
Fell from her eyes and burnt her roses.

I offered her a cup...

And came to paradise...

Ah, sorrow,
When she rose from the waves of wine
I thought she would have killed me
With the swords of her desolation...

Especially as I had tied her girdle
With the wrong bow.

Translated by Powys Mathers[4]

HURRY, FOR THE BEERGARDENS ARE BLOOMING

Hurry, for the beergardens are blooming.
The war still a hill away. Earth
With all its aviary is sitting
In amity with the natural voices.
They sing, till your veins are strings
And a friction begins like recovery.
The soil has come into flower, and wine
(From the bed where an intact leek
And a Roman endlessly reproduce her)
Looks out. If you catch the instant
You will see her nodding.

Translated by Herbert Howarth and Ibrahim Shakrullah[5]

THUS BY THE CAMEL HE LOVES

Thus by the camel he loves
 Upon which is a fine rider
Shaded the brows of the eyes
 The collar of his shirt torn
When she crossed the soft sand
 Vehemence shone in his eye
She chafed the ostrich mother
 When a cold shower hit her
She goes to her eggs in the desert
 In whose hollow is the chick
And by a hand forbidden in mixing
 The wine whose light flames
So when it joins the explosion
 It is like the foamy pearls
He poured it gloriously, pure
 Princes and bold ones grew it
By a basin of a peopled mosque
 How wide and well supported
Its roof does not encompass it
 A mountain alone conceals it
And the camp of Banu Abu Sufyan
 Where the numbers gather
Where the crowds are at home
 And the abodes prepared
The camps of warriors where
 The torrents flow furiously
To houses which are settled in
 Their grief for my soul's one
Sweetest to the eye bekohled
 Whose eye opthalmia circles
Going to her desert and herds
 Returning from her folk
And all struck dead by parting
 As the youth bends his neck
A poet, when he flashes
 A smile, the cold appears
When we arise we pray that

None of us parts from other
I move him when they arise
 And touch him when they sit
The merciful Caliph is not just
 To me when they are praying
And where is Mirbad the ruined
 As described and Jalad
And its trench for the mosque
 Was glorious as was Naḍad
And the camel mart where one
 Drove galloping horses
A place where denying grief
 Was not lacking to me
Some Arabs stripped the place
 Where its sun rose high
When I said: How is life?
 He said: a thick bore
May Allah forbid moderation
 Even if a land shelters them.

Translated by Arthur Wormhoudt[6]

Abu'l Atahiya

VANITY: TO HARUN AL-RASHID

Live securely, as you wish;
the palace heights are safe enough.
With pleasures flooding day and night,
the smooth proves sweeter than the rough.

But when your breath begins to clog
in sharp contractions of your lungs,
then know for certain, my dear sire,
your life was vain as idle tongues.

Translated by James Kritzeck[7]

SURELY SHALL FATE DISJOINT THE PROUDEST NOSE

Surely shall Fate disjoint the proudest nose,
All wears away by movement and repose.
In long experience if wisdom be,
Less than my portion is enough for me.
Eager I take the hopes my soul inspires;
False are these hopes and vain are these desires.
That my hereafter I neglect is clear,
Since I am pleased and happy with things here.
O thou that gloriest in thy worldly state,
Mud piled on mud will never make thee great.
Nay, wouldst thou see the noblest man of all,
Look at a monarch in a beggar's pall!
To him great honour by folk is given,
'Tis he knows how to live on earth for Heaven.

Translate by R. A. Nicholson[8]

VIRTUE CAST AN EYE AT ME COMING

Virtue cast an eye at me coming, and cried.
I swore I was fasting, he laughed till he died.
He leaned on his elbows by the seaside
And talked to himself and the fish and the tide.

Translated by Herbert Howarth and Ibrahim Shakrullah[9]

Dibil

I RECALL THE CAMPSITE AT 'ARAFAH

I recall the campsite at 'Arafah and shed tears at 'Abarah.

The schools where the Qur'an is taught, [there] its recital is no longer; the abodes of Revelation are as vacant courts.

[Oh, how I wish] for the Family of the Prophet of God at al-Khaif at Minā, at the corner of the Ka'bah, at the sacrifice at 'Arafah, and the heaps [at 'Arafah];

[For] the abodes of 'Alī, Husain, Ja'far, Hamzah, and the Worshipper whose knees are calloused—

Abodes effaced by the damage of injustices, not by days and years.

Stop. Let us ask the house, whose people are few, when is the time for fasting and prayer?

Where are they whom distant journeys have estranged from their abode and who have become disordered and dispersed in the lands?

When they trace their lineage, they are the heirs of the Prophet. They are the best leaders and protectors,

Whereas [other] people are envious, liars, hate one another, and are possessed of rancour and revenge.

When they remember those slain at Badr, Khaibar, and Hunain, they shed tears.

The graves at Kufāh, Taibah, and Fakhkh, my prayers reach them!

Others are [buried] in Juzājān, and there is a tomb at Būkhamrā near al-Ghurbah.

In Baghdād is a tomb for a Pure Soul. May God include him in Paradise!

As for these deaf ones, their intrinsic qualities defy my powers of description;

They await the Ressurection, when God will send a Restorer who will scatter their grief and cares.

Souls at the two rivers of Karbalā, whose [final] abode is by the bank of the Euphrates,

The vicissitudes of Time have dispersed them [and], as you see, they have a dust color and are covered with stones.

There is a band of them in Madīnah, who are forever emaciated from need;

Who have few visitors except the male hyena, the eagle, and the vulture;

They are forever asleep in their various beds in the regions of the earth.

They who formerly were the raiders and chosen leaders of the Hijāz and its people,

The distress of years has overtaken their neighborhood, so that a party of
horsemen no longer warm themselves at their fires.

When they joined battle, their spears flashed in the sun—pokers of the coals
of death and woe.

If one day they boasted, they brought forth Muhammad, Gabriel, and the
Furqān, the possessor of the Sūras.

[Beware of] cursing the Family of the Prophet, for, as long as I live, they are
my beloved and the people of my trust.

I choose them as guides for my affairs, for they are the best in all situations.

O God, add clear vision to my firm belief; add the love of them to my other
good qualities.

I swear that you, young and old, are [ever ready] to free slaves and to pay the
bloodwit.

I love my remotest relation out of love for you, and I avoid for your sake my
kin and daughters.

Fearing an enemy, who opposes those alive of the Family of Truth, I hid my
love of you.

Time has surrounded me with evil, and I hope for security after death.

Do you not see me go forth for thirty years, eve and morn, continuously sad?

I see booty divided amongst others; their hands are empty thereof.

The bodies of the Family of the Prophet are lean; the necks of the family of
Ziyād are distended [with food].

The daughters of Ziyād live in palaces; the family of the Messenger of God
lives in the desert.

When they suffer injury, they stretch out to their oppressors hands afflicted
with past injuries.

Were it not for him, who I hope will come today or tomorrow, my sighing for
them would cut my heart.

No doubt an Imām is coming—and Imām who will govern according to the
name of God and the Blessings.

He will distinguish those false and true among us; he will requite with favors
and revenge.

I will restrain my heart from opposing [your enemies], for what I have met of
tears suffices me.

O my soul, delight! O my soul, rejoice! for what cometh is not remote.

If God will delay the time of my death and will bring this event within my
lifespan,

I will recover without damage to my heart, and I will let my lance and sword
water in my enemies.

I wish to transfer the sun from her fixed abode and to cause the hard, bare
 stones to listen.
[However,] many are those who know and do not benefit; many are those
 who are obstinate and incline to their passions and doubts.
My end is that I will die with grief for them—[a grief] which reverberates in
 my throat.
[And] it is as though you saw my ribs become narrow with the intensity of
 [my] sighing.

<div align="right">

Translated by Leon Zolondek[10]

</div>

al-Jahiz

THE BOOK OF PROOF: CONCERNING ASCETICISM

In the name of God the merciful the compassionate. We shall begin, in the name
and by the help of God, with some sayings of the devotees concerning asceti-
cism and with some mention of their characteristics and their exhortations.

'Auf said on the authority of Hasan: "The feet of a son of Adam will not
stir (from the place of Judgment) until he be asked of three things—his youth,
how he wore it away; his life, how he passed it; and his wealth, whence he got
it and on what he spent it."

Yúnus son of 'Ubaid said: "I heard three sayings more wonderful than any I
have ever heard. The first is the saying of Ḥassán son of Abú Sinán—'Nothing
is easier than abstinence from things unlawful: if aught make thee doubt, leave
it alone.' The second is the saying of Ibn Sírin—'I have never envied any one
thing.' The third is the saying of Muwarriḳ al-'Ijlí—'Forty years ago I asked of
God a boon which He has not granted, and I have not despaired of obtaining
it.' They said to Muwarriḳ, 'What is it?' He replied, 'Not to meddle with that
which does not concern me.'"

Ziyád, the slave of 'Aiyásh son of Abú Rabí'a, said, "I am more afraid of
being hindered from prayer than of being denied an answer to my prayer."

Some people said to Rábi'a of (the tribe) Ḳais: "We might speak to the
men of thy family and they would purchase for thee a maid-servant who would
relieve thee of the care of thy house." "By God," said she, "I am ashamed to beg
aught of this world from Him who is the lord of it all: how, then, should I beg
it from one who is not the lord of it?"

A certain ascetic said: "Your dwellings are before you, and your life is after your death."

And Samuel son of 'Ádiyá, the Jew, said in verse:

"Being dead, I was created, and before that I was not anything that dies; but I died when I came to life."

Hassan son of Dínár said: "Hasan (of Basra) saw a man in his death-struggle. 'Surely,' he exclaimed, 'a thing of which this is the end ought not to be desired at the first and ought to be feared at the last.'"

Mujálid son of Sa'íd gives the authority of Sha'bí for the following words spoken by Murra of Hamdán. Mujálid relates that he had himself seen Murra, and that according to Ismá'íl son of Abú Khálid, who told Mujálid that he had never seen the like of him, Murra used to perform prayers of five hundred bowings in a day and a night. Murra would often say: "When (the Caliph) 'Uthmán—may God be well pleased with him!—was killed, I thanked God that I had taken no part in those wars, and I added two hundred bowings. Then after the battle of Nahrawán, at which I was not present, I thanked God and added a hundred bowings; and when the rebellion of Ibn Zubair took place, I thanked God for the same reason and added a hundred more." Now, I ask God to forgive Murra, notwithstanding that we perceive no justification for some of his words, for you will not find amongst orthodox Moslems a single jurist who denies that it is lawful to fight the Khárijites, even as we do not find any of them denying that it is lawful to fight robbers.

'Umar son of 'Abdu'l-'Azíz was questioned concerning those who murdered 'Uthmán and those who deserted him and those who defended him. He answered, "God withheld my hand from that bloodshed, and I prefer not to dip my tongue in it."

Abu'l-Dardá came to visit a sick man and said, "How do you find yourself?" "I am in fear of death." "From whom have you obtained all good?" "From God." "Why, then, are you afraid of Him from whom alone you have obtained all good?" And when Abraham was cast into the fire, Gabriel (on whom be peace!) said to him, "Dost thou want anything, O Friend of Allah?" "From thee, nothing," he replied.

It has been related to me that 'Umar son of Khattáb (may God be well pleased with him!) said: "O people, there came over me a time when I was thinking that those who recite the Qur'an sought thereby only Allah and what is His to give. But now meseems that some of you recite the Qur'an, seeking thereby what is with men. Oh, seek Allah by your recitation and seek Him by your works! Well did we know you when the Revelation was coming down and when the Prophet—God bless him and grant him peace!—was in the midst of

us; but the Revelation hath ceased and the Prophet is gone, and now I know you only by that which I say unto you. Look you, whosoever showeth to us good, we will think good of him and praise him for it; and whosoever showeth to us ill, we will think ill of him and hate him for it. Restrain ye these souls from their lusts, for they are eager in desire, and if ye restrain them not, they will speed you to the most evil end. Verily this Truth is weighty and wholesome, and verily falsehood is light and unhealthy. To abandon sin is better than to strive after repentance. Many a time hath one glance sown the seed of a lust, and the lust of a moment hath left a long grief behind."

Abú Házim the Lame said: "I have found worldly wealth to be two things. One of these is due to me, but I shall never receive it in advance of its appointed term, not though I should demand it with all the might of the heavens and the earth. The other is not due to me: I have not obtained it in the past nor shall I obtain it in the future. What is due to me is withheld from others, just as what is due to others is withheld from me. For which of these twain's sake, then shall I waste my life and bring my soul to perdition?"

Said Jesus son of Mary—the blessings of God be on our Prophet and on him!—"Verily the friends of God have no fear nor do they grieve. They are those who looked to the reality of this life when others looked to its appearance, and to the state hereafter that abideth, when others looked to the life that fleeteth away. They made to die thereof that which they feared would make their spirits die, and they abandoned thereof that which they knew would abandon them."

And seeing him go forth from the house of a harlot, they said, "O Spirit of God, what doest thou here?" Jesus answered, "The physician comes only to the sick."

And he passed by some people and they reviled him. Then he passed by others and they reviled him. And the more they spake evil, the more he spake good. A man of the disciples said to him, "The more they do thee evil, the more thou doest them good: it is as though thou wert setting them on against thee and inciting them to revile thee." Jesus said, "Every man gives of that which he hath not."

Translated by R. A. Nicholson[11]

Abu Tammam

IN PRAISE OF THE CALIPH MU'TASIM

After the Victory at 'Amuriyya

The sword is a better reporter than books
Follow the meteors of lances at war
They drive beyond the seven planets
And further than fables and the perjured
Ornaments of heaven, and sciences
Heady as pine and slight as willow.

The librarian mutters of two months
That stare like crows, of a tailing star at dusk,
Of steady and turned bodies, of poles
And orbits and spaces, mineral gods
By which he disposes his estates,
A heathen in a gown.

Conquest of conquests, outside embrace of language
The day of 'Amuriyya was rich with bags of milk
Islam drove the confounders of faith down the slopes
It was worth the sacrifice of many mothers.

The forelocks of nights had whitened since Alexander
But she was unwrinkled, and no hand had divided
Her virginity. The kings of Anatolia
Had never forced her. The years shook her niggardly
Like old women churning a fine foam
On the pail and spilling nothing.

But a dazzle,
And affliction was on her. First Ankara
Fell, and the squares were empty, the public places
Mournful as monuments. Then the plague came
Through the fields and through the family.
The best men dropped between the walls, their hair

Hot and scarlet, but not for orthodoxy
Not with the Prophet's henna.

The Prince of Believers sold rock and wood
To fire. He departed at midnight
In a forenoon of flame, and one sun
Rose livid as the other died, utterly
Pure of light, except where smoke made haggard
The fringes, trying the private dark.
Time cleared like cloud
The day broiled
Obligation was appeased
Trophies were abundant
Near husbands fallen early
New grooms couched that night.

Vestiges of camps, their pasture plucked,
Where the ballad lovers encouraged their griefs
Were greener than all we left. We liked
Those sores better than the crimson and shamed
Cheeks of girls we took, and the befouled steppe
Better than the vineyards down south.

You feed on victory, Prince, your sword
Drags souls from coverts, your commissars
Fit your armies for many fronts.
God has hurled you on two cities:
Whose marshals said, "No grass will be cropped
By these stray nomads, no roses round here."
They fêted on hope till the antlers of swords
Locked, and swung the frustrating vessels
Of water and bush with death.

A girl in Zibatræa was taken by the Greeks.
As they rent her she shrieked your name.
You heard her beyond the two torrents, and you
Dashed your cup on the marble, and spat out
The saliva of sweet women. The free cities
Crying for help brought even in a summer

Unemployment to cold trickling mouths
And sent you among the fair people
With a sword of fair play and the fare of death to them
And glory to the Arab faces.

Translated by Herbert Howarth and Ibrahim Shakrullah[12]

al-Buhturi

BODIES OF WATER LIKE HORSES

Bodies of water like horses
Breaking from the starter's rope
Hit the bath with a white
Roll of fluid ingots. Wind
Warms overhead creasing it.
The sun doubles it grimacing
Like an uncle. The rain adds
Gum and sorrow to the flow.
But at night the stars descend
In silent order, and you see
The cosmos standing on its hands.

Translated by Herbert Howarth and Ibrahim Shakrullah[13]

Ibn Qutayba

EXTRACTS FROM *UYUN AL-AKHBAR*

When I had become aware of the wide-spread decrease, and disappearance of learning, of Government being too busy to set up a market for Adab, so that it became effaced and erased, I took it upon myself to compose a book on knowledge and on the rectification of tongue and hand for the benefit of those of the scribes whose education was scanty: a book through which I reached my soul's desire for them, and my heart's ease, and in which I registered for their

sake all that God had presented me with for the day of victory. But I impose upon them the condition not only to study it, but also to learn by heart the original sources of the sayings, so as to introduce them as similes into the spaces between their lines when they write, and to make use of their beautiful conceits and elegant expressions when they speak. After having undertaken to look after part of their equipment, zeal called me to satisfy their wants, for I was afraid lest, if I left them to themselves for the remaining needs and trusted them to select it, their perseverance might not last against neglect and out of weakness they might not find their riding beasts easy so that they might turn away from the end, as they had turned away from the beginning; or lest they might attempt this with weakness of purpose and languidness of application so that weakness of natural disposition and disgust at inconvenience might overpower them. Therefore I finished for them what I had begun and coated with plaster the building of which I had laid the foundations; and I behaved towards them like one who acts kindly towards him he loves, rather like a tender father towards a son who shows filial piety. But I shall be satisfied with their casual thanks, relying upon God for reward and remuneration.

This book, although not dealing with Qur'án or Sunna, the religious law or the knowledge of what is lawful and what is forbidden, yet leads on to the heights of things and shows the way to noble character; it restrains from baseness, turns away from ugly things, incites to right conduct and fair management, to mild administration and to rendering the land prosperous. For the way to Allâh is not one nor is all that is good confined to nightprayers and continued fasting and the knowledge of the lawful and the forbidden. On the contrary, the ways to Him are many and the doors of the good are wide; and the soundness of religion depends on the soundness of time and the soundness of time on the soundness of government, whilst the soundness of government depends—beside the help of Allâh—on leading aright and providing proper understanding.

I have arranged these 'Uyûn al-Akhbâr as an eye-opening for those whose upbringing is scanty, as a reminder for the learned, as an education for the leaders of men and those whom they lead, as a place for the kings to rest from the toil of endeavor and weariness. I have classified it into chapters and connected one chapter with one that is like it, one narrative with one that resembles it, one word with its sister; so that he who studies may find it easy to learn, and he who reads remember it, and he who is in search for something may turn to it. Through it the minds of the learned are impregnated, the thoughts of the wise are assisted in being brought forth; it contains the fresh butter of pure milk, the ornament of culture, the fruits of prolonged thought, the choicest words

for the eloquent, the intelligence of poets, the lifestory of kings, the traditions of preceding generations. I have collected for you a great deal in this book of all this, that you may train your soul with the best of it, that you may straighten it with its *thiqâf*, free it from its bad qualities, as you would free the white silver from its dross; and drill it to accept good behavior, upright mode of life, noble culture and grand character, as taught in it. Let it enter your speech when you hold a conference, and your eloquent style when you write; with its help you will succeed in what you ask for, you will use beautiful words in inter-cession, and escape blame by means of the best excuses, when you apologize. For words are the pitfalls of hearts, and lawful sorcery. Make use of its culture in the company of your ruler, and in setting aright administration, in making his policy mild, and in managing his war. Enliven your company through it, whether in earnest or in joke, render your proofs obvious with the help of its similes, humiliate your adversary by taking them into account so that truth may manifest itself in the most beautiful shape and that you reach your aim with the lightest of provision and gain your goal calmly; and that you may overtake the tracked beast, bending part of your rein and walking gently and come in first. All this, provided your natural disposition be compliant, your temper ready and your feeling tractable; should this not be the case, those whose intelligence points out to them the defects of their patience and reflection; who put the remedies of this book on the illness of their natural disposition, drench their soul with its (the book's) water and strike fire from it through its lights, will find this book able to restore the sick and sharpen the blunt and arouse the drowsy and awake the slumbering; until with the help of Allâh even they come near the ranks of those that are gifted by nature.

I did not think it right for this book of mine to be a bequest for those who pursue this world, as opposed to those who pursue the next world; nor the chiefs, as opposed to the masses, nor to the kings as opposed to the subjects. On the contrary, I have given every one of these parties their share and made their part copious. And I have included in the book new examples from the beautiful sayings of the ascetics about the world and its misfortunes, and decay and death; sayings that they quote to each other, whenever they assemble, and which they introduce into their correspondence, when they are separated one from another; sermons and sayings about asceticism, self-restraint, fear of God, certainty of belief and the like of these. Perhaps Allâh will lead back through them those who turn aside, bend towards repentance those who deviate, restrain those who act wrongly, and soften through their delicacies the hard-ness of hearts. But with all this I did not deprive the book of strange curiosities, witty and sagacious sayings, words that please and others that make laugh; lest

there should be omitted from the book any of the roads that travelers have traveled or any way of speech to which speakers have had recourse; and in order to give rest to the reader from the toil of seriousness and the tiring effect of truth for "the ear is wont to reject, while the mind has eager desire" (for what it deems elegant). For if a joke is suitable or almost so, and fitting in with its time and the conditions that bring it forth, it is not bad nor to be disapproved of, belonging neither to the big nor even the small sins, if God will. Therefore, this our book will take you in the end to the chapter on jests and merriment and to such of them as have been handed down from Sharifs and Imâms. If then you, who show a grave mien, come across a saying you hold in light esteem or you find good or you admire or you laugh at, know our method and our mention. Remember also that if you, in your asceticism, can dispense with it, there are others, easygoing in those things in which you exert yourself, who may want it. The book has not been composed for you to the exclusion of others and could not therefore have been arranged according to your outward predilections. Had it been influence by the fear of those that don grave miens, half of its beauty would have gone and half of its juice, and those would have turned away from it whom we should love to turn towards it along with you.

Abú Muhammad said: I wrote a letter to one of the rulers and in one part of it I said: The resolute men have always found sweet the bitter words of the sincere, they have always wished to be guided aright in their faults and to inquire after the right judgment from everybody down to the foolish maidservant. Whilst there are those who are in need of proving the love they claim for him and the purity of their intention, Allâh has made this unnecessary for me through that which compulsion has rendered obligatory; since I have always been hoping for an increase of my present state from the lasting of your privilege and the rising of your scale and the unfolding of your high rank and power.

And in another passage I wrote: In this letter I have taken upon myself a certain amount of blame, and have acted contrary to my own knowledge by offering my judgment without having been asked for advice, and have put myself in the place of the special officers without having been placed there. But my soul burning with anger and feeling uneasy at what it heard, dragged me away from a path right for it, to one right for you, when I saw the tongue of your enemy unfolding itself with its charges against you and its arrows piercing you; whilst I was your friend incapable of arguing since he did not find an excuse, and whilst I saw the common people engage in all kinds of talk regarding you. For there is nothing more harmful for the ruler in some cases nor more useful to him in others, than they; for horsemen carry along what Allâh makes run down their tongues and stories remain and remembrance holds out against time and the ends prevail and

news which has become manifest has more weight in their eyes, than the testimony of trustworthy witnesses.

And again in another passage: He who leads people and manages their affairs is in need of a wide chest and he must gird himself with patience and bear up with the want of culture of the common people; he must make the ignorant understand and satisfy the man against whom the decision has gone and who has been denied his request by pointing out whence he has been denied it; for since people are not universally satisfied, even if all the causes of satisfaction have been put together for their benefit, much less will they be satisfied if some have been withheld from them. And they do not accept obvious excuses, even less dubious ones. And your brother is he who tells you the truth and is grieved for you, not he who follows you in your passion and afterwards disappears from you without bringing you near.

Ziyâd said to a man who consulted him: All those who ask for advice have confidence and every secret has its depository. But there are two things in men that cripple them in their efforts; the squandering of secrets and the venting of advice. There is no room for a secret except in one of two men; the man of Future Life who hopes for God's reward or the man of this world who has nobility in his soul and an intelligence with which to preserve his rank; and I have tested both of them for you.

One of the scribes wrote: Know that he gives you good advice and is anxious for you, who examines for you with his sight the things behind the ends and who shows you the likeness of the things of which you are afraid; who mixes for you the rough and the smooth in his speech and his advice, in order that your fear may equal your hope and your gratitude correspond with the benefit bestowed on you. And know further that he cheats you and instigates others against you, who helps your being seduced, who levels for you the smooth ground of oppression, who runs with you in your bridle obedient to your passion.

And in a passage: If I am suspect in your eyes at present, you will find on reflecting on the various sides of this advice things that will show you that it issued from truth and sincerity.

Ibrâhîm ibn al-Mundhir said: Ziyâd ibn 'Ubeydallâh al-Ḥârithi asked 'Ubeydallâh ibn 'Umar about his brother Abû Bakr as to whether to appoint him a judge, and he advised him to do it. But when he sent to Abû Bakr he refused, whereupon Ziyâd send for 'Ubeydallâh asking him to help him against Abû Bakr. Abû Bakr said to 'Ubeydallâh: "I beseech you by God, do you think it right for me to take charge of the judgeship?" He said, "By God, no." Whereupon Ziyâd said: "God is far from such imperfection! I asked your advice and you advised

me to appoint him and now I hear you forbidding him!" He said: "O Amîr, you asked my advice, so I exerted my judgment for your benefit and gave you my sincere advice, now he asked my advice, so I exerted my judgment for his benefit and gave him my sincere advice."

Naṣr ibn Mâlik was at the head of Abû Muslim's police. When Abû Muslim received Abû Ja'far's leave to come to see him he asked Naṣr's advice and he told him not to go and said: "I do not trust him with regard to you." Abû Ja'far said to him, when he came to him: "Did Abû Muslim ask your advice with regard to coming to see me and did you forbid him?" "Yes." "How is this?" "I heard your brother Ibrâhim the Imâm quote in the name of his father Muhammad ibn 'Alî: 'Men will go on receiving an increase in their judgment, as long as they give sincere advice to those who ask for their advice.' So I behaved to him accordingly, and now I behave toward you as I did toward him."

Mu'âwiya said: "I used to meet an Arab of whom I knew that there was in his heart hatred against me and I used to ask his advice, whereupon he would stir up his hatred against me in the measure he felt it in his soul. While he went on to overwhelm me with insult, I overwhelmed him with forbearance until he turned into a friend whom I asked for help and who gave it, and whom I asked for assistance and who answered my call."

Translated by Josef Horovitz[14]

Ibn al-Rumi

THE CHESS CHAMPION

Mild-handed, dandified, cerebral, arcane,
Typhooning the giants, putting the shrewd on pins
With schemes finer than the composition of winds,
Your record wrecks your man before the game.

Closer than lovers whom on indiscretion
Cautioned to dumbness, you evolve machines
And file them for the tactical moment in
Your cabinet of swift assassination.

You play with your opponents' souls for pieces.

The red board is awash with white blood. You move
Like extinction through the shanks, ennui through love,
Strokes through silence at chosen sacrifices.

Like grey hair under the night of youth advancing
On unspoiled cheeks you progress. You distil
A foreign bubble in a misty cell
To make the serum of the seven adventures.

Unnatural organs at your centre function
And so control your poise of hand, that though
Your eyes in the gallery, you throw
The king and all his knights into confusion.

Translated by Herbert Howarth and Ibrahim Shakrullah[15]

THE COMPROMISE

He dyes
his white hair black
in part,
believing some
will think him wise
and others
young.

Translated by Omar Pound[16]

HE DEFENDS HIMSELF

Think otherwise of me, for it is wrong
To scowl because my praises are so long.
As there lay very little in the well,
I could not use a shorter rope of song.

Translated by Henry Baerlein[17]

al-Tabari

THE BATTLE OF BADR

The Messenger of God and his companions had given order that the attack was not to begin before he released a signal, and until then the enemy was to be prevented from advancing by a screen of arrows. And the Prophet took up his station, Abu Bakr beside him, in a wooden structure from which he could observe the battle.

According to Abu Ga'far, the battle of Badr was fought on a Friday, the seventeenth of Ramadan. The Messenger of God drew up his supporters in files, moving backwards and forwards with a baton in his hand to marshal them. As he passed Sawad Ibn Ghaziyya, he found him out of line, and saying "Get into place, Sawad," thrust the baton into his belly. He answered, "Messenger of God, you have hurt me. God sent you to be the truth, and you should rather lead me." Then the Prophet of God uncovered his stomach and said, "Be led"; whereupon Sawad threw his arms about him and kissed him. "What made you do that, Sawad?" he asked. "Messenger of God," he said, "I saw these great hurts and was not sure I should live; and if this was my last moment with you, I wanted my flesh to touch yours." The Messenger of God wished him well and returning to the scaffolding went up to the platform; and Abu Bakr was with him.

The Messenger of God scrutinized the polytheists and their armament, and compared his own forces, which numbered not more than three hundred. He turned and faced the holy way and prayed to God asking Him to fulfil His promises; warning Him that if the congregation of believers was destroyed it would be an end of His worship on earth. He prayed unremittingly till his garment dropped off; and Abu Bakr, taking it and throwing about him again, said, "Prophet of God, you have invoked your Lord enough. He will surely make good His promises to you." On the instant God inspired His Messenger with the verse "If you summon your Lord He will reply 'I am your reinforcement with a thousand angels mounted on horses.'"

Then the vision was over, and he told Abu Bakr, "God's victory is at hand. I see Gabriel with us holding the reins of his horse, leading it over the rim of the pits." At that moment Maghi', the slave of 'Omar Ibn Khattab, was hit by an arrow and killed, and became Islam's first martyr. He was followed by Haritha Ibn Suraqa of the tribe of Beni 'Adi ibn Nagar who was killed as he drank at the well. The Messenger of God went out to the men to encourage them and stir

them. "By Him who holds the soul of Mohammed in His hands," he said, "each of you that fights and dies, patient, hungry, attacking, never falling back, God admits that man to Paradise." 'Umar Ibn il Hamam, who was eating a few dates he had been carrying, looked up and asked, "Is the only barrier between Paradise and me death at their hands?" And he tossed the dates aside, took his sword, and went and fought the enemy till he died—singing

> Running to God without arrows
> But love and promise and patience
> For all runs out like arrows
> But love of God and guidance.

And Ibn 'Afra' asked the Prophet, "Messenger of God, what would make the Lord smile in the face of His slave?" He answered, "If he dipped his hand in the enemy, naked." At this Ibn 'Afra' slung down the shield he was holding, and went in and fought the enemy till he died.

The Messenger of God picked up a handful of pebbles and threw them at the opposing Quraish, and said, "Their faces are mutilated." Then he turned to his supporters and told them to charge. God slew adversaries and made them victims in great numbers, and it was defeat for the Quraish.

Among those who came to guard the Prophet of God and prevent the enemy reaching his platform, was Sa'ad Ibn Ma'az; and the Prophet saw him standing at the foot of the scaffolding his face creased from repugnance of the work the army was doing.—"As if you hated our men's doing," he said. "Yes," Sa'ad said. "Yes, Prophet of God, this is the first time God has fallen on the polytheists, and the frenzy of the blow of battle is stranger that the way of taking prisoners."

The Prophet of God said that day to his companions, "I understand that the Beni Hisham have been pressed unwillingly into battle against us. Let our men spare any of them they meet. And Abu al Bukhturi Ibn Hisham should be spared, and so should my uncle 'Abdul Mutallib if anyone comes across him." Now Mugadar Beni Zayad found himself confronting al Bukhturi, who had with him a friend from Mecca, Ganada Ibn Tabha. Being told "The Prophet of God has forbidden your death," al Bukhturi asked Mugadar, "What about my friend here?" Mugadar answered, "In God's name no. Your friend shall not survive. The Prophet of God only ordered us to spare you." "Then, by God," said al Bukhturi, "We will die together. The women of the Quraish shall never say of me that love of life made me leave a friend to his fate." And he raised his sword for the fight, reciting:

The good son keeps his laurel crown
Until he cuts a way or is cut down.

And they fought till Mugadar killed him.

Translated by Herbert Howarth and Ibrahim Shakrullah[18]

al-Junayd

THE BOOK OF THE CURE OF SOULS

In the Name of God, the Merciful, the Compassionate.

Praise belongs to God, Who has made clear with manifest demonstration, to the people of gnosis and revelation, what special favours He bestowed upon them, in pre-eternal eternity, before "before" came into being, when there was neither "when" nor "where" nor "how" nor "there", and when there was neither "not-when" nor "not-where" nor "not-how" nor "not-there", by making them worthy of His unification, and the separation of His isolation, who had passed away from the pretence of attaining His limitation. For they were chosen for Himself, and made under His eye, and on them He cast a love from Him and of Him: "and I chose thee for Myself" and "that thou mayst be made under My eye", "and I cast on thee a love from Myself".

Now one of the qualities of those whom God has fashioned for Himself, making them under His eye, and casting on them His love from Himself and of Himself, is this: that their knowledge stays not fixed in one place, nor does their intellect accord with a fixation of a certain intelligence, nor is their resolve directed towards the accomplishment of a single purpose. These are they who are transported by gnosis whither knowledge never transported them—to an infinite aim. Intellects would shrink, minds perish, gnosis be constricted, times pass away, bewilderment would wander in bewilderment, at the description of the first step taken to accord with the quality of a locus for a love, because of the various degrees of knowledge, appointed by God for them through Himself and of Himself, which continued passing over them. For ah! that, which is His, is His through Him being with Him: "whither then will ye depart?" Hast thou not heard of the knowledge of His folding up what He Himself displayed, and His revealing what He himself concealed? Of how

He chose whom He chose to receive the secret of His revelation? "He revealed unto His servant what He revealed; the heart belied not what he saw" "at the highest horizon". He testified to him that he was His servant alone; therefore God did not use him jealously, because of any secret yearning for a desire, or a covert gratification of a lust, or a commerce with a glance, or traffick with a thought: he did not stake a claim by utterance, nor outstrip the just claimants by a spoken word, neither did he for a single instant consider any personal advantage. "He revealed unto him" then "what He revealed"—He made his intellect ready for that which He bestowed on him when He took him to Himself, and chose him for a certain matter, laying on him "what burden he has to bear", and he bore it. "He revealed unto him" then "what He revealed— at the highest horizon": for space was too narrow, and created things shrank, before suffering the revelation that was made to him to pass through them or over them, save "at the highest horizon", "when there covered the lote-tree, what did cover it"—a glance, from the majesty of His glance, which has no object of glance, falling upon the lote-tree, when there covered it what did cover it, and it withstood that which did cover it.

Consider also the mountain, when "He revealed Himself" to it; "He made it dust, and Moses fell swooning, and when he recovered, he said, Glory be to Thee! I have turned unto Thee"—that is, I return to ask of Thee the vision: after experiencing this station, in spite of knowing how enormous his petition was, and despite the fact that, had knowledge met with reality in the time of asking, words would not have been permissible or appropriate. Now in this station there is a knowledge which may not be inscribed, and which it is not appropriate to put in writing.

Consider also how God relates concerning His Beloved: "and he saw him yet another time, at the lote-tree of the utmost boundary." The word "at" here does not imply place: it only implies the moment of revealing the knowledge of the "moment". Consider then the excellence of the two moments, and the variety of the two places, and how the two stations differed, the one being on high, and the other below. So excel the intellects of the Gnostics who believe. Some of them can utter intimate converse, being aware of how near He is Who converses with them and draws them unto Him: whether they be on high or below, the knowledge of the fact does not veil them. Others are not able to do this: with them God makes secondary causes a means to understanding, so that through these they are able to understand when God addresses them, and answer Him. Do not pause at God's saying, "and no man is permitted that God may speak with him, save it be by revelation, or from behind a veil, or that He sendeth a messenger, to reveal by His leave what He wills." These are

matters too vast for narrow knowledge to comprehend, except a man consult with those who enjoy neighbourhood, or occupy himself with knowledge of the winding ways that lead to the sciences of the elect, who are solitary even from their solitudes, and are free from all their desires. For a barrier has been set between them and the objects of their lusts: swept along by the winds of understanding, they were brought down to the seas of wisdom, whence they draw the pure water of life. They fear no mischief thereof, no visitation, they expect, neither are they avid to seek the attainment of any end: nay rather, ends are for them beginnings. What in other men is hidden, in that they are manifest, and they are hidden in that in which other men are manifest. They are the trustees of God's revelation, the preservers of His secret, performing His command, speaking of His truth, acting in obedience to Him. They vie with one another in good works, hastening beforehand to perform them: in the very beginning of their course they preserved excellent manners in their dealings, whatever might be the due which they were required to pay to God. No wise counsel is there, which they have not put into practice, no means to winning God's favour, which they have not employed. Their souls liberally gave all their strength in paying His first due, seeking to come to Him, zealous, leaving nothing, and reserving nothing: rather, they considered that what they owed, at the time of their payment, was greater far than all that their payment had of merit. God's manifest signs to them point, and the sciences of God in them abound. No reproach gives them pause at any visitation, no fear hinders them at any calamity, no covetousness incites them in making any preparation. They preserve God's Book which was entrusted to them, and to it bear witness, for when they perform any duty, they do not turn from seeking refuge in turning to ask God's help, to complete what they set out to do. Their counseling others does not diminish their listening to God addressing them, so long as there remains in them any vestige of the life that is in Him: for they fear lest, knowing what they are required to do for God, they may suffer some vain conceit to enter into the performance of their dues. Therefore they do not hesitate to run forth eagerly when ever the command comes, that act may follow command, without sharp, appreciable division, such as would not be of the nature of the command.

These are the qualities of the elect of God, His beloved friends, whose eye is ever fixed on the saying, which has application to them, impressing the duty of servanthood in true discipline—a discipline which is only condemned in the case of those who undertake it, without performing their obligations under it, failing to practice it.

The souls of practitioners take hastily the knowledge they have, and are veiled by the thought of that knowledge so that they do not know what the

knowledge of that knowledge means to them or what God's favour means in revealing to them the knowledge of that that knowledge is. So veil thickens upon veil, hiding the revelation of the sciences of the veils, and they remain beneath their covering. "Thou wast in heedlessness of this, and we uncovered thy covering, and thy sight to-day is keen"—such a man understands the limits of things, for the Creator uncovers them, and reveals the light of creation in which He clothed them, and the beauty of will, which was manifested in His pervading power, concentrating them and separating them, giving them movement and reality. "It tires Him not to keep them both, for He is High, Mighty. No constraint is there in the faith: guidance has become clear from error."

Translated by A. J. Arberry[19]

al-Hallaj

THREE QASIDAS

I

Here I am! Here I am!
My secret One, my trusted One.
I have answered Your call.
You are my meaning, and my hope.
I call to You...or, no,
You call to Yourself.
Do I say 'It is You'?
Or do You whisper 'It is I'?

You are the distance I must go,
My spring of springs,
My reasoning, my words,
These stammerings.

You are everything I am
My hearing and my sight,
My universe,
My trifling things.

The sum of everything I am
You are. And everything I am
Is Mystery. I have confused You
With my little meaning.

It is You I've been in love with
And been crushed, in moments
When You let Yourself become
My prisoner in love.

I mourn in being exiled
From my home—I chose it so;
My enemies are happy
In my sorrow...

I come near You,
My fear excites me.
Desire steadies me
In my inmost heart...

What can I do with One
With Whom I am this much in love?
O Lord, the doctors say
They're tired of my sickness.
They say, Cure it through Him.
I say to them, O people
What sickness can be cured
By its disease?

My love for my Lord
Consumes and makes me weak.
How can I say to Him,
It is Your doing...

I look...my heart perceives,
But how can I explain
His ways except
By wordless gestures...?

My self's at fault,
O woe to me!
I am the source
Of my own agony...

Like a person drowning
In the sea
Who reaches out for help
With fingertips alone...

Only He Who has come down
To depths known in the heart,
Only He, descends
Into this melancholy.

He knows what I have known
In the long illness;
And in His will I see
My death and resurrection.

O my request and hope,
My home, my very breath,
My faith...
My worldly fate...
Though You are hidden
To my eyes,
My heart perceives You
In the distance...

II

I cry to You for souls whose present witness (I myself)
Now goes beyond the Where to meet the Witness of Eternity.

I cry to You for hearts so long refreshed
By clouds of revelation which once were filled with seas of wisdom.

I cry to hear the Word of God, which since it perished long ago
Has faded into nothingness in our memory.

I cry to You for the inspired speech which silences
The brilliant words of eloquent and learned orators.

I cry to You for signs that have been gathered up by intellects;
Nothing now remains of them in books except debris.

I cry to You, I swear it by Your love, for the Virtues
Of those whose only mount for reaching You was silence.

All have crossed the desert, leaving neither well nor trace behind;
Vanished like the 'Ād tribe and their lost city of Iram.

And after them stumbles an abandoned crowd, looking for their trails,
Blinder even than she-camels, blinder than the dumbest of beasts.

III

Murder me now, my faithful friends,
For in my murder is my Life.

My death would be to go on living
And my Life would be to die.
To me removal of my self
Would be the noblest gift to give

And my survival in my flesh
The ugliest offence, because

My life has tired out my soul
Among its fading artifacts.

So kill me, set aflame
My dried out bones

And when you pass by my remains
In their deserted grave,
You will perceive the secret of my Friend
In the inmost folds of what survives.

One moment I'm a sheikh
Who holds the highest rank,

And then I am a little child
Dependent on a nurse

Or sleeping in a box
Within the brackish earth.

My mother gave her father birth,
Which as a marvel I perceived,

And my own daughters whom I made
Became my sisters in this way to me,

Not in the world of time
Nor through adulteries.

So gather all the parts together
Of the glowing forms

Of air and fire,
And pure water
And sow them in unwatered soil;
Then water it from cups

Of serving maids
And flowing rivulets;

And, then, when seven days have passed,
A perfect plant will grow.

Translated by Herbert Mason[20]

Ibn al-Mu'tazz

IN PRAISE OF CHESS

O thou whose cynic sneers express
the censure of our favourite chess!
Know that its skill is science' self,
its play distraction from distress
It soothes the anxious lover's care,
it weans the drunkard from excess;
It counsels warriors in their art,
when dangers threat and perils press;
And yields us, when we need them most,
companions in our loneliness.

Translated by N. Bland[21]

NIGHT

Our old moon put her horns away and the dark nights were there;
There danced a girl-moon through the clouds, pallid as ivory.
At break of day went Jupiter patrolling down the sky,
Just as the lonely watchman with a lantern passing by.

Translated by Henry Baerlein[22]

WE SHOUTED FOR SERVANTS, BUT ALL SLEPT

We shouted for servants, but all slept.
The palace was quiet and I
Stared at the archer in his eyes
And dropped my head and licked
His trickling fingers, and he fumbled
Dreamily for the jugs and poured
Half and half into our tumblers
Leaning on his elbows he snored.

Translated by Herbert Howarth and Ibrahim Shakrullah[23]

al-Razi

THE REPELLING OF GRIEF

When the passion through the reason pictures the loss of a beloved associate, grief thereby follows. We need a very long and detailed discussion in order to make clear whether grief is an affection of the reason or the passion; but we have already stated at the beginning of this book that we shall not here enter into any discussion unless it be unavoidable in view of the purpose we have here been pursuing. On this account we shall leave aside the discussion of this theme and proceed straight to the purpose at which we have aimed in this book. Still, it may be possible for anyone with the slightest grasp of philosophy to deduce and extract this idea from the sketch we have made of grief at the beginning of the discourse. Now we will have done with that and leave it on one side in order to go after our principal purpose.

Since grief clouds the thought and reason, and is harmful alike to soul and body, it is our duty to endeavour to dismiss and repel it, or at any rate to reduce and diminish it as much as possible. This can be done in two different ways. The first is to be on one's guard against it before it actually comes in or that it may not happen, or if it does, so that it will be as slight as possible. The second is to repel and banish it when it has occurred, either wholly or to the greatest possible extent, and to take precautions betimes either in order that it may not happen, or if it does, so that it will be slight and weak. This may be accomplished by reflecting on the ideas which I am now about to mention.

Since the substance out of which sorrows are generated is simply and solely the loss of one's loved ones, and since it is impossible that these loved ones should not be lost because men have their turns with them and by reason of the fact that they are subject to the succession of generation and corruption, it follows that the man most severely afflicted by grief must be he who has the greatest number of loved ones and whose love is the most ardent, while the man least affected by grief is he whose circumstances are the reverse. It would therefore seem that the intelligent man ought to cut away from himself the substance of his griefs, by making himself independent of the things whose loss involves him in grief; and that he should not be deceived and deluded by the sweetness they impart while they remain in being, but rather keep in mind and image the bitterness that must be tasted when they are lost.

If it be objected that he who takes the precaution of not making and acquiring loved ones, because he is afraid of the grief of losing them, merely hastens

forward the day of grief; the answer would be that even if his precautions and previsions do have this result, the grief such a man hastens forward is by no means equal to that he fears to fall into. A man who has no children cannot be so grief-stricken as the man who loses his child; this is true even if the childless man is of the sort that grieves because he has no child—I leave out of account those who do not trouble or care or grieve about such a matter at all. The grief of him who has no darling is nothing beside the grief of him who loses his darling.

It is said that someone remarked to a philosopher, "If only you took a child!" To this the philosopher replied, "The trouble and grief I have trying to keep this body and soul of mine in health tax me beyond my powers—how then should I add and join to them the like again?" I once heard an intelligent woman remark, "One day I saw a woman terribly distressed over the loss of a child—so much so that she was afraid to go near her husband for fear that she might find herself having another child on whose account she might suffer equal affliction."

Because the possession of the beloved is agreeable and congenial to nature, and the loss thereof is contrary and repugnant to nature, the soul is bound to be more sensitive to the pain of losing the beloved than to the pleasure of having him. In the same way a man may be in good health for a long time and feel no pleasure in being so, yet if he is affected by sickness in one of his members he immediately feels severe pain there. So it is with all loved persons: so long as they are there, or one has their company for a long while, one ceases to feel such pleasure in their existence, but as soon as one loses them one is smitten by severe pain at their loss. It is for this reason that if a man has enjoyed for a long time the possession of a family and a precious child, and is then afflicted by the loss of both, he experiences in a single day, nay, a single hour, a sense of pain exceeding and obliterating the pleasure he formerly enjoyed in having them. This is because nature accounts and reckons all that long enjoyment as her due and right; nay, she counts it as yet less than her right, for even in those circumstances she is never without the feeling that what she possesses is very little, and is constantly and forevermore wanting to have more of it, being as she is so fond and avid of pleasure.

This being so—since the pleasure and enjoyment felt in having loved ones, while they are there, is something so poor, so obscure, so feeble and inconsiderable, whereas the grief, distress and anguish of losing them are so palpable, so huge, so painful and ruinous; what is one to do, but get rid of them altogether, or assert one's independence of them, in order that their evil consequences, their train of hurtful, wasting griefs, may be destroyed or at least diminished?

This is the highest level that can be reached on this topic, and the most effective in amputating the very substance of grief.

After this it follows that a man should picture and represent to himself the loss of his loved ones, and keep this constantly in his mind and imagination, knowing that it is impossible for them to continue unchanged forever. He should never for a moment give up remembering this and putting it into his thoughts, strengthening his resolve and fortifying his endurance against the day when the calamity happens. That is the way to train and gradually to discipline and strengthen the soul, so that it will protest little when misfortunes occur; because one has been little habituated and felt small trust and reliance in the survival of the loved ones during the time they were actually there, and one has frequently represented to the soul and inured and familiarized it with the picturing of those misfortunes before they occurred. It was in this sense that the poet said:

> The man of prudence pictures in his soul
> Ere they descend, what mishaps may befall;
> So, come they sudden, he is not dismayed,
> Having within his soul their image laid.
> He views the matter reaching to its worst,
> And what must hap at last, faces at first.

If however a man is excessively cowardly and extremely inclined to passion and pleasure, and he cannot trust himself to use anything of these twain devices, it is not necessary for him to endeavour to satisfy himself with one beloved out of his many, and to regard her as indispensable and irreplaceable; he should on the contrary adopt several, so as to have one always to stand in the stead (or come near to doing so) of any he may unfortunately lose. In this way it is possible for his sorrow and grief not to be extreme over the loss of any of them.

This is a summary of the precautions that may be taken against the fact and the occurrence of grief. As for the manner in which grief may be repelled or lessened when it has become a reality and has actually happened, we shall proceed to discourse on that subject now.

When the intelligent man examines and considers those things within this world which are affected by the alternation of generation and corruption, when he perceives that their element is changeable and dissoluble and fluid, that nothing is constant or permanent as an individual, but rather that all things pass away and perish and change and decay and vanish; when he reflects on all this, he ought not to take too much to heart or feel too

outraged or stricken by the sudden deprivation of anything. On the contrary, he must reckon the period of their survival to be an advantage, and the enjoyment he has of them a positive gain, seeing that they will inevitably perish and cease to be. Then it will not seem so very terrible or important to him when the need comes, because that is a thing, which must come upon sooner or later. So long as he goes on desiring that they should survive forever, he is yearning for the impossible, and by yearning for the impossible he is bound to bring grief upon himself, and follow the inclinations of his passion rather than his reason. Moreover the loss of those things that are not necessary to the continuance of life does not call for everlasting grief or sorrow; they are soon replaced and made good, and this leads on to consolation and oblivion; gaiety returns, and things come back to what they were before the misfortune happened. How many men we have seen struck down by a terrible and shocking calamity, and presently pick themselves up again, until they became exactly as they were before the blow fell, enjoying life to the full and entirely content with their circumstances!

It therefore behooves the intelligent man to remind himself, when the misfortune is upon him, how it will presently pass and give way and he will return once more to normality; he should present this picture to his mind, and stir within himself the desire for its realization, all the time drawing to himself what may preoccupy and divert his thoughts as much as possible, to speed his emergence into this settled state. The impact of grief can also be greatly lightened and assuaged by reminding oneself of how many there are that share one's misfortunes, and how scarcely a single man is free of them; by remembering too how others have been after the blow has fallen, and the various ways they have consoled themselves; and then by considering his own circumstances and how he has previously consoled himself, when and if misfortunes have come upon him before.

Furthermore, if it be true that the man most severely afflicted by grief is he who has the greatest number of loved ones and whose love is the most ardent, all the same the loss of one of them is bound to result in a corresponding diminution of grief; indeed such a loss relieves his soul of perpetual worry and anticipatory fear, so that he acquires a wariness and fortitude to endure subsequent buffetings. In this way the loss of loved ones actually brings profit in its train, even though the passion may revolt against it; and while the sedative may be bitter to the taste, yet it does in the end afford relief. It was such an idea as this the poet had in mind when he wrote:

> In truth, though we have lost in thee our lord,
> Our cave of refuge, and for thee
> Have grieved and fretted long,
> Yet hath our loss yielded this much reward:
> We can outface calamity,
> Though it be massive strong

As for the man who prefers to follow the dictate of reason and to deny the call of passion, who has complete possession and control of himself, against grief he has one sure protection. The intelligent and perfect man never chooses to continue in a situation that is harmful to him, and therefore he is up betimes to reflect upon the cause of the grief whereby he has been visited. If it be a matter that can be repelled and put an end to, he substitutes for grieving a consideration of the means he may adopt to repel and put an end to that cause. If however it be a matter of diverting his mind from it and trying to forget it, striving to obliterate it from his thoughts and drive it out of his soul. This is because it is passion, not reason, that invites him to continue grieving in those circumstances; for reason only urges one towards a course that yields profit sooner or later. But to grieve over what yields no return whatsoever, but only immediate loss, is bound, so far from proving profitable, to lead to yet further loss in the long run too. The intelligent and perfect man follows only the dictate of reason, and never continues in any state unless he feels free to do so for a definite reason and with a clear justification; he will not follow or go along with his passion when it would lead him in a contrary direction.

Translated by A. J. Arberry[24]

al-Farabi

THE CITY AND THE HOUSEHOLD

The city and the household may be compared with the body of a man. Just as a body is composed of different parts of a determinate number, some more, some less excellent, adjacent to each other and graded, each doing a certain work, and there is combined from all their actions mutual help towards the perfection of the aim in the man's body, so the city and the household are each

composed of different parts of a determinate number, some less, some more excellent, adjacent to each other and graded in different grades, each doing a certain work independently, and there is combined from their actions mutual help towards the perfection of the aim in the city or household, except that the household is part of a city and the households are in the city, so the aims are different. Yet there is combined from these different aims, when they are perfected and combined, mutual help towards the perfection of the aim of the city. This again may be compared with the body, since the head, breast, belly, back, arms, and legs are related to the body as the households of the city to the city. The work of each of the principal members is different from the work of the other, and the parts of each one of these principal members help one another by their different actions toward the perfection of the aim in that principal member. Then there is combined from the different aims of the principal members, when they are perfected, and from their different actions, mutual help towards the perfection of the aim of the whole body. And similarly the situation of the parts of the households with respect to the households and the situation of the households with respect to the city, so that all the parts of the city by their combination are useful to the city and useful for the continued existence of the one through the other, like members of the body.

As the doctor treats any sick member only in accordance with its relation to the whole body and the members adjacent to it and connected with it, since he treats it with a cure by which he affords it health whereby the whole body benefits, and the members adjacent to it and connected with it benefit, so the ruler of the city must necessarily rule the affair of each part of the city, small, like one man, or great, like a household, and treat it and afford it good in relation to the whole city and each of the other parts of the city, by seeking to do what affords that part a good which does not harm the whole city nor any of its parts but a good from which the city as a whole benefits, and each of its parts according to its degree of usefulness to the city. And just as when the doctor does not observe this, aims at providing health to a particular member and treats it without regard to the condition of the other members near it, or treats it with what is bad for all the other members, and affords it health but thereby does something which does not benefit the body as a whole nor the members adjacent to it and connected with it, that member is impaired, as well as the connected members, and the evil permeates the other members, till the whole body is corrupted, and the city also.

Translated by D. M. Dunlop[25]

al-Mas'udi

PEARL-FISHING

The pearl-fishing in the Persian Ocean lasts from the beginning of Nísán (April) to the end of Ailúl (September); there is no fishing during the rest of the year. In our earlier works we have enumerated all the pearl-fisheries in this ocean, which is the only one where pearls are to be found: they are peculiar to the sea that washes the coasts of Abyssinia and Khárak and Ḳuṭur and 'Umán and Sarandíb (Ceylon) and other countries. We have also mentioned how the pearl is formed and the different opinions attributing to its origin to rain-drops and to many things besides, and have described pearls of both sorts, namely, the ancient and those of recent formation, which are called *maḥár* and known as *balbal*. The flesh and fat in the shell is an animal: it feels alarm for the peal within it on account of the divers, as a mother fears for her child. Concerning the manner of diving, we have previously explained that the divers never touch meat, but live on fish and dates and similar foods, and how they slit their ears at the base to make an exit for the breath instead of the nostrils, because they plug the latter with something made of *dhabl*, that is, the shell of the sea-tortoise which is used for making combs, or of horn, but not of wood: it penetrates the nostrils like an iron arrow-head. In their ears they put oiled cotton, and when they are at the bottom of the sea a little of the oil exudes and gives them a bright light. They smear their feet and legs with black pigment for fear of being swallowed by the sea-beasts: the blackness scares these monsters. The divers at the bottom of the sea utter piercing cries like a dog's yelp in order to make themselves heard by one another. All this we have related in our preceding books with much curious information about the divers and the pearl-fishing, the pearl and its animal, and the qualities, marks, prices, the weights of pearls.

CHARACTER OF THE CALIPH MUHTADI

Muhtadí-billah had set himself to lead a virtuous and religious life. He called the men of learning to his court, conferred dignities on the divines, and included them all in his bounty and affection. He used to say, "O sons of Háshim, let me follow the path trodden by 'Umar the son of 'Abdu'l-'Aziz, so that I may be amongst you what 'Umar was amongst the sons of Umaiya." He restricted luxury in articles of dress and furniture and food and drink. By his

command the gold and silver vessels in the treasury were put out and broken and coined into dinars and dirhems; and he gave orders that the painted figures adorning the rooms of the palace should be effaced. He slaughtered the rams which were set to butt against each other in the presence of the Caliphs, and the fighting-cocks, and killed all the wild beasts in the menagerie. He also forbade the use of brocade carpets and every sort of rug or carpet that is not expressly sanctioned by the Mohammedan religious law. It was the custom of the Caliphs before him to spend 10,000 dirhems daily on their table, but Muhtadí abolished that practice and assigned a sum of about 100 dirhems to meet the daily cost of his table and his entire maintenance. Often he would fast for several days at a time. It is said that after he was murdered his baggage was removed from the place where he had sought refuge, and they came upon a small padlocked chest which belonged to him. On opening it, instead of the money or jewels which it was supposed to contain, they found a *jubba* (shirt) of wool or camel's hair and an iron collar. They questioned the attendant, who declared that as soon as darkness fell, the Caliph used to put on the *jubba* and the collar and pray, bowing and prostrating himself, until dawn; and that he would sleep for an hour after the second night-prayer and then rise. Shortly before his assassination, when he had performed the prayer of sunset and was about to break from his fast, one of his intimate friends heard him say, "O God, it is a true saying of Thy apostle Mohammed (God bless him!), that Thou dost never turn away the supplication of a just Imám—and I have taken pains to act justly towards my people; or of one who is wronged—and I am suffering wrong; or of one who has not yet broken his fast—and I am still fasting." Having uttered these words, he began to call down vengeance on his enemies and pray that he might be delivered from their violence.

Translated by R. A. Nicholson[26]

al-Mutanabbi

PARTING HAS JUST TAUGHT OUR EYELIDS SEPARATION

Parting has just taught our eyelids separation
 That bleeds, and associated the heart with grief
I hoped the hour they went for a show of her wrist
 So the tribe perplexed would stay before going
If she appeared to bewilder them shame would draw
 A curtain to guard their wits from her glance
By the camel and its driver and myself! a moon
 Is panting in the curtains from her motion
As for the dress, when one strips its beauty,
 Undressed one clothes her in beauty naked
The musk embraces it with the embrace of a lover
 Until it is wrinkles on the belly wrinkles
I was anxious about my tears because of my sight
 But now after you each dear thing is scorned
The clouds bring their watery breasts for you
 For a beloved there are memories in flashes
When I approached terrors, a heart went with me
 When I wished solace from you it betrayed
I appear and he who thought evil of me bows down
 I do not chide him with forgiveness but scorn
And so I was among my people and in my country
 For what is precious is alien wherever it is
I am envious of virtue, a liar about my mark casts
 Down a hero and meets me when his time comes
I'm not thirsty for what does not bruise desire
 Nor do I reject that which passes as weakness
Nor am I happy when others are praised for that
 Even if you brought me the century full
No one ever attracts my camel toward him
 While I stay alive nor while our saddle rocks
But if I had been able I would have ridden
 All mankind as a camel to Sa'id ibn Abdallah
For the camel is wiser than the people that I see
 As blind to what he sees as benevolence

It is generosity even if bounty is small for him
 Bravery even if he is not content as hero
It is provision what his hand has gained for us
 And if he gives some of it he glorifies us
Time is easy on the tips of his fingers
 Until they are supposed to be times for time
He hurls battles and lances and catastrophes and
 The sword and the guest's open, glad handshake
You imagine from the warmth of heart he is aflame
 From his kindness and cheer that he is drunk
Singing girls trail the skirts of their gowns
 By his bounty, and the horses wear his halters
He gives as a welcome to the clients beforehand
 As one does good to the thirsty with water
Paradise is the reward of the Banu Hasan for they
 In their people are as Adnan's nobility
Allah did not cry glory lost in their ancestors
 And indeed we now see it in them
If written to or met or warred on they are found
 In script and word and battle to be knights
As if their tongues in argument were made,
 Like the lance heads on the spears in jousting
As if they came to drink death out of thirst
 Or smell the Khatti lances a sweet herbs
Beings, for one whose enmity I desire, the worst
 Enemy, and for one I'm friendly with brothers
Natures which if the negroes had they'd change
 Into thin lips, curly hair, and white skins
With souls whose brilliance makes them loved
 Perforce, even if far from you in hate
Whose fathers are unclouded like their foreheads
 And their mothers, their minds and thoughts
O hunter of armies whose flanks are fearful
 Whereas the lions hunt men one by one
As for gifts every hour is time for his giving
 But donors dispense only now and then
You are one who gathers wealth for generous uses
 Then you accept clients for it as treasurers
Responsible to yourself as guardian when alone

You do nothing secretly that you do not openly
I don't seek increase of what in you is noble
 I as one who slept would awaken being awake
Indeed by such as you I shone with magnanimity
 With repulse of the hate of days by content
You are most far reaching in fame and greatest
 In power, and highest of them building glory
Allah has honored earth with you as its dweller
 He honored men since he made men like you.

Translated by R. A. Nicholson[27]

SHAME KEPT MY TEARS AWAY

Shame kept my tears away
But's brought them back again.
My veins and bones seep through the skin
graining *her* iv'ry face
 with lines anew.

Unveiling shows pale veil beneath
as woman's Rhetorick
of inlaid gold and pearl
in filigree marks cheek
 and jowl.

Her night of hair she parts in three
(to make for me four nights of one?);
pale moon reflects her day of face,
that she and I may double see
 as one.

Translated by Omar Pound[28]

COUPLET

Strive always for the highest, you will gain the highest seat,
And have the half-moon's silver for the covering of your feet.

Translated by Henry Baerlein[29]

HOW GLOWS MINE HEART

How glows mine heart for him whose heart to me is cold,
Who liketh ill my case and me in fault doth hold!
Why should I hide a love that hath worn thin my frame?
To Sayfu'l-Dawla all the world avows the same.
Though love of his high star unites us, would that we
According to our love might so divide the fee!
Him have I visited when sword in sheath was laid,
And I have seen him when in blood swam every blade:
Him, both in peace and war the best of all mankind,
Whose crown of excellence was still his noble mind.

Do foes by flight escape thine onset, thou dost gain
A chequered victory, half of pleasure, half of pain.
So puissant is the fear thou strik'st them with, it stands
Instead of thee, and works more than thy warriors' hands.
Unfought the field is thine: thou need'st not further strain
To chase them from their holes in mountain or in plain.
What! 'fore thy fierce attack whene'er an army reels,
Must thy ambitious soul press hot upon their heels?
Thy task it is to rout them on the battle-ground:
No shame to thee if they in flight have safety found.
Or thinkest thou perchance that victory is sweet
Only when scimitars and necks each other greet?

O justest of the just save in thy deeds to me I
Thou art accused and thou, O Sire, must judge the plea.
Look, I implore thee, well! Let not thine eye cajoled
See fat in empty froth, in all that glisters gold!
What use and profit reaps a mortal of his sight,

If darkness unto him be indistinct from light?
My deep poetic art the blind have eyes to see,
My verses ring in ears as deaf as deaf can be.
They wander far abroad while I am unaware,
But men collect them watchfully with toil and care.
Oft hath my laughing mien prolonged the insulter's sport,
Until with claw and mouth I cut his rudeness short.
Ah, when the lion bares his teeth, suspect his guile,
Nor fancy that the lion shows to you a smile.

NAUGHT KILLS THE NOBLE LIKE FORGIVENESS

Naught kills the noble like forgiveness—yet
Where are the noble who no boon forget?
Kindness subdues the man of generous race,
But only makes more insolent the base.
As ill doth bounty in sword's place accord
With honour as in bounty's place the sword.

Translated by R. A. Nicholson[30]

MY SONGS GAVE EYES TO THE BLIND, EARS TO THE DEAF

My songs gave eyes to the blind, ears to the deaf
Set the critics flapping like nightbirds
Set me at rest all night on my bed.

And pay me well if I write you a eulogy
The flatterers will come to you mouthing it.
And desert every voice but mine, for I
Am the singing lark, the rest are echo.
Time is my scribe and my register
It follows me singing the words I drop.
From safe harbours they sailed away
Pre-occupied because of my poems.
The throats that had never spoken trilled
 My scale, the moment before landfall.

AN INDUCTION

They went on, and left me long vague nights,
Longer than bridal nights, and showed me
The regular unwanted moon, and held
The new moon beyond the stretch of roads,
A journey away, and the way doubled
By a stop in existence like a wall.
And for their Hermes of calamity
They made me live when the lovers had gone.

The hot gardens sometimes heard voices
In migrant winds. Like a tree I waited
For the voice to come back. Touching a glass
I sometimes choked because the mind flashed
To fixed steel, that now catches the water
By the one-time camping-place of girls.
I watched the stars on their dark cruises.
Could they not lead to the high clearings?

Has the night not seen your eyes, I cried,
To grow thin and quiet and go?
By the last house I found dawn. The meeting
Healed my limbs and the night died
And the day stood in quick light,
Still wet with gelatine of birth, the sign
That hills were opening, and over lush roads
The sun advancing as your envoy.

HERE IS THE FINAL STRETCH

Here is the final stretch, the instrument
That cuts short the reminiscence
The chatter of what they did to death, the coil
Of it, and the paternal tube of it
And snakiness. At a long paean
The corpse turns over, quicker than hands,
Whose horns state the pain of earning,

Do for time and his slip. He passes
Imperiously, owning the air
And filigree of limbs and soul,
A trap in beauty's structure, that no lover
Could fathom and keep the manacles.
Galenus with his atabrine, the fluting moron
With his goats, went after him. They counted
A similar tally of hours, and the quiet
Was sweeter for the fool. Unbroken drive
Even for welfare is only warfare
And the metal weights on the lungs
Deny the blossoms to the stretch of need.

Translated by Herbert Howarth and Ibrahim Shakrullah[31]

Abu Firas al-Hamdani

THY FIERCEST FOE IS ONE THOU DOST NOT FIGHT

Thy fiercest foe is one thou dost not fight:
Thy kindest friend is one far out of sight.
Much knowledge have I gained of men and days,
Experiment has trained me in their ways.
And from the furthest furthest is my fear;
While danger from the nearest is most near.
The trusted comrade is the foe who harms:
The enemy avowéd least alarms.
That is no home where none has friendly mind:
They are no kinfolk of whom none is kind.
Connexion is connexion of the heart;
Thy neighbour he who distant takes thy part.

GRIEF AMASSES, PATIENCE SCATTERS

Grief amasses, patience scatters;
Love unites, but on some matters
Disagrees; when eyes are sleeping
Mine are waking or are weeping.
Had thy gaze, fair maid, not charmed me,
Never had my vision harmed me.
But on me thy glance went straying:
Then thy folk depart conveying
Far away upon the morrow
Eyes whence all their beauty borrow

Translated D. S. Margoliouth[32]

al-Tawhidi

ARABS AND NON-ARABS

I went to the vizier's house another evening, and the first thing which he addressed to the gathered circle was, "Do you prefer the Arabs over the non-Arabs or the non-Arabs over the Arabs?"

I said, "In the opinion of the learned men, there are four nations: the Greeks, the Arabs, the Persians and the Indians. Three of these are non-Arab, and it is difficult to say that the Arabs by themselves are preferable to the other three, in spite of both their common collections and their differentiations." He said, "However, I like from this group the Persians." And I said, "Before I decide anything, speaking for myself, I will relate a conversation by Ibn al-Muqaffa, who is of pure Persian origin and is deep-rooted among non-Arabs, a man superior among the people of merit..." The vizier said, "Bring me unto the blessing of God and His assistance."

I then related the conversation of Shabib ibn Shabba, who said: We were standing in the courtyard of the camel station (in Basra)—the standing place of the nobles and the meeting place of the people, with the notables of Egypt present—when Ibn al-Muqaffa came into view. There was not among us anyone who did not take delight in him or who did not derive satisfaction in questioning him, and we rejoiced at his appearance. He said, "What keeps you

upon the backs of your animals in this place? By god, if the Caliph were to send out to the people of the earth, seeking the likes of you, he should not locate anyone like you. Now go to the house of Ibn Barthan, in extended shade and shielded from the sun, facing the northerly breeze. Give rest to your animals and servants. We will sit on the ground, for it is a fine carpet, most tread upon." Some of us were listening, for he is the most accomplished of the circle and the most prolific at conversation. So we hastened to do what he had said and alighted from our animals at the house of Ibn Barthan, inhaling the northerly breeze, when Ibn al-Muqaffa drew near to us and said, "Which nation is most intelligent?" We thought that he had in mind the Persians, so we said, "The Persians are the most intelligent," seeking to ingratiate ourselves and having in mind to flatter him. But he said, "Not at all. That ability is not theirs, nor is it among them. They are a people who were taught and who then learned, who were given an example and who then imitated and followed after, who were started on a matter and who then went on to pursue it. They have neither invention nor discovery." So we said to him, "The Greeks." But he said, "It is not them either. Though they have strong bodies and are masters at building and architecture, they do not know anything other than those two, nor have they perfected anything else."

We said, "The Chinese." He replied, "Masters of furniture and crafts, but they have neither thought nor deliberation." We said, "The Turks." He answered, "Lions for quarrel." We said, "The Indians." He responded, "Masters of imagination, trickery, sleight-of-hand, and deception." We said, "The Negroes." He said, "Roving cattle." So we handed over the matter to him, and he said, "The Arabs." We exchanged glances and whispered to one another; that enraged him, his color turning pale. Then he said, "It seems that you suspect me of ingratiating myself with you. By God, I wish that this thing were otherwise, but I would be disgusted if the matter escaped me and its correct solution eluded me. I will not leave you until I explain why I said what I did, in order to clear myself of the suspicion of deception and the imputation of flattery.

"The Arabs did not have a proper condition to follow as a pattern nor a Book to guide them. They are people of a poor land, deserted from mankind; everyone among them, in his loneliness, has need of his thought, his contemplation, and his mind. They knew that their livelihood came from the plants of the earth, so they marked each of them and attributed to each of its type, and they knew the benefit that was in the fresh plant and the dry plant, and their growth cycles, and which its succession and rendered it as spring, summer, and mid-summer and winter. They knew that their drink was from the heavens, so

they invented for them the constellations. And they were aware of the changing of time, so they made for it divisions of the year. They needed to spread out on the earth, so they made of the heavenly stars guides for the sections of the earth and its regions, and followed the land by means of them. And they made among themselves something which would prevent them from doing evil and which would make them desirous of the beautiful, by which they would avoid baseness and which would spur them on to excellent qualities, even to the extent that a member of their nation, though he be in any remote spot of the earth, describes these excellent qualities, not omitting a thing from his description, and he is immoderate in the censure of evil acts and condemns them at length. They do not discourse except in discussion which encourages good deeds, the preservation of the neighbor, the giving away of goods, and the setting up of commendable acts. Everyone of them achieves that by his mind and deduces it by his native intelligence and his thought, without learning or becoming well-mannered; instead, his natural disposition is well-bred and his mind is perceptive. This is why I said they are the most intelligent nation, because of the soundness of natural endowment, correctness of thought, and acuteness of understanding." This was the end of the conversation.

The vizier said, "How good is what Ibn al-Muqaffa said! How good is what you narrated and what you brought! Bring me now what you have heard and have deduced."

I replied, "If what this man, skillful in his manners and excellent of mind, has said is sufficient, then anything added to it would be a superfluity, unnecessary to it, and following it with something similar would be of no use."

The vizier said, "The range of description varies in beautifying and making ugly; the different characteristics depend upon what is thought correct and incorrect. This question—I mean the preference of one nation over another—is, among nations, a thing over which people have contended and have pushed each other around. Nor, since we have exchanged words in this room, have they come to a firm settlement and an apparent agreement."

I responded, "This happens of necessity, for it is not in the Persian's nature nor his custom nor is origin to acknowledge the merit of the Arab, and neither is it in the nature of the Arab nor in his habit that he be delighted at the merit of the Persian. And the same applies to the Indian, the Greek, the Turk, the Dailamite, and others, for the consideration of merit and nobility rests upon two things. The first is that by which one people became distinguished from another, at the time of the creation, by the choice of good and bad, by correct and erroneous opinion, and by the contemplation of the beginning and the end. The matter depends upon this, but secondly, every nation has virtues and

vices and every people has good and bad qualities, and every group of people is both complete and deficient in its industry and its wielding of influence. And it is decreed that bounties and merits and faults be poured forth over all mankind, scattered among them all.

"Thus the Persians have politics, manners of government, restraints, and ceremonies; the Greeks have science and wisdom; the Indians have thought, deliberation, agility, beguilement, and perseverance; the Turks have courage and boldness; the Negroes have patience, the ability for hard labor, and joy; the Arabs have bravery, hospitable reception, fidelity, gallantry, generosity, responsibility to obligation, oratory, and a gift for explanation.

"Moreover, the merits mentioned above, in these famous nations, are not possessed by everyone of their individuals but rather are widespread among them. But there are some in their group who are devoid of all of them and are characterized by their opposite; that is, the Persians do not lack a man ignorant of politics and lacking in manners, found among the riffraff and the rabble. Similarly, the Arabs do not lack a cowardly or an ignorant or a foolish or a miserly or an inarticulate man. And the same holds true for the Indians, the Greeks, and others. Accordingly, when the people of merit and perfection from the Greeks are compared with the people of merit and perfection from the Persians, they come together on an even path. There is no difference between them except in the degrees of merit and the extents of perfection, and those are general rather than specific. In a like manner, when the people of shortcoming and vileness of another nation, they come together on an even path. There is no difference between them except in the degrees and extents. Thus it has become clear from this list that all the nations have divided among themselves merits and shortcomings by the necessity of natural endowment and the choice of thought. Beyond that, people only compete among themselves regarding inheritance, native custom, overwhelming passion of irascible souls, and the angry impulse of emotional force.

"Here is another thing, an important principle which it is not possible to avoid pointing out in our discussion. Every nation has a period of domination over its opponents. This is clearly evident when you imagine for a moment the Greeks at the time of Alexander the Great, when they conquered, governed, ruled, sowed and unsowed, prescribed, managed and commanded, incited and restrained, erased and recorded, acted and reported. Similarly, when you turn your attention to discussing Chosroës Anûshirvân [Sasanid Emperor, 531–578 AD], you find these same conditions...And for this reason, Abû Muslim, when asked which people he found most courageous, said, 'All people are courageous when their fortune is rising.' He had spoken truly. And accordingly, every nation at the beginning of its prosperity is virtuous, courageous, brave,

worthy of glory, generous, outstanding, eloquent, perceptive, and reliable. This point of view is extrapolated from a phenomenon common to all nations, to one universal to each nation at a time, to a thing embracing each group, to one prevalent to each tribe, to something customary in each family, to one special to each person and each man. And this change from nation to nation illustrates the abundance of the generosity of God to all His creation and creatures in proportion to their fulfillment of His demand and their readiness to exert themselves at length in attaining it."

Translated by John Dumis[33]

al-Tanukhi

TABLE TALK

I was told the following by Abu'l-Faraj Babbaghā: Some delay had occurred in the matter of the clothing regularly sent me by the Prince Saif al-Daulah, who liked, enjoyed, and appreciated nothing better than to be asked, when he would give, then to be asked for more, when he would give more, and indeed to be pestered with demands. It was even his habit to put something away behind his back which he meant to give some person. He would then say: I want to give this to So-and-so, and an attendant would go and fetch the man, who was told that he was to have an audience. When the man presented himself Saif al-Daulah would give him nothing; the man would say to him: What is there behind his majesty's cushion?—Saif al-Daulah would ask what business it was of his. The man would say: I am quite sure his majesty has set it aside for me. Saif al-Daulah would deny it, and the man affirm it, and seize it when Saif al-Daulah would try to pull it away. If this were done, Saif al-Daulah would ultimately give it to the man and add some further *douceur*—So, said Babbaghā, I wrote to him, importuning him to send the clothes as usual:

"It is a sign of the courage of the hopeful (God prolong the life of our lord the Prince Saif al-Daulah) if he is satisfied with the person on whom his hopes are set; and the worth of the importuned occupies in his mind. For very different are the degrees and the gradations of men in their assumption of munificence and their cultivation of ambition. Loftiness of morality is to be found in loftiness of pursuit.

> The glory craved by Saif al-Daulah's soul
> Surpasses calculation and control.
> His bounty to my hopes I guaranteed;
> He sent them joyful home, from wandering freed.
> Once I had felt his goodness, I no more
> Needed to haunt the grudging miser's store.
> The rain is jealous of his lavish stream;
> Fate sees with envy my fulfilled dream.

Now my knowledge—God aid him—that I am nearest to him of his suppliants, the one with the strongest claim, the greediest for an increase of his favours, and the most importunate in soliciting his bounty, has encouraged me to approach his heart with a request and to address his munificence in the language of hope:

> If every one knows the position assigned
> The slave in his master's affection and mind,
> Evinced by the robes of distinction he wears
> Discomfiture bringing thereby to his peers;
> How strange that his grant is withheld, when the same
> Who orders, is advocate too for the claim.

May he see to this, please God!"

Translated by D. S. Margoliouth[34]

al-Kalabadhi

THE SUFI DOCTRINE OF VISION

They are agreed that God will be seen with the eyes in the next world, and that the believers will see Him but not the unbelievers, because this is a grace from God: for God says, "To those who do what is good, goodness and an increase." They hold that vision is possible through the intellect, and obligatory through the hearing. As for its being intellectually possible, this is because God exists, and everything which exists may (logically speaking) be seen. For God has implanted in us vision: and if the vision of God had not been possible,

then the petition of Moses, "O Lord, show Thyself to me, that I may look upon Thee", would have been (evidence of) ignorance and unbelief. Moreover, when God made the vision dependent on the condition that the mountain should abide firm—for He says, "And if it abide firm in its place, then shalt thou see Me"—and seeing also that its abiding firm would have been intellectually possible, if God had made it firm; it necessarily follows that the vision which was dependent on this was intellectually permissible and possible. Since therefore it is established that vision is intellectually possible, and as moreover it is shown to be obligatory through the hearing—for God says, "Faces on that day shall be bright, gazing on their Lord", and again, "To those who do what is good, goodness and an increase", and again "Nay, verily, from their Lord on that day they are veiled"—and as the Traditions assert that there is vision, as when the Prophet said, "Verily ye shall see your Lord as ye see the moon on the night of its fullness, without confusion in the vision of Him", concerning which matter the stories are well known and authenticated: it follows that it is necessary to state this, and to believe that it is true.

As for the esoteric interpretation of those who deny the vision of God, this is impossible, as for example those who construe "gazing on their Lord" as meaning "gazing on the reward of their Lord": for the reward of God is other than God. So with those who say "show Thyself to me, that I may look upon Thee" is a petition for a sign: for God had already shown Moses His signs. It is the same with those who interpret "No vision taketh Him in" as meaning that, as no vision taketh Him in in this world, so also in the world to come: God denied that He could be taken in by the vision, for such taking-in would imply modality (*kayfiyah*) and circumscription; He denied, therefore, that which implies modality and circumscription, but not the vision in which there is neither modality nor circumscription.

They are agreed that God is not seen in this world either with the eyes or with the heart, save from the point of view of faith: for this (vision) is the limit of grace and the noblest of blessings, and therefore cannot occur save in the noblest place. If they had been vouchsafed in this world the noblest of blessings, there would have been no difference between this world which passes away, and Paradise which is eternal: and as God prevented His conversant from attaining this in the present world, it is the more proper that those who are beneath him should be likewise (prevented). Moreover, this world is an abode of passing-away: therefore it is not possible for the Eternal to be seen in the abode that passes away. Further, if they had seen God in this world, belief in Him would have been axiomatic (*ḍarūrah*). In short, God has stated that vision will occur in the next world, but He has not stated that it

occurs in this world: and it is necessary to continue oneself to what God has expressly stated.

Translated by A. J. Arberry[35]

al-Hamadhani

THE ASSEMBLY OF QAZWIN

'Ísá ibn Hishám related to us and said: In the year AH 75 I took part in a raid, on the frontier of Qazwín, with those that raided it. We crossed not a rugged upland, but we also descended into a valley, until our march brought us to one of the villages. The scorching noon-day heat impelled us to seek the shade of some tamarisk trees in the centre of which was a spring, like unto the flame of a torch, more limpid than a tear, gliding over the stony ground as glides the restless serpent. We took what food we were inclined to take, then we sought the shade and addressed ourselves to the noon-day nap. But sleep had not yet overcome us when we heard a voice more disagreeable than the braying of an ass and a footfall lighter than that of a camel's colt; accompanying these two was the sound of a drum which seemed to proceed from the jaws of a lion and which drove away the scout of sleep from the people. I opened both my eyes and looked towards him, but the trees intervened between us. So I listened and lo! he was reciting to the beat of the drum:—

'I invite to God, is there an answerer?
To a spacious shelter and luxuriant pasture.
To a lofty garden the fruits whereof cease not to be near to gather and
 never vanish from sight
O people, verily I am a man returning
From the land of infidelity, and wondrous is my story.
If now I have believed, how many nights
Have I denied my Lord and committed the questionable thing?
Ah! many the swine the ends of whose soft bones I have chewed,
And the intoxicant of which I have obtained a share!
Then did God guide me and zealous and effectual endeavour raised me
 from the baseness of unbelief,
But I continued to conceal my religion from my people,

And to worship God with a penitent heart.
I adored the goddess al-Lát, for fear of the enemy,
And in dread of the Watcher, I looked not towards the Ka'ba.
I besought God when night enveloped me and dreadful day wasted me,
Lord, as Thou saved me,
Now deliver me, for I am a stranger among them.
Then did I take the night as my steed,
And I had before me no spare mount, except resolution.
Suffice thee to know of my journey, that it was in a night,
In which the head of a child would almost turn grey,
Until I passed from the enemy's territory
Into the guarded domain of the Faith, and then I shook off fear.
When signs of the Faith came in sight, I said:
Assistance from God and a speedy victory.'

Now, when he reached this verse, he said: "O people! I have entered your dwelling with a resolution which love hath not excited, nor poverty impelled. I have left behind my back gardens planted with trees, and vineyards, damsels of equal age with swelling breasts, and excellent horses, heaped up wealth, equipments, a numerous tribe, mounts and slaves: but I came forth as the serpent issues from its hold, and the bird goes forth from its nest, preferring my religion to my worldly possessions, bringing my right to my left, and joining my day march to my night journey. Now I pray ye will ye combat the fire with its own sparks, and stone the Byzantine empire with its own missiles, and with assistance and aid, with support and succour, and help me in invading them, but not exceeding bounds, every one according to his several ability and in proportion to his wealth? I will not regard a bag of ten thousand dirhems too much; I will accept a mite and not decline a date. For each one from me there will be two arrows, one of which I will sharpen for future recompense, and the other I will notch with prayer and with it from the bow of darkness shoot at the gates of Heaven.' Said 'Ísá ibn Hishám 'His admirable diction excited me, so I cast off the robe of sleep and ran to the company and lo! it was our Shaikh, Abú'l-Fath al-Iskanderí, with a sword which he had drawn, and in a garb which he had adopted as a disguise. Now when he saw me he winked his eye at me and said: 'May God be merciful to him who from his abundance will help us and apportion to us a share of his favours.' Then he took what he got, then I led him aside and said: 'Art thou of the sons of the Nabateans? He answered:—

'As is my state with fate, such is my state with pedigree.
'My genealogy is in the hands of Time, if it is hard upon it, it will change.
In the evening a Nabatean am I, in the morning an Arab.'

Translated by W. J. Prendergast[36]

al-Biruni

DETERMINATION OF THE LENGTH OF RAMADAN

Some years ago, however, a pagan sect started into existence somehow or other. They considered how best to employ the interpretation (of the Qur'an), and to attach themselves to the system of the exoteric school of interpreters who, as they maintain, are the Jews and Christians. For these latter have astronomical tables and calculations, by means of which they compute their months, and derive the knowledge of their fast days, whilst Muslims are compelled to observe the new moon, and to inquire into the different phases of the light of the moon, and into that which is common to both her visible and invisible halves. But then they found that Jews and Christians have no certainty on this subject, that they differ, and that one of them blindly follows the other, although they had done their utmost in the study of the places of the moon, and in the researches regarding her motions (lit. expeditions) and stations.

Thereupon they had recourse to the astronomers, and composed their Canons and books, beginning them with dissertations on the elements of the knowledge of the Arabian months, adding various kinds of computations and chronological tables. Now, people, thinking that these calculations were based upon the observation of the new moons, adopted some of them, attributed their authorships to Ja'far al-sadik, believed that they were one of the mysteries of prophecy. However, these calculations are based not upon the apparent, but upon the mean, i.e. the corrected, motions of sun and moon, upon a lunar year of 354 days, and upon the supposition that six months of the year are complete, six incomplete, and that each complete month is followed by an incomplete one. So we judge from the nature of their Canons, and from the books which are intended to establish the bases on which the Canons rest.

But, when they tried to fix thereby the beginning and end of fasting, their calculation, in most cases, preceded the legitimate time by one day. Whereupon they set about eliciting curious things from the following word of the Prophet:

"Fast, when she (new-moon) appears, and cease fasting when she reappears." For they asserted, that the words "fast, when she appears" mean the fasting of that day, in the afternoon of which new-moon becomes visible, as people say, "prepare yourselves to meet him" which case the act of preparing precedes that of meeting.

Besides, they assert that the month of Ramadan has never less than thirty days. However, astronomers and all those who consider the subject attentively, are well aware that the appearance of new-moon does not proceed regularly according to one and the same rule for several reasons: the motion of the moon varies, being sometimes slower, sometimes faster; she is sometimes near the earth, sometimes far distant; she ascends in north and south, and descends in them; and each single one of these occurrences may take place on every point of the ecliptic. And besides, some sections of the ecliptic sink faster, others slower. All this varies according to the different latitudes of the countries, and according to the difference of the atmosphere. This refers either to different places where the air is either naturally clear or dark, being always mixed up with vapours, and mostly dusty, or it refers to different times, the air being dense at one time, and clear at another. Besides, the power of the sight of the observers varies, some being sharp-sighted, others dim-sighted. And all these circumstances, however different they are, are liable to various kinds of coincidences, which may happen at each beginning of the two months of Ramadan and Shawwâl under innumerable forms and varieties. For these reasons the month Ramadan is sometimes incomplete, sometimes complete, and all this varies according to the greater or less latitude of the countries, so that, e.g. in northern countries the month may be complete, whilst the same month is incomplete in southern countries, and vice versa. Further, also, these differences in the various countries do not follow one and the same rule; on the contrary, one identical circumstance may happen to one month several consecutive times or with interruptions.

But even supposing that the use which they make of those tables and calculations were correct, and their computation agreed with the appearance of new-moon, or preceded it by one day, which they have made a fundamental principle, they would require special computations for each degree of longitude, because the variation in the appearance of new-moon does not depend alone upon the latitudes, but to a great extent also upon the longitudes of the countries. For, frequently, new-moon is not seen in some place, whilst she is seen in another place not far to the west; and frequently she is seen in both places at once. This is one of the reasons for which it would be necessary to have special calculations and tables for every single degree of longitude. Therefore, now,

their theory is quite Utopian, viz. that the month of Ramadan should always be complete, and that both its beginning and end should be identical in the whole of the inhabited world, as would follow from that table which they use.

If they contend that from the (above-mentioned) tradition, which is traced back to Muhammad himself, the obligation of making the beginning and end of fasting precede the appearance of new-moon, follows, we must say that such an interpretation is unfounded. For the particle *Lam* relates to future time, as they have mentioned, and relates to past time, as you say, e.g.: ("dated from this or that day of the month"), i.e. from that moment when days of the month were past already, in which case the writing does not precede the past part of the month. And this, not the first mentioned, is the meaning of that tradition. Compare with this the following saying of the Prophet: "We are illiterate people, we do not write nor do we reckon the month thus and thus and thus," each time showing his ten fingers, meaning a complete month or thirty days. Then repeated his words, saying, "and thus and thus and thus," and at the third time he held back one thumb, meaning an incomplete month or twenty-nine days. By this generally known sentence, the Prophet ordained that the month should be one time complete, and incomplete another time, and that this is to be regulated by the appearance of new-moon, not by calculation, as he says, "we do not write, nor do we reckon (calculate)."

But if they say that the Prophet meant that each complete month should be followed by an incomplete one, as the chronologists reckon, they are refuted by the plain facts, if they will not disregard them, and their trickery in both small and great things, in all they have committed, is exposed. For the conclusion of the first-mentioned tradition proves the impossibility of their assertion, viz. "Fast when she (new-moon) appears, and cease fasting when she re-appears, but if heaven be clouded so as to prevent your observation, reckon the month Sha'bān as thirty days." And in another tradition, the Prophet says, "If a cloud or black dust should prevent you from observing the new moon, make the number thirty complete." For if the appearance of new-moon be known either from their tables and calculations, or from the statements of the authors of the canons, and if the beginning and end of fasting is to precede the appearance of new-moon, it would not be necessary to give full thirty days to the month Sha'bān, or to count the month Ramadan as full thirty days, in case the horizon should be covered by a cloud or by dust. And this (i.e. to give full thirty days to Ramadan) is not possible, except by performing the fasting of the day in the evening of which the new-moon is first seen.

If, further, the month Ramadan were always complete, and its beginning were known, people might do without the observation of new-moon for the

month Shawwál. In the same way, the word of the Prophet: "and cease fasting when she (new-moon) re-appears" is to be interpreted.

However, party spirit makes clear-seeing eyes blind, and makes sharp-hearing ears deaf, and instigates people to engage in things which no mind is inclined to adopt. But for this reason, such ideas would not have entered their heads, if you consider the traditions which occur in the books of the Shi'a Zaidiyya,—may God preserve their community!—and which have been corrected by their authorities,—may God bless them!—as for instance, the following: In the time of the Prince of the Believers ('Ali) people had been fasting twenty-eight days in the month of Ramadan. Then he ordered them still to perform the fasting of one day, which they did. The fact was that both consecutive months, Sha'bān and Ramadan, were imperfect, and there had been some obstacle which had prevented them from observing new-moon at the beginning of Ramadan ; they gave the month the full number of thirty days, and at the end of the month the reality of the case became evident. Then there is the following saying, related to have been pronounced by 'Abu-'Abd-Allah Alsadik: "The month of Ramadan is liable to the same increase and decrease as the other months." Also the following is reported of the same: "If you observe the month Sha'bān without being able to see the new-moon, count thirty and then fast." The same 'Abu-'Abd-Allah Alsadik, on being asked regarding the new-moon, said: "If you see the new moon, fast, and if you see her again, cease fasting." All these traditions in the code of the Shi'a refer only to the fasting.

It is astonishing that our masters, the family of the Prophet, listened to such doctrines, and that they adopted them as a uniting link for the minds of the community of the believers who profess to follow them, instead of imitating the example of their ancestor, the Prince of the Believers ('Ali), in his aversion to conciliating the obstinate sinners, when he spoke: "I did not hold out an arm to those who lead astray" (i.e. I did not lend support to them).

As regards the following saying, ascribed by tradition to Alsadik: "When you observe the new-moon of Rajab, count fifty-nine days, and then begin fasting;" and the following saying ascribed to the same: "If you see the new-moon of the month of Ramadan at the time when she appears, count 354 days, and then begin fasting in the next following year. For the Lord has created the year as consisting of 360 days. But from these he has excepted six days, in which he created the heavens and the earth; therefore they (these six days) are not comprehended in the number (of the days of the year)"—regarding these traditions we say, that, if they were correct, his (Alsadik's) statement on this subject would rest on the supposition, that it (the month Ramadan) was really greater in one place, and did not follow the same rule everywhere, as we have heretofore mentioned. Such

a method of accounting for the six days is something so subtle, that it proves the tradition to be false, and renders it void of authenticity.

In a chronicle I have read the following: "Abu-Jafar Muhammad ben Sulaiman, Governor of Kufa, under the Khalif Mansur, had imprisoned 'Abd-alkarim ben 'Abi-al'auja, who was the uncle of Ma'n ben Za'ida, one of the Manichaeans. This man, however, had many protectors in Baghdad, and these urged Mansur in his favour, till at last he wrote to Muhammad ordering him not to put 'Abd-alkarim to death. Meanwhile, 'Abd-alkarim was expecting the arrival of the letter in his cause. He said to 'Abu-aljabbar confidentially: "If the 'Amir gives me respite for three days, I shall give him 100,000 dirhams." 'Abu-aljabbar told this to Muhammad, who replied: "You have reminded me of him, whilst I had forgotten him. Remind me of him when I return from the mosque." Then, when he returned, 'Abu-aljabbar reminded him of the prisoner, whereupon he (Muhammad) ordered him to be brought and to be beheaded. And now, knowing for certain that he was to be killed, he said, "By God, now that you are going to kill me, I tell you that I have put down 4,000 traditions (in my books), in which I forbid that which is allowed, and allow that which is forbidden. And verily, I have made you break your fast when you ought to have fasted, and I have made you fast when yon ought not to have fasted." Thereupon he was beheaded, and afterwards the letter in his cause arrived.

How thoroughly did this heretic deserve to be the author of this subtle interpretation which they have adopted, and of its original (i.e. the text to which the interpretation refers)!

I myself have had a discussion with the originator of this sect, regarding the Musnad-tradition (i.e. such a tradition as is carried back by an uninterrupted chain of witnesses to Muhammad himself). On which occasion I compelled him to admit that consequences, similar to those here mentioned, follow from his theories. But then in the end he declared, that the subject was one that of necessity resulted from the language (i.e. from the interpretation of the *Lam al-Taukit*), and that the language has nothing whatever to do with the law and its corollaries. Thereupon, I answered: "May God have mercy upon you! Have not God and his Prophet addressed us in the language generally known among the Arabs? But the thing is this, that you have nothing whatever to do with the Arabic language; and also in the science of the law you are utterly ignorant. Leave the law aside and address yourself to the astronomers. None of them would agree with you regarding your theory of the perpetual completeness of the month of Ramadan; none of them thinks that the celestial globe and sun and moon distinguish the moon of Ramadan from among the others, so as to move faster or slower just in this particular month. The luminaries do not mark

out this month in particular as do the Muslims, who distinguish it by perform-
ing their fasting in it.

However, arguing with people who are obstinate on purpose, and persevere
in their obstinacy on account of their ignorance, is not productive of any good,
either for the student or for the object of his researches. God speaks (Sura lii.
44): "If they saw a piece of heaven falling down, they would say, 'it is only a
conglomerated cloud.'" And further (Sura vi. 7): "If we sent down to you a
book (written) on paper, and they touched it with their hands, verily the unbe-
lieving would say, 'This is nothing but evident witchcraft.'" God grant that we
may always belong to those who follow and further the truth, who crush and
expose that which is false and wrong!

Translated by E. Sachau[37]

al-Ma'arri

THE EPISTLE OF FORGIVENESS

"Tell me about the poetry of the jinns" said Ibn Qàrih "for the mortal known
as al-Marzubàni collected a selection of it". "But this" replied the old man "is
trash of no account. Does mortal man know any more about verse than a cow
does of astronomy or geometry? Mortals have only fifteen kinds of metre, and
reciters could scarcely better them; while we have thousands which mortals
have never heard; what they know has been communicated to them by learned
babes among us, who have spat out to them an amount as it were the thin bark
of a jungle-tree of Num'àn.

"I composed a single-rhymed poem and some odes centuries before Adam
was created. I have heard that you are a circle of mortals who admire the poetry
of Imru ul Qais beginning: 'Rise up ye two and let us weep for the memory of
loved one and home' and that you teach it to your youth in the schools. If you
wished, I could recite you a thousand verses in this metre rhyming in *man-
zili* and *haumili*, and a thousand in the same strain rhyming in *manzilu* and
haumilu, and another in *manzila* and *haumila*, and *manzilihu* and *haumilihu*,
and *manzilahu* and *haumilahu*, and *manzilihi* and *haumilihi*.

And all being in honour of a poet of ours who was eternally lost for being
an unbeliever, and he is now blazing in the depths of Hell."

"Old man" said Ibn ul Qàrih "How have you kept your memory?"

"We are not like you, sons of Adam." Replied the Jinn "to be overcome by forgetfulness and damp, for you were created of clay, while we are created of flames of fire".

Ibn ul Qàrih's passion for literature moved him to ask the old man to dictate him some of his poetry. "If you wish" replied he "I will dictate more than all the camels can carry, and which all the books of your world could not contain."

Ibn ul Qàrih was about to write from his dictation, but he thought: "I worried myself in the transitory world with collecting literature, and got no profit out of it. I am now so unsuccessful that I have left the joys of Paradise, and have come to copy the literature of the jinns, although I have enough literature—especially as oblivion is general among the literary men of Paradise, and I have become their greatest poet with the longest memory—to Allah be the praise!"

He then asked the old man what was his eponym that he might honour him by using it.

"Abū Hadrash" replied he. "I have had the descendants that Allah decreed, and they are now many tribes. Some are in Hell-fire and others in Paradise."

"Abū Hadrash" replied Ibn ul Qàrih "how is it that I see you grey-haired, when the denizens of Paradise have perpetual youth?"

"Mortals have had that bestowed on them in Paradise" replied he "while we have been denied it, for we were given power to change our shape in the transitory world, and any one of us if he willed could change into a spotted viper or a sparrow or a pigeon,—though in the eternal world, we have been forbidden to change, being left unchanged as we were created. The sons of Adam have the privilege of being made in a form of beauty. One of the mortal poets in the transitory world said: "We have been given the power of deceit, and jinns the power of change! And truly I have met evil at the hands of the sons of Adam, and they have met the like from me!"

Translated by G. Brackenbury[38]

LETTER TO ABU AHMAD 'ABD AL-SALIM IBN AL-HUSAIN

God prolong your existence till 'Urayya be removed, and till the Arabs speak of the Pleiads without the diminutive form; and continue your prosperity until Irāb turns one morning into a hawk or raven in the sky! Often as I write, my letters do not reach you, and through no fault of mine.

"How fair a mountain is mount Rayyān! And nobler still he who dwells

there! How sweet to those southern breezes that at times reach you from mount Rayyān!"

By Rayyān I mean your dwelling, wherever it may be; and by its inhabitant yourself, wherever you happen to be. And this is allowable in a quotation, just as I may say "there is no hero like 'Amr," though the person whom I mean be not named 'Amr. And my grief at parting from you is like that of the turtle-dove, which brings pleasure to the hot listener, retired in a thickly-leaved tree from the heat of the summer, like a singer behind a curtain, or a great man hedged off from the frivolous conversation of the vulgar; with a collar on his neck almost burst by his sorrow; were he able, he would wrench it with his hand off his neck, out of grief for the companion whom he has abandoned to distress, the comrade whom Noah sent out and left to perish, over whom the doves still mourn. Varied music does he chant in the courts, publishing on the branches the secrets of his hidden woe; if he strike up the note of al-Gharīd, he leaves the lover at death's door; and if he imitate a tune of Ma'bad, he does so wondrous well. He summons mourners, such as invite to melancholy; fie upon them, may they be bereaved, who trust not in the Eternal, whose father moaned for Wadd, and who have inherited his lamenting from generation to generation. Truly they wail excessively, and yet their eyes shed no tears. I know not, and indeed it is a puzzle, whether it be singing or moaning. Every grey-green bird is like an orator, on moist branch, with a band of pitch on its beak, with fire kindled in its heart, and with its feet dipped in blood, with a collar of coals and a garment of cinder.

Or rather my grief is like that of the she-dove, when she perceives the star of the wasted, having dwelt in Yemen till some divine doom brought her to an arid land that had neither dew nor showers; and when she looks at Canopus, it reminds her of companions she had known in a land of Yemen, none of whom had ever dealt unkindly with her; and feeling her throat oppressed with regrets she begins to cry and grieve, alleviating by the emission of these sounds the grief which she feels for the dead; thinking that there is no escape from the confinement of the cage, she wishes that God would change her into a mewing day-cat, or a moaning night-wolf; that she might escape by such deliverance from some of her troubles.

My abode is Ma'arrah of Nu'ān, and civil strife is rife among us; there are spear-thrusts and bow-shots; and by the time summer comes swords will have been drawn as well. Had I been able, I should have used no wood but *markh* for firesticks, and inhabited no city but the capital. However, my camel's legs are tied; and God bless Labīd for saying—

"When Lubad saw the rest of the vultures fly away, he raised his feathers like a poor man who has no arms."

I offer you, my friends, and your children salutation such as would enliven the waste wilderness, and stretch from Syria to Yemen. If it passes by men who are burning a fire of tamarisk, they will think the tamarisk must be aloes, so fragrant will it leave the air.

Translated by D. S. Margoliouth[39]

FROM THE *DIWAN*

Life is a flame that flickers in the wind,
 A bird that crouches in the fowler's net—
 Nor may between her flutterings forget
That hour the dreams of youth were unconfined.

There was a time when I was fain to guess
 The riddles of our life, when I would soar
 Against the cruel secrets of the door,
So that I fell to deeper loneliness.

One is behind the draperies of life,
 One who will tear these tanglements away—
 No dark assassin, for the dawn of day
Leaps out, as leapeth laughter, from the knife.

If you will do some deed before you die,
 Remember not this caravan of death,
 But have belief that every little breath
Will stay with you for an eternity.

Translated by Henry Baerlein[40]

FROM THE *LAZUMIYAT*

Upon the threshing-floor of life I burn
Beside the Winnower a word to learn,
 And only this: Man's of the soil and sun,
And to the soil and sun he shall return.

And like a spider's house or sparrows nest.
The Sultan's palace, though upon the crest
 Of glory's mountain, soon or late must go:
Ay, all abodes to ruin are addrest.

So, too, the creeds of Man: the one prevails
Until the other comes; and this one fails
 When that one triumphs; ay, the lonesome world
Will always want the latest fairy-tales

Seek not the Tavern of Belief, my friend,
Until the Sakis there morals mend;
 The trust of wisdom; better far is doubt
Which brings the false into the light of day.

Or wilt thou commerce have with those who make
Rugs of the rainbow, rainbows of the snake,
 Snakes of a staff, and other wondrous things?
The burning thirst a mirage can not slake.

Religion is a maiden veiled in prayer,
Whose bridal gifts and dowry those who care
 Can buy in Mutakallem's shop of words
But I for such, a dirham can not spare.

Why linger here, why turn another page?
Oh! seal with doubt the whole book of the age;
 Doubt every one, even him, the seeming slave
Of righteousness, and doubt the canting sage.

Translated by Ameen Rihani[41]

'TIS SAID THAT SPIRITS REMOVE BY TRANSMIGRATION

'Tis said that spirits remove by transmigration
From body into body, till they are purged;
But disbelieve what error may have urged,
Unless thy mind confirm the information.

Tho' high their heads they carry, like the palm,
Bodies are but as herbs that grow and fade.
Hard polishings wears out the Indian blade,
Allay thy soul's desires and live calm.

IN THE CASKET OF THE HOURS

In the casket of the Hours
Events deep-hid
Wait on their guardian Powers
To raise the lid.

And the Maker infinite,
Whose poem is Time,
He need not weave in it
A forced stale rhyme.

The Nights pass so,
Voices dumb,
Without sense quick or slow
Of what shall come.

By Allah's will preserving
From misflight,
The barbs of Time unswerving
On us alight.

A loan is all he gives
And takes again;
With his gift happy lives
The folly of men.

THOU ART DISEASED IN UNDERSTANDING AND RELIGION

Thou art diseased in understanding and religion. Come to
 me, that thou mayst hear the tidings of sound truth.
Do not unjustly eat what the water has given up, and do not

desire as food the flesh of slaughtered animals,
Or the white (milk) of mothers who intended its pure draught
 for their young, not for noble ladies.
And do not grieve the unsuspecting birds by taking their
 eggs; for injustice is the worst of crimes.
And spare the honey which the bees get betimes by their
 industry from the flowers of fragrant plants;
For they did not store it that it might belong to others, nor
 did they gather it for bounty and gifts.
I washed my hands of all this; and would that I had perceived
 my way ere my temples grew hoar!

Translated by R. A. Nicholson[42]

Ibn Sina (Avicenna)

CONCERNING THE TEMPORAL ORIGIN OF THE SOUL

We say that human souls are of the same species and concept. If they existed before the body, they would either be multiple entities or one single entity. But it is impossible for them to be either the one or the other, as will be shown later, therefore it is impossible for them to exist before the body. We now begin with the explanation of the impossibility of its numerical multiplicity and say that the mutual difference of the souls before [their attachment to] bodies is either due to their quidity and form; or to the element and matter which is multiple in space, a particular part of which each matter occupies; or to the various times peculiar to every soul when it becomes existent in its matter; or to the causes which dived their matter. But their difference is not due to their quiddity or form, since their form is one, therefore their difference is due to the recipient of the quiddity or to the body to which the quiddity is specifically related. Before its attachment to the body the soul is quiddity or to the body to which the quiddity is specifically related. Before its attachment to the body the soul is quiddity pure and simple; thus it is impossible for one soul to be numerically different from another, or for the quiddity to admit of essential differentiation. This holds absolutely true in all cases for the multiplicity of the species of those things whose essences are pure concepts is only due to the sub-strata which receive them and to what is affected by them, or due only to their

times. But when they are absolutely separate, i.e. when the categories we have enumerated are not applicable to them, they cannot be diverse. It is therefore impossible for them to have any kind of diversity or multiplicity among them. Thus it is untrue that before they enter bodies souls have numerically different essences.

I say that it is also impossible for souls to have numerically one essence, for when two bodies come into existence two souls also come into existence in them. Then either—

1. these two souls are two parts of the same single soul, in which case one single thing which does not possess any magnitude and bulk would be potentially divisible. This is manifestly absurd according to the principles established in physics. Or—

2. a soul which is numerically one would be in two bodies. This also does not require much effort to refute.

It is thus proved that the soul comes into existence whenever a body does so fit to be used by it. The body which thus comes into being is the kingdom and instrument of the soul. In the very disposition of the substance of the soul which comes into existence together with a certain body—a body, that is to say, with the appropriate qualities to make it suitable to receive the soul which takes its origin from the first principles—there is a natural yearning to occupy itself with that body, to use it, control it, and be attracted by it. This yearning binds the soul specially to this body, and turns it away from other bodies different from it in nature so that the soul does not contact them except through it. Thus when the principle of its individualization, namely, its peculiar dispositions, occurs to it, it becomes an individual. These dispositions determine its attachment to that particular body and form the relationship of their mutual suitability, although this relationship and its condition may be obscure to us. The soul achieves its first entelechy through the body; its subsequent development, however, does not depend on the body but on its own nature.

But after their separation from their bodies the souls remain individual owing to the different matters in which they had been, and owing to the different matters in which they had been, and owing to the times of their birth and their different dispositions due to their bodies which necessarily differ because of their peculiar conditions.

Translated by F. Rahman[43]

EPISTLE OF THE SOUL

It descended upon thee from out of the regions above,
That exalted, ineffable, glorious, heavenly Dove.
'Twas concealed from the eyes of all those who its nature would ken,
Yet it wears not a veil, and is ever apparent to men.
Unwilling it sought thee and joined thee, and ye, though it grieve,
It is like to be still more unwilling thy body to leave.
It resisted and struggled, and would not be tamed to haste,
Yet it joined thee, and slowly grew used to this desolate waste,
Till, forgotten at length, as I ween, were its haunts and its troth
In the heavenly gardens and groves, which to leave it was loath.
Until, when it entered the D of its downward Descent,
And to earth, to the C of its centre, unwillingly went,
The eye (I) of Infirmity smote it, and lo, it was hurled
Midst the sign-posts and ruined abodes of this desolate world.
It weeps, when it thinks of its home and the peace it possessed,
With tears welling forth from its eyes without pausing or rest,
And with plaintive mourning it broodeth like one bereft
O'er such trace of its home as the fourfold winds have left.
Thick nets detain it, and strong is the cage whereby
It is held from seeking the lofty and spacious sky.
Until, when the hour of its homeward flight draws near,
And 'tis time for it to return to its ampler sphere,
It carols with joy, for the veil is raised, and it spies
Such things as cannot be witnessed by waking eyes.
On a lofty height doth it warble its songs of praise
(For even the lowliest being doth knowledge raise).
And so it returneth, aware of all hidden things
In the universe, while no stain to its garment clings.

Now why from its perch on high was it cast like this
To the lowest Nadir's gloomy and drear abyss?
Was it God who cast it forth for some purpose wise,
Concealed from the keenest seeker's inquiring eyes?
Then is its descent a discipline wise but stern,
That the things that it hath not heard it thus may learn.
So 'tis she whom Fate doth plunder, until her star
Setteth at length in a place from its rising far,

Like a gleam of lightning which over the meadows shone,
And, as though it ne'er had been, in a moment is gone.

Translated by E. G. Browne[44]

ON PROPHECY

Now it is well known that man differs from all other animals in that he cannot enjoy a good life in isolation and alone, managing all his affairs without any partner to assist him in the fulfilment of his needs. A man must perforce attain satisfaction by means of another of his species, whose needs in turn are satisfied by him and his like: thus, one man will act as conveyor, another as baker, another as tailor, another as sewer; when all unite together, the needs of all are satisfied. For this reason they were constrained to construct cities and societies. Those makers of cities who did not observe the conditions required in their undertaking, confining themselves only to coming together in one community, achieved a kind of life little resembling that which is proper to men, being devoid of those 'perfections' which men require.

This being so, it is necessary for men both to associate with each other, and to behave like citizens. This is obvious; it also follows that it is necessary to the life and survival of mankind that there should be co-operation between them, which can only be realized through a common transaction of business; in addition to all the other means which secure the same purpose. This transaction requires a code of law and just regulation, which is their turn call for a lawgiver and regulator. Such a man must be in the position to speak to men, and to constrain them to accept the code; he must therefore be a man.

Now it is not feasible that men should be left to their own opinions in this matter so that they will differ each from the other, every man considering as justice that which favours him, and as injustice that which works against his advantage. The survival and complete self-realization of the human race requires the existence of such a lawgiver, far more than for instance the growth of hair on the eyelashes and eyebrows, the development of a hollow instep, and such other advantages as are not necessary to survival but are at the most merely useful to that end.

It is entirely possible for a righteous man to exist; and it is not feasible that the Divine Providence should have required the other small advantages, and not have required this which is the foundation of them all; neither is it reasonable to suppose that the First Principle and the Angels should have

been aware of the former and not have known of the latter. Finally it is not likely that this, being a matter known to be existentially possible and actually necessary to establish a beneficent order, should yet not exist; indeed, how should it not exist, seeing that that which depends and is constructed upon its existence does in fact already exist?

It follows therefore that there should exist a prophet, and that he should be a man; it also follows that he should have some distinguishing feature which does not belong to other men, so that his fellows may recognize him as possessing something which is not theirs, and so that he may stand out apart from them. This distinguishing feature is the power to work miracles.

Such a man, if and when he exists, must prescribe laws for mankind governing all their affairs, in accordance with God's ordinance and authority, God inspiring him and sending down the Holy Spirit upon him. The fundamental principle upon which his code rests will be to teach them that they have One Creator, Almighty and Omniscient, Whose commandment must of right be obeyed; that the Command must belong to Him Who possesses the power to create; and that He has prepared for those who obey Him a future life of bliss, but wretchedness for such as disobey Him. So the masses will receive the prescriptions, sent down upon his tongue from God and the Angels, with heedful obedience.

It is not necessary for him to trouble their minds with any part of the knowledge of God, save the knowledge that He is One, True, and has no like; as for going beyond this doctrine, so as to change them to believe in God's existence as not to be defined spatially or verbally divisible, as being neither without the world nor within it, or anything of that sort—to do this would impose a great strain upon them and would confuse the religious system which they follow already, bringing them to a pass wherefrom only those rare souls can escape who enjoy especial favour, and they exceedingly uncommon. The generality of mankind cannot imagine these things as they really are except by hard toil; few indeed are they who can conceive the truth of this Divine Unity and Sublimity. The rest are soon apt to disbelieve in this sort of Being, or they fall down upon the road and go off into discussions and speculations which prevent them from attending to their bodily acts, and often enough cause them to fall into opinions contrary to the good of society and inconsistent with the requirements of truth. In such circumstances their doubts and difficulties would multiply, and it would be hard indeed by words to control them: not every man is ready to understand metaphysics, and in any case it would not be proper for any man to disclose that he is in possession of a truth which he conceals from the masses; indeed, he must not allow himself so much as to hint at any such thing. His

duty is to teach men to know the Majesty and Might of God by means of sym-
bols and parables drawn from things which they regard as mighty and majestic,
imparting to them simply this much, that God has no equal, no like and no
partner.

Similarly, he must establish in them the belief in an afterlife, in a manner
that comes within the range of their imagination and will be satisfying to their
souls; he will liken the happiness and misery there to be experienced in terms
which they can understand and conceive. As for the truth of these matters, he
will only adumbrate it to them very briefly, saying that it is something which
"eye hath not seen nor ear heard", and that there is pleasure awaiting us beyond
the grave which is a mighty kingdom, or pain that is an abiding torment. God
certainly knows the beneficent aspect of all this, and it is always right to take
what God knows exactly for what it implies. There is therefore no harm in his
discourse being interspersed with sundry hints and allusions, to attract those
naturally qualified for speculation to undertake philosophical research into the
nature of religious observances and their utility in terms of this world and the
next.

Now this person, the prophet, is not of the kind that often comes into the
world, in every age; the gross matter able to receive his sort of "perfection" occurs
in but few temperaments. It follows from this that the prophet must devise means
of securing the survival of his code and laws in all the spheres of human welfare.
There is no doubt that the advantage in this is, that men will continue to be aware
of the existence of God and of an afterlife; and the danger of their forgetting
these things, a generation after the prophet's mission, will be circumvented. He
must therefore prescribe certain acts which men should repeat at close intervals,
so that if the time for the performance of one act is missed there may soon be an
opportunity for performing the next like act while the memory is still fresh and
has not yet become obliterated.

These acts must of course be linked up with some means of calling God and
the afterlife to mind, else they will be useless; this mnemonic can only consist
of set words to be uttered, or set resolves to be intended in the imagination.
Men must also be told that these acts are means of winning God's favour and of
qualifying for a great and generous reward: these acts should in fact be of such a
sort, and should be like the religious observances prescribed for men to follow.
In a word, these acts should be reminders; and those reminders must either be
certain motions, or the denial of certain motions resulting in other motions.
The former category may be illustrated by the instance of formal prayers, the
latter by fasting; for though fasting is in itself a negative idea, it stirs nature vio-
lently and so reminds the faster that what he is doing is not meaningless, with

the result that he remembers what his intention is in fasting, namely to win the favour of Almighty God.

He should also if possible mix in with these observances other interests, in order to strengthen and extend the code, and to make their practice generally advantageous in a material sense also. Examples of this are Jehad and Pilgrimage. He should specify certain places in the world as the most suitable for worship, stating that they belong exclusively to God; certain obligatory acts must also be specified as being done for God's sake only—as for instance the offering of sacrifices, which are of great help in this connexion. The place which is advantageous in this context, if it be the town where the lawgiver took refuge and dwelt, will also serve the purpose of bringing him to mind, an advantage second only to that of remembering God and the Angels. This single place of refuge cannot be close at hand for the whole community of the Faith; obviously therefore it must also be prescribed as a place for migration, and for journeying unto.

The noblest of these observances from a certain point of view is that one in which the performer assumes that he is addressing God in private converse, that he is turning to God and standing before Him. This observance is Prayer. Certain steps preparatory to prayer must also be prescribed, similar to these which a man customarily undertakes of his own accord before entering the presence of a human ruler; namely, purification and cleansing. The regulations laid down for these should be effective and impressive. The act of prayer should further be accompanied by those attitudes and rules of conduct usually observed in the presence of kings: humility, quietness, lowering the eyes, keeping the hands and feet withdrawn, not turning about and fidgeting. For every moment of the act of worship, appropriate and seemly rules and usages should be prescribed. All these conditions of religious observance serve the useful purpose of keeping the people's thoughts fixed firmly upon the recollection of God; in this way they will continue in their close attachment to the laws and ordinances of the Faith; without these reminders they will be apt to forget all about it in one or two generations after the prophet's death. These practices will also be of the enormous advantage to them in the hereafter, by purifying and lifting up their souls as we have already shown.

So far as the elect are concerned, the advantage they derive from all these prescriptions is mainly connected with the afterlife. We have established above the true nature of the hereafter, and proved that happiness in the world to come is to be acquired by cleansing and uplifting the soul, through removing it far from such bodily conditions as conflict with the means of securing that happiness. Spiritual elevation is achieved through the acquisition of moral qualities

and virtuous habits, which in their turn are acquired by means of acts calculated to divert the soul from the body and the senses and to remind it of its true substance.

If the soul is frequently turned in towards itself, it will not be affected by the physical circumstances of the body. It will be reminded and helped to do this by acts which are in themselves fatiguing; and outside the usual habit of reason; indeed, the reason itself is stimulated by them to undertake these tasks. They fatigue the body and the animal faculties, destroying their inclination to take things easily, to be slothful and unwilling to go to any trouble, to dull the natural zest and avoid all discipline save for the purpose of getting advantages in the form of bestial pleasures. The soul will be constrained to attempt these motions by the very recollection of God, of the Angels and of the world of perfect happiness, whether it will or no; consequently it will become firmly disposed to chafe at the influences of the body and will acquire the habit of dominating it and not to be merely passive in its control. Bodily actions as they occur will not then affect the soul so powerfully and habitually as would be the case if the soul were satisfied and content to submit to the body in everything. All this proves the truth of the saying, that good habits drive out evil ones. If a man continues in this course, he will acquire the habit of turning automatically towards the true, and away from the false; he will become thoroughly prepared and ready to be delivered into celestial happiness when the body is left behind.

If a man performs these acts without believing them to be a duty imposed by God, and in spite of this his each act is accompanied by the remembrance of God, and a turning away from all other things, he will be worthy to acquire some measure of this spiritual fervour: how much more, then, if he follows this use knowing that the Prophet has come from God to prescribe, he acting in all this as God's agent. For the Prophet was truly charged by God to impose these religious observances upon his followers: observances which are of benefit to men in that they perpetuate among them the Prophet's laws and ordinances, which are the means whereby they live at all, and by stimulating them to spiritual zeal bring them near to the nigh Presence of God in the world to come.

Such a man is richly qualified to dispose the affairs of his fellows in a manner securing the regular provision of their well-being in this world, and their ultimate salvation in the world to come: he is a man distinguished above all his fellows by his Godliness.

Translated by A. J. Arberry[45]

al-Hariri

THE ASSEMBLY OF HAJR

Al Hârith, son of Hammâm, related: I needed a cupping, while I was staying
in Hajr al-Yemâmeh, and accordingly was directed to a Shaykh who cupped
skilfully. So I sent my slave-boy to summon him into my presence and kept
waiting for him, but he was slow to return after he had gone, so that I began
to fancy that he had run away, or met with accident after accident. Then he
came back like one who has failed in his errand and disappointed his master.
Said I to him: "Woe betide thee, for the tardiness of Find, and thy fire-shaft
missing to give a spark." Then he pretended that the Shaykh was busier
than the woman of the two butter-bags and in the midst of a battle like the
battle of Hunain. Now I loathed to go to a cupper's place, and I was at a loss
between sallying forth and lagging behind. Finally I saw that there was no
rebuke upon him who goes to the privy. Thereupon, when I had reached his
shop and got sight of his face, I perceived an old man of cleanly aspect, sur-
rounded by ring upon ring of onlookers and throng upon throng [of custom-
ers]. Before him stood a youth like [the sharp sword] Ṣamṣâmah, about to be
cupped, the Shaykh saying to him: "I see thou hast stretched forth thy head,
before thou bringest out thy scrap, and hast offered me thy nape without
saying to me 'This is for thee.' But I am not of those who sell ready goods for
owed money, nor look out for the shadow after the substance. So if thou dole
out thy coin, thou wilt be cupped in both thy neck-veins, but if thou deem
stinting better, and hoarding more becoming in thyself, then read the Sura,"
he frowned and turned away, "and vanish from out of my sight, or else—"
Then the youth said: "By Him who has forbidden the forging of lies, as He
has forbidden the chase in the two sacred precincts, I am more penniless than
the babe two days old, so trust to the flow of my mountain slope, and grant
me a delay until times have mended with me." Said the Shaykh to him: "Fair
promises are like the shoot of a tree, that has an equal chance that it perish, or
that the fresh date be gathered from it. So what will teach me, whether I am
to reap fruit from thy tree, or to derive from it an ailment? Furthermore what
relying is there that, when thou hast gotten thyself far away, thou wilt fulfil
what thou promisest? For in sooth, treachery has become as the whiteness in
a horse's forefeet amongst the adornments of this generation, so rid me, by
Allah, of thy bothering, and take thee off to where the wolf howls." Then the
lad advanced towards him, overcome with shame, and said: "By Allah, none

breaks faith, save the mean, the contemptible, and none resorts to the pond of treachery but the worthless, and if thou knewest who I am, thou wouldst not let me hear ribald talk; but thou hast spoken in ignorance, and where it behoved thee to prostrate thyself, thou hast foully aspersed, and how abject are exile and poverty, and how beautiful is the speech of him who said:

'The stranger, who trails his skirt pompously, meets but with scorn, how will he fare then abroad, if food and drink fail him?

But no distress brings disgrace upon the high-minded man: camphor and musk, well ye know, though pounded spread fragrance,

The ruby is often tried in Ghada-fire's fiercest glow, the fire abates but the ruby still remains ruby.'

Said the Shaykh to him: "O thou bane of thy father, who causest thy kindred to wail, art thou in a place to brag of, and of an account to be blazed forth? or in the place of a hide to be flayed, and of a nape to be cupped? And granted thy house be such as thou claimest, results therefrom the cupping of the hind-part of thy neck? By Allah, if thy father lorded it over 'Abd al-Manâf, or if 'Abd al-Madâd humbled himself to thy maternal uncle, hammer not cold iron, and seek not that which thou wilt not find, and boast when thou boastest, of thy belongings, not of thy forefathers, and of thy gatherings, not of the roots from which thou springest, and of thy own qualities, not of thy rotten bones, and of thy valuables, not of thy pedigree. Yield not to thy ambition or it will abase thee [bring thee to fall], nor follow thy lust lest it lead thee astray. I commend to Allah him who said to his son:

'Be upright, my dear son, for the straight tree will spread its roots, whereas, when it grows crooked it speedily pines away,

Obey not abasing greed, but behave as a man who bears in silence the pangs of hunger, that gnaw at his vital parts;

And battle against lust that destroys thee, for many who had soared to the stars, enslaved by lust, fell and came to grief.

Be helpful to thy kinsfolk, for shameful it is to see the pinch of distress in those depending upon the free.

And keep to the friend who when the times turn their back on thee, betrays not, but proves faithful, when matters go wrong with thee.

And pardon if thou art strong, for no good is in a man who needlessly wounds, when power of wounding is in his grasp

And guard thee of complaining, thou hearest no man of sense complain, but the fool, who snarls and growls while he checks himself.'

Then the lad said to the onlookers: "How wonderful! What a strange rarity! the nose in the sky and the rump in the water; words sweet as wine and deeds hard as flint stone." Then he assailed the Shaykh with a sharp tongue and in burning rage, saying: "Out upon thee for a fashioner of fine speeches, who swerves from the road of kindliness. Thou preachest benevolence and actest with the ruthlessness of the cat. And if the briskness of thy trade is the cause of thy crustiness, then may Allah strike it with slackness and allow it to be spoiled by thy enviers, until thou art seen more bereft of customers than the cupper of Sabat, and narrower, as far as thy livelihood is concerned, than the eye of the needle." Said the Shaykh to him: "Nay, may Allah visit thee with blisters all over thy mouth, and heat of the blood, until thou art driven to a cupper of mighty roughness, heavy in charges, with blunt cupping-knives, snotty and breaking wind at every moment." Now, when the youth saw that he was complaining to one who would not be silenced, and intent on opening a door that would be kept locked, he desisted from bandying words and made ready for departure. But the Shaykh knew that he deserved blame for what he had said to the youth. So he felt inclined to pacify him, and vouchsafed to submit to his claim and not to ask a fee for cupping him. The lad, however, would not hear but of going and fleeing from his presence, and the twain ceased not from argument and abuse, and tugging each other about, until the youth quaked from the strife and his sleeves got torn. Then he cried aloud over his exceedingly great loss, and the rending of his honour and his rags, while the Shaykh began to make excuses for his excesses, and to quiet the other's tears. But the youth would not listen to his apologies nor abate his weeping until the Shaykh said to him: "May thy uncle (meaning himself) be thy ransom, and that which grieves thee pass over. Art thou not tired of wailing? Wilt thou not learn forbearance? Hast thou not heard of him, who exercised forgiveness, taking after the speech of him who said:

'Quench by thy mercy the fire of anger that recklessly a churl has kindled in thee, and pardon his trespass,
 For mercy is far the best of jewels that grace the wise, and sweetest fruit, culled by man, is ready forgiveness.'

Then the youth said to him: "Forsooth, if thou wert to look at my sordid life, thou wouldst excuse my flowing tears. But the smooth-skinned make light of what the back-sore feels." Then it was as if he became ashamed, and he left off weeping, regaining his composure, and he said to the Shaykh: "I have now conformed with thy wish, so patch up what thou hast rent." Said the Shaykh:

"Get thee gone! thou over-taxest the flow of the streamlets of my bounty: spy for another's lightning, than mine." Then he rose to go from row to row, and begged for the gift of the standers-by, inciting while he was wending his way between them:

'I swear by Mecca's holy house, whither flock in pilgrim's garb the pious from far and wide:

If I possessed but food for one day, my hand would never touch the lancet or cupping-cup.

Nor would my soul, that craves for fair fame with men, contentedly put up with this sign of trade,

Nor had this youth complained of harshness from me or felt the lacerating prick of my sting.

But, lack-a-day, foul fortune's fell fitfulness, left me to grope my way in pitch-darkest night

And poverty brought me to such piteous pass: the blazing pit of hell I would fain prefer!

Is there a man then whom compassion impels, and tender feelings prompt to prove kind to me?'

Said Al Ḥârith, son of Hammâm: Thereupon I was the first to commiserate with his misfortune, and doled out to him two dirhems, saying [within myself], "They are of no account, even though he should be a liar." So he rejoiced at the first-fruit of his gathering, and augured well from them for the obtainment of what he needed; and the dirhems ceased not to pour upon him, and to come to him from all sides, until he had become possessed of verdant plenty, and a well-filled saddle-bag. Then he cheered up at this, and congratulated himself on the event, saying to the youth: "This is a spring-growth of thy sowing, and a milk-flow of which one half belongs to thee; come then to take thy share, and be not abashed." Thus they divided the money between them to the nicety with which the fruit of the dwarf palm splits in two, and rose in perfect agreement, and when the bond of conciliation was tied between them, and the Shaykh bethought himself of going, I said to him: "My blood is heated, and I had directed my steps to thee, so wouldst thou please to cup me and rid me of my ailment?" Then he turned his glance upon me and scanned me sharply, whereupon he came close up to me and incited:

'What think'st thou of my cunning and beguiling, and what occurred 'twixt me and my kid yonder?

That I come off as victor in the contest, and feed on fertile meadows after famine!

Tell me, my heart's core, tell me, pray, by Allah, hast ever thou set eyes upon one like me?

To open by my spell each fastened padlock? to captivate all minds by charm of witchcraft?

To blend the serious with the sportive humour? If Al Iskandari has been before me,

The dew precedes the shower, but the shower excels the dew in fructifying bounty.'

Said the narrator: Then his poetry roused my attention and made me perceive that he was our Shaykh, whom every finger points out. So I rebuked him for his lowering himself and stooping to self-abasement. But he took no notice of what he heard, and minded not my rebuke, saying: "Any shoe suits the bare-footed who walks on flints." Wherewith he stepped away from me contemptuously, and started off, he and his son, like two racehorses.

Translated by F. Steingass[46]

THE ASSEMBLY OF DAMASCUS

al-Hárith son of Hammám related:

I went from 'Irák to Damascus with its green watercourses, in the day when I had troops of fine-bred horses and was the owner of coveted wealth and resources, free to divert myself, as I chose, and flown with the pride of him whose fullness overflows. When I reached the city after toil and teen on a camel travel-lean, I found it to be all that tongues recite and to contain soul's desire and eye's delight. So I thanked my journey and entered Pleasure's tourney and began there to break the seals of appetites that cloy and cull the clusters of joy, until a caravan for 'Irák was making ready—and by then my wild humour had become steady, so that I remembered my home and was not consoled, but pined for my fold—wherefore I struck the tents of absence and yearning and saddled the steed of returning.

As soon as my companions were arrayed, and the agreement duly made, fear debarred us from setting on our way without an escort to guard us. We sought one in every clan and tried a thousand devices to secure a man, but he was nowhere to be found in the hive: it seemed as though he were not amongst

the live. The travellers, being at the end of their tether, mustered at the Jairún gate to take counsel together, and ceased not from tying and unbinding and twisting and unwinding, until contrivance was exhausted and those lost hope who had never lost it.

Now, over against them stood a person of youthful mien, garbed in a hermit's gaberdine: in his hand he held a rosary, while his eyes spake of vigil and ecstasy; at us he was peering, and had sharpened his ear to steal a hearing. When the party was about to scatter, he said to them, for now he had laid open their secret matter, "O people, let your cares be sloughed and your fears rebuffed, for I will safeguard you with that which will cast out dread from your breasts and show itself obedient to your behests." Said the narrator: We demanded of him that he should inform us concerning his gage, and offered him a greater fee than for an embassage; and he declared it was certain words rehearsed to him in a dream of the night, to serve him as a phylactery against the world's despite. Then began we to exchange the furtive glance and wink to one another and look askance. Recognising that we thought poorly of his tale and conceived it to be frail, he said, "Why will ye treat my solemn assurance as an idle toy and my pure gold as alloy? By God, I have traversed many an awesome region and plunged into deadly hazards legion, and it hath enabled me to do without the protection of a guide and to dispense with a quiver at my side. Furthermore, I will banish the suspicion that hath shaken you and remove the distrust that hath o'er taken you by consorting with you in the desert lands and accompanying you across the Samáwa sands. If my promise prove true, then do ye make my fortune new; but if my lips forswear, then my skin ye may tear and spill my blood and not spare!"

We were inspired to give his vision credit and allow the truth to be as he said it, so we refrained from harrying him, and cast lots for carrying him; and at his bidding we cut the loops of delay and put aside fear of harm or stay. When the pack-saddles were tied and the hour of departure nighed, we begged him to dictate the words of the magic ritual, that we might make them a safeguard perpetual. He said, "Let each one of you repeat the Mother of the Qur'an at the coming of eve and dawn; then let him say, with a tongue of meekness and a voice of weakness, 'O God! O quickener of bodies mouldering in their site! O averter of blight! O Thou that shieldest from affright! O Thou that dost graciously requite! O refuge of them that sue for favour in Thy sight! O Pardoner and Forgiver by right! Bless Mohammed, the last of the prophets for ever, him that came Thy message to deliver! Bless the Lights of his family and the Keys of his victory! And save me, O God, from the intrigues of the satanical and the assaults of the tyrannical; from the vexation of the insolent and the molestation of the truculent; from the oppression of transgressors and the transgression of oppressors; from

the foiling of the foilers and the spoiling of the spoilers; from the perfidy of the perfidious and the insidiousness of the insidious! And, O God, protect me from the wrong-doing of them that around me throng and from the thronging around me of them that do me wrong; and keep me from the hands of the injurious, and bring me out of the darkness of the iniquitous, and in Thy mercy let me enter amongst Thy servants that are righteous! O God, preserve me from dangers on my native soil and in the land of strangers, when I roam and come home, when I go in quest and return to rest, in employment and enjoyment, in occupation and vacation! And guard me in myself and my self, in my fame and my aim, in my weans and my means, in my hold and my fold, in my health and my wealth, in my state and my fate! Let me not decline toward fortune's nadir, or fall under the dominion of an invader, but grant me from Thyself a power that shall be my aider! O God, watch over me with Thine eye and Thine help from on high; and distinguish me by Thy safeguarding and Thy bounteous rewarding; and befriend me with Thy favour and Thy blessing alone, and entrust me not to any care but Thine own! And bestow on me a happiness that decayeth not, and allot to me a comfort that frayeth not; and relieve me from the fears of indigence, and shelter me with the coverlets of affluence; and suffer not the talons of mine enemies for Thou art He that hearkeneth to prayer.'"

Then he looked down with an unroving eye, and uttered not a word in reply, so that we said, "An awe hath astounded him, or a faintness hath dumbfounded him." At last he raised his head and heaved his breath and said, "I swear by heaven with its starry train, and by the earth with its highways plain, and by the streaming rain, and by the blazing lamp of the Inane, and by the sounding main, and by the dust-whirling hurricane: truly this is the most auspicious of charms and will stand you in better stead than the men-at-arms: he that cons it at the smiling of the dawn dreads no calamity ere evening's blush comes on; and he that murmurs it to the scouts of darkness as they advance is ensured for the night against any thievish chance."

Said the narrator: So, for our part, we learned it till we knew it by heart, and we repeated it each man to his neighbour, lest we should forget it and lose our labour. Then we marched, speeding the beasts along by prayers, not by the drivers' song, guarding bundle and bale by holy words, not by men in mail; and our friend, although his attention we never lacked, was not, claiming the fulfilment of our pact, until, when the house-tops of 'Ána rose in the distance, he cried, "Now, your assistance! your assistance!" whereupon we brought to him of our goods both the concealed and the revealed, and the corded and the sealed, and said, "Take at thy choice, for thou wilt not find amongst us a dissentient voice." But all his delight was for the light and the fine, nothing pleased his eye but the coin:

'twas a full load he shouldered and bore, enough to keep want from his door; then off he skipped as the cutpurse skips, and away he slipped as quicksilver slips. We were distressed by his defaulting and amazed at his bolting, and we sought everywhere for a clue and inquired after him from false guides and true, till we heard that since foot in 'Ána he set he had never quitted the cabaret. The foulness of this rumour egged me on to test the ore of its mine and meddle with what is not in my line. Long before sunrise I repaired to the tavern in disguise, and lo, amidst jars and vats, there was the old varlet in a robe of scarlet, and around him cupbearers beaming and candles gleaming and myrtle and jessamine and pipe and mandolin: now he would be broaching the jars, now waking the music of guitars, now inhaling sweet flower-smells, now sporting with the gazelles. When I struck upon his guileful way and the difference of his today from his yesterday, I said, "Woe to thee, O accursed one! So soon hast thou forgotten the day of Jaurún." But he guffawed with a will and began merrily to trill:

"I ride and I ride through the waste far and wide, and I fling away pride to be gay as the swallow;
Stem the torrent's fierce speed, tame the mettlesome steed, that wherever I lead Youth and Pleasure may follow.
I bid gravity pack, and I strip bare my back lest liquor I lack when the goblet is lifted:
Did I never incline to the quaffing of wine, I had ne'er been with fine wit and eloquence gifted.
Is it wonderful, pray, that an old man should stay in a well stored seray by a cask overflowing?
Wine strengthens the knees, physics every disease, and from sorrow it frees, the oblivion-bestowing!
Oh, the purest of joys is to live sans disguise, unconstrained by the ties of a grave reputation,
And the sweetest of love that the lover can prove is when fear and hope move him to utter his passion.
Thy love then proclaim, quench the smouldering flame, for 'twill spark out thy shame and betray thee to laughter:
Heal the wounds of thine heart and assuage thou the smart by the cups that impart a delight men seek after;
While to hand thee the bowl damsels wait who cajole and enravish the soul with eyes tenderly glancing,
And singers whose throats pour such high-mounting notes, when the melody floats, iron rocks would be dancing!

Obey not the fool who forbids thee to pull beauty's rose when in full
bloom thou'rt free to possess it;
 Pursue thine end still, though it seem past thy skill: let them say what
they will, take thy pleasure and bless it!
 Get thee gone from thy sire if he thwart thy desire; spread thy nets nor
inquire what the nets are receiving;
 But be true to a friend, shun the miser and spend, ways of charity wend,
be unwearied in giving.
 He that knocks enters straight at the Merciful's gate, so repent or e'er
Fate call thee forth from the living!"

I said to him, "Bravo, bravo, for thy recitation, but fie and shame on thy repro-
bation! By God, whence springeth thy stock? methinks thy riddle is right hard
to unlock,"
 He answered, "I do not wish to explicate but I will indicate:

I am the age's rarity, the wonder of mankind,
I play my tricks amongst them all, and many a dupe I find;
But then I am a needy wretch whom Fortune broke and beat,
And father, too, of little ones laid bare as butcher's meat.
The poor man with a family—none blames him if he cheat."

Said the narrator: Then I knew he was Abú Zaid, the rogue of his race, he that
blackens the face of hoariness with disgrace; and I was shocked by the greatness
of his iniquity and the abomination of his obliquity. "Old man," I said, "is it not
time that thou draw back from thy course of crime?" He growled and scowled
and fumed, and pondered a moment and resumed, "'Tis a night for exulting,
not for insulting, and an occasion for wine-quailing, not for mutual scoffing.
Away with sorrow till we meet tomorrow I." So I parted from him, in fear of
a row, not because I relied on his vow; and I passed my night in the weeds of
contrition for having gained admission to the daughter of the vine, not to a
mosque or a shrine. And I promised God Almighty that nevermore would I
visit a drinking-shop, not though the empire of Baghdád were given me as a
sop, and never see the vats of wine again, even if the season of youth might be
mine again.
 Then we saddled the camels tawny-white in dawn's twilight, and left Abú
Zaid in peace with his old tutor, Iblis.

Translated by R. A. Nicholson[47]

al-Ghazzali

THE BEGINNING OF GUIDANCE

In the name of God, the Merciful and Compassionate!

The words of the Shaykh, the Imam, the learned Scholar, the Proof of Islam and the Blessing of Mankind, Abu Hamid Muhammad ibn Muhammad ibn Muhammad al-Ghazālī aṭ-Ṭūsī—may God sanctify his rest and lighten the darkness of his tomb:

Praise be to God as is His right, and blessing and peace be upon the best of His creatures, Muhammad, and on his house and Companions after him!

With eager desire you are setting out to acquire knowledge, my friend; of yourself you are making clear how genuine is your longing and how passionate your thirst for it. Be sure that, if in your quest for knowledge your aim is to gain something for yourself and to surpass your fellows, to attract men's attention to yourself and to amass this-worldly vanities, then you are on the way to bring your religion to nothing and destroy yourself, to sell your eternal life for this present one; your bargain is dead loss, your trading without profit. Your teacher abets you in your disobedience and is partner in your loss. He is like one who sells a sword to a highwayman, for in the words of the Prophet (God bless and preserve him), "whoever aids and abets a sin, even by half a word, is partner with the sinner in it".

On the other hand, if in seeking knowledge your intention and purpose, between God most high and yourself is to receive guidance and not merely to acquire information, then rejoice. The angels will spread out their wings for you when you walk, and the denizens of the sea will ask pardon from God for you when you run. Above all, however, you must realize that the guidance which is the fruit of knowledge has a beginning and an ending, an outward aspect and an inward. No one can reach the ending until he has completed the beginning; no one can discover the inward aspect until he has mastered the outward.

Here, then, I give you counsel about the Beginning of Guidance, so that thereby you may test yourself and examine your heart. If you find your heart drawn towards it and your soul docile and receptive, go ahead, make for the end, launch out into the oceans of knowledge. If, on the other hand, you find that when you turn to the matter seriously, your heart tends to procrastinate and to put off actually doing anything about it, then you may be sure that the

part of your soul which is drawn to seek knowledge is the evil-inclined irrational soul. It has been roused in obedience to Satan, the accursed, in order that he may lower you into the well by the rope of his deception, and by his wiles lure you to the abyss of destruction. His aim is to press his evil wares upon you in the place where good wares are sold, so that he may unite you with those "who most lose their works, whose effort goes astray in this present life though they think they are doing well" (Q. 18, 103f).

Moreover Satan, to impress you, rehearses the excellence of knowledge, the high rank of scholars and the Traditions about knowledge from the Prophet and others. He thus diverts your attention from sayings of the Prophet (God bless and preserve him) such as the following: "Whoever increases in knowledge and does not increase in guidance, only increases in distance from God"; "the most severe punishment on the day of Resurrection is that of the scholar to whom God gave no benefit from his knowledge"; "O God, I take refuge with Thee from knowledge which does not benefit, from the heart which does not humble itself, from the act which is not lifted up to God, and from the prayer which is not heard"; "during my night-journey I passed some groups of people whose lips were cut by fiery scissors, and I said to them, Who are you?, and they replied, We used to command others to do good and yet ourselves did not do it, and to prohibit others from doing evil and yet ourselves did it.'

Beware then, unfortunate man, of listening to his fair words, lest he lower you into the well by the rope of his deception. Woe to the ignorant man, when he has not learned even once, and woe to the learned man when he has not put into practice what he learned a thousand times!

People who seek knowledge are of three types. There is the man who seeks knowledge to take it as his travelling-provision for the life to come; he seeks thereby only the Countenance of God and the mansion of eternity; such a man is saved. Then there is the man who seeks it for the help it gives in his transitory life in obtaining power, influence and wealth, and at the same time is aware of that ultimate truth and in his heart has some perception of the worthlessness of his condition and the vileness of his aim. Such a man is in jeopardy, for if his appointed term comes upon him suddenly before he repents, a bad end of life is to be feared for him and his fate will depend upon the will (of God); yet, if he is given grace to repent before the arrival of the appointed term, and adds practice to theory, and makes up for the matters he has neglected, he will join the ranks of the saved, for "the man who repents of sin is like the man who has none".

A third man has been overcome by Satan. He has taken his knowledge as a means to increase his wealth, to boast of his influence and to pride himself

on his numerous following. By his knowledge he explores every avenue which offers a prospect of realizing what he hopes for from this world. Moreover he believes in himself that he has an important place in God's eyes because with his garb and jargon he bears the brand and stamp of the scholar despite his mad desire of this world both openly and in secret. Such men will perish, being stupid and easily deceived, for there is no hope of their repentance since they fancy that they are acting well. They are unmindful of the words of God most high, "O ye who have believed, why do ye say what ye do not do?" (Q. 61, 2). To them may be applied the saying of the Messenger of God (God bless and preserve him), "I fear on your account one who is the Dajjāl (or Antichrist) more than I fear the Dajjāl", and when someone said to him, "Who is that?", he replied, "An evil scholar".

The point of this is that the aim of the Dajjāl is to lead men astray. The scholar is similar if he turns men from this world by what he says, yet he calls them to it by what he is and what he does. A man's conduct speaks more eloquently than his words. Human nature is more inclined to share in what is done than to follow what is said. The corruption caused by the acts of this misguided man is greater than the improvement effected by his words, for the ignorant man does not venture to set his desire on this world till the scholars have done so. Thus this man's knowledge has become a cause of God's servants venturing to disobey Him. Despite that his ignorant soul remains confident; it fills him with desire and hope, and urges him to expect a reward from God for his knowledge. It suggests to him that he is better than many of God's servants.

Be of the first group, then, O seeker of knowledge. Avoid being of the second group, for many a procrastinator is suddenly overtaken by his appointed term before repenting, and is lost. But beware, above all beware, of being in the third group and perishing utterly without any hope or expectation of salvation.

If, then, you ask, What is the Beginning of Guidance in order that I may test my soul thereby?, know that the beginning of guidance is outward piety and the end of guidance is inward piety. Only through piety is anything really achieved; only the pious are guided. Piety designates carrying out the commands of God most high and turning aside from what He prohibits, and thus has two parts. In what follows I expound to you briefly the outward aspect of the science of piety in both its parts.

Translated by W. Montgomery Watt[48]

THE FIRST DUTY OF BROTHERHOOD

Know that the contact of brotherhood is a bond between two persons, like the contract of marriage between two spouses. For just as marriage gives rise to certain duties which must be fulfilled when it is entered into, so does the contract of brotherhood confer upon your brother a certain right touching your property, your person, your tongue and your heart—by way of forgiveness, prayer, sincerity, loyalty, relief and considerateness.

In all, this comprises eight duties:

The first duty is the material one.

God's Messenger (God bless him and give him Peace!) said:

— Two brothers are likened to a pair of hands, one of which washes the other.

He chose the simile of the two hands, rather than the hand and the foot, because the pair are of mutual assistance towards a single aim. So it is with two brothers; their brotherhood is only complete when they are comrades in a single enterprise. In a sense the two are like one person. This entails a common participation in good fortune and bad, a partnership in the future as in the present moment, an abandonment of possessiveness and selfishness. In thus sharing one's property with one's brother there are three degrees:

The lowest degree is where you place your brother on the same footing as your slave or your servant, attending to his need from your surplus. Some need befalls him when you have more than you require to satisfy your own so you give spontaneously, not obliging him to ask. To oblige him to ask is the ultimate shortcoming in brotherly duty.

At the second degree you place your brother on the same footing as yourself. You are content to have him as partner in your property and to treat him like yourself, to the point of letting him share it equally. al-Hasan said there was once a man who would split his waist-band between himself and his brother.

At the third degree; the highest of all, you prefer your brother to yourself and set his need before your own. This is degree of the *ṣiddiq* and the final stage for those united in spiritual love.

Self-sacrifice is one of the fruits of this degree. Tradition tells how a Sufi fraternity were slanderously misrepresented to one of the Caliphs, who ordered their execution. Now one of their number was Abu'l-Husayn al-Nuri, who ran forward to the executioner so that he might be the first to be put to death. Asked why, he replied:

— I wished that my brothers rather than I should have that moment to live.

This, to cut a long story short, was the cause of all of their lives being saved.

If you do not find yourself at any of these stages in relation to your brother, then you must realize that the contract of brotherhood is not yet concluded in the Inner. All that lies between you is a formal connexion, lacking real force in reason or religion.

Maymun ibn Mahran said:

-One who is content not to put his brother first.

As for the lowest degree this is also unacceptable to truly religious people. Tradition tells that Utba al-Ghulam came to the house of a man whose brother he had become, saying:

— I need four thousand of your money.

The other said:

— Take two thousand.

Utba declined the offer, saying:

— You have preferred this world to God. Are you not ashamed to claim brotherhood in God when you can say such a thing?

You ought to avoid worldly dealings with one at the lowest stage of brotherhood. Abu Hazim said:

— If you have a spiritual brother do not deal with him in your worldly affairs.

By this he meant 'if he is at this stage'.

As for the highest degree, this corresponds to the description of the true believers given by God (Exalted is He!) when He said:

— They agree their affairs by mutual consultation, and spend freely of what We have bestowed upon them. (*Qur'an*, 41.38)

That is, they are co-owners of worldly goods without distinctions of status. There were those who would shun the fellowship of man who used the expression "*my* shoe", thereby attributing it to himself.

Fath al-Mawsili once came to a brother's house while he was away. Telling his brother's wife to bring out his chest, he opened it and took from it what he needed. When the slave-girl later informed her master he exclaimed:

— If what you say is true you are a free woman for the sake of God!

So delighted was he at his brother's deed.

Once a man approached Abu Hurayra (may God be pleased with him) and said:

— I wish to take you as my brother in God.

— Do you know what brotherhood entails?

— No.

— That you have no greater right to your pounds or your pence than I have.

— I have not yet reached that stage.

— Then begone from me!

Ali son of al-Husayn (may God be pleased with both) said to a man:

— Does one of you put his hand in the pocket or purse of his brother and take what he needs without permission?

— No.

—Then you are not brothers!

Some people called upon al-Hasan (may God be pleased with him!) and asked:

— Abu Sa'id, have you done your *ṣalāt* prayer?

— Yes.

— Because the market folk have not yet prayed

— And who takes his religion from the market folk?

I hear that one of them would refuse his brother a penny. al-Hasan said this as if it amazed him.

A man came to Ibrahim ibn Adham (may God be pleased with him!) as the latter was leaving for Jerusalem, and said:

— I wish to be your traveling-companion.

— On condition that I have more right to your goods than you.

— No.

— I admire your sincerity!

Now this Ibrahim ibn Adham (may God be pleased with him!) would never differ with a man who accompanied him on a journey, and he would only choose for a companion someone who was in harmony with him. His fellow on one occasion was a sandal-thong merchant. At a certain staging-post someone presented Ibrahim with a bowl of broth. He opened his companion's bag, took a bundle of thongs, set them in the bowl and returned it to the giver of the present. When his companion came along he asked:

— Where are the thongs?

— That broth I ate, what did it cost?:

— You must have given him two or three thongs.

— Be generous and generosity will be shown you!

He once gave a donkey belonging to his companion, without his permission, to a man he saw walking. When his companion came along he said nothing and did not disapprove.

Umar's son (may God be pleased with them both!) said that one of the companions of God's Messenger (God bless him and give him Peace!) was given a sheep's head. He said:

—My brother so-and-so needs it more than I do,

and sent it to him. That person sent it on to another. Thus it was passed from one to another till it came round again to the first, after being through seven hands.

Tradition tells that Masruq owed a heavy debt. His brother Khaythama was also in debt, so Masruq went and paid off Khaythama's debt without his knowledge, and Khaythama went and paid off Masruq's debt without *his* knowledge.

When God's Messenger (God bless him and give him Peace!) witnessed the brotherhood between Abd al-Rahman ibn Awf and Sa'd ibn, al-Rabi', the latter offered to put the former first both materially and spiritually. Abd al-Rahman said:

— God bless you in both respects.

thus preferring his brother in the same way as his brother preferred him. It was as if he accepted then returned the compliment. This is equalising, whereas the first gesture was preferment. Preferment is worthier than equalising.

Abu Sulayman al-Darani used to say:

— If I owned the whole world to put in the mouth of a brother of mine I would still deem it too little for him.

He also said:

—I feed a morsel to a brother of mine and find the taste of it in my own throat.

Spending on brothers is even worthier than giving alms to the poor, for Ali (may God be pleased with him!) said:

—Twenty dirhams I give to my brother in God are dearer to me than one hundred I give in alms to the needy.

He also said:

—To make a meal and gather my brothers in God around it is dearer to me than to free a slave.

In putting others first, all follow the example of God's Messenger (God bless him and give him Peace!). He once entered a thicket with one of his companions and gathered two toothpicks, one of them crooked and the other straight. The straight one he gave to his companion, who said:

— O Messenger of God, you are more entitled to the straight one than I!

But he replied:

— When a comrade accompanies a comrade, if only for one hour of the day, he will be asked to account for his companionship, whether he fulfilled his duty to God therein or whether he neglected it.

He indicated by his own example that putting the companion first is to fulfil one's duty to God in fellowship.

On another occasion God's Messenger (God bless him and give him Peace!) went out to a well to wash at it. Hudhayfa ibn al-Yaman took a robe and stood screening God's Messenger while he washed. Then Hudhayfa sat down to wash himself, and God's Messenger (God bless him and give him Peace!) took his turn to stand screening Hudhayfa from view with the robe. But he objected saying:

— My father be your ransom, and my mother too! O messenger of God, do not do it!

Yet he (God bless him and give him Peace!) insisted on holding the robe as a screen while Hudhayfa washed, and he said:

— Each time two people are in company together, the dearer to God is he who is kinder to his companion.

Tradition tells that Malik ibn Dinar and Muhammad ibn Wasi' went together to the house of al-Hasan while he was out. Muhammad ibn Wasi' took out a basket of food from under al-Hasan's bed and began to eat. Malik said to him:

— Clap your hands to fetch the master of the house.

But Muhammad paid no attention to his words and went on eating, for Malik was more for politeness and manners than he. Then al-Hasan arrived and said:

— My dear Malik, we were not used to being so shy one of another till you and your fellows appeared.

With this he indicated that to make oneself at home in one's brothers' homes is part of true brotherhood.

And indeed, God (Exalted is He!) said:

— Or of your friend, or to which you have the keys. (*Qur'an*)

For although one brother would give the keys of his house to another, permitting him to act as he saw fit, a brother felt that piety required him to refrain from eating, until God (Exalted is He!) revealed this Verse and allowed them to help themselves to the food of brothers and friends.

Translated by Muhtar Holland[49]

THE PHYSICAL SCIENCES

The sciences called by the philosophers "physical" are many. We will mention some of them, so that it may be seen that the Sacred Law does not require a dispute over them, except on a few points which we have mentioned.

These sciences are divided into principal and subsidiary sciences, The principal sciences are eight: (i) The discussion of all that relates to body, *qua* body (i.e., division, motion, and change); and all that appertains to movement, or follows from it (i.e., Time, Space, and the Void). This is the subject-matter of the book called Physics. (ii) The inquiry concerning the various kinds of the component parts of the world (e.g., the heavens, and all that is in the hollow of the sphere of the Moon—viz., the four elements); the nature of these things, and the cause of the location of each one of these in a definite place. This, is discussed in the book called *De coelo*. (iii) The inquiry concerning the laws of generation and corruption; development and reproduction and growth and decay; transformations; and the manner of the preservation of species, in spite of the corruption which overtakes individuals because of the two—i.e., Eastward and Westward celestial movements. This is discussed in the book called *De generations et corruptione*. (iv) The inquiry concerning the accidental conditions of the four elements whose mixture results in meteorological phenomena—e.g., clouds, rain, thunder, lightning, the halo, the rainbow, thunderbolts, winds, and earthquakes. (v) The study of the mineral substances. (vi) The science of botany. (vii) The study of animals. It forms the subject of the book called *Historia animalium*. (viii) The study of the animal soul, and the faculties of perception, showing that the soul of man does not die because of the death of the body, but that it is a spiritual substance whose annihilation is impossible.

The subsidiary sciences are seven: (i) Medicine. It aims at discovering the principles governing the human body; its various conditions (e.g., health and disease); the causes of these conditions, and their symptoms—so that disease may be prevented, and health may be preserved. (ii) Astrology. It is an estimate, based on the figures and constellations of stars, as to what will happen to the world and to people; how new-born babes will fare, and how the years will progress. (iii) Physiognomy. It infers moral character from physical appearance. (iv) Interpretation of dreams, which is an elucidation, derived from dream-images, of what the soul has observed of the Hidden World, and the imaginative faculty has represented through a different symbol. (v) The talismanic art, which combines celestial forces with those of some terrestrial bodies, so as to produce from the combination another force which will work wonders in the world. (vi) The art of magic, which combines earthly substances to produce strange things from them. (vii) Alchemy, which aims at changing the properties of mineral substances, so that finally gold and silver may be produced through some controlled device.

The Sacred Law is not necessarily opposed to any one of these sciences.

However, we shall select from them four points on which we have to criticise the philosophers:

(i) Their postulate that the connection observed to exist between causes and effects is a necessary connection, and that it is not possible or feasible to produce a cause which is not followed by its effect, or to bring into existence an effect independently of the cause.

(ii) Their assertion that human souls are self-subsisting substances which are not impressed upon bodies, and that death means the severance of their connection with the bodies; when their directive function ceases. For, they argue, the soul exists in itself in any event. And, they assert, this is known by a rational argument.

(iii) Their assertion that the extinction of these souls is impossible; and that once having been produced, they have an everlasting existence whose annihilation is impossible.

(iv) Their assertion that the return of the souls to the bodies is impossible.

Criticism of the philosophers on the first point is necessary, for on that criticism is to be built the affirmation of the miracles which mark a departure from the usual course of events—e.g., the Rod turning into a serpent; the revivification of the dead; and the splitting of the Moon. He who thinks that the natural course of events is necessary and unchangeable calls all these miracles impossible. Thus, the philosophers interpret the Qur'anic references to the revivification of the dead, saying that it means the supercession of the Death-arising-from-ignorance by the Life-resulting-from-knowledge. Or, they interpret the Rod's devouring the magic of the magicians, by saying that it means the refutation of the doubts of the disbelievers by the Divine proof which was manifested at the hands of Moses. As regards the splitting of the Moon, they often deny the fact, and assert that the transmission of the Tradition has not been continuous and trustworthy.

And it is only on three points that the philosophers affirm extraordinary miracles:

(i) In regard to the faculty of imagination. They assert:
When this faculty becomes mature and strong, and if sensuous preoccupations do not distract it, it catches a glimpse into the Preserved Tablet. Thereupon, the forms of particulars which will take place in the future are impressed upon it. This happens in waking life in the case of the prophets; and only in sleep in the case of all other men. This, then, is the prophetic property of the faculty of imagination.

(ii) In regard to a property of the faculty of theoretical reason. Say the philosophers:

This property actually amounts to an intuitive power—viz. the quickness of transition from one object of knowledge to another. A man who has a sharp intelligence awakens to the proof, when only that which has been proved is mentioned to him; or when only the proof is mentioned to him he awakens to that which has thereby been proved. In other words, he discovers it out of himself. Generally, when the middle term occurs to him, he awakens to the conclusion; or when only the two terms which occur in the conclusion are presented to his mind, the middle term which joins the terms of the conclusion arises in his mind. And people are divided into different classes in respect of this power. There are those whose awakening is self-determined. Then there are those who need some stimulus, however slight, in order to awaken. Finally, there are those who will not awaken, in spite of a stimulus, until they have taken considerable pains. Since it is possible that the side of deficiency should have its extreme end in those who have no intuition at all (so that, in spite of all stimuli, they are incapable of understanding the intelligibles), it is also possible for the side of possession or potency to have its extreme end in one who will awaken to all the intelligibles, or to most of them, in the shortest and the quickest time. And the difference is quantitative as well as qualitative—according as the awakening extends to some problems or to all of them, and according as it is more or less quick and immediate. Therefore, many a pure and holy soul has an intuitive understanding of all the intelligibles, which (understanding) is continuous and takes the shortest time. Such a one is the prophet, whose theoretical faculty is a miracle. He need not be taught the intelligibles; for, as it were, he learns by himself. And that is the quality mentioned in the Verse: 'Its oil would well-nigh give light though no fire were in contact with it, light upon light.'

(iii) In regard to the practical faculty of the soul. Say the philosophers:

This faculty develops to such an extent that physical things can be influenced and controlled by it. For example, when our soul imagines something, the limbs and their faculties serve it, moving towards the direction imagined to be desirable. Thus, when a man imagines something sweet, his mouth waters, and the salivary faculty, which causes saliva to flow from its sources, comes into action. Similarly, when a man imagines sexual intercourse, a certain faculty comes into action, and the (genital) organ becomes excited. Or, when a man walks over a plank which is elevated, with its two sides supported on two walls, he has the possibility of falling

overwhelmingly presented to his imagination. Consequently, his body becomes passive to the imagination; and he falls. If the plank rested on ground, he would walk over it, and would not fall. And this is so, because the bodies and the bodily faculties are created to be the servants and the subordinates of the soul. And the service differs according as the soul is more or less pure and powerful. Therefore, it is not improbable that the power of a soul should be so great that the physical forces outside its own body should have to serve it. For the soul is not impressed upon the body; it has only a certain inclination towards, or interest in, directing it, the inclination or the interest having been created to be part of its nature. If, therefore, the physical parts of its own body can obey the soul, it will not be impossible for such parts outside the body to do the same. This is the reason why when a man's soul contemplates the blowing of winds; the falling of rains; the gathering of thunderbolts, or the trembling of the Earth (in order to swallow up a people)—which are all natural phenomena whose occurrence depends on the appearance of Heat or Cold or Motion in the Air—then such Heat or Cold appears in the soul, and these phenomena arise therefrom, although no perceptible physical cause is present. This is the miracle of a prophet. But such a thing is bound to occur *in* the Air which is prepared to receive it. It is not possible for the miracle to go to such an extent as to transform a piece of wood into an animal, or to split the Moon which is incapable of being split.

Translated by S. A. Kamali[50]

Ibn Rushd (Averroes)

THE LAW MAKES PHILOSOPHIC STUDIES OBLIGATORY

[If teleological study of the world is philosophy, and if the Law commands such a study, then the Law commands philosophy.]

We say: If the activity of "philosophy" is nothing more than study of existing beings and reflection on them as indications of the Artisan, i.e. inasmuch as they are products of art (for beings only indicate the Artisan through our knowledge of the art in them, and the more perfect this knowledge is, the more perfect the knowledge of the Artisan becomes), and if the Law has encouraged

and urged reflection on beings, then it is clear that what this name signifies is either obligatory or recommended by the Law.

[The Law commands such a study.]

That the Law summons to reflection on beings, and the pursuit of knowledge about them, by the intellect is clear from several verses of the Book of God, Blessed and Exalted, such as the saying of the Exalted, "Reflect, you have vision": this is textual authority, for the obligation to use intellectual reasoning, or a combination of intellectual and legal reasoning. Another example is His saying, "Have they not studied the kingdom of the heavens and the earth, and whatever things God has created?": this is a text urging the study of the totality of beings. Again, God the Exalted has taught that one of those whom He singularly honoured by this knowledge was Abraham, peace on him, for the Exalted said, "So we made Abraham see the kingdom of the heavens and the earth, that he might be" [and so on to the end of the verse]. The Exalted also said, "Do they not observe the camels, how they have been created, and the sky, how it has been raised up?", and He said, "and they give thought to the creation of the heavens and the earth", and so on in countless other verses.

[This study must be conducted in the best manner, by demonstrative reasoning.]

Since it has now been established that the Law has rendered obligatory the study of beings by the intellect, and reflection on them, and since reflection is nothing more than inference and drawing out of the unknown from the known, and since this is reasoning or at any rate done by reasoning, therefore we are under an obligation to carry on our study of beings by intellectual reasoning. It is further evident that this manner of study, to which the Law summons and urges, is the most perfect kind of study using the most perfect kind of reasoning; and this is the kind called "demonstration".

[To master this instrument the religious thinker must make a preliminary study of logic, just as the lawyer must study legal reasoning. This is no more heretical in the one case than in the other. And logic must be learned from the ancient masters, regardless of the fact that they were not Muslims.]

The Law, then, has urged us to have demonstrative knowledge of God the Exalted and all the beings of His creation. But it is preferable and even

necessary for anyone, who wants to understand God the Exalted and the other beings demonstratively, to have first understood the kinds of demonstration and their conditions [of validity], and in what respects demonstrative reasoning differs from dialectical, rhetorical and fallacious reasoning. But this is not possible unless he has previously learned what reasoning as such is, and how many kinds it has, and which of them are valid and which invalid. This in turn is not possible unless he has previously learned the parts of reasoning, of which it is composed, i.e., the premises and their kinds. Therefore he who believes in the Law, and obeys its command to study beings, ought prior to his study to gain a knowledge of these things, which have the same place in theoretical studies as instruments have in practical activities.

For just as the lawyer infers from the Divine command to him to acquire knowledge of the legal categories that he is under obligation to know the various kinds of legal syllogisms, and which are valid and which invalid, in the same way he who would, know [God] ought to infer from the command to study beings that he is under obligation to acquire a knowledge of intellectual reasoning and its kinds. Indeed it is more fitting for him to do so, for if the lawyer infers from the saying of the Exalted, "Reflect, you who have vision", the obligation to acquire a knowledge of legal reasoning, how much more fitting and proper that he who would know God should infer from it the obligation to acquire a knowledge of intellectual reasoning!

It cannot be objected; "This kind of study of intellectual reasoning is a heretical innovation since it did not exist among the first believers." For the study of legal reasoning and its kinds is also something which has been discovered since the first believers, yet it is not considered to be a heretical innovation. So the objector should believe the same about the study of intellectual reasoning. (For this there is a reason, which it is not the place to mention here.) But most (masters) of this religion support intellectual reasoning, except a small group of gross literalists, who can be refuted by [sacred] texts.

Since it has now been established that there is an obligation of the Law to study intellectual reasoning and its kinds, just as there is an obligation to study legal reasoning, it is clear that, if none of our predecessors had formerly examined intellectual reasoning and its kinds, we should be obliged to undertake such an examination from the beginning, and that each succeeding scholar would have to seek help in that task from his predecessor in order that knowledge of the subject might be completed. For it is difficult or impossible for one man to find out by himself and from the beginning all that he needs of that subject, as it is difficult for one man to discover all the knowledge that he needs of the kinds of legal reasoning; indeed this is even truer of knowledge of intellectual reasoning.

But if someone other than ourselves has already examined that subject, it is clear that we ought to seek help towards our goal from what has been said by such a predecessor on the subject, regardless of whether this other one shares our religion or not. For when a valid sacrifice is performed with a certain instrument, no account is taken, in judging the validity of the sacrifice, of whether the instrument belongs to one who shares our religion or to one who does not, so long as it fulfils the conditions for validity. By "those who do not share our religion" I refer to those ancients who studied these matters before Islam. So if such is the case, and everything that is required in the study of the subject of intellectual syllogisms has already been examined in the most perfect manner by the ancients, presumably we ought to lay hands on their books in order to study what they said about that subject; and if it is all correct we should accept it from them, while if there is anything incorrect in it, we should draw attention to that.

[After logic we must proceed to philosophy proper. Here too we have to learn from our predecessors, just as in mathematics and law. Thus it is wrong to forbid the study of ancient philosophy. Harm from it is accidental, like harm from taking medicine, drinking water, or studying law.]

When we have finished with this sort of study and acquired the instruments by whose aid we are able to reflect on beings and the indications of art in them (for he who does not understand the art does not understand the product of art, and he who does not understand the product of art does not understand the Artisan), then we ought to begin the examination of beings in the order and manner we have learned from the art of demonstrative syllogisms.

And again it is clear that in the study of beings this aim can be fulfilled by us perfectly only through successive examinations of them by one man after another, the later ones seeking the help of the earlier in that task, on the model of what has happened in the mathematical sciences. For if we suppose that the art of geometry did not exist in this age of ours, and likewise the art of astronomy, and a single person wanted to ascertain by himself the sizes of the heavenly bodies, their shapes, and their distances from each other, that would not be possible for him—e.g., to know the proportion of the sun to the earth or other facts about the sizes of the stars—even though he were the most intelligent of men by nature, unless by a revelation or something resembling revelation. Indeed if he were told that the sun is about 150 or 160 times as great as the earth, he would think this statement madness on the part of the speaker, although this is a fact which has been demonstrated in astronomy so surely that no one who has mastered that science doubts it.

But what calls even more strongly for comparison with the art of mathematics in this respect is the art of the principles of law: and the study of law itself was completed only over a long period of time. And if someone today wanted to find out by himself all the arguments which have been discovered by the theorists of the legal schools on controversial questions, about which debate has taken place between them in most countries of Islam (except the West), he would deserve to be ridiculed, because such a task is impossible for him, apart from the fact that the work has been done already. Moreover, this is a situation that is self-evident not in the scientific arts alone but also in the practical arts; for there is not one of them which a single man can construct by himself. Then how can he do it with the art of arts, philosophy? If this is so, then, whenever we find in the works of our predecessors of former nations a theory about beings and a reflection on them conforming to what the conditions of demonstration require, we ought to study what they said about the matter and what they affirmed in their books. And we should accept from them gladly and gratefully whatever in these books accords with the truth, and draw attention to and warn against what does not accord with the truth, at the same time excusing them.

From this it is evident that the study of the books of the ancients is obligatory by Law, since their aim and purpose in their books is just the purpose to which the Law has urged us, and that whoever forbids the study of them to anyone who is fit to study them, i.e, anyone who unites two qualities, (1) natural intelligence and (2) religious integrity and moral virtue, is blocking people from the door by which the Law summons them to knowledge of God, the door of theoretical study which leads to the truest knowledge of Him; and such an act is the extreme of ignorance and estrangement from God the Exalted.

And if someone errs or stumbles in the study of these books owing to a deficiency in his natural capacity, or bad organization of his study of them, or being dominated by his passions, or not finding a teacher to guide him to an understanding of their contents, or a combination of all or more than one of these causes, it does not follow that one should forbid them to anyone who is qualified to study them. For this manner of harm which arises owing to them is something that is attached to them by accident, not by essence; and when a thing is beneficial by its nature and essence, it ought not to be shunned because of something harmful contained in it by accident. This was the thought of the Prophet, peace on him, on the occasion when he ordered a man to give his brother honey to drink for his diarrhoea, and the diarrhoea increased after he had given him the honey: when the man complained to him about it, he said, "God spoke the truth; it was your brother's stomach that lied." We can even say that a man who prevents a qualified person from studying books of philosophy,

because some of the most vicious people may be thought to have gone astray through their study of them, is like a man who prevents a thirsty person from drinking cool, fresh water until he dies of thirst, because some people have choked to death on it. For death from water by choking is an accidental matter, but death by thirst is essential and necessary.

Moreover, this accidental effect of this art is a thing which may also occur accidentally from the other arts. To how many lawyers has law been a cause of lack of piety and immersion in this world! Indeed we find most lawyers in this state, although their art by its essence calls for nothing but practical virtue. Thus it is not strange if the same thing that occurs accidentally in the art which calls for practical virtue should occur accidentally in the art which calls for intellectual virtue.

[For every Muslim the Law has provided a way to truth suitable to his nature, through demonstrative, dialectical or rhetorical methods.]

Since all this is now established, and since we, the Muslim community, hold that this divine religion of ours is true, and that it is this religion which incites and summons us to the happiness that consists in the knowledge of God, Mighty and Majestic, and of His creation, that [end] is appointed for every Muslim by the method of assent which his temperament and nature require. For the natures of men are on different levels with respect to [their paths to] assent. One of them comes to assent through demonstration; another comes to assent through dialectical arguments, just as firmly as the demonstrative man through demonstration, since his nature does not contain any greater capacity; while another comes to assent through rhetorical arguments, again just as firmly as the demonstrative man through demonstrative arguments.

Thus since this divine religion of ours has summoned people by these three methods, assent to it has extended to everyone, except him who stubbornly denies it with his tongue or him for whom no method of summons to God the Exalted has been appointed in religion owing to his own neglect of such matters. It was for this purpose that the Prophet, peace on him, was sent with a special mission to "the white man and the black man" alike; I mean because his religion embraces all the methods of summons to God the Exalted. This is clearly expressed in the saying of God the Exalted, "Summon to the way of your Lord by wisdom and by good preaching, and debate with them in the most effective manner".

Translated by G. F. Hourani[51]

Usama

THE PROTECTION OF ALLAH

I saw a proof of the goodness of Allâh and of his splendid protection when the Franks (the curse of Allâh upon them!) encamped against us with knights and foot-soldiers. We were separated from one another by the Orontes (*Al Âṣî*), whose waters were so swollen that the Franks could not reach us and we were prevented from reaching them. They pitched their tents on the mountain, while some took up their position in the gardens in their neighbourhood, set their horses free in the meadows and went to sleep. Some young foot-soldiers from Schaizar took off their clothes, took their swords, swam towards these sleepers and killed several of them. Then a number of our enemies rushed at our companions, who took to the water and returned, while the Frankish army rushed down the mountain on horseback like a torrent. Near them there was a mosque, the mosque of Aboû'l-Madjd ibn Soumayya, in which there was a man named Ḥasan az-Zâhid (the ascetic) who lived on a flat roof and used to retire to the mosque to pray. He was dressed in black woollen clothes. We saw him, but we had no means of reaching him. The Franks came, got down at the gate of the mosque and went towards him, while we said, "Power and might belong to Allâh alone! The Franks will kill him." But he, by Allâh, neither stopped praying nor moved from his position. The Franks stopped, turned away, remounted their horses and rode off, while he remained motionless in the same place, continuing to pray. We did not doubt that Allâh (glory be to him!) had blinded the Franks with regard to him and had hidden him from their sight. Glory to the Almighty, the Merciful!

Among the favours of Allâh the Host High was one shown when the king of the Greeks (*Ar-Roûm*) camped before Schaizar in the year 532. A body of infantry came out from Schaizar to fight. The Greeks cut them to pieces, killed some and took others prisoner. Among those who were taken captive was an ascetic of the Banoû Kardoûs, a holy man born a slave of Maḥmoud, son Ṣâliḥ, lord of Aleppo. When the Greeks returned, he was their prisoner. He reached Constantinople (*al-Ḳousṭaṭîniyya*). One day while he was there he met a man who said to him: "Are you Ibn Kardoûs?" "Yes," he answered. The other replied, "Come with me, take me to your master." They went together and Ibn Kardoûs presented to his master his companion, who discussed with him the prisoner's ransom until this was fixed by the two parties at a sum with which the Greek declared himself satisfied. The amount having been paid, the man gave to Ibn

Kardoûs a sum of money in addition, saying to him: "This is to enable you to rejoin your family. Go in peace with Allâh the Most High." Ibn Kardoûs left Constantinople and returned to Schaizar. This deliverance came from Allâh by his mysterious favour. For Ibn Kardoûs did not know who it was who had ransomed him and set him free.

A similar thing happened to me. When, on our departure from Miṣr, the Franks attacked us on the road after they had killed ʿAbbâs, son of Aboû 'I-Foutoûḥ, and his eldest son Naṣr, we fled to a neighbouring mountain. Our men climbed it on foot, leading their horses. As for me, I was on a hack and could not walk. I got on to my mount. Now the sides of this mountain are all jagged rocks and stones which, trampled underfoot by a horse, make its feet bleed. I whipped the hack to make it go up. But it could not, and went down, driven back by the sharp rocks and stones. I dismounted, rested it and stopped, not being able to walk. Then a man came down to me from the mountain, took one of my hands while my hack was in the other, and pulled me to the top. By Allâh, I did not know who he was and I have never seen him since.

In such times of difficulty, people recall to you the least benefits and claim compensation for them. A Turk had given me a little water to drink, in exchange for which I had given him two dînârs. He never ceased, after our arrival at Damascus, to claim from me what he wanted and to ask me to satisfy his wishes because of this little drink that he had given me. Now my benefactor considered himself an angel (may Allâh have mercy upon me!) by whom Allâh had come to my help.

Translated by G. R. Potter[52]

Ibn Tufayl

HAYY ADMIRES THE WORK OF THE CREATOR

Now, when he saw that all things existing were the work of the Creator, he again considered the power of the same, greatly admiring so rare a workmanship, such accurate wisdom and profound knowledge.

There appeared to him in the most minute creatures (much more in the greater) such signs of wisdom and marvels of the work of creation that his mind was filled with the greatest admiration. Then he became assured that all these things must proceed from a voluntary Agent of infinite perfection, even above all

perfection, to whom even the weight of an atom could not be unknown whether in heaven or earth, nor any other thing whether lesser or greater than it.

Thereupon he considered all the different sorts of animals, and how this Agent had given to every one of them such a fabric of body and then taught them what use to make thereof. For if he had not taught them to use the members he had given them for those employments for which they were designed, they would not have derived any benefit or advantage therefrom, but on the contrary would rather have found them a burden.

Hence he knew that he was most bountiful and most gracious of all. And then, when he perceived among the creatures anything that had beauty, perfection, power and strength, or whatever other excellency it had, he concluded that it must necessarily proceed from that voluntary Agent, from his existence and by his operation.

He knew that the qualities that were in him were much greater, more perfect, more absolute, more bountiful, more excellent and more lasting; and there was no comparison between those things that were in him and those that were found in the animals.

Nor did he cease to go on with his search till he had run through all the attributes of perfection, and found that they were all in the Agent and proceeded from him, and that he was worthy of them more than any to whom they should be ascribed.

Also he searched all the attributes of defects, and saw him free from them and void of them. And how was it possible for him to be otherwise, since the notion of imperfection is nothing but mere privation or what depends upon it.

How should he in any degree partake of privation, who is a most simple being, the very essence himself, and giving a being to everything that exists, and besides whom there is no existence. For He is the Existence, He is the Absolute, He is the Perfection, He is the Beauty, He is the Glory, He is the Power, He is the Knowledge, He is He, and all Things perish beside Him. (Qur'an.)

Translated by Paul Brönnle[53]

PLAYING WITH FIRE

But upon a time it hapned* that in a certain dry Wood, Fire chanced to be kindled by the mutual knocking and dashing together of the Boughs of some

* *Note*: 17th-century spelling throughout

Trees, which consisted of a gummy or rosiny Substance. Which when he perceived, he saw somewhat that affrighted him, being a thing which he had never seen before; so that he stood a good while much wondering at it. Yet he ventured to draw nearer and nearer to it by degrees, still observing its glittering Light, and that wondrous great Force, whereby it seized on everything that it touched, and converted it into its own Nature. Then, to satisfie his Wonder yet farther, and being incited also by that innate Courage and Boldness, which God had planted in his Nature, he was induced to put his Hand to it, and had a mind to lay hold thereon. But when he felt that it burnt his Hand, and that he was not able to lay hold on it, he attempted to take a Stick from the burning Tree, which the Fire had not as yet wholly seized upon; and laying hold on that part which was yet untouch'd, (the Fire having possessed the other end only) he easily affected what he intended and desired; and brought the Fire-brand in his Hand to the Place of his Habitation. For he had before retired into a certain Covert, which he had made choice of for himself, as a fit Lodging, and place of Retirement. And when he had brought the Fire thither, he ceased not to feed it with Stubble and dry Sticks, and other combustible Matter. So that partly out of his Admiration at it, and partly out of the Delight he took in it, he would not suffer it to go out, nor could endure to be long absent from it. But the chief Reason that caused him to make so much of it, and frequent it in the Night-time, was this, that it supplied the Place and Office of the Sun, as well in regard of Light as Heat; insomuch that he was extreamly taken with it, and esteemed it the most excellent and useful of all those things which he had about him. When he also observed that the Flame tended upward towards the Heavens, he began to be persuaded that it was of kin to those celestial Bodies which he saw moving and shining above his Head. He tried also the force and strength thereof upon all manner of Bodies, by casting them into it, by which Experiment he found that it prevailed over all of them sooner or later, according to their several Natures and Dispositions, which rendered them more or less combustible.

And among other Experiments, wherewith he made trial of its strength, he put thereinto certain Fishes which the Sea had cast upon the Shore; which being fried, and the Steam thereof coming to his Nose, his Appetite was stirred up, and became quickned thereby, insomuch that he ventured to taste some part thereof; which he found agreeable to his Palate, and agreeable to his Stomach, from thence forward he accustomed himself to eat Flesh; and to that end, used all kind of Arts he could think on which might enable him to hunt both by Sea and Land, and to catch such living Creatures as were fit for him

to feed on, until at length he became to be very expert in them. By this means, his love and regard for the Fire encreased daily, because by the help thereof he provided himself with various sorts of good Food, which he had never afore been acquainted with.

Translated by George Ashwell[54]
(from the Latin rendering by Edward Pocock)

Ibn Jubayr

A DESCRIPTION OF THE MOSQUE OF THE APOSTLE OF GOD AND OF HIS SACRED RAWDAH

The blessed Mosque is oblong in shape, and is surrounded on all four sides by porticos. In its centre is a court covered with sand and gravel. The south side has five rows of porticoes and the west four. The sacred Rawdah is at the eastern extremity of the south side. It extends over two rows of porticoes on the side of the court and projects about four spans into the third. It has five angles and five sides, and its form is so wondrous that one can barely portray or describe it. Four of its sides incline away from the direction of the *qiblah* in an ingenious fashion, and because of this deviation from the *qiblah*, no one is able to face them in his prayers. The sheik, the imam, learned and pious, last of the learned doctors, and pillar of jurisprudents, Abu Ibrahim Ishaq ibn Ibrahim the Tunisian—may God hold him in His favour—told us that 'Umar ibn 'Abd al-'Aziz—may God hold him in His favour—determined this in planning the construction from a fear that men might take them as a place of prayer. From the east side, the Rawdah also covers two rows of porticoes, and thus encloses six portico columns.

The length of the side facing the *qiblah* is twenty-four spans, that of the east thirty, that between the east and the north corners thirty-five, that from the north corner to the west thirty-nine, and that from the west corner to the south twenty-four. On this side is an ebony chest inlaid with sandal-wood, faced with silver and embellished with stars. It is opposite the head of the Prophet—may God bless and preserve him—and is five spans long, three wide and four high. On the side between the north and the west corners is a place over which hangs a curtain that is said to be where the angel Gabriel came down. Upon him be (eternal) happiness.

The circumference of the venerated Rawdah is two hundred and seventy-two spans. It is covered with finely cut marble of splendid quality. The wainscot rises to a third (of its height) or a little less. Above this another third of the blessed walls is daubed with an unguent of musk and other perfumes to a depth of half a span, and blackened, cracked, and accumulated by the passage of time. The walls above this are composed of wooden lattice-work that reaches to the ceiling, for the top of the blessed Rawdah touches the ceiling of the Mosque. The veils (that covers the Rawdah) fall as far as the line of the marble wainscot. They are of azure colour with a check of white quadrangular and octangular figures containing roundels and encircled by white dots. They present a handsome spectacle of novel design. In the upper part runs a band tending to white. In the south wall, opposite the venerated face of the Prophet—may God bless and preserve him—is a silver nail before which men stand to give their salutations. At his feet—may God bless and preserve him—lies the head of Abu Bakr The Faithful—may God hold him in His favour—and the head of 'Umar The Distinguisher (of True from False) is nigh to the shoulders of Abu Bakr The Faithful—may God hold them both in His favour. He who makes his salutation turns his back to the *qiblah* and, looking towards the venerated face, gives his salute. He then turns right towards the face of Abu Bakr, and then towards that of 'Umar—may God hold them both in His favour.

Before this venerated wall hang about twenty silver lamps, and amongst them are two of gold. At the north of the sacred Rawdah is a marbled trough having at its southern end a kind of *mihrab*. It is said that it is the house of Fatimah—may God hold her in His favour—and also reputed to be her grave. God best knows the truth of this. To the right of the venerated Rawdah the noble pulpit stands forty-two paces away from it. It is set in the blessed *haud* which is fourteen paces long, six wide, and a span and a half high, and wholly clothed in marble. Between it and the small Rawdah that lies between the venerated tomb and the pulpit, and which tradition declares to be one of the Rawdahs [gardens] of Paradise, lie eight paces. Into this Rawdah men throng to pray, as indeed it is meet and proper that they should. Beside it, to the south, is a pillar said to enclose a relic of the palm-tree trunk that leant towards the Prophet—may God bless and preserve him. A piece of it can be seen in the pillar and men kiss it and hasten to acquire blessings by touching it and passing their cheeks over it. At the south end of this small Rawdah is the chest (described above).

The venerated pulpit is a man's stature or more in height, five spans wide, five paces long, and has eight steps. The door is in the form of a grille four and a half spans long. It is locked but is opened every Friday. The pulpit is covered with ebony-wood, and the seat of the Prophet—may God bless and

preserve him—can be seen above, covered by an ebony board that does not touch it, but protects it from being sat upon. Men insert their hands beneath it and smooth the venerated seat to acquire blessings by touching it. At the top of the right support of the pulpit, where the preacher puts his hand when delivering the khutbah, is a hollow silver ring, resembling that which the tailor puts on his finger, but only so in shape and not in size, for this is larger and loose and encircles the support. Men say that it was the plaything of al-Hasan and al-Husayn—may God hold them in His favour—when their grandfather [Muhammad]—may God bless and preserve him—delivered the khutbah.

The venerated Mosque is one hundred and ninety-six paces long and one hundred and twenty-six wide. It has two hundred and ninety columns that are like straight props, for they reach the ceiling and have no arches bending over them. They are composed of stone hewn into a number of round, bored blocks, mortised together and with melted lead poured between each pair so that they form a straight column. They are then covered with a coat of plaster and rubbed and polished zealously until they appear as white marble. The portico to the south, which we have mentioned as having five rows of porticoes, is enfolded by a *maqsurah* that flanks its length from west to east and in which there is a *mihrab*. The imam prays in the aforementioned little Rawdah beside the chest. Between this *maqsurah* and the Rawdah and the sacred tomb is a big painted reading-desk on which lies a large Qur'an locked in a case. It is one of the four copies sent by 'Uthman ibn 'Affan—may God hold him in His favour—to the several cities.

Beside the *maqsurah*, to the east, are two large cupboards containing books and Qur'ans endowed as a waqf to the blessed Mosque. Hard by these cupboards, in the second (row of) porticoes and also to the east, is a trap-door fitted to the level of the ground and locked. It covers a subterranean passage, to which one descends by steps, that leads out from the Mosque to the house of Abu Bakr the Faithful—may God hold him in His favour. This is the way that 'A'ishah was wont to use. Fast by this house is that of 'Umar ibn al-Khattab, as well as that of his son 'Abdullah—may God hold them both in His favour. Beyond a peradventure this place is the passage leading to Abu Bakr's house which the Prophet—may God bless and preserve him—especially commanded should be preserved. In front of the sacred Rawdah is another large chest that holds the candles and chandeliers which every night are lit before it.

Towards the east is a wooden structure where some of the guardians of the blessed Mosque sleep. These guardians are Abyssinian eunuchs and slaves of handsome presence, elegantly clad and ornamented. The resident muezzin of the Mosque is a descendent of Bilal—may God hold him in His favour. In the north part of the court is a large pavilion, newly-built called Qubbat

al-Zayt [The Pavilion of the Oil], that acts as a store for the appointments of the blessed Mosque and contains all that is needful for it. Beside it in the court are fifteen palm trees. In the upper part of the *mihrab* that is in the south wall inside the *maqsurah*, is a square yellow stone, one span square and of a bright and shining surface, that is said to be the mirror of Chosroes. God best knows. Above this in the *mihrab* there is a nail driven into the wall, and on it is a kind of small casket of which no one knows the origin but which men say may be the drinking cup of Chosroes. God best knows the truth of all this.

The lower half of the south wall is cased with marble, tile on tile, of varying order and colour: a splendid marquetry. The upper half is wholly inlaid with pieces of gold called *fusayfisa* [Gr., Ψηφοζ] in which the artist has displayed amazing skill, producing shapes of trees in diverse forms, their branches laden with fruits. The whole Mosque is of this style, but the work in the south wall is more embellished. The wall looking on the court from the south side is of this manner, as also is that which does so from the north side. The west and east walls that overlook the court are wholly white and carved, and adorned with a band that contains various kinds of colours. It would take too long to portray and describe the decorations of this blessed Mosque that contains the sacred and unspotted tomb whose charge is more noble and whose resting-place is more exalted than all that adorns it.

The blessed Mosque has nineteen gates of which only four are open. On the west there are two, one called Bab al-Rahmah [Gate of Pity], and the other Bab al-Khashya [Gate of Fear]. On the east there are also two, one called Bab Jibril [Gate of Gabriel]—upon whom be eternal happiness—and the other Bab al-Rakha' [Gate of Plenty]. Facing Bab Jibril – upon whom be eternal happiness—is the house of 'Uthman—may God hold him in His favour—in which he was martyred. Facing the venerated Rawdah on this eastern side is the tomb of Jamal al-Din of Mosul—may God have mercy on his soul—whose story and the monuments of whose generosity are celebrated, and whose memorable deeds we have already recorded. In front of the venerated Rawdah is (a window with) an iron grating opening on the Rawdah from which exudes a perfumed aroma. To the south there is a small locked gate; to the north there are four locked gates; to the west another five, also locked; and to the east yet five more locked, which with the four open gates gives a total of nineteen gates. The blessed Mosque has three minarets, one in the angle between the east and the south, and the other two in the two north corners. They are small and have the form of turrets but the first is like a minaret.

Translated by R. J. C. Broadhurst[55]

Ibn Arabi

THE WISDOM OF VIRTUE IN THE WORD OF LUQMAN

Should the deity wish for Himself sustenance,
> Then the whole of existence is food for Him.

Should the deity wish sustenance for us,
> Then He may be food for us, as He wishes.

His Will is His Wish, so say,
> Of it that He has willed it, so it is what is willed.

He wishes increase and He wishes decrease,
> But what He wills is naught but what is willed.

There is this difference between them, so realize,
> Although from another view they are essentially the same.

God has said, *We brought Luqmān the Wisdom*, and whosoever is brought the Wisdom is granted a great boon. Luqmān, therefore, was the possessor of a great boon, according to the Qur'an and God's own witness. Now Wisdom may be expressed [in words] or may be unexpressed, as when Luqmān said to his son, *O my son, consider this tiny mustard seed, which God would bring forth were it to be [hidden] in a rock, whether in heaven or earth*. This is an expressed wisdom, namely that the bringing forth is God's doing, which is confirmed by God in His Book, the saying not being attributed to the one who uttered it. As for the unexpressed wisdom, it is known by the circumstantial indications, the one for whom the seed is brought forth not being mentioned, since he did not say to his son, "God will bring it forth for you or for someone else." He made the bringing forth general and situated what was brought forth in the heavens or in the earth, to draw the attention of the hearer to His saying, *He is God in the heavens and the earth*. By what was expressed and what was unexpressed, Luqmān realized that God is the essence of everything known, "the known" being a more general term than "the thing," being as indefinite as possible. Then he completes the wisdom and fulfills it, so that its meaning may be perfected, by saying, *Surely, God is Gracious*. It is also of His grace and kindness that He is the essence of the thing, however named or defined, so that it is referred to by its name only by collusion and usage. Thus one speaks of the heaven, the earth, the rock, the tree, the animal, the angel, sustenance or food, the Essence of everything and in everything being One.

The Ash'arites maintain that the Cosmos is substantially homogeneous, being one substance, which is the same as our saying that the Essence is one. They go

on to say that its accidents are different, which is the same as our saying that it is various and multiple in its forms and attributions, so that [its parts] might be distinguished (one from another]. One says of this that it is not that, whether in form, accidental nature, or makeup. One may also say that this is the same as that, with respect to substance, so that the same substance is implicit in defining every form and makeup. We say that it is nothing other than God, while the Ash'arites consider that what is called a substance, even if it is a reality, is not the Reality, which is what is meant by those who understand divine revelation and manifestation. This then is the wisdom of His being Gracious.

Then he [Luqmān] describes Him as being "Experienced", which means knowing by experience, as in His saying, *We will surely test you until We know*, indicating knowledge by immediate experience. God, despite His knowledge of things as they are, speaks [here] of Himself as gaining knowledge, and we cannot deny what God has stipulated of Himself. Here God is distinguishing between knowledge acquired by direct [sensory] experience and absolute knowledge, direct experience being restricted to the faculties. He has said of Himself that He is the very powers of his servant in His saying, "I am his hearing", which is one of the servant's faculties, as also "his sight", and his tongue, foot, and hand, which are his members. It is not merely the faculties that are involved, but also the limbs, which together constitute the servant. Thus the essence of that which is called servant is God, which is not to say that the servant himself is [the same as] the master. That is because the attributions of the essence are differentiated, which is not true of that to which they refer. In fact there is nothing but His Essence in all attributions, for He is the One Essence endowed with relationships, ascriptions, and attributes.

It is of the Wisdom of Luqmān instructing his son that he used the two names *the Gracious, the Experienced* to describe God. This wisdom would have been more perfect had he used the word "is" to denote its being in existence. God relates Luqmān's saying notionally, in the sense that he meant that nothing can add increase to Him. His saying, *God, the Gracious, the Experienced* is God's own saying, since God knew of Luqmān [in eternity] that he would have completed the Wisdom, had he uttered it in a more complete way.

As for His saying, *Even if it be the weight of a mustard seed*, it concerns the one whose food it is, being the same as the "speck" mentioned in His saying, *Whoever does a speck's weight of good will see it, and whoever does a speck's weight of evil, will see it also.* [That which feeds on it] is the smallest feeder, and the mustard seed is the smallest item of food. Were there anything smaller, He would have brought that forth, as in His saying, *God is not shy of coining a similitude, be it a gnat, there being nothing more so.* Because He knows that there is

nothing smaller than a gnat, He says, there being nothing more so, meaning any smaller. This, as also the verse in the Chapter of the Earthquake [concerning the speck], is the speech of God, so understand. We know that God would not have restricted Himself to the weight of a speck, had there been anything smaller, but would have used it for hyperbole; but God knows best.

As for his use of the diminutive of the word "son", it is a diminutive of mercy, seeing that he counsels him concerning things that will bring him felicity, provided he acts on them. As for the wisdom of his counsel prohibiting him from *associating anything with God, for such association is a terrible wrong*, it is that the divine object of this wrong, which the polytheist describes as divided, is but One Essence. He is, in fact, associating with Him what is nothing other than His Essence, which is the height of ignorance. The reason for this is that one who has no spiritual insight into things as they are, or of the true reality of something when its forms appear various in the one essence, and does not realize that this variety occurs in one Essence, associates one form with the other in that state [of oneness] and apportions to each form a part of it. Now, concerning an associate, it is well known that that which distinguishes it from that with which it is associated is not the same as that with which it is associated, since the latter is [similarly] distinguished [in some way]. There is then no associate in reality, since each of them has something of its own, from which it is said that an association exists between them. The reason [for such an assertion] is general association. However, if it is truly general, then the independent activity of any particular part annuls that generality. Say: *Call upon God, or call upon the Merciful*. This is the spirit of the matter.

Translated by R. W. J. Austin[56]

WHOSO KNOWETH HIMSELF ...

In the name of God, the Merciful, the Compassionate, and Him we ask for aid: Praise be to God before whose oneness there was not a before, unless the Before were He, and after whose singleness there is not an after, except the After be He. He is, and there is with Him no after nor before, nor above nor below, nor far nor near, nor union nor division, nor how nor where nor when, nor times nor moment nor age, nor being nor place. And He is now as He was. He is the One without oneness, and the Single without singleness. He is not composed of name and named, for His name is He and His named is He. So there is no name other than He, nor named. And so He is the Name and the Named. He

is the First without firstness, and the Last without lastness. He is the Outward without outwardness, and the Inward without inwardness. I mean that He is the very existence of the First and the very existence of the Last, and the very existence of the Outward and the very existence or the Inward. So that there is no first nor last, nor outward nor inward, except Him, without these becoming Him or His becoming them.

Understand, therefore, in order that thou mayest not fall into the error of the Hululis:—He is not in a thing nor a thing in Him, whether entering in or proceeding forth. It is necessary that thou know Him after this fashion, not by knowledge ('ilm), nor by intellect, nor by understanding, nor by imagination, nor by sense, nor by the outward eye, nor by the inward eye, nor by perception. There does not see Him, save Himself; nor perceive Him, save Himself By Himself He sees Himself, and by Himself He knows Himself. None sees Him other than He, and none perceives Him other than He. His Veil is [only a part of] His oneness; nothing veils other than He. His veil is [only] the concealment of His existence in His oneness, without any quality. None sees Him other than He—no sent prophet, nor saint made perfect, nor angel brought nigh knows Him. His Prophet is He, and His sending is He, and His word is He. He sent Himself with Himself to Himself. There was no mediator nor any means other than He. There is no difference between the Sender and the thing sent, and the person sent and the person to whom he is sent. The very existence of the prophetic message is His existence. There is no other, and there is no existence to other, than He, nor to its ceasing to be (fana'), nor to its name, nor to its named.

And for this the Prophet (upon whom be peace) said: "Whoso knoweth himself knoweth his Lord." And he said (upon him be peace): "I know my Lord by my Lord." The Prophet (upon whom be peace) points out by that, that thou art not thou: thou art He, without thou; not He entering into thee, nor thou entering into Him, nor He proceeding forth from thee, nor thou proceeding forth from Him. And it is not meant by that, that thou art aught that exists or thine attributes aught that exists, but it is meant by it that thou never wast nor wilt be, whether by thyself or through Him or in Him or along with Him. Thou art neither ceasing to be nor still existing. Thou art He, without one of these limitations. Then if thou know thine existence thus, then thou knowest God; and if not, then not.

And most of "those who know God" (al 'urraf) make a ceasing of existence and the ceasing of that ceasing a condition of attaining the knowledge of God, and that is an error and a clear oversight. For the knowledge of God does not presuppose the ceasing of existence nor the ceasing of that ceasing. For things

have no existence, and what does not exist cannot cease to exist. For the ceasing to be implies the positing of existence, and that is polytheism. Then if thou know thyself without existence or ceasing to be, then thou knowest God; and if not, then not.

And in making the knowledge of God conditional upon the ceasing of existence and the ceasing of that ceasing, there is involved all assertion of polytheism. For the Prophet (upon whom be peace) said, "Whoso knoweth himself," and did not say, "Whoso maketh himself to cease to be." For the affirmation of the other makes its extinction impossible, and [on the other hand] that of which the affirmation is not allowable its extinction is not allowable. Thine existence is nothing, and nothing cannot be added to something, whether it be perishing or unperishing, or existent or non-existent. The Prophet points to the fact that thou art non-existent now as thou was non-existent before the Creation. For now is past eternity and now is future eternity, and now is past time. And God (whose name be exalted) is the existence of past eternity and the existence of future eternity and the existence of past time, yet without past eternity or future eternity or past time ever existing. For if it were not so He would not be by Himself without any partner, and it is indispensable that He should be by Himself without any partner. For His "partner" would be he whose existence was in his own essence, not in the existence of God, and whoever should be in that position would not be dependent upon Him. Then, in that case, there would be a second Lord, which is absurd: God (whose name be exalted) can have no partner nor like nor equal. And whoever looks upon anything as being alone with God or apart from God or in God, but subject to Him in respect of His divinity, makes this thing also a partner, [only] subject to God in respect of divinity. And whoever allows that anything exists side by side with God, whether self-subsisting or subsisting in Him or capable of ceasing to exist or of ceasing to cease to exist, he is far from what smells of a breath of the knowledge of the soul. Because, whoever allows that he is existent beside God, subsisting in Him, then in Him becoming extinct, and his extinction becoming extinct, then one extinction is linked to another, and that is polytheism upon polytheism. So he is a polytheist, not one who knows God and himself.

Then if one say: How lies the way to the knowledge of the soul and the knowledge of God (whose name be exalted)?—

Then the Answer is: The way of the knowledge of these two is, that thou understand that God is, and that there is not with Him a thing. He is now as He was.

Then if one say: I see myself to be other than God and I do not see God to be myself.

Then the Answer is: The Prophet (may God bless him and give him peace) meant by the soul thine existence and thy reality, not the "soul" which is named "commanding," "upbraiding," and "pacified"; but in the "soul" he pointed to all that is beside God (whose name be exalted), as the Prophet (may God bless him and give him peace) said: "O my God, show me things as they are clearly", meaning by "things" whatever is beside God (whose name be exalted), that is, "Make me to know what is beside Thee in order that I may understand and know things, which they are—whether they are Thou or other than Thou, and whether they are of old, abiding, or recent and perishing." Then God showed him what was beside Himself, without the existence of what is beside Himself. So he saw things as they are: I mean, he saw things to be the essence of God (whose name be exalted) without how or where. And the name "things" includes the soul and other than it of things. For the existence of the soul and the existence of other things are both equal in point of being "things," that is, are nothing; for, in reality, the thing is God and God is named a thing.

Then when thou knowest the things thou knowest the soul, and when thou knowest the soul thou knowest the Lord. Because he whom thou thinkest to be beside God, he is not beside God; but thou dost not know Him, and thou seest Him and dost not understand that thou seest Him. And when this secret is revealed to thee thou understandest that thou art not what is beside God, and that thou art thine own end and thine own object in thy search after thy Lord, and that thou dost not require to cease to be, and that thou hast continued and wilt continue without when and without times, as we mentioned above. And thou seest all thine actions to be His actions, and all His attributes to be thine attributes. Thou seest thine outward to be His outward and thine inward to be His inward, and thy first to be His first and thy last to be His last, without doubting and without wavering. And thou seest thine attributes to be His attributes and thine essence to be His essence, without thy becoming Him or His becoming thee, either in the greatest or least degree. "Everything is perishing except His Face", that is there is no existent but He, nor existence to other than He, so that it should require to perish and His Face remain; that is, there is nothing except His Face: "then, whithersoever ye turn, there is the Face of God".

It is as if one did not know a thing and afterwards knows it. His existence does not cease, but his ignorance ceases, and his existence continues as it was, without his existence being exchanged for another existence, or the existence of the not knowing person being compounded with the existence of the knowing, or intermixing, but [merely] a taking away of ignorance. Therefore, think not that thou requirest to cease to be. For if thou requirest to cease to be, then thou wouldest in that case be His veil, and the veil other than God (whose name be exalted);

which requires that another than He should have overcome Him in preventing His being seen; and this is an error and an oversight. And we have mentioned above that His veil is [only a part of] His oneness, and His singleness is not other than it. And. thus it is permitted to him who is united to Reality to say, "I am the Truth," and to say, "Praise be to me." But none attains to union except he see his own attributes to be the attributes of God (whose name be exalted), and his own essence to be the essence of God (whose name be exalted), without his attributes or essence entering into God or proceeding forth from Him at all, or ceasing from God or remaining in Him. And he sees himself as never having been, not as having been and then having ceased to be. For there is no soul save His soul, and there is no existence save His existence.

And to this the Prophet (upon whom be peace) pointed when he said: "Revile not the world, for God—He is the world," pointing to the fact that the existence of the world is God's existence without partner or like or equal. And it is related from the Prophet (upon whom be peace) that he said that God (whose name be exalted) said:

"O my servant, I was sick and thou visitedst Me not, I begged of thee and thou gavest not to Me," with other like expressions; pointing to the fact that the existence of the beggar is His existence, and that the existence of the sick is His existence. And when it is allowed that the existence of the beggar and the existence of the sick are His existence, it is allowed that thy existence is His existence, and that the existence of all created things, both accidents and substances, is His existence. And when the secret of an atom or the atoms is clear, the secret of all created things, both external and internal, is clear, and thou dost not see in this world or the next aught beside God, but the existence of these two Abodes, and their name and their named, all of them, are He, without doubt and without wavering. And thou dost not see God as having ever created anything, but thou seest "every day He is in a business", in the way of revealing His existence or concealing it, without any quality, because He is the First and the Last and the Outward and the Inward. He is outward in His oneness and inward in His singleness: He is the first in His essence and His immutability, and the last in His everlastingness. The very existence of the first is He, and the very existence of the last is He, and the very existence of the outward is He, and the very existence of the inward is He. He is His name and He is His named. And as His existence is "necessary," so the non-existence of all beside Him is necessary. For that which thou thinkest to be beside Him is not beside Him. For He will not have aught to be other than He. Nay, the other is He, and there is no otherness. The other is with His existence and in His existence, outwardly and inwardly.

The person to whom this description is applicable is endowed with many qualities without limit or end.

Translated by T. H. Weir[57]

SELECTIONS FROM *TARJUMAN AL-ASHWAQ*

I

Would that I were aware they knew what heart they possessed!
And would that my heart knew what mountain-pass they threaded!
Dost thou deem them safe or dost thou deem them dead?
Lovers lose their way in love and become entangled

II

On the day of parting they did not saddle the full-grown reddish-white
 camels until they had mounted the peacocks upon them,
Peacocks with murderous glances and sovereign power: thou wouldst fancy
 that each of them was a Bilqis on her throne of pearls
When she walks on the glass pavement thou seest a sun on a celestial sphere
 in the bosom of Idris.
When she kills with her glances, her speech restores to life, as tho' she, in
 giving life thereby, were Jesus.
The smooth surface of her legs is (like) the Tora in brightness, and I follow it
 and tread in its footsteps as tho' I were Moses.
She is a bishopess, one of the daughters of Rome, unadorned: thou seest in
 her a radiant Goodness.
Wild is she, none can make her his friend she has gotten in her solitary
 chamber a mausoleum for remembrance.
She has baffled everyone who is learned in our religion, every student of the
 Psalms of David, every Jewish doctor, and every Christian priest.
If with a gesture she demands the Gospel, thou wouldst deem us to be priests
 and patriarchs and deacons.
The day when they departed on the road, I prepared for war the armies of my
 patience, host after host.
When my soul reached the throat (i.e. when I was at the point of death), I

besought that Beauty and that Grace to grant me relief,

And she yielded—may God preserve us from her evil, and may the victorious king repel Iblis!

I exclaimed, when her she-camel set out to depart, "O driver of the reddish-white camels, do not drive them away with her!"

XI

O doves that haunt the *arak* and *ban* trees, have pity! Do not double my woes by your lamentation!

Have pity! Do not reveal, by wailing and weeping, my hidden desires and my secret sorrows!

I respond to her, at eve and morn, with the plaintive cry of a longing man and the moan of an impassioned lover.

The spirits faced one another in the thicket of *ghada* trees and bent their branches towards me, and it (the bending) annihilated me;

And they brought me diverse sorts of storming desire and passion and untried affliction.

Who will give me sure promise of Jam' and al-Muhassab of Mina? Who of Dhat al-Athl? Who of Na'man?

They encompass my heart moment after moment, for the sake of love and anguish, and kiss my pillars,

Even as the best of mankind encompassed the Ka'ba, which the evidence of Reason proclaims to be imperfect,

And kissed the stones therein, although he was a Natiq (prophet). And what is the rank of the Temple in comparison with the dignity of Man?

How often did they vow and swear that they would not change, but one dyed with henna does not keep oaths.

And one of the most wonderful things is a veiled gazelle, who points with red finger-tip and winks with eyelids,

A gazelle whose pasture is between the breast-bones and the bowels. O marvel! A garden amidst fires!

My heart has become capable of every form: it is a pasture for gazelles and a convent for Christian monks,

And a temple for idols and the Pilgrim's Ka'ba and the tables of the Tora and the book of the Qur'an.

I follow the religion of Love: whatever way Love's camels take, that is my religion and my faith.

We have a pattern in Bishr, the lover of Hind and her sister, and in Qays and Lubna and in Mayya and Ghaylan.

XIV

He saw the lightning in the east and he longed for the east, but if it had flashed in the west he would have longed for the west.

My desire is for the lightning and its gleam, not for the places and the earth.

The east wind related to me from them a tradition handed down successively from distracted thoughts, from my passion, from anguish, from my tribulation,

From rapture, from my reason, from yearning, from ardour, from tears, from my eyelid, from fire, from my heart,

That "He whom thou lovest is between thy ribs; the breaths toss him from side to side".

I said to the east wind, "Bring a message to him and say that he is the enkindler of the fire within my heart.

If it shall be quenched, then everlasting union, and if it shall burn, then no blame to the lover!"

XXXVII

O my two comrades, approach the guarded pasture and seek Najd and yonder
 sign that marks the way,
And come down to a well at the tents of the curving sand and beg shade of it
 dal and *salam* trees.
And whenever ye come to the valley of Mina—for them ye have come to that
 in which my heart's being—
Deliver to all who dwell there the greetings of love from me, or only say,
 "Peace be with you!"
And hearken what they will reply, and tell how one who is heartsick
Complains of the ardours of love, while he is hiding nothing, seeking
 information, and asking questions.

Translated by R. A. Nicholson[58]

Ibnu'l Farid

THE MEETING

A summer's night I met my girl on the path
That leads straight to her dwelling and straight to my tent.

We were alone, we two, without watchers or informers,
Far from the tribe, far from jealous eyes and spying ears and harming tongues.

I laid my face on the ground, my brow a footstool for my girl. She said: "Open
your heart with joy, we are without watchers; Come press your lips to my veil."

But my lips would not consent to it.
I felt that I had two honours to guard,
My girl's and mine.

And, as was my desire, we were all night together,
Near to each other, far from the tribe and spying eyes.

And it seemed that I was master
Of all the kingdoms of the world, and that the elements
Obeyed me as slaves.

Translated by Powys Mathers[59]

WHERE EYES ENCOUNTER SOULS IN BATTLE-FRAY

Where eyes encounter souls in the battle-fray
I am the murdered man whom 'twas no crime to slay.
At the first look, ere love in me arose,
To that all-glorious beauty I was vowed,
God bless a racked heart crying,
And lids that passion will not let me close,
And ribs worn thin,
Their crookedness well nigh to straightness shaped
By the glow within,

And seas of tears whence I had never escaped
But for the fire of sighing!
How sweet are maladies which hide
Me from myself, my loyal proofs to Love!
Though after woeful eve came woeful dawn,
It could not move
Once to despair my spirit: I never cried
To Agony, "Begone"
I yearn to every heart that passion shook,
And every tongue that love made voluble,
And every deaf ear stopped against rebuke,
And every lid not dropped in slumbers dull.
Out on a love that hath no melting eyes!
Out on a flame from which no rapture flies!

LO, FROM BEHIND THE VEIL MYSTERIOUS

Lo, from behind the veil mysterious
The forms of things are shown in every guise
Of manifold appearance; and in them
An all-wise providence hath joined what stands
Opposed in nature: mute they utter speech,
Inert they move and void of splendour shine,
And so it comes that now thou laugh'st in glee,
Then weep'st anon, like mother o'er dead child,
And mournest, if they sigh, for pleasure lost,
And tremblest, if they sing, with music's joy,
Birds warbling on the boughs delight thine ear,
The while their sweet notes sadden thee within;
Thou wonderest their voices and their words
Expressive unintelligible tongues!
On land the camels cross the wilderness,
At sea the ships run swiftly through the deep;
And thou behold'st two armies—one on land,
On sea another—multitudes of men,
Clad, for their bravery, in iron mail
And fenced about with points of sword and spear.
The land-troops march on horseback or on foot,

Bold cavaliers and stubborn infantry;
The warriors of the sea some mount on deck,
Some climb the masts like lances straight and tall.
Here in assault they smite with gleaming swords,
There thrust with tough brown shafts of quivering spears;
Part drowned with fire of arrows shot in showers,
Part burned with floods of steel that pierce like flames;
These rushing onward, offering their lives,
Those reeling broken 'neath the shame of rout;
And catapults thou seest hurling stones
Against strong fortresses and citadels,
To ruin them. And apparitions strange
Of naked viewless spirits thou mayst espy,
That wear no friendly shape of humankind,
For genies love not men.
And in the stream
The fisher casts his net and draws forth fish;
And craftily the fowler sets a snare
That hungry birds may fall in it for corn.
And ravening monsters wreck the ships at sea,
And lions in the jungle rend their prey,
And in the air some birds, and in the wilds
Some animals, hunt others. And thou seest
Many a form besides, whose names I pass,
Putting my trust in samples choice, tho' few.
Regard now what is this that lingers not
Before thine eye and in a moment fades.
All thou beholdest is the act of one
In solitude, but closely veiled is he.
Let him but lift the screen, no doubt remains:
The forms are vanished, he alone is all;
And thou, illumined, knowest that by his light
Thou find'st his actions in the senses' night.

Translated by R. A. Nicholson[60]

Ibn Khallikan

HOW THE GAME OF CHESS WAS INVENTED

Sincere in his religious belief and virtuous his conducts Abú Bakr al-Súlí merited the confidence which was always placed in his word. As a chess-player he was without an equal, and, even to the present day, it is said as a proverb of a player, whose skill one wishes to extol, that his game is like that of al-Súlí. I have met many people who believe al-Súlí to have been the inventor of chess, but this is an erroneous opinion, that game having been imagined by Sissa the son of Dáhir, an Indian, for the amusement of King Shihrám.

Ardeshír the son of Bábek, the ancestor of the last royal house of Persia, invented the game of *nard* or backgammon. ... He designed it as an image of the world and its inhabitants, and therefore divided the board into twelve squares to represent the months of the year; the thirty pieces (or men) represented the days of the month, and the dice were emblems of Fate and the vicissitudes thereof with which it conducts the people of the world. But to expatiate on these points would lead us too far and cause us to digress from the subject in which we are now engaged. But as for the game of *nard* the Persians count it as one of the inventions which does honour to their nation.

It is said that, when Sissa invented the game of chess and presented it to Shihrám, the King was struck with admiration and filled with joy; he had chess-boards placed in the temples, and he expressed the opinion that the game was the best thing man could study, inasmuch as it served as an introduction to the art of war, and that it was an honour to the Faith and the World, as well as the foundation of all justice.

The King also manifested his gratitude and satisfaction for the favour which Heaven had granted him in shedding lustre on his reign by such an invention, and, he said to Sissa; "Ask for whatever you desire."—"I then demand," replied Sissa, "that a grain of wheat be placed in the first square of the chess-board, two in the second, and that the number of grains be progressively doubled till the last square is reached: whatever this quantity of wheat may be, I ask you to bestow on me." The King who intended to make him a worthy present exclaimed, that such a recompense would be too little, and he reproached Sissa for asking so inadequate a reward. Sissa declared that he desired no other gift and, heedless of the King's remonstrances, he persisted in his request. The King, at last consented, and gave orders that the required quantity of grain be given to him. When the chiefs of the royal office received their orders they

calculated the amount, and answered that they did not possess near as much wheat as was required. When these words were reported to the King, he was unable to credit them and had the chiefs brought before him; when questioned on the subject they declared that all the wheat in the world would be insufficient to make up that quantity. They were asked to prove the truth of their contention, and by a series of multiplications and reckonings they demonstrated that such was indeed the case. The King then said to Sissa, "Your ingenuity in imagining such a request is even more admirable than your talent in inventing the game of chess."

The way in which the doubling of the grains of wheat is to be done consists in the calculator placing one grain in the first square, two in the second, four in the third, eight in the fourth, and so on, until he comes to the last square, placing in each square double the number contained in the preceding one. I was doubtful of the contention that the final amount could be as great as was said, but when I met one of the accountants employed at Alexandria, I received from him a demonstration which convinced me that their statement was true: he placed before me a sheet of paper, on which he had calculated the amount up to the sixteenth square, obtaining the result 32,768. "Now," said he, "let us consider this number of grains to be the contents of a pint measure, and this I know by experiment to be true"—these are the accountant's words, so let him bear the responsibility—"then let the pint be doubled in the seventeenth square, and so on progressively. In the twentieth square it will become a *wayba*, the *waybas* will then become an *ardeb*, and in the fortieth square we shall have 174,762 *ardebs*; let us consider this to be the contents of a corn-store, and no corn-store contains more than that; then, in the fiftieth square we shall have the contents of 1,024 stores; suppose these to be situated in one city—and no city can have more than that number of granaries or even so many—we shall then find that the number required for the sixty-fourth and last square corresponds to the contents of the granaries of 16,384 cities; but you know that there is not in the whole world a greater number of cities than that." ...

This demonstration is decisive and indubitable.

Translated by Macguckin de Slaine[61]

JA'FAR AND AL-RASHID

Ja'far was in al-Rashid's closest confidence, influenced all his decisions, and acquired a status permitted to no other before or after him. Indeed, the Caliph ordered the tailoring of a special garment which was two suits in one, so that he and Ja'far could wear it together and become like one man.

Al-Rashid could scarcely bear to be separated from his Minister for a moment. But he was also deeply attached to his sister, el 'Abbassa, daughter of el Mahdi. She was the dearest of women in his eyes, and like Ja'far she should never be absent a moment or all his happiness was imperfect. Therefore he married his two friends to one another, in order that it should be lawful for them to meet; but before the ceremony was undertaken he made Ja'far swear never to be with 'Abbassa when he was not their third.

A day came when al-Rashid changed and brought disaster on his former favourite, executing him and imprisoning his brother and; his father, Yahya, and holding them in prison till they died. Historians have advanced conflicting explanations for this reversal of the Caliph's behaviour, and some have connected it with the *mariage de convenance*. Ja'far, they say, kept the condition which al-Rashid had imposed, but after some time el 'Abbassa fell in love with him and tried to seduce him. When her many and varied efforts at persuasion had broken on the barrier of his fear, she determined to approach her object circuitously, and went to Ja'far's mother Itaba, and asked to be submitted to him as a virgin slave-girl such as she knew 'Itaba sent every Friday evening when he was in his cups. The mother refused, but 'Abbassa threatened to communicate certain secrets they shared to the Caliph; and, mixing inducements with threats, added, "If I bear a child to your son, it will bring you great honour. And even if my brother finds out about it, what will he do?" If Ja'far's mother consented and began to work on her son by hinting, every time she met him, that she had a slave-girl in readiness whose looks and wit were equally commendable. At last he began to remind her of this promise, and to ask when it would be fulfilled, and she knew he desired the girl. She sent word to 'Abbassa to arrange herself for that night; which she did, and was brought to Ja'far, who did not know her, for all their previous meetings had been in the presence of al-Rashid, and before the Caliph he did not dare to raise his eyes to her face. After he had slept with her that night, she asked him, "What do you think of the deceit of the daughter of kings?" and when he asked "Which king's daughter are you?" she said, "I am your mistress, el 'Abbassa." Then the drunkenness flew from his head, and he went to his mother and said, "By God, you have sold me cheap."

El 'Abbasaa gave birth to a boy, which she at once entrusted to a nurse and

servant; and when he grew older, and she was afraid the secret would become known, the three were sent away to Mecca.

Now the Caliph's palace and the women's apartments were administered by Ja'far's father, Yahya, who used to lock the gates and put the keys in his pocket, and exercised a severity which annoyed the women. Zubeida, the favourite wife, complained to al-Rashid, who asked Yahya "My father" (that was the title he regularly used when addressing him) "Why is Zubeida complaining of you?" And he said, "Am I accused of a breach of your honour, Prince of Believers?" The Caliph told him he was not. "Then," said Yahya, "do not accept the complaint." And after this episode he was rougher than ever and strict to the point of violence. Zubeida again went to complain to Rashid, who replied, "Yahya stands before me guiltless of staining my honour." "If that were so," she cried, "he would have prevented his son doing what he did." When he asked her to be clearer, she told him about el 'Abbassa, and when he demanded proof he answered, "What proof could be more convincing than the child? There was a boy in this palace, till they were afraid he would be discovered, and he is now at Mecca." He asked whether she was the only one who knew, and she replied, "There's not a single slave-girl in the palace that doesn't know." And he was silent.

He expressed his wish to make a pilgrimage, and set out, Ja'far with him, for Mecca. 'Abbassa wrote to the servant and the nurse to proceed to Yemen, so that when al-Rashid, on arrival in the city, sent his investigators out, they did not find the child. But they found that the story was true. Then the Caliph secreted evil for the Ja'far family.

Abu Nawwas has a couplet on the story:

"The king who would eliminate a twister
Buries the axe and weds him to his sister,"

Other writers explain Ja'far's fall as follows. The Caliph handed over the rebel Yahya Ibn 'Abdullah 'Abdu Hassan to Ja'far under orders to hold him in prison. Yahya asked to see the Minister, and said, "Fear God, Ja'far. Don't make my grandfather, the Prophet Mohammad, your enemy on the day of resurrection. For God knows I have done no wrong." Ja'far had mercy on him, and told him he could depart where he wished, and when the rebel expressed the fear that he would only be recaptured and sent back again, assigned guards as his escort to a distant refuge. This action was reported to al-Rashid, who summoned Ja'far, and exchanged a quite ordinary conversation, but at the end asked, "How is Yahya now?" Ja'far turned the question with, "As he is, sire," but the Caliph

persisted, "Can you swear to his security by my life?" he asked. Then Ja'far's face darkened and he was silent a moment, after which he said "No, by your life. I released him when I discovered he was innocent." "You were right," said the Caliph "You did nothing that I would not have done myself." But when Ja'far rose and left, he followed him with his eyes till at last he was out of sight, and then he said, "Now God murder me if I do not murder you."

It is on record that when Sayyid Ibn Salim was asked the reason of the Barmeki tragedy, he said, "God knows, parts of their downfall are utterly beyond explaining. But their days had lengthened, and everything that is long is tiresome. Men who were the best of men grew tired of the days of 'Omar Ibn Khattab, which were of all days the most just and secure and rich in conquests, and even of the days of 'Osman. And they killed both these good men. Moreover, al-Rashid heard the great praise paid to that family and saw what hopes men centred on it; and kings have been jealous for less than that. So he grew hard and looked, for matter to their discredit, and their enemies like at Fadl Ibn Rabiyya exaggerated anything that was brought to light against them."

Another story refers to an anonymous poem left in al-Rashid's way; which he opened, and read:

Tell God's deputy
Whose hands untie and tie
That Yahya's son is king too
And no distinction left for you
Your orders wait on his, his travel without halt
He has built a house which neither Persians nor Indians built
Its bricks are pearl and ruby, and amber and incense are its silt
And we tremble that if you leave him to thunder when you and death
 combine
Felicity will strain the slave's gross stomach and he will stretch at the divine.

It is also told how 'Aliyya, the daughter of al Mahdi, said to al-Rashid one day in the time after the assassination: "Sire, since the day you killed Ja'far, even your best happiness has been tainted. Why did you kill Ja'far, my lord?" He said, "My life, if I found that the shirt of my body knew the reason, I would tear it to pieces."

Translated by Herbert Howarth and Ibrahim Shakrullah[62]

al-Busiri

THE PROPHET

When he beckoned the trees advanced
Signing with a flourish of body
Their text and engraved tale

A cloud paced his movements
To be his awning at midday
Also the moon divided herself

His cave was light with winds
And concepts of truth and good,
Stoniness to the infidels

Who did not see the bows round him,
The weaving of the spiders
And the doves making circles,

From God, and better than citadels
Or the skins of multiple shields.

Translated by Herbert Howarth and Ibrahim Shakrullah[63]

Part V

AL-ANDALUS – ARAB SPAIN

Ibn Hazm

Among the laudable instincts, noble characteristics and virtuous habits by which men may be adorned, whether they are engaged in love-making or any other activity, Fidelity ranks high. It is one of the strongest proofs and clearest demonstrations of sound stock and pure breed; it differs in degree of excellence according to that variability which is inherent in all created beings. I have a short poem on this subject from which I will quote two separate stanzas: here is the first.

> The deeds of every man advise
> What element within him lies:
> The visual evidence is true—
> Thou needst not seek another clue.

And this is the second.

> And has the oleander's root
> E'er yielded raisins for its fruit,
> Or do the bees so bravely strive
> To treasure aloes in their hive?

The first degree of fidelity is for a man to be faithful to one who is faithful to him. This indeed is an absolute duty, an obligation binding upon lover and beloved alike: no man deviates from it, unless he be of mean extraction and devoid of every grace and virtue. Were it not for the fact that it was not my intention in this essay to discourse upon the human character in general, and the inborn and acquired qualities of man, how the innate characteristics may be increased by cultivation, and the acquired attributes disappear for want of natural aptitude, I would have added here the observations necessary to be set down upon such a subject. But it was only my purpose to speak upon this matter of Love, as you expressly desired of me; to develop the matter in its extremely manifold aspects would have taken an extremely long time indeed.

The most frightful instance of this order of fidelity that I have ever witnessed, and the most terrible in its consequences, concerns a drama which I actually saw enacted before my own eyes. A certain man of my acquaintance

consented to break off relations with a person whom he loved dearly and cherished more fondly than anyone else in the world, so that he would have preferred to die rather than be parted from him a single hour. He agreed to this appalling deprivation in order to guard a secret which had been entrusted to him. His loved one had sworn a solemn oath never to speak to him again, and to have no further commerce with him, unless he divulged that secret to him. Although the person who had committed the secret to his charge was far away, yet the lover refused to betray his trust; he continued to conceal the secret, and his loved one persisted in holding aloof from him, until time parted them forever.

The second degree of fidelity is for a man to be faithful towards one who has betrayed him. This trait appertains to the lover alone, and not to the beloved. The latter has no way here, neither is he under any such obligation; for fidelity is a course of action which can only be attempted by men who are tough, strong, broad-shouldered, magnanimous, of great forbearance and infinite patience, firm in judgement, of noble character and pure intentions. The man who rewards treachery with treachery by no means deserves blame; but the conduct which we have adumbrated excels this latter procedure exceedingly, and surpasses it by far. In this case the object of fidelity is to refrain from paying back injury with injury, and to abstain from matching evil against evil whether in deeds or words; to delay the fatal step of severing the cords of friendship as long as possible, while hope still remains that intimacy may be resumed and the smallest expectation may yet be cherished that relations can be restored, while the least sign of a resumption is still visible the faintest glimmer thereof may be perceived, and its slightest symptom diagnosed. Once despair however has gripped your heart, and resentment dominates your emotions, then you should strive your utmost to ensure that the perfidious friend may for all that be safe from your petty fury, secure from your malice, delivered from the danger of your mischief; let the recollection of what is gone before prevent you from giving vent to your wrath over what has now transpired. To be faithful to old obligations is the assured duty of all intelligent men; and to yearn affectionately for the past, and not to forget the times that are finished and done with, is the surest proof of true fidelity. This is a fine quality indeed, and one which ought to be employed in all human transactions, of whatever kind and in whatever circumstances.

I call to mind a man I once knew, one of my dearest friends, who formed an attachment for a young slave-girl. Their love waxed very strong; then she betrayed his trust, and broke the bonds of their affection. The story was noised widely abroad, and he suffered the most acute distress in consequence.

I once had a friend whose intentions towards me became ignoble, after we

had been united in a firm affection the like of which ought not to be gainsaid. This he allowed to happen, despite the fact that each of us knew all the other's secrets, and all formalities had been dropped between us. When his feelings towards me changed, he divulged all that he had got to know about me, though I knew many times as much to his disadvantage. Then he learned that I had become aware of what he had said concerning me; he was much disturbed, and feared that I would requite him in kind for his base conduct. Hearing of this, I wrote some verses to him to comfort him, assuring him that I did not intend to take reprisals against him.

Here is another reminiscence which belongs to the same category, although in truth neither this nor the preceding paragraph is strictly relevant to the essay and the chapter now being written; all the same it is roughly parallel, in accordance with the general conditions of the discourse which I have laid down. Muhammad ibn Walid ibn Maksir the Civil Secretary was on friendly and indeed devoted terms with me during the viziership of my late father; but when those events took place in Cordova which do not need to be further specified, and circumstances changed, he removed to another district. There he became connected with the local ruler, and attained in due course to a position of affluence, importance and agreeable distinction. I happened to stay in that district on one of my travels, but my friend of other days did not do his duty by me; my presence was unwelcome to him, and he treated me very evilly. During that time I requested him to do me a certain service, but he did not stir a finger to help me, pretending to be otherwise occupied, although the matter on which he claimed to be engaged was nothing urgent at all. I wrote him a poem of reproach, and he replied endeavouring to appease me; but for all that I did not trouble him with any further request. On this topic, though still outside the scope of the present chapter and yet cognate with it, I wrote some verses from which I will now quote.

To hide a secret guarded well
Is no great merit, truth to tell,
But rather to conceal a thing
Which other men are whispering.

So generosity is best
And noblest, when the thing possessed
Is rare, and he who makes the gift
Is famous for his stingy thrift.

The third order of fidelity is when a man is faithful for all that he has despaired completely and finally, death having intervened and sudden decease having unexpectedly removed all hope of further relations. Fidelity under these circumstances is even nobler and finer than during the lifetime of the beloved, when there is still the expectation of another meeting.

A woman in whom I have every confidence once told me that she had seen, in the house of Muhammad ibn Ahmad ibn Wahb, better known as Ibn al-Rakiza, a descendant of Badr who entered Andalusia with the Imam 'Abd al-Rahman ibn Mu'awiya (God be well satisfied with him!), a slave-girl of striking beauty. She had had a master who had died, and was sold with his estate; but she refused to have anything to do with men after him, and no man enjoyed her charms until she met Allah the Omnipotent. She had been a fine singer, but denied all knowledge of the art and was content to be an ordinary servant, and to be excluded from those ladies who are taken for procreation, pleasure and a life of comfort. This she did out of fidelity to the departed, long since committed to earth and with tombstones cemented above him. Her afore-mentioned lord desired to take her to his bed, along with the rest of his concubines, and to bring her out of her position of menial servitude, but she refused. He beat her more than once, and administered corporal correction; but she bore it all with fortitude, persisting in her honourable refusal; this is an extremely rare instance of fidelity.

You must know that the duty of fidelity is incumbent upon the lover more than upon the beloved, and applies to him far more strictly. This is because it is the lover who initiated the attachment, and is the one who proposes the formation of the engagement; he seeks to conform the bond of affection, and petitions for true intimacy. He is the first to strike his claim to preferment, and takes the lead in seeking for enjoyment by striving to acquire the friendship. He it is who fetters himself with the reins of love, binding his soul with the stoutest shackles and bridling it with the strongest muzzle. Who was there to compel him to do all this if he did not wish to complete his part of the bargain, or to oblige him to attract so fond affection if he had not the intention to seal it with fidelity to the one whose love he desired? The beloved, on the other hand, is a person to whom the lover feels drawn and whose affection he seeks; she is free to accept or reject his advances. If she accepts, then that is the fulfilment of all the lover's hopes; if she refuses, she deserves not to be blamed on that account. To propose union, to persist in one's suit, to dispose oneself for anything that may attract the beloved's sympathy, such as readiness to fall in with all her wishes, and a willingness to make all things clear and straight between himself and her, whether present or absent—all this has nothing to do with fidelity. In

seeking her hand it is his own pleasure that he is pursuing, his own happiness he is labouring for; love calls and drives him to this, whether he will or no. Fidelity is only praiseworthy when a man is in a position to be unfaithful.

Fidelity imposes certain conditions upon the lover. The first is that he should keep his troth with the beloved, and protect her secrets; her public and private transactions should be alike sacred to him; he should conceal her evil aspects, advertise her good points, cover up her faults, put her actions in the best light, and overlook her slips; he should acquiesce in whatever the beloved imposes upon him, and for his part not thrust himself upon her so immoderately as to provoke her aversion; when she is eager he should not be languid, neither in her weariness should he be impetuous. The beloved for her part is bound by the same rules, if she fully reciprocates his affection; but if her love is less than his, he must not press her to come up to his level, nor be cross with her in an endeavour to induce her by these means to love him with the same degree of intensity. In that case it is enough for him to keep their relations secret, and not requite her with unpleasantness or threats. If a third situation should exist, namely that she has no corresponding feelings for him whatsoever, let him be content with what he finds, and take whatever he can readily get; let him not demand any conditions, or be importunate for any rights. He can only expect what windfalls his luck may bring, or what fruits his labours may ripen.

You must know that uncomely acts never appear as such to those who perform them, and therefore their repulsiveness is doubly disgusting to others innocent of them. I do not say what I am about to say in order to boast, but simply relying upon the precept of Allah the Omnipotent, Who says, "And as for the bounty of thy Lord, proclaim it abroad" (Qur'an XCIII ii). Now Allah has vouchsafed to me the blessing of fidelity towards every man with whom I have had any connection, even if it be only in a single meeting; He has bestowed on me the gift of protecting any man with whom I have ever entered into an engagement, be it in the conversation of but a solitary hour. For this great boon I thank God and praise Him, petitioning Him to continue and augment His beneficence towards me. There is nothing that I loathe more than treachery. By my life, I have never allowed myself to meditate harming any person with whom I have had the slightest engagement, however great may be his crimes, and however numerous his sins against me. I have suffered not a few grievous blows in this way, but I have ever repaid evil with good: Allah be praised for that!

I take pride in my fidelity in a long poem, in which I have mentioned the calamities which have stricken me, and the sufferings I have had to endure in a life of constant alighting and departing, as I shifted my tent from one encampment to another throughout all the lands. This poem opens as follows:

He went away, and was pursued
By all my noble fortitude:
The tears o'erflowing from his eyes
Betrayed what in his bosom lies.

A weary body, and a heart
Affectionate; which, when to part
Irrevocably doomed, was full
Of sorrow inexpressible.

No home thereafter he possessed,
And in no country found he rest;
The couch whereon he nightly lay
Was warmed not, ere he was away.

Methinks his spirit wears for shroud
The fleecy tissue of a cloud,
By some erratic wind of heaven
To new horizons ever driven.

Or he is like the credo brief
Of unitarian belief
Which infidels so much detest,
They spew it from their miscreant breast.

Of else he is an errant star
Migrating through the heavens far,
Now setting in the west extreme,
Now rising with an orient beam.

Did she reward him (I suppose)
Or lend him succour in his woes,
The flooding tears that she would shed
Should follow him wher'er he fled.

I pride myself on my fidelity in another long ballad which I have reproduced here, although the most of it is not relevant to the subject of this essay. The reason for my composing these verses was that certain of my antagonists, being choked in intellectual debate with me, cast foul reproaches in my face, and

accused me of espousing the cause of untruth; this they did because they were unable to refute my arguments in defence of truth and its champions, and were jealous of my debating prowess. So I invented this spirited poem, and addressed it to an intelligent friend. I will quote a few selections.

> Then take me for thy Moses' rod,
> And bring them one and all by God!
> Be every one a snake, among
> The lote-trees flicking his forked tongue.

Again:

> Their wondrous lies they bravely shout
> When they perceive me not about:
> The lion is a cowering thing—
> Aye, but he bides his time to spring!

Again:

> The wildest hopes they entertain
> For what they surely will not gain;
> Their master, think the Rafidis,
> Can do impossibilities

Again:

> If my resolve and self-control
> Inhabited each timorous soul,
> The eyes of beauties languishing
> Would little influence on them bring:
>
> Scorning, as verbs intransitive,
> In mean dependency to live,
> Like prepositions, that refuse
> Their verbs to govern as they choose.

Again:

> My judgement pioneers its way
> Through all things hidden from the day,
> As pulsing arteries do all
> Traverse the body physical:
> Detecting with a simple glance

The labrynthine track of ants,
While it is hidden from their sight
Where elephants do crouch at night!

OF BETRAYAL

As Fidelity is a most lofty attribute and a truly noble quality, so Betrayal is base
and detestable in the extreme. The term is only to be applied to those who take
the initiative in treachery; to repay betrayal with like betrayal, though it be equal
as regards the action itself, is not true treachery, and the man who so acts is not
deserving of blame, for Allah Himself says, "And the recompense of an evil act is
an evil act like unto it" (Qur'an XLII 38). Now we know of course that the second
act is not evil; it is only because it appears to be of the same order as the first that
the name "evil" is given to it. This shall be expounded at length in the chapter on
Forgetting, if Allah wills.

Because betrayal is so common a characteristic of the beloved, fidelity on
her part has come to be regarded as extraordinary; therefore its rare occurrence
in persons loved is thought to counterbalance its frequency among lovers. I
have a little poem on this subject.

Small faithfulness in the beloved
Is most exceedingly approved,
While lovers' great fidelity
Is taken unremarkably.

So cowards, rarely brave in war,
Are more applauded when they are
Than heroes, who sustain all day
The heat and fury of the fray.

A particularly base type of betrayal is when the lover sends an emissary to the
beloved, entrusting all his secrets to his keeping, and then the messenger strives
and contrives to convert the beloved's interest to himself, and captures her affec-
tion to the exclusion of his principal. I put this situation in rhyme as follows.

I sent an envoy to thee,
Intending so my hopes to gain;

I trusted him too foolishly;
Now he has come between us twain.

He loosed the cords of my true love,
Then neatly tied his own instead;
He drove me out of all whereof
I might have well been tenanted.
I, who had called him to the stand,
Am now a witness to his case:
I fed him at my table, and
Now hang myself upon his grace.

The cadi Yunus ibn 'Abd Allah told me once the following story. "I remember in my youth a certain slave-girl belonging to one of the great houses, who was passionately loved by a young man of high culture and princely blood. She reciprocated his feelings, and the two corresponded together, their messenger and postman being one of his companions of a like age, who had ready access to her. In due course the girl was offered for sale, and her royal lover desired to purchase her; but he was beaten to the bargain by the youth who had been his envoy. One day he entered her apartment, and found her opening a casket belonging to her, and searching for some personal effect. He came up and began turning out the box with her; and a letter fell out which was written in the hand of the youth who had been in love with her, all daubed with ambergris and treasured with tender care. He cried angrily, "Where did this come from, strumpet?" "You yourself conveyed it to me", she answered. "Perhaps this has arrived newly, since that time", he said. "Oh no", she replied. "It is one of those old letters, which you know all about." The cadi concluded: "It was just as though she had popped a stone in his mouth. He was utterly confounded, and could not utter another word."

Translated by A. J. Arberry[1]

ANXIETY

I am a man who has always been uneasy about the impermanency and constant instability of fortune. Concerns of this sort have occupied me during the greater part of my life, and I have preferred to spend it in pursuing these matters studiously, rather than in looking for delights of the senses or the

accumulation of great wealth, which most seem to prefer. In this book I have gathered teachings suggested by experience, in order that those into whose hands it should chance to fall may derive a little benefit from what has cost me so much anguish and meditation.

In my investigations I have constantly tried to discover an end in human actions which all men unanimously hold as good and which they all seek. I have found only this: the one aim of escaping anxiety. I have not only discovered that all humanity considers this good and desirable, but also that, notwithstanding the contradictory variety of opinions, designs, wishes, and purposes of men, no one is moved to act or resolves to speak who does not hope by means of action or word to release anxiety and drive it from his spirit. Now it is clear that some err in their choice of the right path leading to this end; others deviate from it; still others, and they are always in a minority, achieve it; yet escape from anxiety has always been the common purpose of men of all races and peoples since the world began and will be until it ends. All their desires have their unique foundation in this purpose.

Other ends do not seem to command the unanimous approbation of men. There are, for example, those who do not desire goodness, faith, or truth; there are those who prefer to satisfy their passions in a dark corner rather than to enjoy fame's flatteries; there are those who do not desire riches but prefer to be poor, as do most philosophers and devout people; there are those who, as if by natural inclination, detest sensual delights and hold as imperfect those who crave them; there are many who prefer ignorance to knowledge. One must reckon these things among the ends of human actions. Still, no one considers anxiety to be a good thing; every man seeks release from it.

Those who crave riches seek them only in order to drive the fear of poverty out of their spirits; others seek for glory to free themselves from the fear of being scorned; some seek sensual delights to escape the pain of privations; some seek knowledge to cast out the uncertainty of ignorance; others delight in hearing news and conversation because they seek by these means to dispel the sorrow of solitude and isolation. In brief, man eats, drinks, marries, watches, plays, lives under a roof, rides, walks, or remains still with the sole aim of driving out their contraries and, in general, all other anxieties.

Yet each of these actions is in turn an inescapable hotbed of new anxieties; unexpected obstacles to its realization raise difficulties according to the occasion...loss of what was gained, inability through misfortunes to reach a happy conclusion, unpleasant consequences which come with satisfaction, fear of competition, criticism of the jealous, theft by the covetous, aversion to seeing what we desire in the hands of an enemy, slanders, and the like.

After grasping this sublime truth and comprehending this weighty secret, I sought to find a sure method of arriving at this end which all men alike, ignorant and learned, holy and wicked, seek and hold as good. I discovered that this method consists in nothing else but directing one's self towards a Supreme Goodness by means of good works conducive to immortal life.

For, as I investigated, I observed that all things tended to elude me, and I reached the conclusion that the only permanent reality possible consists in good works useful for another, immortal life. Every other hope that I desired to see realized was followed by melancholy, sometimes because what was ardently desired escaped me, sometimes because I decided to abandon it. It seemed to me that nothing escaped these dangers but good works, directed by a Supreme Goodness. These alone were always followed by pleasure in the present and ill in the future: in the present because I was freed from numberless anxieties which disturbed my tranquility, and, moreover, friends and enemies concurred in commending me; and in the future because these works promised immortality.

The good work, one profitable for an immortal life, stands innocent of all defect, free of all imperfection, and is, moreover, a sure way to put aside every anxiety effectively. I have, indeed, observed that everyone who works for this end, even though he undergoes unpleasant tests on the road of life, not only is free of care but rejoices, because the hope which he holds for the end of his present life helps him to seek what he longs for and incites him to follow in this direction, the end in which he believes. And if any obstacle stands in his way, I have likewise observed he has no anxiety about it, because as he has not consecrated himself to what he sought, he does not consider the obstacle as a punishment inflicted on him. I have seen, too, that if anyone damages him he is joyful, and if any calamity comes about he is no less happy; and more, if he experiences sorrow or weariness in what he has done, he is still full of joy. He lives, in point of fact, in constant unending joy, while quite the contrary holds for other men.

The pleasure which the intelligent man experiences in the exercise of his reason, the learned man in his study, the prudent man in his discreet deliberation, and the devout man in his ascetic combat is greater than the delight which is felt by the glutton in his eating, the toper in his drinking, the lecher in his incontinence, the trader in his gainful bargaining, the gamester in his merriment, and the leader in the exercise of his authority. The proof of this lies in the fact that intelligent, learned, prudent, and devout men also experience those other delights which have just enumerated in the same way as one who lives only to wallow in them but they tend to abandon and separate

themselves from them, preferring instead the quest for permanent release from anxiety through good and virtuous works.

It seems unworthy of a man to consecrate himself to something which is not higher than he is, that is to say, a Supreme Goodness. The intelligent person would account any lower price on himself as unworthy. Therefore he will consecrate himself to good works, to leading his brothers to truth, to the defence of sacred things, to avoiding any despicable humiliation which is not imposed on men by necessity of nature, and to protecting victims of injustice. One who consecrates himself to lesser things is like one who trades a precious gem for a pebble.

Do not forget, then, that only one thing deserves to be sought by men, and that is the absence of care; and the unique avenue which leads to it is built of good works done for the sake of the Supreme Goodness. All else is a foolish waste of time.

Translated by James Kritzeck[2]

TWICE TIMES THEN IS NOW

You ask how old am I
bleached by the sun
my teeth all gone.
How old am I?

I have no guide
no calendar inside
except a smile
and little kiss
she gave me
by surprise
upon my brow.

And now,
that little while
is all my life
and all reality, how long or brief
it seems to be.

Translated by Omar Pound[3]

Ibn 'Abd Rabbihi

MODEST BLUSH

Never, never did I see
Neither have I heard the same,
That a pearl can turn for shame
Into red chalcedony.

When you gaze with awe profound
On the beauty of his brow
Lo, you see your beauty now
In its liquid lustre drowned.

Translated by A. J. Arberry[4]

Ibn Zaydun

POEM TO WALLADA

To-day my longing thoughts recall thee here;
The landscape glitters, and the sky is clear,
So feebly breathes the gentle zephyr's gale,
In pity of my grief it seems to fail.
The silvery fountains laugh, as from a girl's
Fair throat a broken necklace sheds its pearls.
Oh, 'tis a day like those of our sweet prime,
When, stealing pleasures from indulgent Time.
We played midst flowers of eye-bewitching hue,
That bent their heads beneath the drops of dew.
Alas, they see me now bereaved of sleep:
They share my passion and with me they weep.
Here in her sunny haunt the rose blooms bright,
Adding new luster to Aurora's light;
And waked by morning beams, yet languid still,
The rival lotus doth his perfume spill.

All stirs in me the memory of that fire
Which in my tortured breast will ne'er expire.
Had death come ere we parted, it had been
The best of all days in the world, I ween:
And this poor heart, where thou art every thing,
Would not be fluttering now on passion's wing.
Ah, might the zephyr waft me tenderly,
O treasure mine, if lover e'er possessed
A treasure! O thou dearest, queenliest!
Once, once, we paid the debt of love complete
And ran an equal race with eager feet.
How true, how blameless was the love I bore,
Thou hast forgotten but I still adore!

Translated by R. A. Nicholson[5]

al-Mutamid

THE MOON, THE STARS, AND A KING

When the moon in splendour glides
In the darkened west,
The stars advancing at her sides
Raise a flag the whole world sees
—The glittering Pleiades

So I a king on earth, between
My dark battalions and
The loveliest girls this world has seen,
Behold their shields dispersing night
And these whose wine brings light.

And though to a zither slaves may sing
A soft seductive tune,
For all that, my young men can ding
A music that still merrier goes
On the helmets of their foes!

Translated by Harold Morland[6]

Abu'l Hasan Ali ibn Hisn

THE PIGEON

A bough is weeping in the stream.
Green island, green... And I dream.
A pigeon moans, disquiets me...

Her breast is lapis lazuli,
Her throat a pale pistachio-green,
Hazel the wing she turns to preen.
Her throbbing throat disquiets me.

Over the ruby of her eyes
She flickers lids of pearl
With an edge of gold...
But when she cries
Her note disquiets me...

She sits the branch as if a throne,
Hiding her throat within a fold
Of her bright wing...
And still her moan
Is in the air, disquieting me.

But when my tears are my reply,
Above the branch she spreads her wings
Bearing my heart away, to fly
Above despair and mortal things
Where I can never go...
Ah where? a weeping bough, I do not know.

Translated by Harold Morland[1]

Ibn Hamdis

THE ANDALUSIAN FOUNTAINS

And lions people this official wood
 encompass the pools with thunder
and profuse over aureate-banded
 bodies their skulls gush glass
Lions like stillness stirred
 questing mobility there
or trophies of carnivores
 proper those deployed haunches
Sun is tinder to the stirred
 colours, is light to long tongues,
is a hand to unsheath the lunging
 blades that shiver out in a splash.
By a zephyr damp and thread
 are woven and, corsleted
on a branch sits sorcery netted
 like incandescent birds from space
That lest they fall to freedom
 are forcibly propped, lest their songs
start a whistling on the ponds
 and a warbling in the mercurial trees
And they dipped in cascades
 of crysolite and tossed pearl
and they chatter an astral .
 mischief: while expert armourer
Garnish with gilt hoods
 the gates: and an invert
terrace or stalactites
 glows in a submarine recess.
This specialist brocade
 is a mere hallucination
its azure and sun and plantation
 ephemeral as fine skies
Some with beasts in the wood.
 some with the fowl in disaster

are the antique lineal masters
　　　　　hunting their sperm down ornate galleries.

Translated by Herbert Howarth and Ibrahim Shakrullah[8]

FLOWING STREAM

The surface of the flowing stream
Is polished by the prying wind,
Resolved to publish, it would seem.
The secrets hidden in its mind.

The jagged pebbles gash its flanks,
And as the waters swell again
And ever o'er the river's banks
It murmurs fretfully in pain.
As if a serpent, terrified
Beneath the bubbles as it sleeps,
Awakens suddenly, to slide
Impetuously in its deeps.

Translated by A. J. Arberry[9]

Abus Salt

THE INCENSE BURNER

Though its heart was all aflame.
Yet it never knew that same
Grief of parting, and that woe
Sundered lovers know.

When the lightning of the wine
Bathed the drinkers in its shine,
What a brave cloud billowed thence
Sweet with frankincense!

Never saw I, all my days,
Such a conflagration blaze
To persuade the revellers
Paradise was theirs.

Ibn Quzman

THE RADISH

The radish is a good
And doubtless wholesome food,
But proves, to vex the eater,
A powerful repeater.

This only fault I find:
What should be left behind
Comes issuing instead
Right from the eater's head!

Translated by A. J. Arberry[10]

Ibn Hayyun

THE GIRL WITH THE BEAUTY-SPOTS

Once when her beauty-spots had snared
 My breathless heart
I said: Is all your whiteness shared
Sweet favours on your part?
And do these spots that stain
 Now image your disdain?

She answered with a smile
Of roguish guile:

My father is a royal scribe,
And once when I came near
He thought that I should probe
State-secrets and, in fear,
He flicked his pen and on my face
 Left this inky trace...

Ibn Sa'ad al-Khair

THE DRAW-WELL

Dear God!
 The draw-well overflows
 With sweet, sad water
Down to a garden where the trees
Heavily fruited groan...
And doves tell it their moan
With a throbbing throat,
 And it replies
 With a singing tone.

It seems a lover inconsolable
That endlessly walks on
And on about the one sweet spot
Where love was born, and unforgot
For ever cries on her that's gone.

And like the channels grooved by grief
 In human cheeks,
Its conduits give the sad relief
 That a deep heart seeks.

Translated by Harold Morland[11]

Ibn al-Faras

MOON OF BEAUTY

She came in beauty beaming,
Like a full moon gleaming
Her face, beneath the veil
Of dusk approaching, pale.

She came, serene and stately,
The veil so delicately
Drawn above her brow,
No veil was there, I trow.

I deemed her veil the shimmer
Of waters pure, a-glimmer
Therein, for all to see,
Truth's naked purity.

Ibn Said

THE GUARDIANS

Such churlish brutes his guardians be,
Well-schooled in incivility,
Sworn to do battle, when they can,
With every cultivated man.

Whene'er ambitious lover would
Draw nigher to his neighbourhood,
The jealous watchers swiftly rise
And whisk their moon into the skies.

But I have learned a gambit fit
The keenest guardian to outwit,

A stratagem to mollify
The most inexorable spy.

It needs the succour of a shower
For earth to show her guarded flower,
And their hostility relents
When watered with sufficient pence.

Translated by A. J. Arberry[12]

Ibn Maimon (Moses Maimonides)

GUIDE FOR THE PERPLEXED

Part II
Chapter XXXIII

It is clear to me that what Moses experienced at the revelation on Mount Sinai was different from that which was experienced by all the other Israelites, for Moses alone was addressed by God, and for this reason the second person singular is used in the Ten Commandments; Moses then went down to the foot of the mount and told his fellow-men what he had heard. Comp., "I stood between the Lord and you at that time to tell you the word of the Lord" (Deut. v. 5). Again, "Moses spake, and God answered him with a loud voice" (Exod. xix. 19). In the Mechilta our Sages say distinctly that he brought to them every word as he had heard it. Furthermore, the words, "In order that the people hear when I speak with thee" (Exod. xix. 9), show that God spoke to Moses, and the people only heard the mighty sound, not distinct words. It is to the perception of this mighty sound that Scripture refers in the passage, "When ye hear the sound" (Deut. v. 20); again it is stated, "You heard a sound of words" (*ibid*. iv. 12), and it is not said "You heard words"; and even where the hearing of the words is mentioned, only the perception of the sound is meant. It was only Moses that heard the words, and he reported them to the people. This is apparent from Scripture, and from the utterances of our Sages in general. There is, however, an opinion of our Sages frequently expressed in the Midrashim, and found also in the Talmud, to this effect: The Israelites heard the first and the second commandments from God, i.e., they learnt the truth of the principles

contained in these two commandments in the same manner as Moses, and not through Moses. For these two principles, the existence of God and His Unity, can be arrived at by means of reasoning, and whatever can be established by proof is known by the prophet in the same way as by any other person; he has no advantage in this respect. These two principles were not known through prophecy alone. Comp., "Thou hast been shown to know that," etc. (Deut. iv. 34). But the rest of the commandments are of an ethical and authoritative character, and do not contain [truths] perceived by the intellect. Notwithstanding all that has been said by our Sages on this subject, we infer from Scripture as well as from the words of our Sages, that the Israelites heard on that occasion a certain sound which Moses understood to proclaim the first two commandments, and through Moses all other Israelites learnt them when he in intelligible sounds repeated them to the people. Our Sages mention this view, and support it by the verse, "God hath spoken once; twice have I heard this" (Ps. lxii. 11). They state distinctly, in the beginning of *Midrash Ḥazita*, that the Israelites did not hear any other command directly from God; comp. "A loud voice, and it was not heard again" (Deut. v. 19). It was after this first sound was heard that the people were seized with the fear and terror described in Scripture, and that they said, "Behold the Lord our God has shown us, etc., and now why shall we die, etc. Come thou near," etc. Then Moses, the most distinguished of all mankind, came the second time, received successively the other commandments, and came down to the foot of the mountain to proclaim them to the people, whilst the mighty phenomena continued; they saw the fire, they heard the sounds, which were those of thunder and lightning during a storm, and the loud sound of the shofar: and all that is said of the many sounds heard at that time, e.g., in the verse, "and all the people perceived the sounds," etc., refers to the sound of the shofar, thunder, and similar sounds. But the voice of the Lord, that is, the voice created for that purpose, which was understood to include the diverse commandments, was only heard once, as is declared in the Law, and has been clearly stated by our Sages in the places which I have indicated to you. When the people heard this voice their soul left them; and in this voice they perceived the first two commandments. It must, however, be noticed that the people did not understand the voice in the same degree as Moses did. I will point out to you this important fact, and show you that it was a matter of tradition with the nation, and well known by our Sages. For, as a rule, Onkelos renders the word *va-yedabber* by *u-mallel* ("and God spake"); this is also the case with this word in the beginning of the twentieth chapter of Exodus, but the words *ve-al yedabber immanu elohim*, "let not God speak to us" (Exod. xx. 19), addressed by the people to Moses, is rendered *vela yitmallel immanu*

min kodam adonai ("Let not aught be spoken to us by the Lord"). Onkelos makes thus the same distinction which we made. You know that according to the Talmud Onkelos received all these excellent interpretations directly from R. Eliezer and R. Joshua, the wisest men in Israel. Note it, and remember it, for it is impossible for any person to expound the revelation on Mount Sinai more fully than our Sages have done, since it is one of the secrets of the Law. It is very difficult to have a true conception of the events, for there has never been before, nor will there ever be again, anything like it. Note it.

Part III
Chapter XXVII

The general object of the Law is twofold: the well-being of the soul, and the well-being of the body. The well-being of the soul is promoted by correct opinions communicated to the people according to their capacity. Some of these opinions are therefore imparted in a plain form, others allegorically: because certain opinions are in their plain form too strong for the capacity of the common people. The well-being of the body is established by a proper management of the relations in which we live one to another. This we can attain in two ways: first by removing all violence from our midst: that is to say, that we do not do every one as he pleases, desires, and is able to do; but every one of us does that which contributes towards the common welfare. Secondly, by teaching every one of us such good morals as must produce a good social state. Of these two objects, the one, the well-being of the soul, or the communication of correct opinions, comes undoubtedly first in rank, but the other, the well-being of the body, the government of the state, and the establishment of the best possible relations among men, is anterior in nature and time. The latter object is required first; it is also treated [in the Law] most carefully and most minutely, because the well-being of the soul can only be obtained after that of the body has been secured. For it has already been found that man has a double perfection: the first perfection is that of the body, and the second perfection is that of the soul. The first consists in the most healthy condition of his material relations, and this is only possible when man has all his wants supplied, as they arise; if he has his food, and other things needful for his body, e.g., shelter, bath, and the like. But one man alone cannot procure all this; it is impossible for a single man to obtain this comfort; it is only possible in society, since man, as is well known, is by nature social.

The second perfection of man consists in his becoming an actually intelligent being; i.e., he knows about the things in existence all that a person perfectly developed is capable of knowing. This second perfection certainly does not include any action or good conduct, but only knowledge, which is arrived at by speculation, or established by research.

It is clear that the second and superior kind of perfection can only be attained when the first perfection has been acquired; for a person that is suffering from great hunger, thirst, heat, or cold, cannot grasp an idea even if communicated by others, much less can he arrive at it by his own reasoning. But when a person is in possession of the first perfection, then he may possibly acquire the second perfection, which is undoubtedly of a superior kind, and is alone the source of eternal life. The true Law, which as we said is one, and beside which there is no other Law, viz., the Law of our teacher Moses, has for its purpose to give us the twofold perfection. It aims first at the establishment of good mutual relations among men by removing injustice and creating the noblest feelings. In this way the people in every land are enabled to stay and continue in one condition, and every one can acquire his first perfection. Secondly, it seeks to train us in faith, and to impart correct and true opinions when the intellect is sufficiently developed. Scripture clearly mentions the twofold perfection, and tells us that its acquisition is the object of all the divine commandments. Comp., "And the Lord commanded us to do all these statutes, to fear the Lord our God, for our good always, that he might preserve us alive as it is this day" (Deut. vi. 24). Here the second perfection is first mentioned because it is of greater importance, being, as we have shown, the ultimate aim of man's existence. This perfection is expressed in the phrase, "for our good always." You know the interpretation of our Sages, "that it may be well with thee" (*ibid.* xxii. 7), namely, in the world that is all good, "and that thou mayest prolong thy days" (*ibid.*), i.e., in the world that is all eternal." In the same sense I explain the words, "for our good always," to mean that we may come into the world that is all good and eternal, where we may live permanently; and the words, "that he might preserve us alive as it is this day," I explain as referring to our first and temporal existence, to that of our body, which cannot be in a perfect and good condition except by the co-operation of society, as has been shown by us.

Part III
Chapter LIII

This chapter treats of the meaning of three terms which we find necessary to explain, viz., *ḥesed* ("loving kindness"), *mishpat* ("judgment"), and *ẓedakah* ("righteousness").

In our Commentary on the Sayings of the Fathers (chap. v. 7) we have explained the expression *ḥesed* as denoting an excess [in some moral quality]. It is especially used of extraordinary kindness. Loving-kindness is practised in two ways: first, we show kindness to those who have no claim whatever upon us; secondly, we are kind to those to whom it is due, in a greater measure than is due to them. In the inspired writings the term *ḥesed* occurs mostly in the sense of showing kindness to those who have no claim to it whatever. For this reason the term *ḥesed* is employed to express the good bestowed upon us by God: "I will mention the loving-kindness of the Lord" (Isa. lxiii. 7). On this account, the very act of the creation is an act of God's loving-kindness. "I have said, The Universe is built up in loving-kindness" (Ps. lxxxix. 3); i.e., the building up of the Universe is an act of loving-kindness. Also, in the enumeration of God's attributes, Scripture says: "And abundant in loving-kindness" (Exod. xxxiv. 6).

The term *ẓedakah* is derived from *ẓedek*, "righteousness"; it denotes the act of giving every one his due, and of showing kindness to every being according as it deserves. In Scripture, however, the expression *ẓedakah* is not used in the first sense, and does not apply to the payment of what we owe to others. When we therefore give the hired labourer his wages, or pay a debt, we do not perform an act of *ẓedakah*. But we do perform an act of *ẓedakah* when we fulfil those duties towards our fellow-men which our moral conscience imposes upon us; e.g., when we heal the wound of the sufferer. Thus Scripture says, in reference to the returning of the pledge [to the poor debtor]: "And it shall be *ẓedakah* (righteousness) unto thee" (Deut. xxiv. 11). When we walk in the way of virtue we act righteously towards our intellectual faculty, and pay what is due unto it; and because every virtue is thus *ẓedakah*, Scripture applies the term to the virtue of faith in God. Comp., "And he believed in the Lord, and he accounted it to him as righteousness" (Gen. xv. 6); "And it shall be our righteousness" (Deut. vi. 25).

The noun *mishpat*, "judgment," denotes the act of deciding upon a certain action in accordance with justice which may demand either mercy or punishment.

We have thus shown that *ḥesed* denotes pure charity; *ẓedakah* kindness, prompted by a certain moral conscience in man, and being a means of attaining perfection for his soul, whilst *mishpat* may in some cases find expression in revenge, in other cases in mercy.

In discussing the impropriety of admitting attributes of God (Part I., chap. liii., seq.), we stated that the divine attributes which occur in Scripture are attributes of His actions; thus He is called *ḥasid*, "kind," because He created the Universe; *ẓaddik*, "righteous," on account of His mercy with the weak, in providing for every living being according to its powers; and *shofet*, "judge," on account of the relative good and the great relative evils that are decreed by God's justice as directed by His wisdom. These three names occur in the Pentateuch: "Shall not the judge (*shofet*) of all the earth," etc. (Gen. xviii. 25); "Righteous (*ẓaddik*) and upright is he" (Deut. xxxii. 4); "Abundant in loving-kindness" (*ḥesed*, Exod. xxxiv. 6).

We intended in explaining these three terms to prepare the reader for the next chapter.

Translated by Michael Friedlander[13]

Saadia Gaon

CONCERNING HOW IT IS MOST PROPER FOR MAN TO CONDUCT
HIMSELF IN THIS WORLD

Exordium

The principle which forms the subject of this treatise is a matter that many men have attempted to fathom but of which only a few have reached a satisfactory view. Let me, therefore, state by way of introduction, that, inasmuch as the Creator of the universe, exalted and magnified be He, is essentially one, it follows by logical necessity that His creatures be composed of many elements, as I have made clear in the foregoing.

At this point, now, I would say that the thing that generally gives the appearance of constituting a unity, whatever sort of unit it be, is singular only in number. Upon careful consideration, however, it is found to be of a multiple

nature. To reduce this generalization to simpler terms, when the substances of all beings are analyzed, they are found to be endowed with the attributes of heat and cold and moisture and dryness. When the substance of a tree is examined, it is found to include in addition to the aforementioned, branches and leaves and fruits, and all that is connected therewith. When the human body, again, is examined, it is found to be composed, besides the elements listed above, of flesh and bones and sinews and arteries and muscles and all that goes with them. This is a matter about which no doubt can be entertained and the reality of which is not to be denied.

All these phenomena are in accord with the laws of creation: namely, that the Creator, exalted and magnified be He, be one and His works manifold. That is also borne out by such statements of the Scriptures as *How manifold are Thy works, O Lord! In wisdom hast Thou made them all* (Ps. 104:24). Even heaven is made up of various parts, dimensions, forms, colors, and movements without number. That is what makes it heaven, as is stated in Scripture: *Who maketh the Bear, Orion, and the Pleiades, and the champers of the south* (Job 9:9).

Chapter 1

Having made this preliminary observation, I say now that the same thing applies to the tendencies exhibited by man. He evinces a liking for many things and a dislike for others. This is borne out by such statements of Scripture as *There are many devices in a man's heart; but the counsel of the Lord, that shall stand* (Prov. 19:21).

Now just as the material objects do not consist of just one of the four elements [of which they are said to be composed], and the body of the trees cannot exist with only one of the parts mentioned by us, and man cannot live if he has bone or flesh alone—in fact, even the heavens are not illuminated by just one star—so, too, man's conduct in the course of his lifetime cannot logically be based on just a single trait. But just as in each instance the final product is the result of a combination of ingredients in larger or smaller proportions, so too, is man's behavior the result of a combination of his likes and dislikes in varying proportions.

Man acts as though he were a judge to whom the disposal of the different tendencies is submitted for decision, as Scripture says: *Well is it with the man that dealeth graciously and lendeth, that ordereth his affairs rightfully* (Ps. 112:5). Or his position might be compared to that of one who would weigh these impulses with a balance and give each its due measure, as Scripture also puts it:

Balance the path of thy feet (Prov. 4:26). When, then, a person behaves in this manner, his affairs will be properly adjusted and well regulated.

What impelled me to put this theme at the beginning of the present treatise is the fact that I have seen people who think—and with them it is a firm conviction—that it is obligatory for human beings to order their entire existence upon the exploitation of one trait, lavishing their love on one thing above all others and their hatred on a certain thing above the rest. Now I investigated this view and I found it to be extremely erroneous for sundry reasons.

One of these is that if the [exclusive] love for one thing and its preference [above all others] had been the most salutary thing for man, the Creator would not have implanted in his character the love for these other things. Also if that were so, God could have created man out of one element and of one piece, and He would have done likewise for the other creatures so that they would have been similarly constituted. Seest thou not how individual functions cannot very well be executed by the use of a single medium? Still less is this possible in human conduct in general.

Another argument [that might be advanced against the exclusive cultivation of one trait] is that, if an architect were to build a house of stones or teakwood or mats or pegs alone, it would not be as well constructed as if he had built it of all these materials put together. The same might be asserted with regard to cooking, food, drink, dress, service, and other matters. Must not the person who notes that all these items which exist for the purpose of serving man's needs and well-being are not composed of just one ingredient open his eyes and realize how much less that would be possible in the case of the inclinations of his soul and its characteristics?

Chapter II

Now it is also necessary for me to explain that the evil resulting from such a one-sided choice is not trivial but quite serious, as I shall illustrate. I say, then, that there are people who give themselves up to long mountain trips, which leads to their becoming insane. Others indulge in excessive eating and drinking, which causes them to contract hemorrhoids. Others, again, lavish all their energies on the gathering of wealth, only to accumulate it for other men. Furthermore, there are those who dedicate themselves entirely to satisfying their thirst for revenge, with the consequence that their vindictiveness reacts against themselves. I might also cite other such instances, as I shall explain in the middle of this treatise with the help of God.

Let me, however, state here, prior to that discussion that it is for the above-mentioned reasons that man stands in constant need of a wisdom that would regulate his conduct and behavior, as Scripture says: *When thou walkest, it shall lead thee* (Prov. 6:2). Principally that consists, in this particular instance, in his exercising control over his impulses and having complete mastery over his likes and dislikes, for each has its distinctive role in which it must be made to function. Once, then, he recognizes the role belonging to a given impulse, he must give it full opportunity to discharge its function in the required measure. On the other hand, he must restrain it until the ground for such restraint no longer exists for him. All this is to be done with due deliberation and with the power to release or hold, at will, as Scripture has said: *He that is slow to anger is better than the mighty; and he that ruleth his spirit than he that taketh a city* (Prov. 16:22).

I have already stated previously that the soul has three faculties—the appetitive, the impulsive, and the cognitive. As for the appetitive faculty, it is that whereby a human being entertains the desire for food and drink and sexual intercourse and for seeing beautiful sights and smelling fragrant odors and for wearing garments that are soft to the touch. The impulsive faculty is that which renders a person courageous and bold, and endows him with zeal for leadership and championing the common weal, and makes him vindictive and vainglorious, and other such things. As for the cognitive faculty, again, it exercises judgment over the two other faculties. When any one of them or of their subdivisions is aroused, the cognitive faculty takes it under consideration and investigates it. If it notes that it is sound from beginning to end, it points this fact out, not to speak of the case where the consequences are desirable.

Any person, then, who follows this course of giving his cognitive faculty dominion over his appetites and impulses, is disciplined *by the discipline of the wise,* as Scripture says: *The fear of the Lord is the discipline of wisdom* (Prov. 15:33). Any man, on the other hand, who permits his appetites and impulses to dominate his faculty of cognition, is undisciplined. And if someone wrongly calls such conduct discipline, it is *the discipline of the foolish,* as Scripture says: *But the foolish despise...discipline* (Prov. 1:7), and also: *Or as one in fetters to the discipline of the fool* (Prov. 7:22).

Chapter III

Having demonstrated, then, in this introductory statement how logical necessity leads to the assumption of the existence of an All-Wise Being who arranged

for us the order of these our likes and dislikes and indicated to us the manner of our procedure with them, let me say that the sage Solomon, the son of David, may peace be upon them both, has fathomed this subject for the purpose of enabling us to attain what is best. He says, namely: *I have seen all the works that are done under the sun; and, behold, all is vanity and striving after wind* (Eccles. 1:14).

Now he does not refer, when he makes the remark: *All is vanity and striving after wind*, to the union and combination of all works, for it was the Creator, exalted and magnified be He, who established them and set them up, and it is not fitting for a sage like Solomon to say of what the Creator, exalted and magnified be He, has established: *It is vanity*. What he meant to say was, rather, that any act that a human being undertakes to carry out in isolation—that is to say, every one of the acts of man that receive exclusive attention—is as futile for him as associating with the wind.

With reference to this sort of one-sided procedure, he says also: *That which is crooked cannot be made straight; and that which is wanting [cannot be number]* (Eccles. 1:15). That is to say any act practiced exclusively constitutes a distortion from what is straight and is lacking in completeness, while in their combination [with the full range of pious works, single acts] do not constitute a *deficiency* but rather completion and perfection.

The correctness of the foregoing interpretation is confirmed by the fact that the author presents three classes of objects of mundane ambition, each of which he decides is *hebhel*, the meaning of which is " vanity." This [rendering of the word] is borne out by such statements of Scripture as *They lead you unto vanity (mahbilim)* (Jer. 23:16); that is: "They deceive you with vain hopes"; and *Trust not in oppression, and put not vain hope ('al tehbalu) in robbery* (Ps. 62:11).

The first of these [strivings that Solomon considers futile] is the exclusive devotion to wisdom to the neglect of all other objects of [human] desire. He says, namely, in reference thereto: *And I applied my heart to know wisdom, and to know madness and folly—I perceived that this also was a striving after wind* (Eccles. 1:17). As his reason for regarding it thus he gives the fact that as a person's knowledge increases, there is also an increase for him of sorrow. That is due to the circumstance that with the increase in knowledge there are revealed to him the flaws in things concerning which he was fully at ease before they became evident to him. That is the import of his remark: *For in much wisdom is much vexation; and he that increaseth knowledge increaseth sorrow* (Eccles. 1:18).

He next repeats [this observation] with reference to the exclusive cultivation of mirth and gaiety, saying that if a person gave all his attention and devotion to them alone, they, too, would prove a disappointment to him. Thus he

says: *I said in my heart: "Come now, I will try thee with mirth and enjoy pleasure";* *and, behold this also was vanity* (Eccles. 2:1). As his reason for this conclusion he gives the fact that a person experiences, when he laughs and jests, a sense of degradation and debasement putting him on a level with the behavior of the beasts. That is the import of this declaration: *I said of laughter: "It is mad"; and of mirth; "What doth it accomplish?"* (Eccles. 2:2).

After this he makes the same remark for the third time about the upbuilding of the material world and he informs us that the preoccupation therewith, too, is vanity. He does this in his statement: *I made me great works; I builded me houses; I planted me vineyards; I made me gardens and parks* (Eccles. 2:4) and all the other things that he relates about his doings until the end of the passage in question. The reason he gives as his objection to all this sort of activity is that he has to leave whatever he has achieved to those that will come after him and that, therefore, his labor will have been wasted. Thus he says: *And I hated all my labour wherein I laboured under the sun, seeing that I must leave it unto the man that shall be after me* (Eccles. 2:18).

Having, then, enumerated these three types, he desists from mentioning other worldly strivings lest he be diverted thereby from his central theme. Yet in the very midst of his discussion of these types he hints at the need for the proper balancing of these three strivings. This is to be effected by devoting some attention to the cultivation of wisdom and to indulgence in pleasure without neglecting to inquire into what is best for man. Thus he says: *I searched in my heart how to pamper my flesh with wine, and my heart conducting itself with wisdom, [how yet to lay hold on folly, till I might see which it was best for the sons of men that they should do]* (Eccles. 2:3).

Translated by Samuel Rosenblatt[14]

Solomon ibn Gabirol

THE ETHICS OF SOLOMON GABIROL

Part II
Chapter 1: On the Quality of Love

It is almost impossible for any man to be secure from this "accident," O God, save he whose intellect is master of his nature. None such exists; and if any (be found to) exist, he is undoubtedly one of the most excellent (men). Lust is a constituent element in the nature of man, and if he desire to be master and ruler, let him cast away lust (passions), make no use of it whatever, ignore it and do without it, for it is one of the baser qualities. It is well known that the qualities of the wise are not perfected until their souls gain the mastery over their desires. The deeds of him whose intellect prevails over his lustfulness are commendable. Upon the realization of desires there ensues the penalty of misfortune. One of the signs of him, who is overcome by his lust, is that he is very changeable, restless, and fickle of speech. Especially if, added to this, the bloody temper prevail in his constitution and he be in the period of youth and the season of spring, then it proves too strong for him. Therefore the wise man must shrink from this quality lest he make use of it and turn away from it, for there is connected with it no inconsiderable harm. Thou knowest how contempt, obscurity, and abasement come upon its devotee, and that finally its outcome is evil. This thou knowest from the story of Amnon and what happened to him when he hastened after his desire. Man ought to employ this quality only in service of God and His divine Law, as it is written (Ps. i. 2), "And his delight is in the law of the lord," and again (*id.*, cxix. 97), "How I love thy law," etc. Necessarily, one who occupies himself with the quest of knowledge and moral science (theoretical science and the practical arts), will be (so busy as to be) kept from his lusts. The wise one said, "If aught befall thee and no one occur to thee whom thou mightest consult with reference thereto, avoid it and bring it not near to thy passion, for passion in an enemy of the heart." And he said, "He who is submissive to his lust is routed, and he who rebels against it gains the victory." This quality is preferred by foolish men only because of the imminence (immediateness) of its delight and for the sake of the amusement and merriment and the hearing of the mirthful songs which they get through it. They heed not the suffering and the wretchedness that follow in its train, and therefore incline in accord with their natural impulses

to the attainment of present pleasure, as it is said (Prov. xiii, 19), "The desire accomplished is sweet to the soul"—turning aside from wisdom and the service of the Lord, because of what appears to be the remoteness of the delight and pleasurableness of these things. Verily, in their opinion, these are remote. Yet these are not remote, but near at hand. They are remote only in their mind. Therefore man must devote this quality of love to God, exalted may He be, as it is written (Deut. xi. 1), written (I Sam. xx. 17), "For he loved him as he loved his own soul"; to his relatives as it is written (Gen. xxix. 18), "And Jacob loved Rachel"; to his offspring, as it is written (*id.,* xxxvii.3), "Israel loved Joseph"; to his country, as it is written (Num. x. 30), "but I will depart to my own land and to my kindred"; to his companion, as spake David to Jonathan (II Sam. i. 26), "Very pleasant hast thou been unto me"; to his wife (Prov. v. 19), "Let her be as the loving hind and the pleasant roe"; to wisdom, as it is written (Prov. xxix. 3), "The man that loveth wisdom rejoiceth his father." The moral application of this quality is, man must evince it (in his dealings) with all men. It has been said, "he who desires to be endeared to men should conduct himself with regard to them in the best possible manner. Benefit occasions love even as injury begets hatred." Moreover, included under this quality are wishes and unattainable desires. It is right for the man of understanding that he train himself (to keep aloof) therefrom. The following is part of what the poets have said concerning such wishes as cannot be realized, and wherefrom the soul realizes naught except possibly weariness of spirit, continual disquietude, and protracted restlessness:

"My day is a day which is common to men until the darkness of the night is fallen, and then my couch wearies me. I spent my day in entertainment and in desire but the night brought me altogether to grief."

Among other things which have been said with reference to devoting one's self wholly to pleasure and passion, the blameworthy outcome of this, and the trouble which is associated therewith, the poet says:

"We have drunk of the dregs of the wine as if we were kings of the two Iraks and the sea; but when the sun shone brightly, thou mightest have found me with my riches flown, and poverty once more my own."

When this quality obtains the mastery of the soul, the senses become blunted and man is not conscious because of his being given over to pleasure. He is as those of whom it is said (Isa. v. 20), "Woe unto them that call evil good and good evil." The maxim of the sage is, "Thy love of anything renders thee blind and deaf." One sage, writing to another on the subject of subduing the lusts, said, "thou shalt not attain what thou lovest until thou suffer much from what thou loathest, until thou suffer much through that which thou lovest."

Chapter IV: Treating of Hard-Heartedness. This is the Eighth Chapter of the Book.

I do not find this quality among righteous or superior men. But it is (to be found) in him whose nature resembles that of a lion, for he is one who is never sated. These are the ones of whom it is said (Deut. xxviii. 50), "A nation of fierce countenance." Upon my soul, this is a wholly detestable quality, whether (its measure be) great or small. It comes into being when the spirit of wrath prevails over a man. This quality is exercised for the purpose of wreaking vengeance upon enemies. There is no harm in making use of it in a manner, although the intelligent man ought not endeavor to be avenged upon his enemies. For this is not befitting. Thus saith the sage (Prov. xxiv. 17), "Rejoice not when thy enemy fall-fellow-man, to kill him, or to lay hold of the possessions of one who has given no offence, is reprehensible. From such as these may God preserve me, for of their ilk, the Saint said (Ps. cxxiv., 1 and 3), "If it had not been the Lord who was on our side, now may Israel say": "Then they had swallowed us up quick, when their wrath was kindled against us." A proof that this quality is only found in the wicked is the expression (Prov. xii. 10), "But the tender mercies of the wicked are cruel." Plato, the author of the laws in regard to vengeance, said, "He who desires to be revenged upon his enemies should add (a degree of) excellence to himself."

End of Part II

Translated by Stephen S. Wise[15]

Part VI

THE AGE OF DEPRESSION

Ibn Battuta

I left Tangier, my birthplace, on Thursday, 2nd Rajab, 725 [14th June, 1325], being at that time twenty-two [lunar] years of age, with the intention of making the Pilgrimage to the Holy House [at Mecca] and the Tomb of the Prophet [at Madína]. I set out alone, finding no companion to cheer the way with friendly intercourse, and no party of travellers with whom to associate myself. Swayed by an overmastering impulse within me, and a long-cherished desire to visit those glorious sanctuaries, I resolved to quit all my friends and tear myself away from my home. As my parents were still alive, it weighed grievously upon me to part from them, and both they and I were afflicted with sorrow.

On reaching the city of Tilimsán [Tlemsen], whose sultan at that time was Abú Táshifín, I found there two ambassadors of the Sultan of Tunis, who left the city on the same day that I arrived. One of the brethren having advised me to accompany them, I consulted the will of God in this matter, and after a stay of three days in the city to procure all that I needed, I rode after them with all speed. I overtook them at the town of Miliána, where we stayed ten days, as both ambassadors fell sick on account of the summer heats. When we set out again, one of them grew worse, and died after we had stopped for three nights by a stream four miles from Miliána. I left their party there and pursued my journey, with a company of merchants from Tunis. On reaching al-jazá'ir [Algiers] we halted outside the town for a few days, until the former party rejoined us, when we went on together through the Mitíja to the mountain of Oaks [Jurjúra] and so reached Bijáya [Bougie]. The commander of Bijáya at this time was the chamberlain Ibn Sayyid an-Nás. Now one of the Tunisian merchants of our party had died leaving three thousand dinars of gold, which he had entrusted to a certain man of Algiers to deliver to his heirs at Tunis. Ibn Sayyid an-Nás came to hear of this and forcibly seized the money. This was the first instance I witnessed of the tyranny of the agents of the Tunisian government. At Bijáya I fell ill of a fever, and one of my friends advised me to stay there till I recovered. But I refused, saying, "If God decrees my death, it shall be on the road with my face set toward Mecca." "If that is your resolve," he replied, "sell your ass and your heavy baggage, and I shall lend you what you require. In this way you will travel light, for we must make haste on our journey, for fear of meeting roving Arabs on the way." I followed his advice and he did as he had promised—may God reward him! On reaching Qusantínah [Constantine] we

camped outside the town, but a heavy rain forced us to leave our tents during the night and take refuge in some houses there. Next day the governor of the city came to meet us. Seeing my clothes all soiled by the rain he gave orders that they should be washed at his house, and in place of my old worn headcloth sent me a headcloth of fine Syrian cloth, in one of the ends of which he had tied two gold dinars. This was the first alms I received on my journey. From Qusantínah we reached Bona where, after staying in the town for several days, we left the merchants of our party on account of the dangers of the road, while we pursued our journey with the utmost speed. I was again attacked by fever, so I tied myself in the saddle with a turban-cloth in case I should fall by reason of my weakness. So great was my fear that I could not dismount until we arrived at Tunis. The population of the city came out to meet the members of our party, and on all sides greetings and questions were exchanged, but not a soul greeted me as no one there was known to me. I was so affected by my loneliness that I could not restrain my tears and wept bitterly, until one of the pilgrims realized the cause of my distress and coming up to me greeted me kindly and continued to entertain me with friendly talk until I entered the city.

The Sultan of Tunis at that time was Abú Yahyá, the son of Abú Zakaríya ii, and there were a number of notable scholars in the town. During my stay the festival of the Breaking of the Fast fell due, and I joined the company at the Praying-ground. The inhabitants assembled in large numbers to celebrate the festival, making a brave show and wearing their richest apparel. The Sultan Abú Yahyá arrived on horseback, accompanied by all his relatives, courtiers, and officers of state walking on foot in a Stately procession. After the recital of the prayer and the conclusion of the Allocution the people returned to their homes.

Some time later the pilgrim caravan for the Hijáz was formed, and they nominated me as their qádí (Judge). We left Tunis early in November, following the coast road through Súsa, Sax, and Qábis, where we stayed for ten days on account of incessant rains. Thence we set out for Tripoli, accompanied for several stages by a hundred or more horsemen as well as a detachment of archers, out of respect for whom the Arabs kept their distance. I had made a contract of marriage at Sfax with the daughter of one of the syndics at Tunis, and at Tripoli she was conducted to me, but after leaving Tripoli I became involved in a dispute with her father, which necessitated my separation from her. I then married the daughter of a Student from Fez, and when she was conducted to me I detained the caravan for a day by entertaining them all at a wedding party.

At length on April 5th (1326) we reached Alexandria. It is a beautiful city, well-built and fortified with four gates and a magnificent port. Among all

the ports in the world I have seen none to equal it except Kawlam [Quilon] and Cálicút in India, the port of the infidels [Genoese] at Súdáq in the land of the Turks, and the port of Zaytún in China, all of which will be described later. I went to see the lighthouse on this occasion and found one of its faces in ruins. It is a very high square building, and its door is above the level of the earth. Opposite the door, and of the same height, is a building from which there is a plank bridge to the door; if this is removed there is no means of entrance. Inside the door is a place for the lighthouse-keeper, and within the lighthouse there are many chambers. The breadth of the passage inside is nine spans and that of the wall ten spans; each of the four sides of the lighthouse is 140 spans in breadth. It is situated on a high mound and lies three miles from the city on a long tongue of land which juts out into the sea from close by the city wall, so that the lighthouse cannot be reached by land except from the city. On my return to the West in the year 750 [1349] I visited the light-house again, and found that it had fallen into so ruinous a condition that it was not possible to enter it or climb up to the door. Al-Malik an-Násir had started to build a similar lighthouse alongside it but was prevented by death from completing the work. Another of the marvellous things in this city is the awe-inspiring marble column in its outskirts which they call the "Pillar of Columns." It is a single block, skilfully carved, erected on a plinth of square stones like enormous platforms, and no one knows how it was erected there nor for certain who erected it.

One of the learned men of Alexandria was the qádí, a master of eloquence, who used to wear a turban of extraordinary size. Never either in the eastern or the western lands have I seen a more voluminous headgear. Another of them was the pious ascetic Burhán ad-Dín, whom I met during my stay and whose hospitality I enjoyed for three days. One day as I entered his room he said to me "I see that you are fond of travelling through foreign lands." I replied "Yes, I am " (though I had as yet no thought of going to such distant lands as India or China). Then he said "You must certainly visit my brother Faríd ad-Dín in India, and my brother Rukn ad-Dín in Sind, and my brother Burhán ad-Dín in China, and when you find them give them greeting from me." I was amazed at his prediction, and the idea of going to these countries having been cast into my mind, my journeys never ceased until I had met these three that he named and conveyed his greeting to them.

During my stay at Alexandria I had heard of the pious Shaykh al-Murshidí, who bestowed gifts miraculously created at his desire. He lived in solitary retreat in a cell in the country where he was visited by princes and ministers. Parties of men in all ranks of life used to come to him every day and he would supply

them all with food. Each one of them would desire to eat some flesh or fruit or sweetmeat at his cell, and to each he would give what he had suggested though it was frequently out of season. His fame was carried from mouth to mouth far and wide, and the Sultan too had visited him several times in his retreat. I set out from Alexandria to seek this shaykh and passing through Damanhúr came to Fawwá [Fua] a beautiful township, close by which, separated from it by a canal, lies the shaykh's cell. I reached this cell about mid-afternoon, and on saluting the shaykh I found that he had with him one of the sultan's aides-de-camp, who had encamped with his troops just outside. The shaykh rose and embraced me, and calling for food invited me to eat. When the hour of the afternoon prayer arrived he set me in front as prayer-leader, and did the same on every occasion when we were together at the times of prayer during my stay. When I wished to sleep he said to me "Go up to the roof of the cell and sleep there" (this was during the summer heats). I said to the officer "In the name of God," but he replied [quoting from the Qur'an] "There is none of us but has an appointed place." So I mounted to the roof and found there a straw mattress and a leather mat, a water vessel for ritual ablutions, a jar of water and a drinking-cup, and I lay down there to sleep.

That night, while I was sleeping on the roof of the cell, I dreamed that I was on the wing of a great bird which was flying with me towards Mecca, then to Yemen, then eastwards, and thereafter going towards the south, then flying far eastwards, and finally landing in a dark and green country, where it left me. I was astonished at this dream and said to myself "If the shaykh can interpret my dream for me, he is all that they say he is." Next morning, after all the other visitors had gone, he called me and when I had related my dream interpreted it to me saying: "You will make the pilgrimage [to Mecca] and visit [the Tomb of] the Prophet, and you will travel through Yemen, 'Iráq, the country of the Turks, and India. You will stay there for a long time and meet there my brother Dilshád the Indian, who will rescue you from a danger into which you will fall." Then he gave me a travelling-provision of small cakes and money, and I bade him farewell and departed. Never since parting from him have I met on my journeys aught but good fortune, and his blessings have stood me in good stead.

We rode from here to Damietta through a number of towns, in each of which we visited the principal men of religion. Damietta lies on the bank of the Nile, and the people in the houses next to the river draw water from it in buckets. Many of the houses have steps leading down to the river. Their sheep and goats are allowed to pasture at liberty day and night; for this reason the saying goes of Damietta, "Its walls are sweetmeats and its dogs are sheep."

Anyone who enters the city may not afterwards leave it except by the governor's seal. Persons of repute have a seal stamped on a piece of paper so that they may show it to the gatekeepers; other persons have the seal stamped on their forearms. In this city there are many seabirds with extremely greasy flesh, and the milk of its buffaloes is unequalled for sweetness and pleasant taste. The fish called búrí is exported thence to Syria, Anatolia, and Cairo. The present town is of recent construction; the old city was that destroyed by the Franks in the time of al-Malik as-Sálih.

From Darnietta I travelled to Fáriskúr, which is a town on the bank of the Nile, and halted outside it. Here I was overtaken by a horseman who had been sent after me by the governor of Damietta. He handed me a number of coins, saying to me "The Governor asked for you, and on being informed about you, he sent you this gift"—may God reward him! Thence I travelled to Ashmún, a large and ancient town on a canal derived from the Nile. It possesses a wooden bridge at which all vessels anchor, and in the afternoon the baulks are lifted and the vessels pass up and down. From here I went to Samannúd, whence I journeyed upstream to Cairo, between a continuous succession of towns and villages. The traveller on the Nile need take no provision with him, because whenever he desires to descend on the bank he may do so, for ablutions, prayers, provisioning, or any other purpose. There is an uninterrupted chain of bazaars from Alexandria to Cairo, and from Cairo to Assuan in Upper Egypt.

I arrived at length at Cairo, mother of cities and seat of Pharaoh the tyrant, mistress of broad regions and fruitful lands, boundless in multitude of buildings, peerless in beauty and splendour, the meeting-place of comer and goer, the halting-place of feeble and mighty, whose throngs surge as the waves of the sea, and can scarce be contained in her for all her size and capacity. It is said that in Cairo there are twelve thousand water-carriers who transport water on camels, and thirty thousand hirers of mules and donkeys, and that on the Nile there are thirty-six thousand boats belonging to the Sultan and his subjects, which sail upstream to Upper Egypt and downstream to Alexandria and Damietta, laden with goods and profitable merchandise of all kinds. On the bank of the Nile opposite Old Cairo is the place known as The Garden, which is a pleasure park and promenade, containing many beautiful gardens, for the people of Cairo are given to pleasure and amusements. I witnessed a fete once in Cairo for the sultan's recovery from a fractured hand; all the merchants decorated their bazaars and had rich stuffs, ornaments and silken fabrics hanging in their shops for several days. The mosque of 'Amr is highly venerated and widely celebrated. The Friday service is held in it, and the road runs through it from east to west. The madrasas [college mosques] of Cairo cannot be counted for multitude. As

for the Máristán [hospital], which lies "between the two castles" near the mausoleum of Sultan Qalá'ún, no description is adequate to its beauties. It contains an innumerable quantity of appliances and medicaments, and its daily revenue is put as high as a thousand dinars.

There are a large number of religious establishments ("convents"), which they call *khánqahs*, and the nobles vie with one another in building them. Each of these is set apart for a separate school of darwíshes, mostly Persians, who are men of good education and adepts in the mystical doctrines. Each has a superior and a doorkeeper and their affairs are admirably organized. They have many special customs, one of which has to do with their food. The steward of the house comes in the morning to the darwíshes, each of whom indicates what food he desires, and when they assemble for meals, each person is given his bread and soup in a separate dish, none sharing with another. They eat twice a day. They are each given winter clothes and summer clothes, and a monthly allowance of from twenty to thirty dirhams. Every Thursday night they receive sugar cakes, soap to wash their clothes, the price of a bath, and oil for their lamps. These men are celibate; the married men have separate convents.

At Cairo too is the great cemetery of al-Qaráfa, which is a place of peculiar sanctity, and contains the graves of innumerable scholars and pious believers. In the Qaráfa the people build beautiful pavilions surrounded by walls, so that they look like houses. They also build chambers and hire Qur'an-readers, who recite night and day in agreeable voices. Some of them build religious houses and madrasas beside the mausoleums and on Thursday nights they go out to spend the night there with their children and women-folk, and make a circuit of the famous tombs. They go out to spend the night there also on the "Night of mid-Sha'bán," and the market-people take out all kinds of eatables. Among the many celebrated sanctuaries [in the city] is the holy shrine where there reposes the head of al-Husayn. Beside it is a vast monastery of striking construction, on the doors of which there are silver rings and plates of the same metal.

The Egyptian Nile surpasses all rivers of the earth in sweetness of taste, length of course, and utility. No other river in the world can show such a continuous series of towns and villages along its banks, or a basin so intensely cultivated. Its course is from south to north, contrary to all the other [great] rivers. One extraordinary thing about it is that it begins to rise in the extreme hot weather, at the time when rivers generally diminish and dry up, and begins to subside just when rivers begin to increase and overflow. The river Indus resembles it in this feature. The Nile is one of the five great rivers of the world, which are the Nile, Euphrates, Tigris, Syr Darya and Amu Darya; five other rivers resemble these, the Indus, which is called Panj Áb [*i.e.* Five Rivers], the river of

India which is called Gang [Ganges]—it is to it that the Hindus go on pilgrim-
age, and when they burn their dead they throw the ashes into it, and they say
that it comes from Paradise—the river Jún [Jumna, or perhaps Brahmaputra]
in India, the river Itil [Volga] in the Qipchaq steppes, on the banks of which is
the city of Sará, and the river Sarú [Hoang-Ho] in the land of Cathay. All these
will be mentioned in their proper places, if God will. Some distance below
Cairo the Nile divides into three streams, none of which can be crossed except
by boat, winter or summer. The inhabitants of every township have canals led
of the Nile; these are filled when the river is in flood and carry the water over
the fields.

From Cairo I travelled into Upper Egypt, with the intention of crossing to
the Hijáz. On the first night I stayed at the monastery of Dayr at-Tín, which
was built to house certain illustrious relics—a fragment of the Prophet's
wooden basin and the pencil with which he used to apply kohl, the awl he
used for sewing his sandals, and the Qur'an belonging to the Caliph 'Ali
written in his own hand. These were bought, it is said, for a hundred thou-
sand dirhams by the builder of the monastery, who also established funds to
supply food to all comers and to maintain the guardians of the sacred relics.
Thence my way lay through a number of towns and villages to Munyat ibn
Khasíb [Minia], a large town which is built on the bank of the Nile, and most
emphatically excels all the other towns of Upper Egypt. I went on through
Manfalút, Asyút, Ikhmím, where there is a *berba* with sculptures and inscrip-
tions which no one can now read—another of these *berbas* there was pulled
down and its stones used to build a madrasa—Qiná, Qús, where the gover-
nor of Upper Egypt resides, Luxor, a pretty little town containing the tomb
of the pious ascetic Abu'l-Hajjáj, Esná, and thence a day and a night's journey
through desert country to Edfú. Here we crossed the Nile and, hiring camels,
journeyed with a party of Arabs through a desert, totally devoid of settle-
ments but quite safe for travelling. One of our halts was at Humaythira, a
place infested with hyenas. All night long we kept driving them away, and
indeed one got at my baggage, tore open one of the sacks, pulled out a bag of
dates, and made off with it. We found the bag next morning, torn to pieces
and with most of the contents eaten.

After fifteen days' travelling we reached the town of Aydháb, a large town,
well supplied with milk and fish; dates and grain are imported from Upper
Egypt. Its inhabitants are Bejás. These people are black-skinned; they wrap
themselves in yellow blankets and tie headbands about a fingerbreadth wide
round their heads. They do not give their daughters any share in their inher-
itance. They live on camels' milk and they ride on Meháris [dromedaries].

One-third of the city belongs to the Sultan of Egypt and two-thirds to the King of the Bejás, who is called al-Hudrubí. On reaching Aydháb we found that al-Hudrubí was engaged in warfare with the Turks [i.e. the troops of the Sultan of Egypt], that he had sunk the ships and that the Turks had fled before him. It was impossible for us to attempt the sea-crossing, so we sold the provisions that we had made ready for it, and returned to Qús with the Arabs from whom we had hired the camels. We sailed thence down the Nile (it was at the flood time) and after an eight days' journey reached Cairo, where I stayed only one night, and immediately set out for Syria. This was in the middle of July, 1326.

Translated by H. A. R. Gibb[1]

Ibn al-Khatib

TIME OF MEETING

If there is rain may it enrich you
She has consented to
The Andalusian hour

Which drifts through sleep vaguely,
Your meeting, remote profit
Of prying irises

The time is flying pennants,
Tatters of wishes,
Pointing a track for you
Where driblets of lovers skip in the season.

Hesitation like a beam
Opens the lip of flowers

The anemones repeat the lessens
Of the water between clouds
Talking the language of classrooms
Dear to the few who gathered from far
Framed by dark, the garden still is lit

By luminous stones within. A star
Brims out of a black cup. Falls
Felicitous, sheer, unacquainted
With any unchastity but haste.
Here what is sociable is still sweet
Mornings still career like lancers
And out of caves the meteors gashed
Steam is just climbing, the eyes
Of flowers just turning into queens.

A garden broader than the hills
Found enough fidelity in the world
To hide itself there.

Translated by Herbert Howarth and Ibrahim Shakrullah[106]

Ibn Khaldun

FIVE EXTRACTS FROM *MUQADDIMAH*

Prolegomena showing the excellence of the science of History, establishing the methods proper to it, and glancing at the errors into which Historians fall, together with some account of their causes.

Know that the science of History is noble in its conception, abounding in instruction, and exalted in its aim. It acquaints us with the characteristics of the ancient peoples, the ways of life followed by the prophets, and the dynasties and government of kings, so that those who wish may draw valuable lessons for their guidance in religious and worldly affairs.

The student of History, however, requires numerous sources of information and a great variety of knowledge; he must consider well and examine carefully in order to arrive at the truth and avoid errors and pitfalls. If he rely on bare tradition, without having thoroughly grasped the principles of common experience, the institutes of government, the nature of civilisation, and the circumstances of human society, and without judging what is past and invisible by the light of what is present before his eyes, then he will often be in danger of stumbling and slipping and losing the right road. Many errors committed by historians,

commentators, and leading traditionists in their narrative of events have been caused by their reliance on mere tradition, which they have accepted without regard to its (intrinsic) worth, neglecting to refer it to its general principles, judge it by its analogies, and test it by the standard of wisdom, knowledge of the natures of things, and exact historical criticism. Thus they have gone astray from the truth and wandered in the desert of imagination and error. Especially is this the case in computing sums of money and numbers of troops, when such matters occur in their narratives; for here falsehood and exaggeration are to be expected, and one must always refer to general principles and submit to the rules (of probability). For example, Mas'údí and many other historians relate that Moses—On whom be peace!—numbered the armies of the Israelites in the wilderness, after he had reviewed all the men capable of bearing arms who were twenty years old or above that age, and that they amounted to 600,000 or more. Now, in making this statement he forgot to consider whether Egypt and Syria are large enough to support armies of that size, for it is a fact attested by well-known custom and familiar experience that every kingdom keeps for its defence only such a force as it can maintain and furnish with rations and pay. Moreover, it would be impossible for armies so huge to march against each other or fight, because the territory is too limited in extent to allow of it, and because, when drawn up in ranks, they would cover a space twice or three times as far as the eye can reach, if not more. How should these two hosts engage in battle, or one of them gain the victory, when neither wing knows anything of what is happening on the other? The present time bears witness to the truth of my observations: water is not so like to water as the future to the past.

The Persian Empire was much greater than the kingdom of the Israelites, as appears from the conquest of the latter by Nebuchadnezzar, who attacked their country, made himself master of their dominions, and laid waste Jerusalem, the chief seat of their religion and power, although he was only the governor of a Persian province: it is said that he was the satrap of the western frontiers. The Persians ruled over the two 'Iráks, Khurásán, Transoxania, and the lands opening on the Caspian Sea—an empire far more extensive than that of the Israelites; yet their armies never equalled or even approached the number mentioned above. Their army at Kádisíya, the greatest they ever mustered, was 120,000 strong, and each of these was accompanied by a retainer. Saif, by whom this is related, adds, that the whole force exceeded 200,000. According to 'Á'isha and Zuhrí, the troops under Rustam who were opposed to Sa'd at Kádisíya were only 60,000 strong, each man having a follower.

Again, if the Israelites had reached this total, vast would have been the extent of their kingdom and wide the range of their power. Provinces and

kingdoms are small or great in proportion to the numbers of their soldiery and population, as we shall explain in the chapter concerning empires in the First Book. Now, it is well-known that the territories of the Israelites did not extend, in Syria, beyond al-Urdunn and Palestine, and in the Hijáz, beyond the districts of Yathrib (Medina) and Khaibar.

Furthermore, according to the trustworthy authorities, there were only four fathers (generations) between Moses and Israel. Moses was the son of ʿImrán the son of Yas-hur the son of Káhat or Káhit the son of Láwí or Láwá the son of Jacob or Isráʾilu ʾllah (Israel of God). This is his genealogy as given in the Pentateuch. The length of time separating them is recorded by Masʿúdí, who says that when Israel entered Egypt and came to Joseph with his sons, the (twelve) Patriarchs and their children, seventy persons in all, they abode in Egypt under the dominion of the Pharaohs, the kings of the Copts, two hundred and twenty years until they went forth into the wilderness with Moses, on whom be peace. It is incredible that in the course of four generations their offspring should have multiplied so enormously.

2

That being so, the rule for distinguishing the true from the false in history is based on possibility or impossibility; that is to say, we must examine human society, by which I mean civilisation, and discriminate between the characteristics essential to it and inherent in its nature and those which are accidental and unimportant, recognising further those which cannot possibly belong to it. If we do that, we shall have a canon for separating historical fact and truth from error and falsehood by a method of proof that admits of no doubt; and then, if we hear an account of any of the things that happen in civilised society, we shall know how to distinguish what we judge to be worthy of acceptance from what we judge to be spurious, having in our hands an infallible criterion which enables historians to verify whatever they relate.

Such is the purpose of the First Book of the present work. And it would seem that this is an independent science. For it has a subject, namely, human civilisation and society; and problems, namely, to explain in succession the accidental features and essential characters of civilisation. This is the case with every science, the intellectual as well as those founded on authority.

The matter of the following discourse is novel, original, and instructive. I have discovered it by dint of deep thought and research. It appertains not to the science of oratory, which is only concerned with such language as will convince the

multitude and be useful for winning them over to an opinion or persuading them to reject the same. Nor, again, does it form part of the science of civil government, i.e. the proper regulation of a household or city in accordance with moral and philosophical laws, in order that the people may be led to live in a way that tends to preserve and perpetuate the species. These two sciences may resemble it, but its subject differs from theirs. It appears to be a new invention; and indeed I have not met with a discourse upon it by any one in the world. I do not know whether this is due to their neglect of the topic—and we need not think the worse of them for that—or whether, perhaps, they may have treated it exhaustively in books that have not come down to us. Amongst the races of mankind the sciences are many and the savants numerous, and the knowledge we have lost is greater in amount than all that has reached us. What has become of the sciences of the Persians, whose writings were destroyed by 'Umar (may God be well-pleased with him!) at the time of the conquest? Where are those of Chaldaea, Assyria, and Babylonia, with all that they produced and left behind them? Where are those of the Copts and of peoples yet more ancient? We have received the sciences of but one nation, the Greeks, and that only because Ma'mún took pains to have their books translated from the language in which they were composed. He was enabled to do this, by finding plenty of translators and expending large sums on the work. Of the sciences of other peoples we know nothing.

* * *

Now we shall set forth in this Book the various features of civilisation as they appear in human society: kingship, acquisition of wealth, the sciences, and the arts. We shall employ demonstrative methods to verify and elucidate the knowledge spread amongst all classes, to refute false opinions, and to remove uncertainties.

Man is distinguished from the other animals by attributes peculiar to himself. Amongst these are:

(1) The sciences and arts produced by the faculty of reflection, which distinguishes men from the animals and exalts him above the rest of created beings.

(2) The need for an authority to restrain and a government to coerce him. Of the animals he is the only one that cannot exist without this. As for what is said concerning bees and locusts, even if they have something of the sort, they have it by instinct, not from reflection and consideration.

(3) The labour and industry which supply him with diverse ways and means of obtaining a livelihood, inasmuch as God has made nourishment necessary to him for the maintenance of his life and has directed him to seek it and search after it. *"He gave unto all things their nature: then He directed."*

(4) Civilisation, i.e. settling down and dwelling together in a city or in tents for the sake of social intercourse and for the satisfaction of their needs, because men are naturally disposed to help each other to subsist, as we shall explain presently. This civilisation is either nomadic (*badawí*) or residential (*ḥaḍarí*). The former is found in steppes and mountains, among the pastoral tribes of the desert and the inhabitants of remote sands; the latter in towns, villages, cities, and cultivated tracts, whither men resort for safety and in order to be protected by walls. In all these circumstances it exhibits the phenomena characteristic of a social state. Accordingly, the matter of this Book must be comprised in six chapters:

(i) Human society in general, its various divisions, and the part of the earth which it occupies.

(ii) Nomadic civilisation, with an account of the wild tribes and peoples.

(iii) Dynasties, the Caliphate, kingship, and the high offices of government.

(iv) The settled civilisation of countries and cities. Crafts, means of livelihood, and the various ways of making money.

(v) The sciences, and how they are acquired and learned.

3

The tribes of the desert are kept off from each other by the authority of their chiefs and elders, whom they respect greatly. For the defence of their encampments against a foreign enemy, each tribe has a troop of warriors and knights famous for their prowess; but they would not make a firm resistance and defence unless they were united by kinship and a feeling of solidarity (*'aṣabíya*). That is what renders them so strong and formidable. *Esprit de corps* and devotion to one's kin is of supreme importance. The affection which God has put in the hearts of His servants towards those of their own flesh and blood is inherent in human nature: it leads them to help and succour one another and inspires their foes with terror. The Qur'an gives an example in the story of the brothers of Joseph (on whom be peace!), when they said to their father, *"If the wolf devour him, when we are banded together (for his protection), we shall be weaklings indeed,"* i.e., it is inconceivable that violence should be done to anyone so long as he has devoted partisans. In those who are not drawn together by the bonds

of kinship this feeling towards their comrades is seldom aroused; when dark war-clouds threaten disaster, every man will slip away in alarm to look after his own safety, because he fears to be forsaken by his allies. Such a people cannot live in the desert: they would fall an easy prey to any race that attacked them. Now, if this is clear with regard to those dwelling together, who must needs defend and protect themselves, similarly you will see that it holds good in the case of any enterprise that excites hostility, such as the mission of a prophet or the founding of a kingdom or the propaganda of a sect. An object of this kind is only attained by fighting for it, since opposition is natural to man; and in order to fight with success, there must be a feeling of solidarity as we said just now. Let this principle be your guide in perusing the observations which we are about to make. God aids us to arrive at the truth.

4

On the inability of the Arabs to establish an empire unless they are imbued with religion by a prophet or a saint, or generally inspired by religious enthusiasm.

The reason of this is that, being naturally wild, they are of all peoples the most reluctant to submit to one another owing to the rudeness of their manners, their arrogance, their high spirit, and their jealousy of authority. Seldom, therefore, are they unanimous. But when they follow a prophet or a saint, they are restrained by something within themselves; their pride and jealousy depart from them, submission and concord are no longer difficult. Religion brings them together: it takes away their rudeness and insolence, it removes envy and jealousy from their hearts. If there be among them the prophet or saint who urges them to fulfil the command of God, and requires that they shall abandon their evil ways and cleave to the good, and bids them be of one voice to make the truth prevail, they will become completely united and gain victory and empire. Moreover, no people is so quick to receive the truth and the right. Their natures are uncorrupted by vicious habits and free from base qualities; and as for their savagery, it is conformable and adaptable to good in consequence of its having preserved the original constitution of man (which renders him capable of accepting the true religion), and because it is remote from the bad habits and dispositions which stamp themselves on men's souls. For, according to the Apostolic Tradition already quoted, "Every one is born with a capacity for receiving the truth."

5

Showing that empires, like individuals, have their natural term of life.

You must know that physicians and astrologers declare the natural life of man
to be a hundred and twenty years of the kind which astrologers call "the great-
est years of the moon"; but it varies in every race according to the conjunc-
tions of the planets, so that sometimes it is more than this and sometimes less.
Those born under certain planetary conjunctions live a full century, others fifty
years or seventy or eighty; and stargazers believe that all this is indicated by the
position of the heavenly bodies. In the Moslem community, as is recorded in
Traditions of the Prophet, life runs to sixty or seventy years. The natural life, i.e.
120 years, is rarely exceeded: such cases as that of Noah (on whom be peace!),
and a few of the people of 'Ád and Thamúd, depend on extraordinary positions
in the celestial sphere. The lives of empires, too, vary according to the con-
junctions of the planets; but as a rule an empire does not last more than three
generations—reckoning a generation as the middle life of an individual, i.e. 40
years, a period which marks the end of the body's growth and development:
God has said, "*Until when he reaches his age of strength and attains unto forty
years...*" For this reason we said that the length of a generation is the (middle)
life of an individual. Our statement is confirmed by what we have already men-
tioned touching the Divine wisdom which decreed that the Israelites should
pass forty years in the wilderness, and the purpose thereof, namely, that the
generation then living might decease and another grow up, which had never
known the abasement (of slavery). That indicates that forty years, which is the
(middle) life of an individual, is the length of a generation.

An empire, as we remarked, seldom outlives three generations. The first
maintains its nomadic character, its rude and savage ways of life; inured to
hardships, brave, fierce, and sharing renown with each other, the tribesmen
preserve their solidarity in full vigour; their swords are kept sharp, their
attack is feared, and their neighbours vanquished. With the second gener-
ation comes a change. Possessing dominion and affluence, they turn from
nomadic to settled life, and from hardship to ease and plenty. The author-
ity, instead of being shared by all, is appropriated by one, while the rest, too
spiritless to make an effort to regain it, abandon the glory of ambition for the
shame of subjection. Their solidarity is weakened in some degree; yet one may
notice that notwithstanding the indignity to which they submit, they retain
much of what they have known and witnessed in the former generation—the
feelings of fierceness and pride, the desire for honour, and the resolution to

defend themselves and repulse their foes. These qualities they cannot lose entirely, though a part be gone. They hope to become again such men as their fathers were, or they fancy that the old virtues still survive amongst them.

In the third generation the wandering life and rough manners of the desert are forgotten, as though they had never been. At this stage men no longer take delight in glory and patriotism, since all have learned to bow under the might of a sovereign and are so addicted to luxurious pleasures that they have become a burden on the state; for they require protection like the women and young boys. Their national spirit is wholly extinguished; they have no stomach for resistance, defence, or attack. Nevertheless they impose on the people by their (military) appearance and uniform, their horsemanship, and the address with which they manœuvre. It is but a false show: they are in general greater cowards than the most helpless women, and will give way at the first assault. The monarch in those days must needs rely on the bravery of others, enroll many of the clients (freedmen), and recruit soldiers capable, to some extent, of guarding the empire, until God proclaims the hour of its destruction and it falls with everything that it upholds. Thus do empires age and decay in the course of three generations.

Translated by R. A. Nicholson[3]

A SIGN OF ROYAL AUTHORITY

A sign of (the qualification of an individual for) royal authority is his eager desire to acquire praiseworthy qualities, and vice versa.

The existence of group feeling without the practice of praiseworthy qualities would be a defect among people who possess a "house" and prestige. All the more so would it be a defect in men who are invested with royal authority, the greatest possible kind of glory and prestige. Furthermore, political and royal authority are (God's) guarantee to mankind and serve as a representation of God among men with respect to His laws. Now, divine laws affecting men are all for their good and envisage the interests (of men). This is attested by the religious law. Bad laws, on the other hand, all result from stupidity and from Satan, in opposition to the predestination and power of God. He makes both good and evil and predetermines them, for there is no maker except Him.

He who thus obtained group feeling guaranteeing power, and who is known to have good qualities appropriate for the execution of God's laws concerning

His creatures, is ready to act as (God's) subsitute and guarantor among man-
kind. He has the qualifications for that. This proof is more reliable and solid
than the first one.

It has thus become clear that good qualities attest the (potential) existence
of royal authority in a person who (in addition to his good qualities) pos-
sesses group feeling. Whenever we observe people who possess group feeling
and who have gained control over many lands and nations, we find in them an
eager desire for goodness and good qualities, such as generosity, the forgiveness
of error, tolerance toward the weak, hospitality toward guests, the support of
dependents, maintenance of the indigent, patience in adverse circumstances,
faithful fulfillment of obligations, liberality with money for the preservation
of honor, respect for the religious law and for the scholars who are learned in
it, observation of the things to be done or not to be done that (those scholars)
prescribe for them, thinking highly of (religious scholars), belief in and venera-
tion for men of religion and a desire to receive their prayers, great respect for
old men and teachers, acceptance of the truth in response to those who call to
it, fairness to and care for those who are too weak to take care of themselves,
humility toward the poor, attentitiveness to the complaints of supplicants,
fulfillment of the duties of the religious law and divine worship in all details,
avoidance of fraud, cunning, deceit, and of not fulfilling obligations, and simi-
lar things. Thus, we know that these are the qualities of leadership, which (per-
sons qualified for royal authority) have obtained and which have made them
deserving of being the leaders of the people under their control, or to be leaders
in general. It is something good that God has given them, corresponding to
their group feeling and superiority.

Translated by Franz Rosenthal[4]

The Romance of Antar

ANTAR GOES TO MECCA

At night, when all was still, Antar, mounted on Abjer, and accompanied by his brother Shiboob, departs for the Holy Shrine. As they travelled through the deserts, the hero's reflections found expression in these verses:

> If, O tear! thou canst not relieve me in my sorrow,
> perhaps thou mayst quench the flame that consumes me,
> O heart! if thou wilt not wait patiently for a meeting—
> die, then, the death of a woe-begone, wandering stranger!
> How long must I defy the evils of Fortune, and encounter
> the vicissitudes of night with the Indian blade?
> I serve a tribe, whose hearts are the reverse of
> what they exhibit in their fondness for me.
> I am, in the field, the prince of their tribe; but, the
> battle over, I am more despised than a slave.
> O that could annihilate this affection of a lover! how it
> humiliates me!—it agonizes my heart—it enfeebles my courage.
> But soon will I seek the Sacred Shrine, and complain of my
> ill-usage to the Judge against whose decrees there lies no appeal.
> I will renounce the days when my tears deceived me;
> and I will aid the widowed and plaintive dove.
> On thee, O daughter of Malik! be the peace of God!—
> the blessing of a sorrowing, heart-grieved lover !
> I will depart; but my soul is firm in its love for thee have
> pity, then; on the cauterised heart of one far away!
> Soon will my tribe remember me when the horse advance—
> every noble warrior trampling and stamping over them:
> Then, O daughter of Malik! will agony be plainly
> evident, when the coward gnaw his hands in death!

Their journey was marked with no particular incident until they drew near Mecca, when Shiboob observed to his brother that it was strange they had met with no adventure on the way. Antar replied that he was harassed with encountering danger; and his heart was disgusted at fighting and he quoted these verses:

Retire within yourself, and be familiar with solitude;
When you are alone, you are in the right road.
Wild beasts are tamed by gentle treatment;
But men are never to be induced to abandon their iniquity.

But presently they hear, in the calmness of the night, a female voice crying out, evidently in sore distress; upon which Antar slackens his bridle, and gallops in the direction whence proceeded the cries. He discovers a lady, who informs him that she is of the noble tribe of Kondeh; her husband, As-Hath, the son of Obad; that a famine having visited their land, they were proceeded, with their family, to the country of Harith, whence they intended to settle, having a daughter married there, when they were attacked by a horseman of the desert, called Sudam, the son of Salheb, with forty plundering Arabs, who had slain her three sons, wounded her husband, and taken herself and her three daughters captive; and that the brigands were about to convey them to the mountains of Toweila, there to sell them as slaves. Consigning the ladies to the care of his brother, Antar grasped his spear, and turned to meet Sudam and his followers, whom he now saw hastily advancing towards him. The hero is assailed by several of the brigands at once, but he cuts them down on either side, and at length encounters Sudam, and, striking him on the breast with his cleaving Dhami, the chief falls to the ground dead, weltering in his blood.

The three damsels and their mother crowd round their deliverer, kissing his hands and thanking him for having saved them from dishonour; and Antar, desiring the damsels to veil themselves, and having bound up the old sheikh's wounds, sat down to rest himself after the fatigues of his conflict. The old sheikh, grateful for the good service rendered his family by Antar, offers him his choice of his three daughters but Antar courteously declines the compliment, saying to the damsels:

Were my heart my own, I should desire nothing beyond you—
 it would covet nothing but you.
But it loves what tortures it; where no word, no deed encourages it.

Having escorted the old sheikh and his family to the land of Harith, Antar took leave of them, and, in company with Shiboob, proceeded to Mecca. "He alighted in the Sacred Valley, and there he resided; passing his days in hunting to relieve his sorrows and afflictions, and his nights with Shiboob, in talking over old stories and past events.

PRINCE SHAS IN CAPTIVITY

The friends of Antar were much troubled at his departure, and searched for him in all directions; but his uncle was especially gratified, since it left him free, as he thought, to dispose of Abla; and accordingly she is again betrothed to Amarah—the contract being formed by Abla's father and Amarah shaking hands. But Prince Malik, grieved at this great injustice to his absent friend, vows that he will never permit Amarah to marry Abla, while he lives to thwart his wicked plans, and those of the maiden's sordid and crafty father; and he predicts that evil will befall his brother Shas for his share in the infamous transaction.

When the Absians reached the lake of Zat-ul-irsad, Prince Shas with ten horsemen went into the desert in pursuit of the antelope. There they are met by a troop of warriors led by Maisoor, son of Zecad, of the clan of Hazrej, a branch of Harith, and the little band of Absians are all slain, with the exception of Shas, who is taken prisoner, and barbarously treated by Maisoor, whose brother the Prince had killed in the conflict.

Prince Malik and the others arrive in safety at the dwellings of their tribe, and the King is indignant when he learns how the noble Antar has been again deceived by Abla's father. He severely rebukes him for his scandalous conduct, and causes Amarrah to be scourged as a punishment for espousing Abla, when he knew that she was already betrothed to Antar, and that her father was in possession of the rich dowry which the hero had brought from Irak. The absence of Prince Shas causes the King great uneasiness. Having sent horsemen into the desert in quest of him without success, his affliction increases, and he declares that if Shas is slain, he will strike off the head of Amarah, and hang Malik, the son of Carad, because they had incited his son to act basely towards Antar.

In the meantime Shas is a prisoner in the land of Harith, and daily tortured by Maisoor, who "enclosed him between four bars of iron, and stationed a guard of slaves over him; and whenever he went out he kicked him, and whenever he entered he thumped him with his fists." The chief of the clan, however, hearing of this shameful treatment of a noble Arab, sends for Maisoor, and advises him to relax his severities towards his prisoner, which he does, in this manner: he hastens back to Shas and unties his hands, but binds his feet: then he kicks him in the rear and places a slave over him.

ANTAR SUMMONED FROM MECCA TO RESCUE SHAS

The unhappy Prince, however, finds a friend in need in the old lady of Kendeh, who, with her family, had been rescued from the brigand Sudam, by Antar, on his way to Mecca. Misfortune had taught Shas a salutary lesson, and he now bitterly repented of his conduct towards the noble hero: he assured the old lady that if ever he gained his freedom he would henceforth befriend Antar, and further his union with Abla. Perceiving the advantages which Antar would derive from the friendship of Shas, the good old lady despatches her husband, As-hath, to Mecca, to acquaint the hero of Shas' condition.

"With all haste he travelled the plains till he reached Mecca, where he inquired for Antar; and being directed to his residence he introduced himself, and told what had happened to Shas, and how he had left him in despair.—'May God never deliver him from peril or death!' cried Shiboob; 'for my brother has no such enemy among the Absians as he.'—'Brother,' said Antar, 'bear malice against no man;' and he repeated these verses:

> Do not bear malice, O Shiboob!—renounce it, for no good ever came of malice.
> Violence is infamous: its result is ever uncertain, and no one can act justly when actuated by hatred.
> Let my heart support every evil, and let my patience endure till I have subdued all my foes.

"When Antar had finished, the old man was amazed at such clemency towards his enemies, strong and powerful as he was. That night they reposed; but early next morning Antar said to As-hath, 'Let us depart, O Sheikh, before my lord Shas be reduced to the last extremity and be killed.' The sheikh and Antar were soon mounted, and Shiboob started in front of them, making the wild beasts and antelopes fly before him."

But before Antar can come to his deliverance, Maisoor has determined to hang Prince Shas without further delay, and the old lady of Kendeh therefore enables him to escape, in the disguise of a slave, directing him to take the road to Mecca. Having rested during the night in a mountain-cave, the Prince resumes his flight at daybreak, and meets with a party of the tribe of Riyan, one of whom mistakes him for a slave who lately stole his horse. He tells them that he is Shas, the son of Zoheir; but unfortunately his captors are enemies of his tribe; and they are about to put him to death, then they discover a man running towards them with the speed of the wind, and close behind him two horsemen.

These are Shiboob and the noble Antar and As-hath. The hero, with his sword Dhami, and Shiboob, with his arrows, soon make all the warriors to bite the dust, save one, who escapes on a swift camel.

Prince Shas expresses his contrition to Antar, and promises to make him ample amends for the past. Antar having presented to As-hath all the horses and plunder, the old sheikh takes leave, and departs for his own country; while the hero and Prince Shas begin their journey to the land of Hejaz, with the trusty Shiboob for their guide. On the fifth day they reached the waters of the tribe of Akhram, where they rested for the night. Antar had a delightful dream of his beloved Abla, and in the morning, when he awoke, he thus recited:—

THE dear image of Abla visited in sleep the victim of love, intoxicated with affliction.

I arose to complain of my sufferings from love, and the tears from my eyes bedewed the earth.

I kissed her teeth—I smelled the fragrance of musk and the purest ambergris.

I raised up her veil, and her countenance was brilliant, so that Night became unveiled.

She deigned to smile, and looked most lovely; and I saw in her eye the lustre of the full moon.

She is environed with swords and calamitous spears, and about her dwelling prowls the lion of the land.

O Abla! love for thee lives in my bones, with my blood; as long as life animates my frame, there will it flow.

O Shas! I am persecuted with a deadly passion, and the flame of the fire blazes still fiercer,

O Shas! were not the influence of love over-powering every resolution, thou wouldst not thus have subdued Antar!

Translated by Terrick Hamilton[5]

'ABLA'S TREASURE RESTORED

When it became known to Rabia that 'Abla had escaped from the net he had spread for her, his anger was dark as the desert is dark at the approach of a dust storm, dry and menacing and blown on the eastern wind. And Rabia vowed vengeance upon Bashara and plotted also to threaten the lord Zuhair himself with the enmity of King Numan. But at the Abs camp the rejoicing lasted many days, until finally Zuhair, in conference with his sons, Shas, Malik the Prince and Qais, summoned 'Antar and Sheddad to discuss with them the retrieval of 'Abla's jewels, which would in honour have to be restored to the tribe, And Rabia's name was muttered in contempt by many, but 'Antar said, in the nobility of his heart, "Nay, my brothers, he gave to temptation as many of us have done before now, and if he but admits his guilt we must not condemn him." And it was at this time that he wrought the famous poem which begins:

"There is a time for passion
There is a time for forgetting,
O my people, my heart leans towards mercy."

'Abla's father and her brother also approached the lord Zuhair about the jewels, and Zuhair sent Qais to negotiate privately with Rabia, hoping to hide from other tribes the disgrace which Rabia had brought upon them all.

Now Rabia was a witty and resourceful man, and when he was challenged by Qais over the question of the jewels he asked, "Why uncle, what have I to do with this? Ask my fair cousin if she can swear to seeing me either at the lakeside where you say she was abducted, or at the meeting place where last her jewels were seen. She is honesty itself, and I have no fear of her answer." But Bashara spoke up before Zuhair, saying, "My lord, there is confusion here. For although the two men who set upon me were muffled and spoke little, it happened that when the fair 'Abla was sheltering in my mother's tent disguised as a youth, and when I sought out Rabia and found him and Mufarraj, they had discarded their kefiyehs, and I showed them the bloodstained clothes 'Abla had been wearing, stained now with the blood of a sheep, and I could see the evil pleasure gleaming in Rabia's eyes, and indeed I shrank before it." And all believed him.

Then Rabia and his men left camp to avoid further trouble, but fighting nevertheless took place between him and those who supported 'Antar, and all was shame, chaos and animosity. But Zuhair finally resumed authority and he forced Qais to expel Rabia, and commanded that Shas expel 'Antar: but as can be imagined, 'Antar had already left in rage and anguish at the whole ignoble affray.

With him travelled Bashara, carried in a litter after injury in the combat, and Rabiat to care for him, and Sheddad, and 'Abla and her mother Sheriya, and many others, and they repaid Rabia for his trouble-making by capturing flocks belonging to the Zaiyad and Fazara people. Yet tempers cooled: and finally a conference was held at Rikaya. 'Antar decided to approach Numan on the matter of the jewels, and to harass those who had aided Rabia in 'Ablas capture. And Shiboob recommended the safety of the valley Raml, high in the mountain Radm, as a base for this venture. "For this is a country," said Shiboob, "in which we can find safe shelter and also a bountiful supply of fodder, and even of firewood, and game and birds of many kinds for our nourishment." And sure enough, after many days, they came upon the Great River, and far beyond it the wooded hill slopes of Iraq, and here they installed themselves in the Raml valley, burning a swathe of trees to render themselves safe from attack. And the fires burned for six days.

When all was secure, and the camp surrounded by a fair space to discourage reckless invaders, 'Antar travelled on with a hundred and fifty men to seek Mufarraj and the Shaban, leaving Sheddad with but a few men to guard the camp.

Thus was Abs divided by strife and distance, and worse was to come. For Mufarraj learned of the trick by which he had lost his treasure, and his hatred of Bashara and of the Abs almost choked him. He determined to enlist the support of Numan and to fight Zuhair. And war might have followed immediately had it not been that about this time, the lord Numan learned of the incomparable beauty of Mutajerida, daughter of Zuhair and Temadhur, and Numan desired her for his wife.

Numan was influenced by Mufarraj's anger, which was bitter as water from the Dead Sea, when he received news also of 'Abla's escape. And Numan addressed a letter to Zuhair, couched in haughty and undiplomatic terms:

Sire,

We are told by our friend Mufarraj that his property bas been filched from him by a trick, and that the perpetrator of this trick, the slave Bashara, is under your protection. We request that you therefore hand over the slave and restore the property of our friend; and it is our wish that the transfer be made by your own tribe's servant. 'Antar the Negro, who is said to have cooperated with the slave Bashara in robbing one who enjoys our protection.

Once this affair is settled, we would approach you, Sire, upon a happier

issue, for it is our desire to bind the ties between our two peoples through marriage with your daughter, Mutajerida, of whose beauty we have often heard.

When you have complied with our requests we will consider any demand you may make for a brideprice for your daughter.

Now the arrogance of this letter affronted the lord Zuhair, and he replied briefly that he had no daughter available for marriage, and that had he had one, he would not send her so far from home, nor did he know anything of the property of Numan's protégé, Mufarraj. He added that his noble nephew 'Antar was away from the camp, and he sent Numan's messenger home with nothing but a present of clothing to show for all the long journey and the arrogant demands.

And now the armies of the desert were on the move, for Zuhair advanced against Numan. Rabia enlisted his friend, Hadifa from the Farzara country and Dhalim ibn Harith of the Murra tribe, he who wielded the great sword of Dhu al Hayat, the Lord of Life, heirloom of Jaban ibn Himvar, ruler of the universe. Rabia intended supporting Nuan against both Zuhair and 'Antar and Mufarraj was ready to join him in the battles to come. And on Numan's side also was his valiant brother Aswad. But Numan's resolve was weakened by his desire to marry Mutajerida. And Zuhair's and 'Antar's forces were weakened by separation

So it was that Rabia and Mufarraj were enabled, with a band of men, to steal unperceived in to the sand Raml valley, where Sheddad guarded the camp. And when 'Antar and his men retuned one evening from a foray with Numan's scouts, they found only emptiness, and the sound of the warm wind blowing over the aromatic turf; and on the tallest tree the body of Bashara, the beautiful slave, was hanged. And already it had been half devoured by the wheeling vultures.

There was an evil about Bashara's passing which shocked them all. And they were aghast to find that 'Abla and all the women, together with Sheddad and his few fighting men, were gone. And afterwards the story was told—how Rabia and Mufarraj had surprised the camp, and had avenged themselves in the hanging of Bashara, and how a greater enemy, sent to the valley by Numan, had then come upon them. Ma'adi Kereb, friend, and supporter of the widowed Jaida whom 'Antar had wronged, and Jaida herself commanding a fine force. Rabia and Mufarraj had fled and escaped, but Sheddad and the Abs women were taken, and Jaida beat her captives soundly before heading east for Hira. And, indeed, troubles fell thick upon Abs, for the lord Zuhair, leading his

forces into battle against Numan's main army under Aswad, was captured with his fighting men and his old men, his women and children, and his servants, for he had had none to spare guarding camp and all were with him. So of all the Abs tribe, only 'Antar and a small force were free men.

And now, O my listeners, we hear of the Battle of the Pools of Akhrem. Aswad brought his great host, and his Abs prisoners, across the desert route, and he sent men before him on fast camels to bring water back to the main army, but Shiboob, with a few followers, slipped in among them by night and slit the waterskins. Then Aswad sent a second party of men, but these were now enfeebled by thirst, and 'Antar seized them and their arms and their camels and their waterskins, and 'Antar rode by a roundabout way to the rear of Aswad's army. And there he freed, and refreshed, and armed Zuhair and his men. Whereupon Aswad's men had to sue for peace if they were to obtain safety and water for survival. Ma'adi Kereb came to their aid indeed, but he and 'Antar settled the differences between them in single combat and they fought as knights should fight, and parted in friendship and respect, with honour satisfied.

It seemed now that power was balanced between Numan and the Abs, Numan held 'Abla and her jewels, and Sheriya and Sheddad and other noble men and women. Yet his desire for Mutajerida offset his triumph. Zuhair, with 'Antar's help, had defeated Numan's main army under Aswad—yet he longed in secret to wed his daughter to such a noble and powerful ally. But enmity still lay between the forces, for Numan was ignorant of Rabia's duplicity and his heart was bitter against 'Antar to whom his father, Mundhir, had shown such generosity over the flying camels. Yet he was a statesman, and he offered now to exchange his prisoners (despite Jaida's protests) for Aswad and his men-at-arms. And this was arranged. But so grim was 'Antar's wrath that, releasing the captives, be stripped them and sent them forth, bare foot, bare headed and naked, even cropping their hair. And, moreover, he gave them no sustenance for their journey to Hira.

Among these men was Dhalim of the Murra tribe, whose son, Harith, was to bring tragedy to all, and 'Antar might indeed have acted less savagely had he known the outcome of his deeds. But the One God in mercy and justice hides the future from our blind eves.

Numan's heralds reproached 'Antar for causing such shame, but 'Antar rebuked them even more strongly for the ignorance behind their enmity and for their constant abuse. And Shiboob, in furious indignation, produced an old wreck of a camel for Prince Aswad, who, as furiously, refused it. And so the humiliated prisoners reached Hira, and Numan feared that Chosroes would assuredly choose another than himself to subdue these fiery desert men.

Zuhair and his forces, with 'Abla safe, the jewels recovered and honour restored, could not yet return home since Numan's armies were still strong enough to bar the way. So he retired to the Valley of the Torrents. Then, gradually, tempers cooled, and only Aswad's shame and anger lay like a shadow between the opponents. Then Aswad captured Sheddad, and would have killed him in Numan's presence. Yet did the lord Numan hesitate, and he released Sheddad, and sent him with secret messages to Zuhair, and Zuhair summoned 'Antar, saying, "Here now, is a chance of a truce between our armies, and of peace strengthened by marriage, between two peoples." And 'Antar replied, "O my lord, Numan has released my father and subdued my price by his liberality. As for your daughter, she must surely marry, and could find no nobler match than King Numan, vice-regent to the Emperor Chosroes Nushirvan."

So it was settled, and the animosity between the two peoples dissipated with the realization of the true causes of their quarrels. Only Aswad could not face his conqueror 'Antar, and he departed to live among the Fazara, there marrying Miriam, sister of Hadifa, their leader. And there appeared to be peace between Fazara and Abs, but it was a hollow peace.

Then Zuhair at last agreed to the marriage of Numan with his daughter, Mutajerida, and he led his tribe back to their own grazing lands—eager, all of them, to celebrate the marriage of the noble warrior 'Antar to his fair cousin 'Abla. And among the tribes this year is known as the year of the two marriages.

Translated by Diana Richmond[6]

The Arabian Nights

THE TALE OF THE BIRDS AND BEASTS AND THE CARPENTER

QUOTH she. It hath reached me. O auspicious King, that in times of yore and in ages long gone before, a peacock abode with his wife on the seashore. Now the place was infested with lions and all manner wild beasts, withal it abounded in trees and streams. So, cock and hen were wont to roost by night upon one of the trees, being in fear of the beasts, and went forth by day questing food. And they ceased not thus to do till their fear increased on them and they searched for some place wherein to dwell other than their dwelling-place; and in the course of their search, behold, they happened on an island abounding in streams and trees. So they alighted there and ate of its fruits and drank of its waters. But whilst they were thus engaged, Lo! up came to them a duck in a state of extreme terror, and stayed not, faring forwards till she reached the tree whereon were perched the two peafowl, when she seemed reassured in mind.

The peacock doubted not but that she had some rare story; so he asked her of her case and the cause of her concern, whereto she answered. "I am sick for sorrow, and my horror of the son of Adam; so beware, and again I say beware of the son of Adam!" Rejoined the peacock, "Fear not now that thou hast won our protection:' Cried the duck, "Alhamdolillah! glory to God, who hath done away my cark and care by means of you being near! For indeed I come of friendship fain with you twain." And when she had ended her speech the peacock's wife came down to her and said. "Welcome and fair cheer! No harm shall hurt thee; how can son of Adam come to us and we in this isle which lieth a middlemost of the sea? From the land he cannot reach us, neither can he come against us from the water. So be of good cheer and tell us what hath betided thee from the child of Adam:" Answered the duck. "Know, then, O thou peahen, that of a truth I have dwelt all my life in this island safely and peacefully, nor have I seen any disquieting thing, till one night, as I was asleep, I sighted in my dream the semblance of a son of Adam, who talked with me and I with him. Then I heard a voice say to me, 'O thou duck, beware of the son of Adam and be not imposed on by his words nor by that he may suggest to thee; for he aboundeth in wiles and guiles; so beware with all wariness of his perfidy, for again I say, he is crafty and right cunning even as singeth of him the poet:

He'll offer sweetmeats with his edged tongue.
And fox thee with the foxy guile of fox

And know thou that the son of Adam circumventeth the fishes and draweth them forth of the seas; and he shooteth the birds with a pellet of clay, and trappeth the elephant with his craft. None is safe from his mischief and neither bird nor beast escapeth him; and on this wise have I told thee what I have heard concerning the son of Adam.'

"So I awoke, fearful and trembling, and from that hour to this my heart hath not known gladness, for dread of the son of Adam, lest he surprise me unawares by his wile or trap me in his snares. By the time the end of the day overtook me, my strength was grown weak and my spunk failed me; so, desiring to eat and drink, I went forth walking, troubled in spirit and with a heart ill at ease. Now when I reached yonder mountain I saw a tawny lion-whelp at the door of a cave; and sighting me he joyed in me with great joy, for my colour pleased him and my gracious shape; so he cried out to me, saying, 'Draw nigh unto me.' I went up to him and he asked me, 'What is thy name, and what is thy nature?' Answered I, 'My name is Duck, and I am of the bird-kind'; and I added, 'But thou, why tarriest thou in this place till this time?' Answered the whelp, 'My father hath for many a day warned me against the son of Adam, and it came to pass this night that I saw in my sleep the semblance of a son of Adam.' And he went on to tell me the like of that I have told you.

"When I heard these words. I said to him, 'O lion, I take asylum with thee, that thou mayest kill the son of Adam and be steadfast in resolve to his slaughter; verily I fear him for myself with extreme fear and to my fright affright is added for that thou also dreadest the son of Adam, albeit thou art Sultan of savage beasts.' Then I ceased not, O my sister, to bid the young lion beware of the son of Adam and urge him to slay him, till he rose of a sudden and at once from his stead and went out and he fared on, and I after him, and I noted him lashing flanks with tail. We advanced in the same order till we came to a place where the roads forked and saw a cloud of dust arise which, presently clearing away, discovered below it a runaway naked ass, now galloping and running at speed and now rolling in the dust, when the lion saw the ass, he cried out to him, and he came up to him in all humility. Then said the lion, 'Hark ye, crackbrain brute! What is thy kind and what be the cause of thy coming hither?' He replied. 'O son of the Sultan! I am by kind an ass—Asinus Caballus—and the cause of my coming to this place is that I am fleeing from the son of Adam.' Asked the lion-whelp, 'Dost thou fear then that he will kill thee?' Answered the ass, 'Not so, O son of the Sultan, but I dread lest he put a cheat on me and mount upon me; for he hath a thing called Pack-saddle, which he setteth on my back; also a thing called Girths, which he bindeth about my belly; and a thing called Crupper, which he putteth under my tail, and a thing called Bit, which

he placeth in my mouth; and he fashioneth me a goad and goadeth me with it and maketh me run more than my strength. If I stumble, he curseth me, and if I bray, he revileth me; and at last, when I grow old and can no longer run, he putteth on me a pannel of wood and delivereth me to the water-carriers, who load my back with water from the river in skins and other vessels, such as jars, and I cease not to wane in misery and abasement and fatigue till I die, when they cast me on the rubbish-heaps to the dogs. So what grief can surpass this grief, and what calamities can be greater than these calamities?'

"Now, when I heard, O peahen, the ass's words, my skin shuddered, and became as gooseflesh at the son of Adam; and I said to the lion-whelp, 'O my lord, the ass of a verity hath excuse and his words add terror to my terror.' Then quoth the young lion to the ass, 'Whither goest thou?' Quoth he, 'Before sunrise I espied the son of Adam afar off, and fled from him; and now I am minded to flee forth and run without ceasing for the greatness of my fear of him, so haply I may find me a place of shelter from the perfidious son of Adam.' Whilst the ass was thus discoursing with the lion-whelp, seeking the while to take leave of us and go away, behold, appeared to us another cloud of dust, whereat the ass brayed and cried out and looked hard and let fly a loud fart. After a while the dust lifted and discovered a black steed finely dight with a blaze on the forehead like a dirham round and bright, handsomely marked about the hoof with white and with firm strong legs pleasing to sight, and he neighed with affright. This horse ceased not running till he stood before the whelp, the son of the lion who, when he saw him, marvelled and made much of him and said, 'What is thy kind, O majestic wild beast, and wherefore fleest thou into this desert wide and vast?'

"He replied, 'O lord of wild beasts, I am a steed of the horse-kind, and the cause of my running is that I am fleeing from the son of Adam.' The lion-whelp wondered at the horse's speech and cried to him, 'Speak not such words, for it is shame to thee, seeing that thou art tall and stout. And how cometh it that thou fearest the son of Adam, thou, with thy bulk of body and thy swiftness of running, when I, for all my littleness of stature, am resolved to encounter the son of Adam and, rushing on him, eat his flesh, that I may allay the affright of this poor duck and make her dwell in peace in her own place? But now thou hast come here and thou hast wrung my heart with thy talk and turned me back from what I had resolved to do, seeing that for all thy bulk, the son of Adam hath mastered thee and hath feared neither thy height nor thy breadth; albeit, wert thou to kick him with one hoof thou wouldst kill him, nor could he prevail against thee, but thou wouldst make him drink the cup of death.'

"The horse laughed when he heard the whelp's words and replied, 'Far, far

is it from my power to overcome him, O Prince. Let not my length and my breadth nor yet my bulk delude thee with respect to the son of Adam; for that he, of the excess of his guile and his wiles, fashioneth me a thing called Hobble and applieth to my four legs a pair of ropes made of palm fibres bound with felt, and gibbeteth me by the head to a high peg, so that I being tied up remain standing and can neither sit nor lie down. And when he is mindeth to ride me, he bindeth on his feet a thing of iron called Stirrup and layeth on my back another thing called Saddle, which he fasteneth by two Girths passed under my armpits. Then he setteth in my mouth a thing of iron he calleth Bit, to which he tieth a thing of leather called Rein; and, when he sitteth in the saddle on my back, he taketh the rein in his hand and guideth me with it, goading my flanks the while with the shovel-stirrups till he maketh them bleed. So do not ask, O son of our Sultan, the hardships I endure from the son of Adam. And when I grow old and lean and can no longer run swiftly, he selleth me to the miller, who maketh me turn in the mill, and I cease not from turning night and day till I grow decrepit. Then he in turn vendeth me to the knacker, who cutteth my throat and flayeth off my hide and plucketh out my tail, which he selleth to the sieve-maker; and he melteth down my fat for tallow candles.'

"When the young lion heard the horse's words, his rage and vexation redoubled and he said, 'When didst thou leave the son of Adam?' Replied the horse, 'At mid-day, and he is upon my track.' Whilst the whelp was thus conversing with the horse, Lo! there rose a cloud of dust and, presently opening out, discovered below it a furious camel gurgling and pawing the earth with his feet and never ceasing so to do till he came up with us. Now, when the lion-whelp saw how big and buxom he was, he took him to be the son of Adam and was about to spring upon him when I said to him, 'O Prince, of a truth this is not the son of Adam; this be a camel, and he seemeth to be fleeing from the son of Adam.' As I was thus conversing, O my sister, with the lion-whelp, the camel came up and saluted him; whereupon he returned the greeting and said, 'What bringeth thee hither?'

"Replied he, 'I came here fleeing from the son of Adam.' Quoth the whelp, 'And thou, with thy huge frame and length and breadth, how cometh it that thou fearest the son of Adam, seeing that with one kick of thy foot thou wouldst kill him?' Quoth the camel, 'O son of the Sultan, know that the son of Adam hath subtleties and wiles, which none can withstand nor can any prevail against him, save only Death; for he putteth into my nostrils a twine of goat's hair he calleth Nose-ring, and over my head a thing he calleth Halter; then he delivereth me to the least of his little children, and the youngling draweth me along by the nose-ring, my size and strength notwithstanding. Then they load

me with the heaviest of burdens and go long journeys with me and put me to hard labour through the hours of the night and the day. When I grow old and stricken in years and disabled from working, my master keepeth me not with him, but selleth me to the knacker, who cutteth my throat and vendeth my hide to the tanners and my flesh to the cooks. So do not ask the hardships I suffer from the son of Adam.'

"'When didst thou leave the son of Adam?' asked the young lion; and he answered, 'At sundown, and I suppose that, coming to my place after my departure and not finding me there, he is now in search of me; wherefore let me go, O son of the Sultan, that I may flee into the woods and the wilds!' Said the whelp, 'Wait awhile, O camel, till thou see how I will tear him, and give thee to eat of his flesh, whilst I crunch his bones and drink his blood.' Replied the camel, 'O King's son, I fear for thee from the child of Adam, for he is wily and guileful.' And he began repeating these verses:

'When the tyrant enters the lieges' land
Naught remains for the lieges but quick remove!'

"Now, whilst the camel was speaking with the lion-whelp, behold, there rose a cloud of dust which, after a time, opened and showed an old man, scanty of stature and lean of limb; and he bore on his shoulder a basket of carpenter's tools and on his head a branch of a tree and eight planks. He led little children by the hand and came on at a trotting pace, never stopping till he drew near the whelp. When I saw him, O my sister, I fell down for excess of fear; but the young lion rose and walked forward to meet the carpenter, and when he came up to him the man smiled in his face and said to him, with a glib tongue and in courtly terms, 'O King who defendeth from harm and lord of the long arm, Allah prosper thine evening and thine endeavouring and increase thy valiancy and strengthen thee! Protect me from that which hath distressed me and with its mischief hath oppressed me, for I have found no helper save only thyself.' And the carpenter stood in his presence, weeping and wailing and complaining.

"When the whelp heard his sighing and his crying he said, 'I will succour thee from that thou fearest. Who hath done thee wrong, and what art thou, O wild beast, whose like in my life I never saw, nor ever espied one goodlier of form or more eloquent of tongue than thee? What is thy case?' Replied the man, 'O lord of wild beasts, as to myself, I am a carpenter; but as to who hath wronged me, verily he is a son of Adam, and by break of dawn after this coming night he will be with thee in this place.' When the lion-whelp heard these words of the carpenter, the light was changed to night before his sight and he

snorted and roared with ire and his eyes cast forth sparks of fire. Then he cried out, saying, 'By Allah, I will assuredly watch through this coming night till dawn, nor will I return to my father till I have won my will.' Then he turned to the carpenter and asked, 'Of a truth I see thou art short of step and I would not hurt thy feelings for that I am generous of heart; yet do I deem thee unable to keep pace with the wild beasts. Tell me, then, whither thou goest?' Answered the carpenter, 'Know that I am on my way to thy father's Wazir, the lynx; for when he heard that the son of Adam had set foot in this country he feared greatly for himself and sent one of the wild beasts on a message for me, to make him a house wherein he should dwell, that it might shelter him and fend off his enemy from him, so not one of the sons of Adam should come at him. Accordingly, I took up these planks and set forth to find him.'

"Now, when the young lion heard these words, he envied the lynx and said to the carpenter, 'By my life, there is no help for it but thou make me a house with these planks ere thou make one for Sir Lynx! When thou hast done my work, go to him and make him whatso he wisheth.' The carpenter replied, 'O lord of wild beasts, I cannot make thee aught till I have made the lynx what he desireth; then will I return to thy service and build thee a house as a fort to ward thee from thy foe.' Exclaimed the lion-whelp, 'By Allah, I will not let thee leave this place till thou build me a house of planks.' So saying, he made for the carpenter and sprang upon him, thinking to jest with him, and cuffed him with his paw, knocking the basket off his shoulder; and threw him down in a fainting fit, whereupon the young lion laughed at him and said, 'Woe to thee, O carpenter, of a truth thou art feeble and hast no force; so it is excusable in thee to fear the son of Adam.' Now, when the carpenter fell on his back, he waxed exceeding wroth; but he dissembled his wrath for fear of the whelp and sat up and smiled in his face, saying, 'Well, I will make for thee the house.'

"With this he took the planks he had brought and nailed together the house, which he made in the form of a chest after the measure of the young lion. And he left the door open, for he had cut in the box a large aperture, to which he made a stout cover, and bored many holes therein. Then he took out some newly wrought nails and a hammer and said to the young lion, 'Enter the house through this opening, that I may fit to thy measure.' Thereat the Whelp rejoiced and went up to the opening, but saw that it was strait; and the carpenter said to him, 'Enter and crouch down on thy legs and arms!' So the whelp did thus and entered the chest, but his tail remained outside. Then he would have drawn back and come out; but the carpenter said to him, 'Wait patiently a while till I see if there be room for thy tail with thee.' The young lion did as he was bid, when the carpenter twisted up his tail and, stuffing it into the chest,

whipped the lid on to the opening and nailed it down; whereat the whelp cried out and said, 'O carpenter, what is this narrow house thou hast made me? Let me out, sirrah!' But the carpenter answered, 'Far be it, far be it from thy thought! Repentance for past avails naught, and indeed of this place thou shalt not come out.' He then laughed and resumed, 'Verily thou art fallen into the trap and from thy duresse there is no escape, O vilest of wild beasts!' Rejoined the whelp, 'O my brother, what manner of words are these thou addressest to me?' The carpenter replied, 'Know, O dog of the desert! that thou hast fallen into that which thou fearedst. Fate hath upset thee, nor shall caution set thee up.'

"When the Whelp heard these words, O my sister, he knew that this was indeed the very son of Adam, against whom he had been warned by his sire in waking state and by the mysterious Voice in sleeping while; and I also was certified that this was indeed he without doubt; wherefore great fear of him for myself seized me and I withdrew a little apart from him and waited to see what he would do with the young lion. Then I saw, O my sister, the son of Adam dig a pit in that place hard by the chest which held the whelp and throwing the box into the hole, heap dry wood upon it and burn the young lion with fire. At this sight, O sister mine, my fear of the son of Adam redoubled and in my affright I have been these two days fleeing from him."

But when the peahen heard from the duck this story, she wondered with exceeding wonder and said to her, "O my sister, here thou art safe from the son of Adam, for we are in one of the islands of the sea whither there is no way for the son of Adam; so do thou take up thine abode with us till Allah make easy thy case and our case." Quoth the duck, "I fear lest some calamity come upon me by night, for no runaway can rid him of fate by flight." Rejoined the peahen, "Abide with us, and be like unto us"; and ceased not to persuade her, till she yielded, saying, "O my sister, thou knowest how weak is my resistance; but, verily, had I not seen thee here, I had not remained." Said the peahen, "That which is on our foreheads we must indeed fulfil, and when our doomed day draweth near, who shall deliver us? But not a soul departeth except it have accomplished its predestined livelihood and term."

Now, the while they talked thus, a cloud of dust appeared and approached them, at sight of which the duck shrieked aloud and ran down into the sea, crying out, "Beware! beware! though flight there is not from Fate and Lot!" After a while the dust opened out and discovered under it an antelope; whereat the duck and the peahen were reassured and the peacock's wife said to her companion, "O my sister, this thou seest and wouldst have me beware of is an antelope, and here he is, making for us. He will do us no hurt, for the antelope

feedeth upon the herbs of the earth and, even as thou art of the bird-kind, so is he of the beast-kind. Be therefore of good cheer and cease caretaking; for care-taking wasteth thy body." Hardly had the peahen done speaking, when the antelope came up to them, thinking to shelter him under the shade of the tree; and, sighting the peahen and the duck, saluted them and said, "I came to this island to-day and I have seen none richer in herbage nor pleasanter for habitation." Then he besought them for company and amity and, when they saw his friendly behaviour to them, they welcomed him and gladly accepted his offer. So they struck up a sincere friendship and sware thereto; and they slept in one place and they ate and drank together; nor did they cease dwelling in safety, eating and drinking their fill, till one day there came thither a ship which had strayed from her course in the sea.

She cast anchor near them and the crew came forth and dispersed about the island. They soon caught sight of the three friends, antelope, peahen and duck, and made for them; whereupon the peahen flew up into the tree and thence winged her way through air; and the antelope fled into the desert, but the duck abode paralysed by fear. So they chased her till they caught her and she cried out and said, "Caution availed me naught against Fate and Lot!"; and they bore her off to the ship. Now, when the peahen saw what had betided the duck, she removed from the island, saying, "I see that misfortunes lie in ambush for all. But for yonder ship, parting had not befallen between me and this duck, because she was one of the truest of friends." Then she flew off and rejoined the antelope, who saluted her and gave her joy of her safety and asked for the duck, to which she replied, "The enemy hath taken her and I loathe the sojourn of this island after her." Then she wept for the loss of the duck and began repeating:

> The day of parting cut my heart in twain:
> In twain may Allah cut the parting-day!

And she spake also this couplet:
> I pray some day that we re-union gain,
> So may I tell him Parting's ugly way.

The antelope sorrowed with great sorrow, but dissuaded the peahen from her resolve to remove from the island. So he abode there together with him, eating and drinking, in peace and safety, except that they ceased not to mourn for the loss of the duck; and the antelope said to the peahen, "O my sister, thou seest how the folk who came forth of the ship were the cause of our severance

from the duck and of her destruction; so do thou beware of them and guard thyself from them and from the wile of the son of Adam and his guile." But the peahen replied, "I am assured that nought caused her death save her neglecting to say Subhan' Allah, glory to God; indeed, I often said to her, 'Exclaim thou, Praised be Allah, and verily I fear for thee, because thou neglectest to laud the Almighty; for all things created by Allah glorify Him on this wise, and whoso neglecteth the formula of praise, him destruction waylays.'" When the antelope heard the peahen's words, he exclaimed, "Allah make fair thy face!" and betook himself to repeating the formula of praise, and ceased not therefrom a single hour. And it is said that his form of adoration was as follows: "Praise be to the Requiter of every good and evil thing, the Lord of Majesty and of Kings the King!"

Translated by Richard F. Burton[7]

THE STORY OF THE ENVIER AND THE ENVIED

Know, O my master, that there was a certain man who had a neighbour that envied him; and the more this person envied him, so much the more did God increase the prosperity of the former. Thus it continued a long time; but when the envied man found that his neighbour persisted in troubling him, he removed to a place where there was a deserted well; and there he built for himself an oratory, and occupied himself in the worship of God. Numerous fakeers assembled around him, and he acquired great esteem, people repairing to him from every quarter, placing full reliance upon his sanctity; and his fame reached the ears of his envious neighbour, who mounted his horse, and went to visit him; and when the envied man saw him, he saluted him, and paid him the utmost civility. The envier then said to him, I have come hither to inform thee of a matter in which thou wilt find advantage, and for which I shall obtain a recompense in heaven. The envied man replied, May God requite thee for me with every blessing. Then said the envier, Order the fakeers to retire to their cells, for the information that I am about to give thee I would have no one overhear; So he ordered them to enter their cells; and the envier said to him, Arise, and let us walk together, and converse; and they walked on until they came to the deserted well before mentioned, when the envier pushed the envied man into this well, without the knowledge of anybody, and went his way, imagining that he had killed him.

But this well was inhabited by Jinn, who received him unhurt, and seated

him upon a large stone; and when they had done this, one of them said to the others, Do ye know this man? They answered, We know him not.—This, said he, is the envied man who fled from him who envied him, and took up his abode in this quarter, in the neighbouring oratory, and who entertaineth us by his zikr and his readings; and when his envier heard of him, he came hither to him, and, devising a stratagem against him, threw him down here. His fame hath this night reached the Sultan of this city, who hath purposed to visit him to-morrow, on account of the affliction which hath befallen his daughter.— And what, said they, hath happened to his daughter? He answered, Madness; for Meymoon, the son of Demdem, hath become inflamed with love for her; and her cure is the easiest of things. They asked him, What is it?—and he answered, The black cat that is with him in the oratory hath at the end of her tail a white spot, of the size of a piece of silver; and from this white spot should be taken seven hairs, and with these the damsel should be fumigated, and the Marid would depart from over her head, and not return to her; so she would be instantly cured. And now it is our duty to take him out.

When the morning came, the fakeers saw the Sheykh rising out of the well; and he became magnified in their eyes. And when he entered the oratory, he took from the white spot at the end of the cat's tail seven hairs, and placed them in a portfolio by him; and at sunrise the King came to him, and when the Sheykh saw him, he said to him, O King, thou hast come to visit me in order that I may cure thy daughter. The King replied, Yes, O virtuous Sheykh.— Then, said the Sheykh, send some person to bring her hither; and I trust in God, whose name be exalted, that she may be instantly cured. And when the King had brought his daughter, the Sheykh beheld her bound, and, seating her, suspended a curtain over her, and took out the hairs, and fumigated her with them; whereupon the Marid cried out from over her head, and left her; and the damsel immediately recovered her reason, and, veiling her face, said to her father, What is this, and wherefore didst thou bring me to this place? He answered her, Thou hast nothing to fear;—and rejoiced greatly. He kissed the hand of the envied Sheykh, and said to the great men of his court who were with him, What shall be the recompense of this Sheykh for that which he hath done? They answered, His recompense should be that thou marry him to her.—Ye have spoken truly, said the King,—and he gave her in marriage to him, and thus the Sheykh became a connection of the King; and after some days the King died, and he was made King in his place.

And it happened one day that this envied King was riding with his troops, and he saw his envier approaching; and when this man came before him, he seated him upon a horse with high distinction and honour, and, taking him to

his palace, gave him a thousand pieces of gold, and a costly dress; after which he sent him back from the city, with attendants to escort him to his house, and reproached him for nothing.—Consider, then, O 'Efreet, the pardon of the envied to the envier, and his kindness to him, notwithstanding the injuries he had done him.

Translated by Edward William Lane[8]

MEN IN THE JUDGMENT OF THEIR WIVES

One day certain noble women of Yemen met at my house and agreed on oath to tell the whole truth concerning their husbands, without dissimulation whether for good or evil.

The first said: 'My husband, is it? An ugly and inaccessible man, as it were camel meat perched on a difficult mountain. And so dry with it all, that there is not a morsel of marrow to be found in him. A worn straw mat!'

The second said: 'Even to speak of mine is sickening to me. An intractable brute, he threatens divorce if I answer him one word; and, if I keep silence, he bustles me until I feel as if I were balanced on a naked lance point.'

Then said the third: 'Here is a description of my charming lord: if he eats he licks the bottoms of the plates, if he drinks he sucks out the last drop, if he stoops he squats like a parcel, if he kills for our food it is ever the dryest and leanest of the flock. Otherwise he is nothing; even his hand does not touch me to find out how I do.'

The fourth said: 'Be he far off from me! He is a heavy burden upon my eyes and upon my heart, both day and night. He is a storehouse of defects, extravagances, idiocies. He will give you a slap over the side of the head as soon as look at you, or prick and tear your belly, or rush at you, or slap and tear and rush at the same time. A dangerous animal, Allāh destroy him!'

But the fifth said: 'My man is both good and pleasant, like the fairest of the nights of Tihāmah; he is as generous as the rain, he is honoured and feared by all our warriors. He is a lion going forth in his magnificence. His heart burns for all men; the column of his name is high and glorious. He hoards his hunger even at feast times; he watches in the night of danger. He has built his house near the public square so that it shall be the first resort of every traveller. Oh, he is great and handsome! His skin is a soft rabbit silk, it tickles me deliciously. The perfume of his breath is the scent of the zarnab; yet, in spite of all these things, I do as I like with him.'

The sixth lady of Yemen smiled sweetly, as she said: 'My husband is Mālik Abū Zār, that Abū Zār whom the tribes love. He found me the child of a poor house, he led me to his tent of colours, and enriched my ears with rings of splendour; he put ornaments upon my breasts, and his love brought fatness to my wasted arms. He honoured me as his bride, he led me to a dwelling filled with the singing of lively songs and the shining of the lances of Samhar. Ever in my ears I hear the noises of horses, and of camels collected in great parks, the noise of milling and threshing, the noise of twenty flocks. With him I speak to my desire and he does not check me. When I lie down he does not leave me dry, and when I sleep he lets me sleep on. He has quickened my flanks with an excellent little son, so small that his bed seems a sliver of reed plucked from the mat, so behaved that the ration of a new-born kid suffices him, so delightful that, when he walks, balancing in his little coat of mail, he drags after him the hearts of all beholders. And the daughter which Abū Zār gave me! The delicacy, the jewel of our tribe! Her plumpness exquisitely fills her garment, she is bound in her small mantle like a tress of hair. Her belly is firm and straight, the line of her body is a pleasure under her coat, her thighs are rich and free, her little arms are rounded. She has a wide and open eye, a deep black eye with brows of gentle arch. Her nose is curved a little, the blade of a costly sabre. Fair and sincere is her mouth, beautiful and generous are her hands, her gaiety flashes in freedom. Her speech refreshes like a shadow at noonday, her breath is softer than silk, a soul-ensnaring musk. May Allāh keep them for my tenderness and joy, the daughter of Abū Zār, the son of Abū Zār, and Abū Zār!'

When the sixth had thus spoken, I thanked all my guests for the pleasure they had given me and then, taking up the discourse, said:

'My sisters, may Allāh the highest preserve the Prophet for our blessing! My mouth is not pure enough to sing his praise; I will content myself with repeating words of his concerning us, us women who are for the most part fuel for the fires of Hell. One day I begged him to give me counsel which should lead me into the path of righteousness, and he said to me:

"O Āishah of my heart, let the women of the Mussulmāns keep watch upon themselves, to have patience in adversity and to be not unmindful in the day of their fortune, to give many children to their husbands, to surround their husbands with honour and attention, and never to be ungrateful for the gifts of Allāh. For God shall drive out from His mercy the ungrateful woman. Also that woman who looks with an insolent regard upon her husband, saying to him or concerning him: 'An ugly face! A hideous body!' God will twist out one of her eyes on the Day of Judgment, He will lengthen and deform her body, He

will cause it to know an ignoble heaviness, to be a repulsive mass of flaccid flesh, dirtily lumped upon a rumpled, hanging base. Also the woman who opposes her husband in the marriage bed, or vexes him with bitter words, or profanes his mood, Allāh shall pull forth her tongue upon the last day into a foul and fleshy thong, sixty cubits in length, which shall wind its horrible, livid meat about her neck.

"But the virtuous woman, who never troubles the peace of her husband, who never stays from the house at night without permission, who despises dear-bought garment, and precious veils, who wears no costly circles about her arms and ankles, who does not angle for the glances of Believers, who is content with the natural beauty God has given her, whose words are soft, whose riches lie in works of charity, who eagerly foresees in all that concerns her husband, who has a tender love for her children, who keeps good counsel for her neighbour, and who is well disposed to each creature of Allāh—that woman, my dear Āishah, shall enter into Paradise with the prophets and the chosen of the Lord!'

Then I was moved to cry: 'O Prophet of Allāh, you are dearer to me than the blood of my father and mother!'

Translated by Powys Mathers[9]

ADVENTURE OF THE CALIPH HAROON AL-RUSHEED

YOUR majesty cannot but have experienced, that we are sometimes in such extraordinary transports of hilarity, that we communicate cheerfulness to those about us, or easily partake of theirs; and sometimes our depression of spirits is so great, that we are insupportable to ourselves, and are so incapable of giving any one reason for our ennui who should ask it, that we cannot account for it to ourselves.

The caliph was one day in one of these latter fits, when his faithful and favourite grand vizier Jaafer came to him. This minister finding him alone, which was seldom the case, and perceiving as he approached that he was in a very melancholy humour, and never lifted up his eyes, stopped till he should vouchsafe to look at him. At last the caliph turned his eyes towards him, but presently withdrew them again, and remained in the same posture motionless as before.

The grand vizier observing nothing in the caliph's eyes which regarded him personally, took the liberty to speak to him, and said, Commander of the

THE AGE OF DEPRESSION 273

faithful, will your majesty give me leave to ask whence proceeds this melancholy, of which you always seemed to me so little susceptible?

Indeed, vizier, answered the caliph, brightening up his countenance, I am very little subject to it, and had not perceived it but for you, but I will remain no longer in this hippish mood. If no new affair brought you hither, you will gratify me by inventing something to dispel it.

Commander of the faithful, replied the grand vizier, my duty obliged me to wait on you, and I take the liberty to remind your majesty, that this is the day which you have appointed to inform yourself of the good government of your capital and environs; and this occasion very opportunely presents itself to dispel those clouds which obscure your natural gaiety.

You do well to remind me, replied the caliph, for I had entirely forgotten it; go and change your dress, while I do the same.

They each put on the habit of a foreign merchant, and under that disguise went out by a private door of the palace-garden, which led into the country. After they had gone round part of the city to the banks of the Euphrates, at some distance from the walls, without having observed anything disorderly, they crossed the river in the first boat they met, and making a tour on the other side, crossed the bridge, which formed the communication betwixt the two parts of the town. At the foot of this bridge they met an old blind man, who asked alms of them; the caliph turned about, and put a piece of gold into his hand. The blind man instantly caught hold of his hand, and stopped him: Charitable person, said he, whoever you are, whom God hath inspired to bestow alms on me, do not refuse the favour I ask of you, to give me a box on the ear, for I deserve that, and a greater punishment. Having thus spoken, he let the caliph's hand go, that he might strike, but for fear he should pass on without doing it, held him fast by his clothes.

The caliph, surprised both at the words and action of the blind man, said, I cannot comply with your request. I will not lessen the merit of my charity, by treating you as you would have me. After these words, he endeavoured to get away from the blind man. The blind man, who expected this reluctance of his benefactor, exerted himself to detain him. Sir, said he, forgive my boldness and importunity; I desire you would either give me a box on the ear, or take your alms back again, for I cannot receive it but on that condition, without breaking a solemn oath, which I have sworn to God; and if you knew the reason, you would agree with me that the punishment is very slight.

The caliph, unwilling to be detained any longer, yielded to the importunity of the blind man, and gave him a very slight blow: whereupon he immediately let him go, thanked and blessed him. When the caliph and vizier had

got some small distance from the blind man, the caliph said to Jaaffer, This blind man must certainly have some very uncommon reasons, which make him behave himself in this manner to all who give him alms. I should be glad to know them; therefore return, tell him who I am, and bid him not fail to come to my palace about prayer-time in the afternoon of to-morrow, that I may have some conversation with him.

The grand vizier returned, bestowed his alms on the blind man, and after he had given him a box on the ear, told him the caliph's order, and then returned to the caliph. When they came into the town, they found in a square a great crowd of spectators, looking at a handsome well-shaped young man, who was mounted on a mare, which he drove and urged full speed round the place, spurring and whipping the poor creature so barbarously, that she was all over sweat and blood.

The caliph, amazed at the inhumanity of the rider, stopped to ask the people if they knew why he used the mare so ill; but could learn nothing, except that for some time past he had every day, at the same hour, treated her in the same manner. As they went along, the caliph bade the grand vizier take particular notice of the place, and not fail to order the young man to attend the next day at the hour appointed to the blind man. But before the caliph got to his palace, he observed in a street, which he had not passed through a long time before, an edifice newly build, which seemed to him to be the palace of some one of the great lords of the court. He asked the grand vizier if he knew to whom it belonged; who answered he did not know, but would inquire; and thereupon asked a neighbour, who told him that the house was that of one Khaujeh Hassan, surnamed Al Hubbaul, on account of his original trade of rope-making, which he had seen him work at himself, when poor; that without knowing how fortune had favoured him, he supposed he must have acquired great wealth, as he defrayed honourably and splendidly the expenses he had been at in building.

The grand vizier rejoined the caliph, and gave him a full account of what he had heard. I must see this fortunate rope-maker, said the caliph, therefore go and tell him to come to my palace at the same hour you have ordered the other two. Accordingly the vizier obeyed. The next day, after afternoon prayers, the caliph retired to his own apartment, when the grand vizier introduced the three persons we have been speaking of, and presented them to the caliph. They all three prostrated themselves before the throne, and when they rose up, the caliph asked the blind man his name, who answered, it was Baba Abdoollah.

Baba Abdoollah, replied the caliph, your manner of asking alms seemed so strange to me yesterday, that if it had not been for some private considerations

I should not have complied with your request, but should have prevented you from giving any more offence to the public. I ordered you to come hither, to know from yourself what could have induced you to make the indiscreet oath you told me of, that I may judge whether you have done well, and if I ought suffer you to continue a practice that appears to me to set so ill an example. Tell me freely how so extravagant a thought came into your head, and do not disguise anything from me, for I will absolutely know the truth.

Baba Abdoollah, intimidated by his reprimand, cast himself a second time at the foot of the caliph's throne, with his face to the ground, and when he rose up, said, Commander of the faithful, I most humbly ask your majesty's pardon for my presumption, in daring to have required, and almost forced you to do a thing which indeed appears so contrary to reason. I acknowledge my offence, but as I did not then know your majesty, I implore your clemency, and hope you will consider my ignorance. As to the extravagance of my action, I own it, and own also that it must seem strange to mankind; but in the eye of God it is a slight penance I have enjoined myself for an enormous crime of which I have been guilty, and for which, if all the people in the world were each to give me a box on the ear, it would not be sufficient atonement.

Translated by Jonathan Scott[10]

Part VII

AL-NAHDA – RENAISSANCE OF ARABIC LITERATURE

Abd al-Rahman al-Kawakibi

THE VIRTUES OF THE ARABS

Because the society [of Umm al-qura] is concerned only with the religious renaissance, it has found it necessary to pin its hopes on the Arabian Peninsula and its dependencies, and on its people and their neighbors, and to lay before the eyes of the Muslim nation the characteristics of the peninsula, of its people and of the Arabs in general, in order to eliminate political and racial fanaticism as well as to explain why the society has shown preference for the Arabs. We therefore say:

The peninsula is the place from which the light of Islam originated.

It contains the exalted Kaaba.

In it is found the Prophet's Mosque and the holy ground of his house, pulpit, and grave.

The peninsula is the most suitable center for religious policy, since it lies halfway between the Far East of Asia and the Far West of Africa.

Of all countries it is the most free of racial, religious, or sectarian inter-mixture.

It is the most removed of all Muslim countries from the vicinage of foreigners.

The peninsula is most worthy to be a land of free men, owing to its remoteness and natural poverty which preserve it from the greedy and the ambitious.

The Arabs of the peninsula have Islamic unity because religion appeared among them.

The habit of religion has become ingrained in them because religion is more compatible with their social customs than with those of others.

Of all Muslims they are the most knowledgeable in the principles of Islam as they are the oldest to practice it; many hadiths give witness to the strength of their faith.

The Arabs of the peninsula are the most zealous of all Muslims in preserving religion, in supporting it, and in glorying in it, especially as that zeal for the Prophet's cause is still alive among them in the Hijaz, in the Yemen, in Aman, in Hadramaut, in Iraq, and in Africa.

The religion of the peninsula Arabs is still governed by the right example of the ancients, free of excess and confusion.

Of all other Muslims, the peninsula Arabs possess the strongest *esprit de corps* and are the most proud because of the Bedouin characteristics which they possess.

The princes of the peninsula Arabs descend from noble fathers and mothers and are married to noble consorts of good birth; their honor remains untainted.

The peninsula Arabs are the most ancient of nations in having a polished civilization, as is shown by the proliferation and the excellence of their wisdom and their literature.

Of all Muslims, the peninsula Arabs are the best able to bear hardships in order to attain their aims, and to undertake travel and residence abroad, because they have not succumbed to the servile habits of luxury.

The peninsula Arabs preserve better than all other peoples their race and customs, for though they mingle with others they do not mix with them.

The peninsula Arabs are, of all the Muslim nations, the most jealous of their freedom and independence and those who most reject oppression.

Of the Arabs in general, their language, of all the languages of the Muslims, takes greatest care of knowledge; it is preserved from extinction by the noble Qur'an.

The language of the Arabs is the language common to all the Muslims, who number 300 million souls.

The language of the Arabs is the native language of 100 million people, Muslim and non-Muslim.

The Arabs are the oldest of nations in following the principles of equality in rights and in eschewing great disparities in society.

The Arabs are the oldest peoples to practice the principle of consultation in public matters.

The Arabs know best, of all people, the principles of socialist living.

The Arabs are amongst the most noble of people in respecting treaties, and the most human in keeping faith, and the most chivalrous in respecting the rights of vicinage, and the most generous in doing of good deeds.

The Arabs are of all nations the most suitable to be an authority in religion and an example to the Muslims; the other nations have followed their guidance at the start and will not refuse to follow them now.

Translated by Sylvia G. Haim[1]

Ahmad Shawqi

FROM ACT I OF *MAJNUN LAYLA*

Qays:

How still the night! It stirs within me yearning
And poetry. The desert is all night,
And love, and poetry. God, thou has filled
The heaven and earth with passion in this desert,
And I alone am laden with that passion.
Yearning has seized me for the tents of Layla;
I have no guide, no convoy but my passion
Suddenly swells like an unpleasing spring.
If she is far, it pities; when she is near,
Its yearning is rekindled. Ah, the pity,
The yearning of my heart! My people sent me,
Saying, Go seek a coal from Layla's people
Which they have kindled. God have mercy on her;
Layla has laid a burden on my heart,
A blazing fire; I cannot come to her.

Munazil:

What is this wraith approaching through the darkness?
I hear the hum of voices in the shadows.
It is Mulawwah's son: his leanness marks him
And faltering steps. He is my enemy,
Though between us and ours there be no stiffness
Desert and town alike recite his verse,
Mine none rehears: he loves and is loved by Layla,
Yet I am more deserving of that passion.
In all the land men honour him: he is mad,
But with a madness that augments the reason,
I make pretence to love him: but my heart
Rages with hidden hate. I envy him,
And know not which is more unfortunate
By reason of my envy. Who rides the night?
Is it my brother Qays?

Qays:

Well met Munazil!

Munazil:

Do I see Qays come to the shadow of tents?
The Qays I knew befriends the wilderness.

Qays:

Whence comest thou, Munazil?

Munazil:	From being with her,
	From her delightful and beloved assembly.
Qays:	Com'st thou from Layla with thy dragging skirts?
	'Fore God, thou liest!
Munazil:	Nay, I do speak truly.
Qays:	A shame upon thee! When didst thou speak truth?
	What was thy occupation?
Munazil:	As men wont:
	We made amusement. There is ever a throng
	At Layla's gathering: thou couldst not reckon
	The number of her tribesmen; and she gives
	Her favours as she wishes, or withholds them.
	(Qays springs at him)
Ziyad:	Munazil! Qays! Get thee back, Qays! Leave me
	To school this boy.
Munazil:	Wouldst thou school me, Ziyad,
	Thou madman's shadow, mouthpiece of a raver?
	Dost thou assert I am a match for Qays?
	My other ills suffice me: spare me this!
Ziyad:	Who ever said thou art a match for Qays?
	Then life's a jest. Come out with me, thou scoundrel.
	(Exeunt fighting)
Qays:	Layla!
	(al-Mahdi comes out of the tent)
al-Mahdi:	Who calls? Is't Qays? Why tarriest thou,
	When all have gone?
Qays:	I was at home, until
	Our fire was spent. There was no wood on the hearth;
	The winds have taken all, and guests, and neighbours.
al-Mahdi:	Layla! Wait, Qays. Layla!
Layla:	What ails my father?
(from the tent)	
al-Mahdi:	Thy cousin's here: they have no fire at home.
	(Layla appears at the tent door)
Layla:	My cousin Qays! We bid thee welcome, Qays!
Qays:	God give the life and all thy heart's desires!
Layla:	'Afra!
'Afra:	My mistress?
Layla:	Hither! We have dues

	To pay. Come fill a pot with wood for him.
	(*Exeunt*)
Qays:	Layla has granted me this casual need:
	Why grants she not my heart's needs? She has gone
	Seeking a coal for me, whose tents do blaze
	With fire! How many a simulated cause,
	Pretexts how numerous, and invented reasons,
	Bring me to Layla!
	(*Layla enters*)
Layla:	Qays!
Qays:	If only Layla
	Were at my side, my cup would be o'erflowing.
Layla:	Well are we met, and this fair hour that joins us
	Is worth the whole of life.
Qays:	Meanest thou this?
Layla:	My heart's not stone or iron. Thou hast a heart:
	Ask it, and it will tell thee. I have suffered
	In this my yearning more than heart can bear.
Qays:	My mind is all distraught: how shall I speak,
	How utter my complaint? Shall I set forth
	My passions tale complete, or tell it briefly?
Layla:	Nay, tell me this: why lovest thou the desert?
	Thou singest odes therein, whose fame has spread
	Beyond the desert's borders. Every deer
	That thou hast met is necklaced now with pearls:
	And does thy love for other antelopes
	Console thy loss of me?
Qays:	Art jealous, Layla,
	Of antelopes? They do not envy thee.
	How lovely is the desert, being peopled
	With forms of thee! Thy softness does surpass
	A woman's softness, as the desert moon
	Outshines all other moons.
	(*Layla see the flame of the torch almost at his sleeve*)
Layla:	What do I see?
	Qays!
Qays:	Layla?
Layla:	Have a care!
Qays:	How many a dawn breeze

	I have asked. Breath'st thou this morn? How many a

I have asked. Breath'st thou this morn? How many a
Trails me thy scented skirt [sic]: how many a deer,
Whose lids have robbed and shelter thy dark eyes!

Layla: Peril assails thee. Fling away the coal:
Its flame laps thy right wrist!

 (*Qays flings away the brand; then, angrily*)

Qays: And many a wolf,
That rolled its friendly tooth and claw in my hand,
Is tenderer, Layla, than thy jealous kinsfolk.

Layla: O Qays, thou didst not know thy hand was burning.

Qays: Thou kindles in my heart a fire of passion
Until it blazed in flame: and dost thou fear
A little coal, that flesh and hair consumes?

 (*He reels, and is about to faint*)

Layla: What ails thee. Qays? O, speak: say what assails thee!

Layla: Help, father, help! Qays has been burnt, he lies
Upon our threshold.

 (*Her father comes from the tent*)

Father, thou hast come:
Assist me, father. He is burnt, I shake him,
But he does not revive.

al-Mahdi: We are watched, Layla.

Layla: Think not of watchers: they see naught but us,
They will not guess our secret. None's more worthy
Than Qays thy love and pity. Ah, my breast
Cannot support him longer: take him, father,
And lean him on thy breast.

al-Mahdi: Now God preserve thee,
And give thee guerdon for thy patience, Layla.
For me, I fear the people; but for thee
I fear my heart. How I have screened thee, Layla,
An made excuses: yet I am not hard,
Nor covetous for thy dowry. O my son,
God guard thee from all ill, and bless thy days.
Thy poetry has brought me down to sorrow,
Yet I rehearse no poetry but thine:
'Tis like God's words, that charm the infidel
Past his desire. Qays!

 (*Qays tries to stand, and is supported by Layla*)

Qays:	Yes, uncle?
al-Mahdi:	Enough:
	Now get thee gone, and do not treat this threshold
	After tonight
Layla:	My father, do not wrong him!
al-Mahdi:	Shall I not wrong him, seeing he wronged his own?
Layla:	Seest thou not, father, he is like a branch
	Withered and wasted, pale as westering sun?
	Look at his hands and mantle; thou wilt find
	The fire is in them yet. Let him rest, father!
al-Mahdi:	Child, leave us: do not fan my kindled wrath
	Into a fiercer blaze.
Qays:	Layla, enough:
	Abase thyself no more. Conjure him not,
	Nor plead excuses. Sir, what is my sin?
Layla:	How did Qays sin?
al-Mahdi:	Hast thou forgot men's tales?
Qays:	Uncle, they lie.
al-Mahdi:	The thicket—was 't at night
	Thou camest to it, or by day? What chanced
	The night of the thicket, that thou hast composed
	Prelude and verses on it?
Qays:	Not alone
	We were: a company of lads and girls
	Had come together in the thicket meadows,
	Like evening talkers in a tribe's enclosure.
	We greeted, and then parted: she to the right,
	And I to the left.
al-Mahdi:	Get thee gone, Qays. Begone!
	Cover not Layla with this shame and scandal
	I know what tales will run upon this burning:
	Verses will publish it, and all the tribe
	Will see me clothed in new humiliation;
	Nay, the whole world will know it. Go, Qays, go.
Qays:	Uncle, be merciful to Qays and Layla:
	Be not a tyrant. Fear the wrath of God;
	Beware his anger, uncle.
al-Mahdi:	Get thee gone.
	Thou cam'st both seeking fire, and bearing it:

Tarriest thou till the whole house be lit?
(*Exit Qays*)

Translated by A. J. Arberry[2]

TO A LATE COMPOSER

Every day another reception and garlands of rhetoric over a tomb.
This man taught the nation nothing, planted no deserts with pylons.
We remnants are enriched, but his friends and family were impoverished
Slander arrested him in kennels of aphrodisiac and hashish

But beams make tears of what they play on. He filled ears and throat
With the turmoil of his presence first, then with his stiff quiet.
Unthought stresses of voice and instrument replaneted his firmament
Beyond the mason on the site he built for duration
Set for perpetuity more than the seedsman, explored properties
Rare in the luckiest tendril or the talented stone.

The sands were dry and ready for the fall.
An Alexandrian nightingale with sky-nest
Lighted on the shore from a dark flowering hill
He chose where only the kites circled in a cleft
An hour when the food-gatherers were away busy
He chose to struggle with the two horizons
And alert as a parrot he intercepted.
The surprise of the world's shouts and whispers.

A frenzy in the sands was fretting
For his harangues and elegiac speech.
For soliloquies on the reed
And sighs which through gaping notches
Achieve the slopes and parapets
In continents of the pure dead.

The house of earth was opened, down its corridors of art
Consolation was blown from the cool belts. And do not lament
For art. There is always nourishment streaming in the crevices of air,

The calendar's quickening restores the corpses, and the meteors
In the shafts of Karnak make bonfires among the pillars
And what washes through Egypt is tired and brilliant as wax.

The master, relaxed: the end of his blaze was disaster.
He quitted his disquiet, even the random and epilectic
Revelations, by which be committed more monuments to us
Than legions have left banners in this sand.
 Still in the lay kingdom chants a boy,
 Frail as bamboo, pink with tossing
The ball of twine that cradles space
He clings to the suburbs, restless, locking his hands
—And the premise of art is an alabaster blush.

Translated by Herbert Howarth and Ibrahim Shakrullah[3]

THE FEAST OF TIME

To God all religions belong—whomever
He wills, He guides,
Calling each single soul through the voice
Of Faith to His side,
The many Faiths that exist, no hostile
Feeling or strife
Ever must quicken to birth in those to
Whom he has given life.
All creeds and holy books, all messengers
From God's hand,
Are treasures beyond price to those who
Understand.
The essence of all true Faiths, are God's
Love and His fear,
The rock beneath His laws to all who serve
Him here.
In what those laws decree all goodness is
Enshrined,
Their interdicts ward off all evil for
Mankind.

Among their virtues, tolerance shines forth
With brightest gleam,
In holiness sublime, it crowns them all
Supreme.

Translated by Suheil Bushrui[4]

AN ANDALUSIAN EXILE

O bird crying on the acacia tree, alike are our sorrows
Should I grieve for your troubles or lament my own?
What tale have you to tell me?—only that the self-same hand
That laid my heart has pinioned your wing.
Exile has cast us both, fellow strangers,
In a grove not our own, where our kind never meet
Parting has struck us—you with a knife, me with a barbed arrow.
Roused by long, neither of us can move,
Our broken wings too weak to answer our will.
Child of the valley, nature has set us apart,
And yet affliction has brought us together.
You have not forsaken your drink for unquenched longing,
Sad memory, or countless similar sorrows,
Dragging your feet on the boughs, and your tail behind you,
You go in search of one who might heal you.
There are many to heal the body if we but seek them,
But where, O where the skillful healer of the soul?

Translated by M. Mustafa Badawi and John Heath-Stubbs[5]

Hafiz Ibrahim

ELEGY TO MUSTAFA KAMIL

Oh martyr of high purpose,
 That voice of yours is sounding
Unchanged, today just as it
 Was yesterday resounding.
It shouts out, saying "This is
 A building I erected:
Consign not to destruction
 This same thing I erected."
It cries "Let not the people
 Feel I am gone for ever,
And that those who survive me
 Are quit of all endeavour."
It orders us: "In God's name,
 Be ye not disunited:
Behave like men, and make not
 Your enemies delighted.

My spirit, from this high place,
 Looks down on you, surveying
Your actions for me, though I
 Am here below decaying.
Sadden it not: my fear is,
 Through promises forsaken,
By manifold misfortunes
 You may be overtaken."
Yes! You who for our welfare
 The path of good presented,
Our whole life long, we're ready;
 So you may sleep contented.
Your building still is standing,
 Your spirit still beside us;
Your voice we still are hearing,
 Though distance may divide us.
We never saw you weeping,

You hated it when others
In neighbouring lands were weeping,
 Among our suffering brothers.
Allow us one day's weeping!
 Then you will find us ready,
At dawn, as you would have us,
 Like mountains, firm and steady.
Oh River Nile! If you should
 Not flow, after his going,
Blood-red, I swear you will not,
 Oh Nile, be truly flowing.

Oh grave! This guest you welcome
 Gave hopes to a whole nation.
So praise God, and receive him,
 Respectful, in prostration.
Our honour 'tis Mustafa
 To see within you shaded,
A martyr to high purpose,
 In manhood's flower fast faded.
If we had lost him only,
 Were he the sole departed,
Then could we find some solace
 From sorrow brokenhearted.
We lost not but him only;
 We lost all else beside him!
Oh would that fate could send him
 A second life provide him!
Oh you who ask where honour
 And manliness appear now?
Where wisdom, and sound judgement?
 Alas! You see them here now.
How lucky for the English!
 No more let them be frightened
Of any shouter, now that
 The loudest shout is quietened!
Now he is dead—that man who
 Revived in men their feeling;
Leading them on to glory,

Their shattered spirits healing.
I praised you in your life-time,
How weak my eulogizing!
Now you are dead, how strongly
I speak in elegizing!
For you we sorrow—therefore,
In sorrow unifying,
For you we weep—or wherefore
Is this whole nation crying?
Curer of human minds, he
Himself could not recover
From human ills within him
No cure could he discover.
You were alive and watchful,
While we were soundly sleeping:
You, when grief dulled our senses,
Were still your vigil keeping.

Egypt, if you his mem'ry
Fail to keep fresh within you
Until the Day of Judgement,
Your weakness will continue.
Egyptians, if you know not
The man we are regretting,
Know that the Star of Fortune
Has sunk unto its setting.
Thirty odd years your life-span,
Like thirty pearls all gleaming,
Strung on night's necklace, brightly
Across the heavens streaming.
Their story will report you
Were no mere stripling, lacking
Companions to support you,
But a whole host, attacking!

Translated by John A. Haywood[6]

Khalil Mutran

THE ARAB AWAKENING

O noble company of Arabs! ye
My pride and boast, o'er every company,
Long have I hid your carelessness and sloth,
Yet not as one that might despise, or loathe,
But candidly, as if to wake a friend
Unconscious of vast perils that impend.
Long nights of intercession, and of pleas,
Your slumber kept me wakeful with unease,
Till I would cry, "Had ever nation kept
Its bed such centuries, as ye have slept?
Do ye not know, 'tis loss for those that drowse
Till noon, the spoils to them who early rouse?
Already ye outsleep, in countryside
As in built town, all men that ever died!
Ye are a folk whose chronicles abound
With noble deeds, since valour was renowned,
Yea, from when Qahtan found a hero's grave
Even to Shaiban's Qais, and Antar brave,
To that Quraishite orphan, who was lord
Of wisdom marvellous, and mighty sword,
Vessel of God's revealing, battling down
Kisra, and spoiling Caesar of his crown;
And then that hero of the Arab host,
His wisdom mightiest his experience most,
And next the incomparable ruler, he
Who spread the bounds in peerless equity;
And Affan's glorious son, who as he read
The scriptures, o'er the script his blood was shed;
And Ali, his bright sword to battle bared,
His voice from pulpit rapturously heard;
Those flashing stars innumerable that be,
Great generals, and dauntless soldiery;
Wise governors, that with accomplished skill
Revolved the world's affairs upon their will;

Scholars profound, who shed true learning's light
On human hearts, to guide mankind aright."

All this I whispered in my people's ear,
Softly persuasive, or cried loud and clear;
And all the while reverted, with the grief
Of one who would, but cannot, bring relief,
Unslumbering, yet through the nighttime drear
My faith and hope still gave my spirit cheer,
Like the pole-star immovable, a light
That lit my thoughts, and shone upon my sight.
In vain I hid; until the terror struck,
A ghost of malice, dusty locks that shook
Upon the wind, in armour helmeted
And terribly arrayed, with treacherous tread,
Able to soar in air, to march, to ride,
To see in murk, to traverse ocean wide.
"Now is the hour of peril come!" I said,
"That shall awake them! O my soul, be glad!
Danger's the thing to stir a frozen soul,
A people's screwed-up virtue to unroll!"

Translated by A. J. Arberry[7]

Ma'ruf al-Rusafi

FAIREST

Thou charmedst angels, ere that man was made,
 The sun desired thee, while the moon yet slept,
Ere sight descried, the ear in thee was glad,
 The poem sang thee, ere the strings were swept:
Maiden so lovely, and so nobly staid!

The soul of love flutters to view thy face,
 The argent moon yearns to behold thee rise
To rise like thee with more majestic grace.

The breeze of dawn watches with wondering eyes
To breathe as softly as thy whispering pace.

The wine of coquetry (O sweet delight!)
 Swayeth thee lissom in thy symmetry;
Beauty in thee ascends the throne of might,
 And orders with imperious majesty
Our minds, that in his chains are fettered tight.

Whene'er thy beauty is to eye displayed.
 love seeketh quarter, and in reverence bows;
Before this light the lights of heaven fade,
 Proud Time surrenders to thy gleaming brows,
Yea, Fate itself submits to thee, fair maid!

Translated by A. J. Arberry[8]

Ilya Abu Madi

ENVOI

Dear companion! But for thee
Never flowed my melody;
Whensoe'er I sang, apart,
Thou wast dwelling in my heart.
Gardens put on brave array
To be gathered in, one day;
Let thy spirit's ear attend
To my spirit's echoes, friend;
Keep what beauty soundeth there,
And reject what is not fair—
Art may be in listening,
As it taketh art to sing—
And thou'lt prove a fecund field,
Seeded little, much to yield.
Quickened by the wind's caress,
Clouds o'erbrim with fruitfulness;

So through thee such wealth I won
Is to greater riches grown.
What denotes the uttered word,
If by ear it not be heard?
Dawn hath brighter radiancy
When thou watchest it with me;
If thou walkest in my vine,
Greater yield, and peace, are mine.
Lo, I pour thee all the cup;
Drink it freely, drink it up,
And let others quaff thereof—
Fear not to offend my love;
As thou emptiest my bowl,
Sooner is it freshly whole;
To survive is more to give,
As, withheld, it cannot live.

LIFE AND LOVE

God willed that we should lovers be
When loveliness created He;
The love He fashioned in thy heart
This same to mine He did impart.
Such was His will, as we confess:
His will cannot be purposeless;
What sin is then to disapprove,
If thou or I should chance to love?

Let the censorious have his say,
The spiteful lie, as lie he may:
What, shall the rivulet flow free,
The flower bloom in fragrancy,
Shall birds be ardent for the Spring
And April's feast of blossoming,
And is the heart forbidden yet
To love, and to be passionate?
Come hither, then! Love's diety
Invites thee to the wood, and me,

That he may pour us, soul to soul,
Like wine and spices in a bowl.
There in the wood the light divine
Shall be thy raiment, love, and mine:
What, wilt thou hearken what men say,
And men's Creator disobey?

Love wills, that we with laughter gay
Should greet the laughing dawn of day;
Come, let us laugh, and lightly leap
With leaping brook, and river deep;
Come, let us sing, as biddeth love,
With nightingale and turtle-dove;
Who knoweth, when this day is o'er,
What dark adventures lie before?

Come hither, ere the blackbirds hush
Their golden song in golden bush,
Ere myrtle and narcissus fade,
And willow be in ruin laid,
Come, love, before the storms descend
And all my dreams are at an end,
No dawn to greet, no wine to take,
No bowl to pass, when we awake.

Translated by A. J. Arberry[9]

THE PHOENIX

I am not the first one infatuated with the glorious maiden, for she is the
 Dream of all mankind.
I searched for her in the folds of dawn and darkness, I stretched my
 Hands out even to the stars.

I was told, "Be pious, for she evades all but the pious ascetic."
So I buried my joys, divorced my desires, and silenced all signs of passion
 In my heart.

I smashed my flask before I was quenched, and refrained from eating
 When I was still hungry.
I thought I was approaching her speedily, but found that I had
 Approached only my ruin.
Like a garden denying itself its wealth of flora
To feel the sunlight in its soil and meet the breeze unmasked,
Only to find autumn creeping on it like night pitching a tent over a waste-
 Land;
I was like a bird that stripped itself of its shiny plumage
To become lighter, only to fall to the ground and be attacked by ants.
I lay me down to sleep hoping she was the daughter of dreams; but I
 Woke up mocking those who slept
For the world of slumber was not all joy, fearful things abounded in it.
When I dreamt of her I dreamt of a flower that could not be plucked, and
 A star that did not rise
On waking I saw nothing around me but my error, my bed, and my
 Room,
For he who drinks of the rivers of his fancy travels life with an insatiable
 Thirst.

Spring passed and she was not in the singing river or the fertile garden.
Winter came and she was not in its weeping clouds or crying thunder.
I glimpsed the flash of lightning and thought she was in it, but she was
 Not there.
Empty-handed, led astray by youth and conniving,
I felt my hopes to find her were dashed, my sturdy moorings cut off.
Sorrow pressed upon my soul, and it tearfully flowed. It was then that I
 Caught a glimpse of her and perceived her in my tears.
I learned, when learning was late, that she whom I had lost was always
 Here with me.

Translated by Issa Boullata and Naomi Shihab Nyei[10]

Gibran Kahlil Gibran

THE POET

A link between this world and the next; a sweet fountain from which all thirsty souls drink; a tree planted on the river bank of beauty covered with ripened fruits desired by hungry hearts; a nightingale flitting among branches of words and singing melodies that fill the heart with gentleness and peace; a white cloud appearing in the twilight and rising and growing and filling the face of heaven and then pouring rain upon the flowers in the field of life; an angel sent by the gods to teach men divine knowledge; a bright lamp that no darkness can overcome, nor any bushel hide, filled with oil by Astarte, the goddess of love, and lit by Apollo, the god of music.

Clad in simplicity and fed upon gentility, he sits alone in nature's lap to learn the miracle of creation and remains awake in the stillness of the night awaiting the descent of the spirit. He is the husbandman sowing the seeds of his heart in the fields of [feelings] so that mankind may feed upon the plentiful yield. This is the poet whom men ignore in this life and only recognize when he forsakes this world for his sublime abode. It is he who asks naught of men but a mere smile and whose breath rises and fills the horizon with beautiful living images; yet he is refused both bread and refuge by his fellow-men.

How long, O man, how long, O universe, will you erect mansions in honour of those who cover the face of the earth with blood, and ignore those who give you peace and joy and the beauty of themselves? How long will you glorify murderers and tyrants who have bent necks with the yoke of slavery, and forget the men who spend the light of their eyes in the darkness of the night to teach you the glory of daylight, those that spend their life a prey to misery so that no pleasure may pass you by? And you, O poets, who are the very essence of life, you have conquered the ages despite the cruelty of the ages; and you have won the laurels of glory plucked out from the thorns of vanity; you have built your kingdom in the hearts, and your kingdom has no end.

Translated by S. B. Bushrui[11]

FROM A SPEECH BY KHALIL THE HERETIC

From the depths of these depths
We call you, O Liberty—hear us!
From the corners of this darkness
We raise our hands in supplication—turn your gaze towards us!
On the expanse of these snows
We lay ourselves prostrate before you, have compassion upon us!

We stand now before your terrible throne
Wearing the blood-smeared garments of our fathers;
Covering our heads with the dust of the tombs mingled with their remains;
Drawing the swords which have been sheathed in their entrails;
Raising the spears that have pierced their breasts;
Dragging the chains that have withered their feet;
Crying aloud cries that have wounded their throats,
And lamentations that have filled the darkness of their prisons;
Praying prayers that have sprung out of the pain of their hearts—
Listen, O Liberty, and hear us!

From the sources of the Nile to the estuary of the Euphrates
The wailing of souls surging with the scream of the abyss rises;
From the frontiers of the peninsula to the mountains of Lebanon
Hands are outstretched to you, trembling in the agony of death;

From the coast of the gulf to the ends of the desert
Eyes are uplifted to you with pining hearts
Turn, O Liberty, and look upon us.

In the corners of huts standing in the shadow of poverty and humiliation,
Breasts are being beaten before you;
In the emptiness of houses erected in the darkness of ignorance and folly,
Hearts are cast before you;
And in the corners of houses buried in the clouds of oppression and tyranny,
 Spirits are longing for you—
Look upon us, O Liberty, and have compassion.

In schools and offices
Despairing youth calls upon you;

In the churches and mosques
The forsaken book invites you;
In the councils and courts
The neglected law implores you—
Have pity, O Liberty, and save us.

In our narrow streets
The merchant barters his days only to pay the thieves from the West,
And none is there to advise him!
In our barren fields
The peasant ploughs the earth with his finger-nails,
And sows the seeds of his heart and waters them with his tears,
And nothing does he harvest save thorns and thistles,
And none is there to teach him!
In our empty plains
The Bedouin walks bare-foot, naked and hungry
And none is there to have mercy upon him—
Speak, O Liberty, and teach us...

From the very beginning the darkness of the night has descended upon our
 souls How long until the dawn?
From prison to prison our bodies move, and the mocking ages pass us by—
How long are we to bear the mockery of the ages?
From yoke to heavier yoke our necks do pass
And the nations of the earth look at us and laugh—
How long shall we endure the mockery of nations?
From fetters to fetters our path leads us
And neither do the fetters disappear nor do we perish—
How long shall we remain alive?...

From the grasp of Pharaoh
To the claws of Nebuchadnezzar;
To the nails of Alexander;
To the swords of Herod;
To the claws of Nero;
To the fangs of the devil;
Whose yoke is going to enslave us now?
And when shall we fall within the grasp of death to find comfort away from
 the silence of nonexistence?

With the strength of our arms they erected the pillars of their temples and
 shrines to glorify their gods;
On our backs they brought clay and stones to build castles to strengthen their
 strongholds;
And with the power of our bodies they built pyramids to render their names
 immortal;
How long are we to build castles and palaces
And live but in huts and caves?
How long are we to fill granaries and stores
And eat nothing but garlic and clover?
How long are we to weave silk and wool
And be clad in tattered cloth?
Through their cunning and treachery they have set clan against clan;
Have separated group from group;
Have sown the seeds of hate twixt tribe and tribe—
How long are we then to wither like ashes before this cruel hurricane,
And fight like hungry young lions near this stinking carcass?

In order to secure their power and to rest at heart's ease they have armed the
 Durzi to fight the Arab;
Have instigated the Shi'i against the Sunni;
Have incited the Kurd to slaughter the Bedouin;
Have encouraged the Mohammadan to fight the Christian—
How long is a brother to fight his brother on the breast of the mother?
How long is a neighbour to threaten his neighbour near the tomb of the
 beloved?
How long are the Cross and the Crescent to remain apart before the eyes of
 God?

Listen, O Liberty, and harken unto us
Turn your gaze towards us, O mother of the earth's inhabitants,
For we are not the offspring of your rival;
Speak with the tongue of any one of us
For from one spark the dry straw catches fire;
Awaken with the sound of your wings the spirit of one of our men
For from one cloud one lightning flash illuminates valley-lanes and mountain-
 tops.
Disperse with your resolve these dark clouds;
Descend as a thunderbolt,

Destroy like a catapult
The props of those thrones erected on bones and skulls,
Plated with the gold of taxes and bribery
And soaked in blood and tears.
Listen to us, O liberty
Have compassion on us, O Daughter of Athens,
Rescue us, O Sister of Rome,
Save us, O Companion of Moses,
Come to our aid, O beloved of Mohammad,
Teach us, O bride of Jesus,
Strengthen our hearts that we may live;
Or strengthen the arms of our enemies against us
That we may wither, perish and find peace.

Translated by S. B. Bushrui[12]

Ameen Rihani

LIGHT

Light! Light! Let it shine in our hearts, however dark the world
 may be.
Let it flow forth from our hearts, however sombre the horizons
 may be.
Though I have only a hut in the valley, lit in the night by a
 meagre candle,
my eye reflects in the hut all the light it beholds in the world.
And should the storm blow and uproot my hut as it uproots the
 trees,
carrying it to the river's mouth,
there is a cave there among the rocks impregnable to the storm,
 and there
is the light of the sun and the stars.
And should the heavens darken and the planets and stars be
 eclipsed,
still in this human heart is light eternal.
Let light shine in our hearts, however sombre the horizons may be.

Translated by Mounah A. Khouri and Hamid Algar[13]

SUPPLICATION: A PRAYER

O Immortal Majesty! Bestow upon me a portion of Thy glory!
O Eternal Light! Assist me with a shaft of Thy refulgence!
O Illimitable Potency! Imbue me with a measure of Thy might!

I am the Source of immortal Life,
The Fountain-head of Love and Power;
I am alive in thee, attentive unto thy supplications.

Thou art the whole of life,
Both in the beginning and in the end,
And I, truly, find my life in Thee.

I am the Source of human understanding,
And I shall increase thine understanding
That thou art a part of Me.

O God! Assist me to devote my powers,
Whether spiritual, intellectual or physical,
In the pathway of Truth, of Love, and of Wisdom.

O son of man! I, in truth, do hearken unto thee,
Accord thee freedom in thine actions,
And bestow upon thee My grace.

O Eternal Fountain,
From whence well forth the lights of love,
From whence gush forth the streams of life and well-being!
I open unto Thee my heart and my mind,
And lay bare my soul before Thee.
Deny me not, then, Thine overflowing bounties,
Nor remove me from Thy copious fountains.

My fountains are amidst the stars,
And in that which binds them one unto another,
And in the strength and health that grow therefrom,
And in the flowers that blow therein,
And in the scent they breathe of love and beauty

—All these are before thine eyes and beneath thy grasp,
The grasp of the discerning mind and of the immortal soul.

Thou art my Lord and there is no God besides Thee.

I am the pulse of life within thee,
The spirit of love within thee,
The light of wisdom within thee,
Be thou faithful thereunto,
For they are the reality of Divinity, whether sought as Truth or as Religion.

Translated by S. B. Bushrui[14]

Mikhail Naimy

A NEW YEAR

The village of Yarboub is famous for many things. Anyone who knows that verse of King David in praise of "wine that maketh glad the heart of man" will tell you how excellent is its wine and arak. Any silk mill-owner in Lebanon will tell you of the fine quality of the silkworm cocoons bred there. A farmer who wished to buy a really good milch cow or a sturdy bull would unhesitatingly head first for Yurboub, confident he would find there just what he sought. And likewise a lad who, having passed a certain age and realised that life does not open her girt-bag and shower her bounties upon bachelors in this world, decided to hitch the remainder of his life to that of one of the daughters of his forebear Eve, would rise with the dawn, before his neighbours and fellow-villages were astir, and follow the morning star to this selfsame village. After spending a night and a day there he would seldom, if ever, return without having given his heart to his bride-to-be.

But wine, arak, silkworms, cattle and nubile maids were not the only things that gained for Yarboub such an exalted reputation in the eyes of her neighbours. There was another factor that raised it above its peers. This was, its sheikh, Butrus al-Naqous, or as the villagers, their neighbours and the local officials called him Abu Nasif.

Abu Nasif had inherited his Sheikhdom from his father and grandfather before him. Other sheikhs who had known his father as the feudal lord affirmed

unanimously that he was superior to the late sheikh in several respects. For a start, Abu Nasir could read and write, whereas his father's only claim to literacy had been to dip his little finger in the inkwell, smear it over the end of his signet ring, then slowly and deliberately press it onto the paper; and there in elegant Persian script would appear the words: "Elias Butrus al-Naqous, Sheikh of the village of Yarboub." Many people wondered how the engraver could possibly have included all those names on an ordinary, small-size signet ring, but this was one of those little things that reassured the late Sheikh that he was greater and more important then anyone else around him.

Secondly, the late Sheikh had lived his whole life sleeping on the floor and eating from a straw tray with a wooden spoon or with his hands. But Abu Nasif had acquired a bed and a mosquito net, a dining table, chairs and so on. When an important visitor called on him, more often than not he would bring out of his chests a collection of knives, forks and spoons, even though—according to those in the know—he preferred to follow in his father's footsteps and would often leave aside knife and fork and fall back on his fingers, even before guests. Similarly, he preferred to sleep on the floor.

Thirdly, the old Sheikh had worn throughout his life an old-fashioned tarboosh with a blue turban wrapped round it, baggy trousers of dyed calico and a belt that he always tucked under his pillow when he resigned himself to the arms of Morpheus (some there are who say that this belt was under his pillow when he died). Abu Nasif, however, was never seen walking abroad in anything but a stylish, turbanless tarboosh, a long robe and a silken sash, and fashionable boots. On high holidays, or when entertaining dignitaries such as an Ottoman government official or the Archbishop, it was by no means unusual to see him in a European suit and a dress shirt, with his tarboosh pushed forward at a rakish angle (I was told by someone who knows the Sheikh well that once when he appeared to welcome the *qaimmaqam*—the local governor—he had a gold watch dangling at his chest, but when His Excellency asked him the time he blushed and stammered that his watch had stopped; and thereafter he was never seen wearing the gold watch-and-chain again).

There were many ways in which Abu Nasif was an improvement on his late father, as anyone you asked in Yarboub and its environs would tell you. You would learn, for instance, that unlike his father Abu Nasif inspired awe and respect in any assembly and his word was law in the courtroom, and that whenever the people of the village got into some difficulty or predicament, Abu Nasif was there to help, and in no time at all differences would be smoothed out and problems solved.

Yet another advantage Abu Nasif had over his villagers was that when they counted off all the households from which someone had emigrated to America, they would get to the Sheikh's house and stop; for this was the only house in Yarboub that had not yet paid its tithe to Columbus.

Children, youths and old men all respected and revered Abu Nasif. There were just a few gossiping women who, out of envy or malice, would pass on to one another in their secret sessions some unsavoury tales about the Sheikh: how they sometimes heard screams from the Sheikh's house, and often saw the Sheikha with her face swollen and bruised and tearstained. There was one called Barbara, who would sometimes whisper to her cronies how once, when she took a pail of milk for the Sheikh, she found him gripping the Sheikha's throat with venom in his eyes, his moustache quivering, as she lay sprawled on the floor with her hair spread over her face. This same Barbara had many tales to tell about the Sheikh. Such as finding the Sheikha one day locked in the stable with the cows and horses, starving to death, and fetching her a loaf of bread. And how the Sheikh had "sentenced" his wife to death; and so on. Hardly surprising, for women have tremendous capacity for inventing news.

But one truth that could not be hidden from anyone in the village was that the Sheikh had seven daughters; and that he did not like anyone to mention his daughters in front of him, and would change the subject whenever someone asked him about the Sheikha. Moreover, he would bow his head in silence whenever he came across a woman carrying a male child in her arms, and would swallow hard whenever anyone gave him the glad news he was the father of a son. He had dedicated half his vineyards to Saint Elias if he would give him a son. And now the Sheikha was pregnant and expected to give birth very shortly.

In this year 1908 as in 1907 before it, the village of Yarboub has succumbed to howling winds and roaring torrents. Now the storm mourns above what is left of it, darkness shrouds it and the heavens are spreading a white blanket over its tombstone to welcome in the year 1909.

In the village, a few lights are still gleaming through windows and chinks in doors. One or two boys and youths gather together to try their luck at games of chance—variously for walnuts, almonds or small change—and from time to time can be heard their loud bursts of laughter, which are promptly snatched up by the wind and buried in the valley bottom.

Night comes on and the lamps begin to go out one by one as if the spirit of the old year declined to withdraw before the face of the new under the slightest shred of illumination and refused to transmit its last testament concerning the village of Yarboub in the hearing of anyone of its inhabitants. And even before the old year has breathed its last and the new year emerged from the cocoon

of eternity, the whole village—old, young, children and dogs—has sunk into a deep sleep. Goodnight, dear Yarboub, goodnight!

But a solitary, faint light still shines from one of the houses as if struggling against extinction—flares up, then flickers low. Is that the howling of the gale, pounding at the windows of yonder house, to turn back as a long-drawn, agonized moan? Or is it a human voice rising from a breast racked with pain?

The storm howls and the sky weeps, and from time to time through this tumult can be heard fragments of screams issuing from the windows of the house with the light. They are indeed cries from a human breast, cries for help: "Oh, Jesus! Virgin! Saint Elias!"

This is the house of Abu Nasif, and it is his wife the Sheikha crying for help, as she lies in labour with a boy or a girl. There is no-one with her but the midwife, an old woman of nearly seventy who is apparently a past-mistress of her profession and familiar with all the acts and scenes that make up this kind of drama. The passage of time has not marked her handsome face, except for a few lines that alternately wrinkle up and relax, revealing her state of mind. There is no doubt that she is at present greatly agitated, for the lines are wrinkled rather than relaxed. She realizes that the New Year has begun and that if this time she delivers a boy for the Sheikh, she might not leave the house with less than a gold sovereign and a frock; she might even get a pair of new slippers... She has been awaiting this chance for some time, and perhaps she has been praying for it to Saint Elias and Saint George more than the Sheikh and the Sheikha both. She would rather die than have to tell Abu Nasif for the eighth time that he is the father of a girl rather than a boy, to see him scowl and fume and stamp and give her only a few piastres. Yet, she would sooner die.

Meanwhile Abu Nasif is pacing up and down in the next room, his head bowed under the pressure of thoughts that condense before his eyes into living persons, filling up the room so as to leave him no space to move. Voices ring in his ears, shapes pass before his eyes. A furnace in his head, a tempest in his sod. And this mad hurricane that shrieks and howls and dances around the house, making the windows and doors dance with it—what does it want from him, and what news does it bring him: a boy or a girl?

The phantoms wheel about with him and circle round him like dancers at a wedding or mourners at a funeral. All roads are barred to him, his feet shackled to the spot, and he stands bolt upright in the middle of the room like an idol with thousands of worshippers massed around him, closing their ranks like the waves of a sea lashed by the eruptions of submarine volcanoes. And these waves are rushing at him from every side. Now they sweep over him up to his chest and he feels as if the whole of Mount Sannin is crushing him; now they cling

round his neck and bear down on him with full force: "A girl...?"

His breathing grows laboured his head heavy, his eves dim. He is drowning.
—"Jesus!"

Abu Nasif falls to his knees, raising his hands and eyes to a crucifix on the
wall. The waves subside, Sannin returns to its place and the dancer-mourners
cease. The storm dies and the phantom shapes vanish. Abu Nasif is alone in
the room, staring at the crucified Christ and the robbers on either side. The
robbers disappear from view and he sees only the crucified man in the middle,
the blood flowing from his side and from his hands and feet nailed to the cross.
The colours and lines merge before his eves and he no longer sees the head
bowed beneath the crown of thorns, or the hands and feet, or the cross; just the
drop of blood oozing from His side. The whole picture is transformed in his
eyes into a pool of blood. Suddenly the surface of the pool is ruffled and from
the blood emerges a small, downy head, followed by hands, body and legs. The
figure twitches restlessly. The image is no longer that of three crucified men,
but of a male child. The child stretches out his little arms towards Abu Nasif.
He descends from the wall and steps towards him; he is no longer a child, but
a youth in the first bloom of life. Abu Nasif opens his arms and clasps him to
his breast and kisses him more fervently than anyone has ever kissed anyone
before. Yes, this is his son Nasif. This is the Alpha and the Omega of his hopes.
This is the dream of his life, the prop of his old age, the heir to his fortune and
the refurbisher of the honour of his line. The seal of the Sheikhdom will not
now fall into the hands of strangers. When the Archbishop visits the village
of Yarboub he will not lodge elsewhere but at the house of Naqous, And his
neighbour Elias Hundaqouq will never again lord it over him with his five sons.

And his wife Umm Nasif! Ah, he will kiss her feet every morning and night
and beg her forgiveness a thousand times every day for his past sins against her,
and will swear by Nasif's life never again to touch a hair of her head in anger
or malice. He will shed tears of blood for her sake, he will make her the belle
of the town.

Today is New Year's Eve, and tomorrow the news will spread of the birth of
a son to the Sheikh. The village will come, old and young, to share in his joy.
And right welcome they will be! For Abu Nasif will cause the wine to flow in
rivers and the roasts to rum for weeks.

But supposing it were a girl...?

This thought settles over the room like a black cloud; Abu Nasif trembles in
every limb and is momentarily blinded.

"Saint...Elias...!"

Light floods back into Abu Nasif's heart and the clouds clear from his eyes,

and Nasif appears once again in his father's presence. No, no, Saint Elias will answer a broken heart just this once. Saint Elias whom Abu Nasif reveres above all saints, by whose name alone he swears, in whose church alone he prays and who never sees a Sunday or a holiday go by without Abu Nasif's dropping a ten-para piece into his offertory tray. Saint Elias, to whom Abu Nasif has presented a silver candlestick and a gilded icon, Yes, Saint Elias knows that the Sheikh deserves a male child more than any one in the village and moreover Abu Nasif is ready to endow him with half his vineyards if he grants his wish. Saint Elias will not refuse him this favour.

"Holy...Virgin...!"

Again the trembling in Abu Nasif's body, again the emptiness in his heart and the darkness before his eyes. Nasif disappears and is replaced by a diabolical image—that of a baby girl tossing and turning in her cradle. The picture lunging on the wall that shows a woman holding a child in her arms begins to move, to shudder, and then mother and child fall to the floor. The woman gazes at him tenderly, comes towards him, her lips moving as if she is trying to speak to him. The child in her arms is not a boy, but a girl. What does this woman want of him and what does she wish to tell him? Abu Nasif explodes with rage and his hand goes up to strike her. But she smiles, opens her mouth, and this smile inflames Abu Nasif's fury. He summons up the last of his strength to restrain himself from hitting her. "Speak to me! Speak to me!"

"A girl! A girl! A girl!"

The room is suddenly filled with these words. Abu Nasif feels them as fangs that stay fixed in his flesh however he twists and turns, "A girl! A girl! A girl"

"Get out, you traitress! It's a boy, a boy, a boy!"

Abu Nasif resumes his pacing more furiously than before, his head heavier than Mount Sannin and the storm resumes its funeral procession around the house, seeming to Abu Nasif as if it is burying his hopes, repeating: "A girl! A girl! A gi-i-irl !"

"Wa-a-aah!"

Abu Nasif's heart skips a beat and he freezes to the spot as if paralyzed. He wants to take a step, but his legs will not obey him; he wants to cross himself, but his hand betrays him.

A boy or a girl? Shall he wait until the midwife comes to announce the birth of Nasif, or shall he go himself to welcome his son and heir and the light of his life?

And if it should be a girl? "Strangle her!"

An infernal gleam lights Abu Nasif's eyes and a demonic power drives him from the spot towards the room where mother and midwife wait.

"What...?" His tongue will not consent to say more.

The mother stops her sobbing and the midwife holds her breath, and the child, too, seems to share in their suspense, uttering only a single "waah!"

"What?" The Sheikh repeats his question after a moment that seems to him an age. A silence deeper than the silence of the grave reigns once more in the room, while the Sheikh writhes inwardly with fury.

"A girl?" The word falls from his lips like a thunderclap in that dead silence. The midwife's bowels shudder in her terror. She moves her lips in an effort to speak, but her lips fail her and can stammer only a single sound before relapsing into silence.

Abu Nasif's eyes again gleam with the same infernal fire, and in a flash he has pounced upon the midwife like an eagle on a lure, snatched the child from her arms, run to the door and out to the stable, where he seizes a spade and heads straight towards the pines behind the church.

The winds are howling, the snow is falling, the trees are swaying and Abu Nasif is digging...

Dawn breaks and the villagers begin wishing each other a Happy New Year. In the graveyard behind the church the trees are mourning, the storm wailing and the sky weeping icy tears as the church bell peals out: "Happy New Year!"

If you saw Barbara from the village of Yarboub, she would tell you that the village is still famous for its excellent wine, arak and cattle. That young men back from America still make pilgrimages there before anywhere else. That the seal of the sheikhdom is still in the hands of Abu Nasif and that everyone pities poor Abu Nasif, because a son was born to him dead and he gave him a solitary burial with his own hands. But *she*, Barbara, will tell you a secret told to her by the midwife, who has revealed it to no-one else: that the child was a girl, and that Abu Nasif gave the midwife two gold sovereigns to spread the word that it had been a stillborn boy. That the Sheikh had gone on beating his wife until she went out of her mind and he will not now let her out of the house. That from that time forth, he—the Sheikh—has never set foot in the grounds of Saint Elias' church, and some say he might even have changed his faith and left Yarboub for good.

Yes, the village of Yarboub is famous for many things.

Kana ma kana

Translated by J. R. Perry[15]

COMRADE!

Comrade, the warrior in the west
Returning boasts what he achieved,
And hallows the heroic best
Whereof his country is bereaved.
Praise not the victors, nor revile
Rejoicing the defeated foe;
Kneel silently with me awhile
And let your heart be bowed in woe
And bleed,
As we lament our dead.

Comrade, the soldier from the wars
Comes to his fatherland again
To find him healing for his scars,
And friends to ease him of pain.
Look not to find, if you shall come
Homeward, old comrades waiting here;
Hunger has left us with loving cheer
Beside
The ghosts of those who died.

Comrade, the farmer to his field
Returns to plough and sow once more,
After long exile to rebuild
The cottage shattered by the war.
Our hearth is wrecked by misery,
Our water-wheels are choked with sand,
The malice of our enemy
Has left no seedling in our land,
No thing
Save our dead, mouldering.

Comrade, this had not come to pass
Except we wished it so to be;
Ruin is over all, because
Ourselves willed this catastrophe.
Then shed no tears, my comrade; save

Your tale of sorrow none will hear,
But follow me, and dig a grave
With pick and shovel, and inter
With me
Our dead, where none may see.

Comrade, what men are we? No land
Is ours, no neighbors, kindred none,
And let us sleep, or let us stand,
Shame is our covering alone.
Whether we dead or living be,
The world is noisome with our stench;
Come, bring a spade, and follow me,
And let us dig another trench
To lay
Our living in the clay

Translated by A. J. Arberry[16]

Taha Hussein

AN EGYPTIAN CHILDHOOD

He was from the outset of an inquisitive nature, regardless of what he encountered in the finding out of what he did not know, and that cost him much discomfort and trouble. But one incident in particular curbed his curiosity, and filled his heart with a shyness which lingers even yet.

He was sitting down to supper with his father and brothers, and his mother, as was her custom, was superintending the meal and directing the servant and her daughters, who were assisting the servant, in bringing the dishes required for the meal. And he was eating just as the others were eating, when a strange thought occurred to him! What would happen if he took hold of a morsel of food with both hands instead of one as was customary? And what was there to prevent him from making this experiment? Nothing. Lo! he took a morsel in both hands. Then he raised it to his mouth.

At once his brothers burst out laughing. His mother was on the point of tears. His father said in a soft and sorrowful tone, "That is not the way to eat

your food, my son!" And he himself passed a troubled night.

From that time his movements were fettered with infinite caution, fear and shyness. And thenceforth he realised that he had a strong will and also abstained from many kinds of food which he only allowed himself when he was over twenty-five years old. He gave up soup and rice, and all dishes which had to be eaten with spoons because he knew that he could not wield a spoon nicely, and so he didn't want his brothers to laugh at him, his mother to weep or his father to reproach him, albeit softly and sadly.

This incident helped him to understand correctly a traditional story about Abu-l-'Alā [al-Ma'arri].

They say that one day he was eating treacle, some of which, unbeknown to him, fell down the front of his garment. When he went out therefore to lecture to his students, one of them said to him, "Sir, you have been eating treacle." Abu-l-'Alā quickly put his hand on his chest and said, "Yes! God save us from gluttony!" Thereafter he gave up eating treacle for the rest of his life.

This incident also led him to appreciate more fully other actions of Abu-l-'Alā. For example he understood the reason why he used to eat unseen by anybody, not even his servant, and that he used to eat in a tunnel under the ground, ordering his servant to lay his meals there and then go away, so that he was left alone with his food and could eat it as he liked.

They also say that one day his students were talking about the melons of Aleppo and saying how excellent they were. Abu-l-'Alā took the trouble to send someone to Aleppo to buy some for them.

When the students ate, the servant kept a piece of melon for his master and put it in the tunnel. But it seems that he did not put it in the place where he usually put the old man's food, and the latter not liking to ask for his share of the melon, it remained in that place until it went bad and he never tasted it at all.

Our friend understood completely these features of the life of Abu-l-'Alā, because therein he saw himself. How often as a child he used to long to be able to eat by himself, but he never dared communicate this desire to his people. However, he was left alone with portions of the food frequently in the month of Ramadan and at the great festivals of the year, when his family used to partake of various kinds of sweet dishes, such as must be eaten with spoons. Then he used to refuse his portion of them at the table, and his mother, not liking this abstinence of his, would set aside for him a special dish and leave him alone with it in a special room in which he could shut himself up so that nobody was able to see him while he ate.

When at length he reached years of discretion, he made this his general rule.

He pursued this course of seclusion when he travelled to Europe for the first time, feigning fatigue and refusing to go to the dining-saloon on board ship, so that food was brought to him in his cabin. Then when he got to France, it was his rule on arrival at a hotel, or when staying with a family, that his food should be brought to him in his room without his bothering to go to the common dining-room. Nor did he abandon this habit until he got married, when his wife broke him of many habits he had grown into.

This incident, again, caused him many kinds of hardship. It made him a by-word among his family and those who knew him before he passed from family life into society.

He was a small eater, not because he had no great appetite, but because he had a horror of being called a glutton or of his brothers winking at one another on account of him. At first this caused him much pain, but it was not long before he got accustomed to it, so that he found it difficult to eat as others ate.

He used to take exceedingly small helpings of food. Now there was an uncle of his who was much vexed with him about it, whenever he saw it, and used to get enraged and rebuke him, urging him to take larger helpings; so that his brothers laughed. This caused him to hate his uncle with a deadly hatred.

He was ashamed to drink at table, fearing that the glass might upset in his hand or that he would take hold of it clumsily when it was handed to him. Therefore he always ate his food dry at the table until such time as he got up and went to wash his hands at the tap, drinking there to his heart's content. Now the water was not always clean, nor was this way of quenching his thirst beneficial to the health. So things went on until he got stomach trouble and no one was able to tell the reason of it.

Moreover, he abstained from all kinds of sports and games, except those which did not give him much trouble, and such as exposed him neither to ridicule nor to sympathy. His favourite was to collect a number of iron rods, take them to a quiet corner of the house, and then put them together, separate them and knock one against the other. Thus he would while away hours until he wearied of it. Then he would fall back on his brothers and friends, who were playing a game in which he would join with his mind but not with his hand. Like that he knew numerous games without ever taking part in them.

Now this abstention of his from play led him to become fond of one kind of diversion, and that was listening to stories and legends. His great delight was to listen to the songs of the bard or the conversation of his father with other men or of his mother with other women, and so he acquired the art of listening. His father and some of his friends were very fond of story-telling. As soon as ever they had finished their afternoon prayers they all collected round one of them,

who would recite to them tales of raids and conquests, and of the adventures of Antarah and Zahir Baibars, and narratives about prophets, ascetics and pious folk; and he would read them books of sermons and the religious law.

Our friend would sit at a respectful distance from them, and although they were oblivious of his presence, he was in no way unmindful of what he heard or even of the impression these stories made upon the audience. So it was that when the sun set, people went to their food, but as soon as they had said their evening prayers they assembled again and conversed for a great part of the night. Then came the bard and began to recite the deeds of the Hilalies and Zanaties to him, and our friend would sit listening during the early part of the night just as he did toward the close of the day.

The women in the villages of Egypt do not like silence, nor have they any talent for it, so that if one of them is by herself and cannot find anyone to talk she will divert herself with various kinds of speech; if glad, she will sing, and if she is sad by reason of bereavement she will lament the deceased; for every woman in Egypt can mourn when she wishes. Best of all when they are by themselves do the village women like to recall their troubles and eulogise those who have departed this life and very often this eulogising causes them to shed real tears.

Our friend was the happiest of mortals when he was listening to his sisters singing or his mother lamenting. However, the song of his sisters used to annoy him and left no impression on him because he found it inane and pointless, without rhyme or reason, whereas the lamentations of his mother used to move him very much and often reduced him to tears. Somewhat after this fashion our friend learnt by heart many songs, many lamentations and many tales both serious and amusing. He learnt something else which had no connection at all with this, to wit passages of the Qur'an which his old blind grandfather used to recite morning and evening.

This grandfather of his was to him an unattractive and odious person, who used to spend every winter at the house. He became pious and ascetic when life drove him to it, and so he used to pray the regular five times a day and the mention of God was incessantly on his tongue. He would get up toward the end of the night in order to recite the collect for the dawn and would sleep at a belated hour after the evening prayer and recite all manner of collects and prayers.

Now our friend slept in a room adjoining that of the old man and thus could hear him intoning and learn by heart what he intoned, so that he memorised a great number of these collects and prayers.

Moreover, the people of the village were very fond of Sufism and used to perform the zikr. Our friend liked this propensity of theirs because he enjoyed

the zikr and the incantations of the chanters during it.

So it was that before he was nine years old he had accumulated a very fair collection of songs, lamentations, stories, poems about the Hilalies and Zanaties, collects, prayers and dervish incantations, and learnt them by heart, and in addition to all that he had learnt the Qur'an,

* * *

Strange to relate, he does not know how he memorised the Qur'an, nor how he began it, nor how he went over it a second time, although of his life in the village school he remembers numerous episodes, many of which make him laugh even now, while others sadden him.

He recalls the time when he used to go to school carried on the shoulder of one of his brothers because the school was a long way away and he was too weak to go such a distance on foot.

He cannot remember, either, when he began to go to the village school. He sees himself in the early part of the day sitting on the ground in front of "Our Master", surrounded by a collection of shoes, with some of which he was playing, and he remembers how patched they were. Now "Our Master" sat on a small, wooden dais that was neither particularly high nor particularly low; it stood on the right of the door as you came in, so that everyone who entered passed "Our Master". As soon as "Our Master" entered the school, it was his custom to take off his cloak, or more accurately his overcoat, and having rolled it up into the shape of a cushion he put it on his right side. Then he would take off his shoes and, sitting cross-legged on his dais, light a cigarette and begin to call the roll.

Now "Our Master" never discarded his shoes until it was absolutely necessary. He used to patch them on the right side and on the left and on the top and the bottom. Whenever one of his shoes needed patching he would call one of the boys of the school, and taking the shoe in his hand say to him, "You will go to the cobbler who lives near by and say to him, 'Our Master says that this shoe needs a patch on the right side. Look, do you see? Here where I put my finger.' The cobbler will reply, 'Yes I will patch it.' Then you will say to him, 'Our Master says that you must choose a strong, coarse, new piece of leather and that you must put it on neatly so that it is invisible or nearly so.' He will reply, 'Yes I will do that.' Then you will say to him, 'Our Master says that he is an old customer of yours, so please take that into account,' and whatever he says to you don't agree to pay more than a piastre. Now go and come back again in the twinkling of an eye."

So the boy would depart and "Our Master" would forget all about him. By the time that he did return, "Our Master" would have twinkled his eye times without number.

Nevertheless, although this man opened and shut his eye, he could not see anything, or at any rate very little, for he was completely blind except for the faintest glimmer of sight in one eye, so that he could discern shapes without being able to distinguish between them. Not but what he was very pleased with this dim sight of his, and deceived himself into imagining that he could see as well as other people. However, this did not prevent him from relying on two of his pupils to guide him on his way to and from the school, putting an arm on the shoulder of each.

Thus they would proceed three abreast along the street, which they occupied to the detriment of other pedestrians, who had to make way for them: Strange indeed was the sight of "Our Master" on his way to the school or his house in the morning and evening. He was a bulky, corpulent man and his overcoat increased his bulk. As we mentioned above he put his arms over the shoulders of his two companions, and as the three of them marched along, the earth resounded beneath their tread.

Now "Our Master" used to choose the most intelligent of his pupils, and those with the best voices, for this important task. This was because he was fond of singing and liked to give singing lessons to his pupils. He would deliver his lesson to them all along the street. Thus he would sing, and at times his companions would begin to accompany him (in song) or merely listen to him at others; or one of them he would charge to sing, and "Our Master" and his other companion would accompany him.

"Our Master" did not sing with his voice and tongue alone, but with his head and body also. He used to nod his head up and down and waggle it from side to side. Moreover he sang with his hands also, beating time upon the chests of his two companions with his fingers. Sometimes when the song was particularly agreeable to him, and he found that walking did not suit him, he would stop till it was finished. The best of it was that "Our Master" thought he had a very beautiful voice, though our friend does not think that God ever created an uglier voice than his.

Whenever he read the verse: "Verily the most unpleasant sound is the braying of asses": he invariably thought of "Our Master" while he was beating time to the verses of the *al-Burda* on his way to the mosque to pray at noon or on his way home to the house from the school.

Our friend pictures himself, as described above, sitting on the ground playing with the shoes around him, while "Our Master" hears him recite

Surat-ar-Rahman, but he cannot remember whether he was reciting it for the first time or the second.

Indeed on another occasion he sees himself sitting not on the floor among the shoes, but on the right of "Our Master" on another long dais, and the latter is hearing him recite: "Do ye enjoin good works on others and yourselves forget to do them? Do ye read the book and then do not understand?" To the best of his belief he had finished reciting the Qur'an through once and was beginning to do it a second time.

It is not to be wondered at that our friend forgets how he learnt the Qur'an, since at the time of its completion he was not nine years old. He remembers very clearly the day on which he concluded his study of the Qur'an, and "Our Master" telling him some days before, how pleased his father would be with him and how he would make his stipulations for it and demand his past dues. For had he not taught four of our friend's brothers before him, of whom one had gone to al-Azhar and the others to various schools? So that our friend was the fifth.... Did "Our Master" not have many claims upon the family?

These claims "Our Master" always detailed in terms of food, drink, clothes and money.

The first of all of these dues, of which he would demand payment, when our friend had finished the Qur'an, would be a rich supper; then a gown and caftan, a pair of shoes, a Maghraby tarbush, a cotton cap of the material of which turbans are made and a golden guinea—he would not be satisfied with anything less than that...if they did not pay him all this, he would disown the family and would not take anything from them. Nor would he have any more to do with them. This he swore with the most binding oaths.

It was Wednesday, and "Our Master" had announced in the morning that our friend would conclude the Qur'an that day. They set forth in the afternoon, "Our Master" leading the way supported by his two companions, and behind him our friend, led by one of the orphans in the village. At last they reached the house and "Our Master" gave the door a push and uttering the customary cry "Ya Sattar" (O Veiler), made his way to the guest-room, where was the sheikh, who had just finished his afternoon prayers and was reciting some private prayers as was his wont. He greeted them smilingly and confidently. His voice was soft and that of "Our Master" raucous. Meanwhile our friend said nothing and the orphan was smiling from ear to ear.

The sheikh signed to "Our Master" and his two companions to be seated, and placed a silver coin in the orphan's hand. Then having called the servant and bidden him take the orphan to a place where he would find something to eat, he patted his son on the head and said, "May God open his ways to you!

Go and tell your mother that 'Our Master' is here."

His mother must have heard the voice of "Our Master", for she had prepared such things as were necessary for an occasion like this: a tall and wide mug of unadulterated sugared water. It was brought to "Our Master" and he gulped it down. His two companions also drank two mugs of sugared water. Then coffee was brought and then "Our Master" urged the sheikh to examine the lad in the Qur'an, but the sheikh replied, "Leave him to play. He is yet young." "Our Master" got up to go, whereupon the sheikh said "We will say the sunset prayer together, if God wills," which was of course an invitation to supper.

I cannot recollect that "Our Master" received any other reward in return for our friend completing the Qur'an, for he had known the family twenty years and received presents from them regularly, and did not stand on ceremony with them. Indeed, he was confident that if he was unlucky with the family this time, he would not be so unlucky some other time.

Translated by E. H. Paxton[17]

FROM *THE STREAM OF DAYS*

For the first two or three weeks of his stay in Cairo he was lost in bewilderment. All he knew was that he had left the country behind him and settled in the capital as a student attending lectures at the Azhar. It was more by imagination than by sense that he distinguished the three phases of his day.

Both the house he lived in and the path that led to it were strange and unfamiliar. When he came back from the Azhar he turned to the right through a gateway which was open during the daytime and shut at night; after evening prayer there was only a narrow opening left in the middle of the door. Once through it, he became aware of a gentle heat playing on his right cheek, and a fine smoke teasing his nostrils; while on the left he heard an odd gurgling sound which at once puzzled and delighted him.

For several days, morning and evening, he listened curiously to this sound, but lacked the courage to inquire what it might be. Then one day he gathered from a chance remark that it came from the bubbling of a *narghile* smoked by tradesmen of the district. It was provided for them by the proprietor of the café from which the gentle heat and the fine smoke-cloud issued.

He walked straight on for a few steps before crossing a damp, roofed-in space in which it was impossible to stand firmly because of the slops thrown there by the café proprietor. Then he came out into an open passage-way; but

this was narrow and filthy and full of strange, elusive smells, which were only moderately unpleasant early in the day and at nightfall, but as the day advanced and the heat of the sun grew stronger, became utterly intolerable.

He walked straight on through this narrow passage; but rarely did he find it smooth or easy. More often than not his friend would have to push him either this way or that so as to avoid some obstacle or other. Then he would continue in the new direction, feeling his way towards a house either to left or right, until he had passed the obstacle and taken the old direction again. He hurried along nervously at his companion's side, breathing the nauseous smells, and half-deafened by the medley of sounds that came from all sides at once, left and right, above and below, to meet in mid-air, where they seemed to unite above the boy's head, layer upon layer, into a single fine mist.

There was in fact a remarkable variety of sounds. Voices of women raised in dispute, of men shouting in anger or peaceably talking together; the noise of loads being set down or picked up; the song of the water-carrier crying his wares; the curse of a carter to his horse or mule or donkey; the grating sound of cart-wheels: and from time to time this confused whirl of sounds was torn by the braying of a donkey or the whinnying of a horse.

As he passed through this babel, his thoughts were far away, and he was scarcely conscious of himself or of what he was doing; but at a certain point on the road he caught the confused sound of conversation through a half-open door on the left; then he knew that a pace or two further on he must turn to the left up a staircase which would bring him to his lodging.

It was an ordinary sort of staircase, neither wide nor narrow, and its steps were of stone; but since it was used very frequently in both directions, and no one troubled to wash or sweep it, the dirt piled up thickly and stuck together in a compact mass on the steps, so that the stone was completely covered up, and whether you were going up or coming down the staircase appeared to be made of mud.

Now whenever the boy went up or down a staircase he was obliged to count the steps. But long as were the years he stayed in this place, and countless the times he negotiated this staircase, it never occurred to him to count the number of its steps, He learnt at the second or third time of climbing it that after going up a few steps he had to turn a little to the left before continuing his ascent, leaving on his right an opening through which he never penetrated, though he knew that it led to the first floor of the building in which he lived for so many years.

This floor was not inhabited by students, but by workers and tradesmen. He left the entrance to it on his right, and went on up to the second floor.

There his harassed spirit found rest and relief; lungfuls of fresh air drove away the sense of suffocation with which he had been oppressed on that filthy staircase; and then too there was the parrot, whistling on without a break, as if to testify before all the world to the tyranny of her Persian master, who had imprisoned her in an abominable cage, and would sell her tomorrow or the day after to another man who would treat her in exactly the same way. And when he was rid of her and had laid hands on the cash, he would buy a successor for her who would be cooped up in the same prison pouring forth the same curses on her master, and waiting as her sister had waited to be passed on from hand to hand, and from cage to cage, while everywhere she went that plaintive cry of hers would delight the hearts of men and women.

When our friend reached the top of the staircase he breathed in the fresh air that blew on his face, and listened to the voice of the parrot calling him towards the right. He obeyed, turning through a narrow corridor, past two rooms in which two Persians lived. One of these was still a young man, while the other was already past middle age. The one was as morose and misanthropic as the other was genial and good-natured.

At last the boy was home. He entered a room like a hall, which provided for most of the practical needs of the house. This led on to another room, large but irregular in shape, which served for social and intellectual needs. It was bedroom and dining-room, reading-room and study, and a room for conversation by day or by night. Here were books and crockery and food; and here the boy had his own particular corner, as in every room he occupied or visited at all frequently.

This place of his was on the left inside the door. After advancing a pace or two he found a mat spread on the ground, and above that an old but quite serviceable carpet. Here he sat in the daytime, and here he slept at night, with a pillow for his head and a rug to cover him. On the opposite side of the room was his elder brother's pitch, a good deal higher than his own. He had a mat spread on the ground, and a decent carpet on top of that, then a felt mattress, and above that a long, wide piece of bedding stuffed with cotton, and finally, crowning all, a coverlet. Here the young sheikh would sit with his close friends. They were not obliged to prop up their backs against the bare wall, as the boy did, having cushions to pile up on the rugs. At night this couch was transformed into a bed on which the young sheikh slept.

Translated by Hilary Wayment[18]

Abbas al-Aqqad

DRINKING SONG

Now is Time's good tiding come:
Raise thy hopes, so long in tomb,
To the music of the strings
And good comrades' clamourings.

Call the wine, to flow again
Joyous in each joyful vein;
Bid it mingle with the heart,
Banishing all sorrow's smart.

"Slain thou wast by treachery,
And so long they buried thee;
Come, renew that life to-day
In the barrel past away!

"Get thy life in us anew;
If thou livest, so we do,
Yea, and we long years shall live
In this hour that Fate may give.

"Pour upon the wounded soul
Healing draughts, to make it whole;
Eden's vine thy parent is,
Thou art mother of all bliss.

"Lift us far from lowly earth,
Bring us nigh immortal mirth;
Thou, like us, art sprung from there,
Saplings of one soil we were.

"From this ruin make us rise
To the triumph of the skies;
Turn our grief to living glee,
Man unto Divinity.

"Teach us all the manner of
That angelic life above;
Let the ramparts of the world
To oblivion be hurled.

"Man's endeavour is a veil,
Thou the gateway, thou the pale
Whence the body's dust may view
Mortal ruin, mortal rue.

"Ah, what joy to dying men,
Likeness of the gods to gain:
Shall they not a while be free
From the curse of misery?"
Pass and pour the cup my friend;
Hope is barren in the end;
Life is such an ancient ill
And defeats the highest skill.

Cheer a spirit bowed by woes
Wrought alike of friends and foes;
Save in wine, where shall he find
Pleasure to console the mind?

Count it not to us for shame,
To this refuge that we came;
Lovely ladies stole away
All we look to win to-day

And if Love our wounds had healed,
Ne'er to wine-cup would we yield:
What's the comfort, wine to sip
Banished from the maiden's lip?

If the world had not proved less
Than our looked-for happiness,
Never had we sought to flee
Its long shadow's company.
Ah, but whither should we roam?

Is not earth our only home,
Where the glad and grieving breast
May alone discover rest?

Drink, my comrade, drink with cheer
For the joy that thou art clear
Of this load of grief and care
Thy poor brother has to bear.

Patience; bear with me, my brave,
If awhile I seem to rave;
Thou art drunk but singly; I
Twice intoxicated lie!

DOUBLE TROUBLE

They said 'twas better
I should forget her
And spare my weeping,
Since she preferred
In love not keeping
Her plighted word.

Alas! my trouble
In love is double
My heart's adoring
Unmerited,
My tears outpouring
Far best unshed.

Who mourneth over
The faithful lover,
At least he reapeth
This much relief
That she he weepeth
Deserved his grief.

Translated by A. J. Arberry[19]

May Ziadah

REJOICE

In the temple of human sorrows the Great Master stood to speak to the people and I heard him say:

If you are rich, rejoice! Experience of weighty matters has served you well, your good deeds are praised and generosity is expected of you. You have become powerful and no one can harm you. Prosperity has put up a shield round your domain, protecting your independence and freedom.

If you are poor, rejoice! You have been spared the spiritual stupor which overcomes the avaricious and you are safe from the jealousy and hatred attracted by the rich. Men's hearts do not burn with envy on account of your prosperity, nor do they gaze at your possessions with jaundiced eyes.

If you are charitable, rejoice! You have filled empty hands, clothed naked bodies and endowed those who have nothing. These achievements have brought you pleasure and you have wished to share that singular pleasure with hundreds so that it might be multiplied by the number of those whom it benefits.

If you cannot extend charity, rejoice! The hour will never come when you witness ingratitude from the one you have helped, who has fashioned your kindness into a weapon to threaten you, thinking it courageous to be aggressive and clever to be fickle. You will avoid that hour which must inevitably come to the generous man, bringing tension to his nerves, provoking his rage, hardening his feelings, drying up the springs of his generosity and creating within him a hatred for men and a despair of their reform. All this he must endure before he can attain the peak of sublime forgiveness and forbearance.

If you are young, rejoice! The sap is rising in the tree of your desires. The goal of your aspirations lies far ahead. If you are worthy of your dreams, their realisation can be easy.

If you are old, rejoice! You have striven with time and men and, because of your discretion and foresight, you have been entrusted with the management of affairs. Everything you have done can bear fruit at your command. The minutes of your life are equal to years so full are they of experience, wisdom and accurate judgement. It is as if those minutes were autumn fruit: fully mature, succulent, and imbued with perfection, plenitude and passion.

If you are a man, rejoice! In the vigour of manhood lies the greater meaning of life.

If you are a woman, rejoice! Woman is the desire of man; her nobility is his support, her sweetness the source of his consolation and her smile the reward for his labours.

If you are of noble birth, rejoice! You have gained the confidence of the multitude unaided by anyone's patronage.

If you are of low birth, rejoice! It is better to make a name for yourself than to bear a great name reluctantly and without having contributed to its fame.

If you have many friends, rejoice! You will find yourself present in every one of them. They will reflect the brilliance of your success or sweeten the bitterness of failure. To attract men's hearts you must have qualities and abilities rarely found except in those who are truly great. Of these the most important is the capacity to break out of the restrictions of selfishness to discover the nobility, compassion and intelligence that others possess.

If you have many enemies, rejoice! Your enemies are the ladder of your ascendance and they are the surest proof of your importance. The more strongly they oppose and attack you, the more you will feel your greatness. The more various their slanderous criticisms, the more scope you will have to discern what truth there may be in their intended poison, which you can then imbibe as the greatest of tonics. The remainder of their libel you can see to be fallacious and that part you can gracefully ignore, for it is nothing more than the product of impotence and deception. Does the eagle soaring in the heights take any heed of the conspiracies hatched by the dung beetles of the ground?

If you enjoy good health, rejoice! In you the universal law has found its balance and has qualified you to deal with difficulties and overcome impediments.

If you suffer from ill-health, rejoice! In you the two great forces of the universe have found a battlefield. It is for you to choose the victor and, if you choose correctly, you can be healed.

If you are a genius, rejoice! A resplendent ray from the most sublime realm has shone upon you. The glance of the Merciful is reflected in the thought radiating from your forehead; there is mystery in your eyes and enchantment in your voice. The expressions of others that are mere sounds, mere mutterings and syllables, have become, by your touch and on your lips, a fire and a light, stinging and illuminating, burning and soothing, humbling and exalting, humiliating and stimulating, hurting and healing, rebuking and bewildering. No sooner do you inspire the birth of meaning than it exists.

If you are not a genius, rejoice! Men's tongues are not sharp when they mention you nor are their eyes afire with carping and criticism when they turn towards you. The summit is there for you to attain if you can and, if you cannot, there is satisfaction in supporting others on their way up. For

the luxurious mansion could not stand without small bricks. You will enjoy a comfort reserved only for those whose lips taste Life's waters while their souls bathe in the floods of inspiration.

If your friend is faithful, rejoice! The world has bestowed upon you its richest treasure.

If your friend is faithless, rejoice! He has not been ready to listen to the parable you have offered to teach him. None forsakes the mansion of love but to vacate it for another, worthier and better than himself.

If you are free, rejoice! In liberty strength finds its exercise; faculties are reinforced and opportunities increased.

If you are enslaved, rejoice! Slavery is the best school in which to learn the lessons of liberty and acquire the qualities to earn it.

If you live in surroundings that cherish and respond to you, rejoice! There you will find second youth and new strength; your spirit will grow to astonish you by its realm of wide oceans and towering heights.

If you live in primitive and inferior surroundings, rejoice! You are free to take wings to rise above them to a place where you can create from the shadows of yourself a world that can satisfy the hunger of your thought and quench the thirst of your soul.

If you are in love and are loved, rejoice! Life has indeed pampered you and has included you among its chosen sons. Divine Power has revealed to you its compassion contained in the exchange of hearts. Two halves wandering in the darkness of the unknown have at last become united and unto them the wonders of daybreak have been disclosed; the suns have gladdened their hearts with that which they had not yet found in their orbits among the planets. The Ether has divulged to them its very secrets and so they know the way when he who is empty of love can go astray; they are silent when he speaks, in jest when he is serious. They divine the lines of eternity where he cannot even see shadows.

If you are in love and are not loved, rejoice! He who has spurned you does, in his highest being, truly love you with a love that cannot be matched by his infatuation for the one he apparently loves. To be rejected in love is an experience full of meaning and mystery; it lowers inflated desires and purifies polluted feelings, leaving the heart transparent, glittering and resplendent as the vessel from which the gods drink of immortality. You are bound to win the one you love, if not in this remote and worldly form then in another form. Be ready for love no matter how heavy the burden of your feelings, for love is unpredictable and you know not the hour of its passage. Be great so that you may be chosen by a great love and lest your lot be a love that feeds on dust and wallows in the mud, either leaving you unchanged or lowering you to its depths instead

of raising you as high as the towers that are out of human sight, whose wonders are beyond our dreams. The edifice of our desires is founded on imaginary plans invented by our longing.

Rejoice! The doors of happiness are many in number, the gates of good fortune are countless and the paths of life are renewed minute by minute.

Rejoice always! However you may find yourself, rejoice!

Translated by S. B. Bushrui[20]

Ahmad al-Safi al-Najafi

TO A CLOCK

O Clock, worn out by regularity!
Rest and repose are all forbidden thee;

Thou hurriest, since no crowd hindereth
Thy running footsteps, swift and sure as death.

Our nights and daytimes are thy properties,
And thou destroyest them, like enemies.
Sleep is a sword that cutteth our lives through,
And dost thou never slumber as we do?

If it would make thee drunk, I'd pour thee wine!
The months and years should share that draught of thine,

And, when men slumbered, ye would take repose.
The wine would sleep, yea, and the cup should doze;

Then, while ye couched, our nights and days would be
Naught but soft dreams that in your sleep ye see,
And in those dreams, your fancies would be—we!

Translated by A. J. Arberry[21]

Mahmud Taymur

THE FARE

Among the facts of life which go on behind the veil of secrecy are disgrace-
ful and painful things. The story-writer whose motto is ever to describe
things as they are, considers it his duty to reveal these disgraceful and pain-
ful deeds, however grim they may be.

Umm Labība went in to see her mistress, Madam Iqbāl, and told her that the
cabman was at the door, demanding his fare. Madam Iqbāl frowned, and told
Umm Labība to go and tell the cabman to come back that afternoon. Umm
Labība went off, worried, hoping she would be successful in her attempt to
persuade the cabman to defer collection of his bill till the afternoon. No sooner
was she face to face with him, than he spoke first, using coarse language indica-
tive of his contempt. She informed him, in accordance with her mistress's com-
mand. But being put off like this aroused his wrath, and he began to curse and
swear.

The cabman was angry, and he had every right to be. On six occasions he
had taken the Lady out for a drive to visit her "companions in arms". His total
fare had now reached 300 piastres, of which he had received so far not one
piastre. Now this cabman had a wife and children, who had difficulty in getting
adequate food and clothing. It was only natural that he should shout angrily
when demanding the dues of which he was being deprived, this bad debt. He
had come for the sixth time, to be greeted only with procrastination and delay.

The cabman returned to his rank shrieking with anger, despairing for getting
anywhere with his shouts and insults. He was determined to get what he was
owed that afternoon, cost what it may. But Madam Iqbāl thought no more of the
incident, as if she was long accustomed to it. She went to the mirror, tidied her
hair, took out a tin of rouge, and began to paint her wrinkled face, heaving a sigh
from time to time.

She was thirty-eight, and had been a model of beauty and decorum in her
youth. At eighteen she had married a young reprobate, a gambler and drunkard.
He stayed with her eight years, then left her tarred with his own brush. Madam
Iqbāl was left a widow in her twenties. Her husband, by the time he died, had
led her astray, obsessed her with wickedness and vice, poisoning her mind with
obscenity and immorality. While she was still young, her husband had driven
her on the "primrose path", and deliberately led her to immorality. For it was

he who had incited her, nay commanded her, to drink and take drugs. He it was who offered her to any of his friends who wanted her for a trifling "quid pro quo". He it was who induced her to make a bit on the side by prostitution.

The young husband died, leaving his young wife to bear in her heart the ulcers of sorrow and shame, and on her body the pains of disease. At thirty-eight, she was more like fifty-eight. Her frame was thin, her face pallid, her skin yellow, and suffering had given her bags under the eyes. The modest, beautiful and chaste girl of yesterday, Madam Iqbāl, had today become a disgraceful gambler, riddled with disease, fond of all drugs and stimulants, particularly alcohol and cocaine. She had a son of seven, by an unknown father, who had grown up amidst unhappiness and misfortune, and spent his youth in an atmosphere of prostitution and vice. Madam Iqbāl had now reached a state of desperation and despair. Her beauty had faded, and men, young and old, generally shunned her. She took up the profession of "go-between", bringing together young men and profligate women, when she realized that her original business was on the decline. And in so doing, she returned to her former condition, menaced by impending poverty and overwhelming want, which were always on the point of overpowering her. Today she lived in a house whose tattered trappings of prostitution were insufficient to lure even the mean spirited and impoverished. So she lived from day to day—no, from hour to hour, closing her eyes to what the future would bring.

The cabman returned at the prearranged time in the afternoon, and began to rant, demanding his fare. But no-one answered. He left his cab in charge of some boy or other, and dashed across the small garden, till he reached the door. He began to knock on it, shouting loudly and angrily. Madam Iqbāl was, as usual, in her bedroom, titivating herself up, wearing her transparent night-dress, a relic of the days of her affluence. Her hair was hanging down, she was barefooted, and her shrivelled breasts were showing from her exposed chest. She heard the cabman ranting, but merely smiled and ignored it. Umm Labība came in, and told her that the cabman was on the point of storming the "harem", and was hurling embarrassing abuse without ceasing. Madam Iqbāl replied quietly:

"What do you want me to do about it? I've no money."

At that point, the cabman succeeded in opening the door, and rushed into the holy harem! He entered the hall, shouting, demanding settlement of his account. Umm Labība ran to him, telling him off for his cheek and nerve, restraining him from his evil intention, telling him to be gone! The two of them kept abusing each other in stinging language for a quarter of an hour, until the maid despaired of getting the better of him, and realized that he was

about to get the better of her. So she shouted for help to her mistress. At that moment, the bedroom door opened, and Madam Iqbāl appeared in the doorway, wearing the transparent night-dress, done up to the nines, her legs and wrists bare. She spoke as if she had not quite realized as yet what was happening in her own house:

"What's the matter, Umm Labība?"

The cabman did not allow Umm Labiba to reply, but forestalled her, by shouting and asking to be paid as usual. But Madam Iqbāl spoke in a tone of assumed innocence and gentleness.

"Why all this aggressiveness, cabman? Come and take your fare."

The cabman was astonished at the changed situation, and looked hard at her, trying to size her up, not knowing whether she was lying or telling the truth. When she saw his hesitation, she came out of the room, took him by the hand, and led him in. He, meanwhile, was amazed, not knowing what to say. She said to him:

"Come and take your fare. Why do you not want to enter the room with me? Are you a stranger?"

The cabman, whose name was Shahhata, went into the room, Madam Iqbāl holding his hand, leading him like a condemned prisoner.

Now this cabman Shahhata was a tough, brawny man of fifty-eight, who had learned nothing in his life but how to drive a cab. He had begun as a stable-lad, living in the stables, sweeping up the droppings, cleaning the harness, and washing down the coaches and horses. Then he was promoted to cabman, sitting on the high seat, wearing the coat and jacket obtained at the uniform-seller's. The profit he made from his horses and cab was not sufficient to feed and clothe his five children, and his wife whom sickness confined to the home. He was swarthy, with an ashen beard which he only shaved when in the money. His appearance was dirty, his clothes torn, his toes peeping out of his worn-out shoes. His trousers were tied up with a dirty red scarf. On his head he wore a tarbush which had a black band, with no button. Yet despite the indications of poverty which pervaded his mind and were written all over his clothes and face, he knew of nothing but "luck", which was the one subject of his conversation, and the one aim of his endeavours. When he was aloft on the fine driving seat, you might hear him singing popular love songs or comic ditties. When a pretty girl of his own class passed in front of him, he would tilt his black-banded tarbush, and start wiggling his tattered shoes, smiling, giving the "glad-eye", and saying:

"Sweetheart! Sweetheart! Slow down a bit! My heart's on fire!"

He often saw upper-class girls wearing the black transparent veil, or the

light barqa' which reveals the features of the face, even endowing it with radiant beauty, swinging in their alluring gait! He would stare at them flirtatiously, murmuring to himself:

"What wouldn't I give for..."

If by chance his fares should be a pair of lovers or sweethearts, and he heard the sound of loving laughter, the moving music of kisses, and the movements of love-making, the heat of passion would be awakened in him. He would shout from the very depths of his heart, talking to himself, cursing his wife with a sigh, and saying:

"Oh how I pity you, Mother Ahmad!"

Then he would feel the eagerness of love, but find no means of quietening his nerves except on the thin, tired horses. So he rained lashes and curses on them!

Cabman Shahhata entered the room, not knowing whether she was serious or joking in what she was doing. He smelled the powder and perfume which permeated the atmosphere, and his frayed nerves were appeased, and his eyes lost their flashing evil look. He began to inspect, with his eyes, the body of Madam Iqbāl, while she paced the room, looking for the key of her money-box. Then she opened the box, and emptied the money from it to give him his fare. He looked at her avidly, then his mouth broadened into a smile which clearly conveyed his animal urge.

The cabman Shahhata had never before met a white woman of this class—the bogus aristocracy—in the same room. He had never met one of these girls in these circumstances and in this attire. For had he ever seen any other woman but his crippled wife, brown-skinned, bad tempered, wearing a dirty blue dress, and a torn black veil? And before today, had he ever seen in front of him such a slender figure unclothed, hidden only by a diaphanous nightdress, through which could be descried those soft, slender legs, that white skin tinted with deep red, that painted face, those alluring eyes? Indeed...Cabman Shahhata had never in his life seen such bare feet, such hair in a fringe over the forehead, such prominent white breasts!

At that moment, Cabman Shahhata did not see Madam Iqbal as she really was, with her thin body, pasty face, and hollow eyes, disguised by powder and paint and the trappings of seduction. What he saw was a girl such as he had dreamed about; a white girl who conceals her fine face under a transparent black veil or a light white barqa'...the same sort of girl whose charming laughter he had heard in his cab, whose body had swayed before him in the street, whose beautiful sweet voice, with its alluring tone, had saddened him.

Madam Iqbal approached him gracefully, affecting coyness, and said to him meekly and humbly:

"I haven't any money today, cabman. Will you come back tomorrow?"

She gave him an imploring look, which contained something of the coquettish and the "come hither". Shahatta's eyes caught a glimpse of a strange gleam. Then he said to her wantonly:

"I can't leave here, Lady. As the saying goes, 'the pigeon doesn't enter the same way as it leaves.'"

Madam Iqbal smiled, guessing what was in his mind. She rushed at him, forgetting his dirtiness and foul smell, giving him a kiss on the mouth which intoxicated him, and almost made him faint.

Madam Iqbal's son, Jamāl, who was seven years old, returned home, looked through the bedroom keyhole, then burst out laughing. As he went away, he met Umm Labība, pulled her head to his, and began to tell her, in his childish language, the secret he had seen in the room...the secret of Cabman Shahhata's remission of the debt due to him by these easy and marvelous means.

Translated by John A. Haywood[22]

Tewfiq al-Hakim

SONG OF DEATH
A play in one act

Cast
Asakir, a widowed peasant woman
Mabruka, her sister-in-law
Simeida, son of Mabruka
Ilwan, son of Asakir

A peasant hut in an Upper Egyptian village. Asakir and Mabruka, both dressed in black, are sitting near the entrance, with heads bowed in silence. Close by them a calf and a kid are seen eating herbage and dried clover. The whistle of a train is heard.

Mabruka (raising her head). There's the train.
Asakir (without moving). Do you think he has come on it?
Mabruka. Didn't he say he would, in his letter? Sheikh Isnawi. the school-teacher, read it out for us yesterday.
Asakir. Are you sure you've told no one at all that he's my son?
Mabruka. Do you think I've gone mad? Your son Ilwan died when he was a mere child of two. He was drowned in the sluice of the water wheel. The whole village knows that.
Asakir. But they no longer believe it.
Mabruka. Who are "they"? The Tahawis?
Asakir. Didn't your son Simeida tell you what he heard in the market the other day?
Mabruka. No. What did he hear?
Asakir. He heard someone say to a group of people "Either the Azizes have no more men left among them or else they're concealing a man in order to take revenge, a man closer to the victim then his nephew Simeida." And who but a man's own son can be any closer than his nephew?
Mabruka. Oh yes: Simeida told me about that. If it hadn't been for this rumor he would never have been able to hold up his head in the village.
Asakir. Well, let them know now that the dead man's son is still alive. We've no fear for him now that he's a grown man. I'm not the one who is afraid now. It's them that fear keeps awake of a night. Hurry up, train, and bring him soon.

I've waited a long time—seventeen years, I've counted them hour by hour. Seventeen whole years and I've milked them out of Time's udders, drop after drop, with all the hard tugging you'd need if you were milking a cow that's far gone in her age.

Mabruka (listening to a far-off sound). There's the train arrived in the station. He'll find my son Simeida waiting to meet him.

Asakir (as if talking to herself). That's right.

Mabruka (turning to her). What's the matter with you, Asakir? You're trembling.

Asakir (as if to herself). Simeida's song will tell me.

Mabruka. Tell you?

Asakir. That he's come.

Mabruka. Did you tell my son to sing as a sign that Ilwan was here?

Asakir. Yes, as soon as they set foot across the village bounds.

Mabruka. Patience, Asakir, be patient. The worst is over now.

Asakir. It's not fear nor weakness that I'm feeling now.

Mabruka. The fearsome days have now gone. Gone forever, they are. I shan't ever forget the day when you hid your son Ilwan—and he a mere child of two then—hid him in the flour basket and carried him under cover of darkness out of the village. Took him all the way to Cairo, and gave him into the care of that kinsman of yours, the flour merchant who kept shop in the spice dealer's row near the mosque of our blessed Hussein.

Asakir. Bring him up as a butcher, I said to him. Let him learn to use the knife like a master.

Mabruka. But he never did as you asked him.

Asakir. He did that! Soon as he was seven years old he placed him in a butcher's shop. But run away, he did, some time later,

Mabruka. And went into the Holy al-Azhar as a student.

Asakir. That's it. When I visited him last year I saw him in his gown and turban looking most dignified. 1 said to him: If only your father could have seen you looking like that, he'd have been mighty proud. But they didn't spare him to enjoy watching his son grow up.

Mabruka. Wouldn't it have been better if he'd stayed on in the butcher's shop?

Asakir. What makes you say that, Mabruka?

Mabruka. I don't know. It's only a thought that came into my head.

Asakir. I reckon I know your thought.

Mabruka. What is it, then, Asakir?

Asakir. It grieves you to see my son in gown and turban while yours goes on wearing his woolly skull cap and his smock.

Mabruka. By the memory of the dear departed, I give you my oath, nothing of the kind was in my mind.

Asakir. Why then don't you like Ilwan to be at the Holy al-Azhar?

Mabruka. I give you my oath, it isn't that I don't like it, it's just that I'm afraid.

Asakir. Afraid?

Mabruka. That he might not be such a master at wielding his knife.

Asakir. Set your mind at rest, Mabruka. When you see Ilwan now, a full-grown man, you'll realize that he has the lean strong-thewed arm of the Aziz family.

Mabruka (listening to the train whistle). The train's moving out of the station now.

Asakir. Let it go where it will, so long as it's brought us Ilwan to force the murderer's soul out of his body, and to leave him for the farm dogs in scattered gobbets of flesh.

Mabruka. What if he hasn't come?

Asakir. Why do you say that, Mabruka?

Mabruka. I don't know. Just a feeling I've got.

Asakir. What would stop him coming?

Mabruka. What would drive him to leave Cairo and the city life and the Holy al-Azhar and come to this—?

Asakir. This is where he was born, where blood is calling out to him.

Mabruka. Our village is a long, long way away from Cairo! Can blood make itself heard as far as the cities?

Asakir. Do you really think he hasn't come?

Mabruka. I know no more about it than you do.

Asakir. And what about the letter that the schoolmaster read out to us?

Mabruka. Don't you recall his words: "I hope to come if my circumstances allow it." Who knows whether or not his circumstances have allowed it?

Asakir. Don't dampen my spirits, Mabruka, Don't dash my hope. I've just heard the train whistle turning into trills of joy in my heart, announcing that the end is near of this long mourning. Ilwan not come? What would become of me if that were true? And how much longer would I have to wait then?

Mabruka. The station isn't so far from here, nor the main road. If he'd arrived, Simeida would be singing now.

Asakir. Perhaps they're taking their time, chatting. After all they haven't seen each other for more than three years...since your son was in Cairo last during the Fair of the blessed Hussein.

Mabruka. If he'd come, my son's heart would have brimmed over with joy and he'd have started his singing even before he'd reached the main road.

Asakir. Perhaps he's forgotten to sing.

Mabruka. It's impossible: he can't forget.

Asakir (listening). I can hear no one singing.

Mabruka (listening). Nor I neither.

Asakir (continuing to listen). There's no one singing, not even a shepherd lad. There's not a single creature singing, not even the owl over in the ruins. You're right, Mabruka, he hasn't come.

Mabruka (as if to herself). My heart tells me things.

Asakir. No, not yours—mine. Mine, that's as secret as the grave, as hard as rock, is now beginning to tell me things.

Mabruka. What things?

Asakir. Things that will happen.

Mabruka. Do tell me.

Asakir (listening intently). Hush! Listen, listen. Can you not hear, Mabruka? Can you not hear?

Mabruka. Simeida singing.

Asakir. The heavens be thanked for that!

(They listen for a while to Simeida's song which grows increasingly clearer)

Simeida (sings):
O my dear one,
Your bitter voice accuses:
Repentance and excuses
Were all I ever gave!
You reproached me then the more,
And out of grief
My clothes
To shreds I tore.
When they told me of your father,
It was my silent shame
Which set unmanly cheeks aflame,
Where eyes ran dry
And made a desert of my face.

Asakir. He's come, Ilwan is here! And now it's off with the shirt of my shame and on with my garment of honor.

Mabruka. And now we can hold the true rites over the body of the dear one— and may he rest in peace.

Asakir. And sacrifice to his spirit the kid and the calf.

Mabruka. O joy! O happiness! *(Makes as though to give out a loud trill)*

Asakir (restrains her). Not now. Otherwise we'll be known to the world too early.

Mabruka. Your hours are numbered, Suweilam Tahawi!

(A knock on the door. Asakir rushes to open it: Simeida appears carrying a bag)

Simeida. I have brought you Sheikh Ilwan. (*Puts the bag on the floor and is soon followed in by Ilwan*)

Asakir (with open arms). Ilwan, my son.

Ilwan (kisses her head). Mother.

Asakir (to her son). Say your greetings to your aunt Mabruka.

Ilwan (turns to Mabruka). Are you well, Aunt Mabruka?

Mabruka. You can see for yourself, Ilwan, You are our only hope now.

Simeida. Let us go home now, mother.

Mabruka. Come. It's close now, Asakir—the hour of relief.

(Mabruka and Simeida go out)

Asakir. You must be hungry, Ilwan. I've a bowl of sour milk.

Ilwan. Thank you, mother. No, I'm not hungry. I had some hard-boiled eggs and some barley-cake on the train.

Asakir. You'll be thirsty then?

Ilwan. No, not thirsty either.

Asakir. Of course you haven't come here for food or drink. You've come to eat of his flesh and drink of his blood.

Ilwan (as if in a trance). I have come here to do something truly great, mother.

Asakir. I know, I know, my son. Wait till I bring you something: something you've never set your eyes on before. (*Rushes to an inner room where she disappears for a while*)

Ilwan (casting a look around the room). My eyes can still see animals and their droppings in your houses. The dirty water jar, firewood and dried stalks of maize forming a shaky roof.

Asakir (emerges from the inner room holding a saddlebag which she lays before her son). Here. For seventeen years I have kept these things for you.

Ilwan (looks at the saddlebag without moving) What is this?

Asakir. The saddlebag that your father's body was sent to me in, carried on his donkey. In this pouch I found his severed head, and in the other one the rest of his body, hacked to pieces. With his own knife they stabbed him to death—the knife he was carrying, then they put knife and body in the saddlebag. See, here is the knife. I left the blood on it until it's turned to

just as you can see. As for the donkey that brought me the body of your murdered father, tracing its steps back to this house by force of habit, with its head bowed down, as if it was grieving over its master—I couldn't keep it alive for you. It couldn't endure for all these years: it's died.

Ilwan. Who did this?

Asakir. Suweilam Tahawi.

Ilwan. How do you know?

Asakir. The whole village knows.

Ilwan. I know you've told me that. You've told that name to me over and over again, whenever you came to visit me in Cairo. I was too young to think then or to argue. But now my reason needs to be satisfied. What's the evidence? Did the police ever look into the crime?

Asakir. Look into the crime?

Ilwan. Yes. What did you say to the Public Prosecutor?

Asakir. Public Prosecutor? The shame of it! We say anything to the Public Prosecutor? We the Azizes do that? Did ever the Tahawis ever do that?

Ilwan. Didn't the Public Prosecutor ask you any questions?

Asakir. Of course. But we said we knew nothing about the business, that we'd seen no corpse. Meantime we had buried your father in secret under cover of darkness.

Ilwan (as if addressing himself). So that we may exact requital with our own hands.

Asakir. With the self-same knife that stabbed your father.

Ilwan. And the murderer?

Asakir. Alive and hearty. There's not a saint or a holy man in the neighborhood but whose shrine I visited. I held on to the railings of their sanctuary, uncovered my head and heaped dust from their ground over my hair, and I prayed to them to beseech our God for me that He might prolong the slayer's days until you, my son, should take his life—with your own hands,

Ilwan. Are you sure, mother, that he was the murderer?

Asakir. We've no enemies beside the Tahawis.

Ilwan. But how do you know it was Suweilam himself who did it?

Asakir. Because he believed it was your father who'd murdered his father.

Ilwan. And is that true? Did my father kill his father?

Asakir. God alone knows.

Ilwan. But what started this family feud in the first place?

Asakir. I don't know. Nobody knows. It's something far gone in the past. All that we know is that there's always been blood spilt between us.

Ilwan. The cause may well be that one of our calves happened to drink from a

water-channel in a field that belonged to their ancestors!

Asakir. God alone knows. As for us mortals, all that we know is that between the Azizes and Tahawis rivers of blood have flown.

Ilwan. Rivers that water neither crop nor fruit.

Asakir. Rivers that stopped flowing only with the death of your father. And that became of your tender age. Years then went past dry as the thirsty season, and people whispered lies and false rumors, while I was writhing in the flames of my hidden anger, waiting for this hour. And now the hour has come, so get up, son, and put out my fire and slake my thirst for the blood of Suweilam Tahawi.

Ilwan. Has this Suweilam Tahawi got a son?

Asakir. Yes. Fourteen years old.

Ilwan. So I have no more than another four or five years to live.

Asakir. What is it you are saying?

Ilwan. ...Only until he grows strong enough to do to me what I am supposed to do to his father.

Asakir. Do you fear for your life, Ilwan?

Ilwan. And what about you, mother? Do you fear for my life?

Asakir. The Lord be my witness, how I fear for every hair on your head.

Ilwan. You really care about my life, mother?

Asakir. Has my life any worth without yours? Or for that matter, the lives of all the Azizes. It's your life alone has made it possible for every one of us to live through the past seventeen years.

Ilwan (*bows his head*). I see.

Asakir. How often we suffered shame and humiliation. But as soon as your image crossed our minds our energy would revive, our resolution would strengthen and we were united in the hope that we placed upon you.

Ilwan (*his head still bowed and as if talking to himself*). You certainly need my life.

Asakir. Even your father's funeral waits for you, Ilwan. These sacrifices here are ready for the slaughter. My lamentation which I've been choking down in my throat all these years is waiting for you to set it free, My frock which I've kept myself from tearing open all that time is waiting for you, too. Everything in our existence is dead. Stagnant. Locking to you to breathe life into it.

Ilwan. Is this how life is breathed into you?

Asakir. Yes, Ilwan. Bring the appointed hour closer. Be quick.

Ilwan (*in wonder*). The appointed hour?

Asakir. I've forgotten nothing. Even the stone to whet the rusty knife I've

brought for you and hidden in this room.

Ilwan. But how am I to know this Suweilam? I've never set eyes on him in the whole of my life.

Asakir. Simeida will show you where to find him. He'll point him out to you.

Ilwan (*looks at his clothes*). Am I to commit this deed while I'm dressed in this way?

Asakir. Take off those clothes. I've a cloak that belonged to your father. I've kept it for you. (*She runs to go into the inner room*)

Ilwan (*stops her*). Just a minute, mother. Why the hurry?

Asakir. Every breath Suweilam draws while you are here is a gift which you are granting to him,

Ilwan. And what harm is there in that?

Asakir. It's taken from our breaths; it's drawn out of our wellbeing. Against our wishes we were forced to extend his life by as much as nearly brought us to the grave. Look at your mother, Ilwan. I was a young woman when your father died. But look what all those years have done to me. It is as if they were forty years, not seventeen. The sap of my youth has dried up and my bones have grown weak. All I have left is a memory that can never forget and a heart that cannot relent.

Ilwan (*as if to himself*). What a price it costs to avenge one's blood.

Asakir (*uncomprehending*). What did you say, Ilwan?

Ilwan. I said that God the Mighty Avenger is merciful to us. He offers to relieve us of this burden without any cost to us.

Asakir (*in a suspicious tone*). What do you mean?

Ilwan. Nothing, mother, nothing.

Asakir (*decisively*). Take off those clothes. I'll bring you the cloak and sharpen the knife for you myself.

Ilwan. Isn't there a mosque nearby?

Asakir. We've only a little chapel next to Sheikh Isnawis school-house.

Ilwan (*moving*). I'll go there and say my evening prayers.

Asakir. At this hour?

Ilwan. I think the sun is about to set.

Asakir. Do you want to be seen in the mosque by everyone in the village?

Ilwan. That would be the best opportunity for my purpose.

Asakir (*stares him in the face*). Have you gone mad, Ilwan?

Ilwan. It's most important for me to meet the villagers, Haven't I just told you that I have come to do something truly great?

Asakir (*as if mocking him*). I shouldn't imagine you'll want to reveal to the village the reason for your coming here?

Ilwan. It's essential to let them all hear what I have to tell.

Asakir. Ilwan, my son! What is it that I hear you say? Are you serious? Are you in your right mind? What is it that you want to tell them?

Ilwan (*as if in a dream*). I'll tell them what I have come here to say. I have often thought about my village and its people, in spite of the long time I've been away from it. There, at al-Azhar, when the classes were over, we—the students, that is—we'd gather together and read the newspapers. And we'd think of the places we'd come from. We were very homesick. And we often worried about when our people in the countryside would be able to live like human beings, in clean houses where they wouldn't share their meals with animals. When the roofs of their houses would be something better than dry stalks of cotton and maize, and the walls painted with something better than mud and the droppings of their beasts. When the water pot would disappear and there would be clean running water to the house. When electric lights would replace the oil lamp. Was that too much to ask for our people? Don't they have the same rights as others?

Asakir (*as if uncomprehending*). What is all this you're saying, Ilwan?

Ilwan. This is what the people of the village ought to know. And these of us who were educated in Cairo—it's our duty to make them see and realize their human rights. It shouldn't be difficult for them to achieve this aim: if only they would unite, join hands and co-operate. They ought to set up a council. Elect a council, that's it, from amongst themselves. And they could tax those who had money enough to pay. They'd form a team of able-bodied men to spend those long hours when there's nothing doing in making dykes and bridges and other constructive things. Not wasting time in squabbles and feuds. Why, if they worked together like that, if they would only make the effort, we'd make this a model village. And it would soon be an example for all the other villages in the country to follow.

Asakir. You're talking the language of books. You can keep that for later. For when you have your evening talk with Sheikh Muhammad Isnawi. He can understand it—I can't. As for the present, there's something more important that we've to do, Ilwan.

Ilwan (*shocked*). What is it that's more important?

Asakir. No. Don't go to the mosque to pray tonight. Else our plan might fail. Pray here tonight, if you wish to. Go and take off those clothes. I'll fetch water from the water-pot for you to prepare for your prayers. Put on the cloak and help me sharpen the knife.

Ilwan (*his head bowed, whispers*). Your mercy, O God, Your favor and forgiveness!

Asakir. What are you saying, Ilwan?

Ilwan (raises his head). I am saying that I have come here only to make you see and realize what life is, to bring you life.

Asakir. And that's exactly what we've been waiting for patiently for all these long nights. For seventeen years all the Azizes have been dead, waiting for your return to bring life back to them.

Ilwan (whispers with his head bowed down). God! What am I to do with these people?

Asakir. What is wrong with you, Ilwan? You keep bowing your head. Come on. Get up. Don't waste any more time.

Ilwan (raises his head and takes courage). Mother, I will not kill.

Asakir (tries to conceal her distress). What do I hear?

Ilwan. I will not kill.

Asakir (in a rough voice). The blood of your father!

Ilwan. It's you yourselves who left it spilt and wasted by hiding the crime from the government. It's up to the authorities to punish.

Asakir (beside herself). The blood of your father!

Ilwan. My hand wasn't made to destroy a human being.

Asakir (as if in a trance). The blood of your father!

Ilwan (alarmed at her condition). Mother, mother: what is the matter with you?

Asakir (as if she can see nobody in front of her). The blood of your father! Seventeen years. The blood of your father. Seventeen years...!

Ilwan. Mother, calm yourself. Of course it's a shock to you. But you must realize that I could never be an assassin and use my knife on a man.

Asakir (whispers as if out of her mind). Seventeen years...Vengeance for your father's murder...Seventeen years...

Ilwan (as if to himself). Mother, I know that you've stood it patiently for so long. If only this patience and endurance of yours were given up to a useful cause you would perform miracles! But you must understand that I—

Asakir (with a quaver in her throat). The blood of your father!

Ilwan (rushes towards her, alarmed). Mother! Mother! Mother!

Asakir (recovers awareness of her surroundings). Who are you?

Ilwan. Your son, Ilwan. Your son.

Asakir (screams). Son? My son? No, no! Never, never, never!

Ilwan (astonished). Mother!

Asakir. I'm not your mother. I don't know you. No son has ever been born out of my womb. No son have I ever given birth to.

Ilwan (pleading). Please, mother! Try to understand that—

Asakir. Out of my house...God's curse be upon you to the Day of Judgment.

Out of my house.

Ilwan. Mother!

Asakir (*screams*). Out of my house…or else I'll ask the help of our men to throw you out. We still have men. There are still men among the Azizes. But you—you're not one of them. Out of my house with you.

Ilwan (*picks up his bag*). I'll go to the station and go back to where I came from. And I'll pray to God that your disturbed soul may find peace, and that I may see you in Cairo soon to explain my way of looking at things, in quiet, far away from here. Goodbye, mother.

(*He leaves. His mother remains motionless in her place. After a while, Simeida enters, first putting his head round the door, then gently pushing it open*)

Simeida. Was it you screaming, Aunt Asakir?

Asakir (*with determination: she is fully recovered now*). Come here, Simeida.

Simeida (*looks round*). Where's Ilwan? Where's your son?

Asakir. I have no son. I never bore a son.

Simeida. What are you saying, Aunt Asakir?

Asakir. If I had a son he'd now be avenging his father's murder.

Simeida. Where has he gone?

Asakir. To the station. On his way back to Cairo.

Simeida. My mother was right. As soon as she saw him just now, she said , as we were leaving, "That turbaned preacher will never kill Suweilam Tahawi."

Asakir. I wish my womb had been torn to shreds before it brought such a son into the world!

Simeida. Don't upset yourself, aunt. There are still men among the Azizes.

Asakir. Our hope is now in you, Simeida.

Simeida. A nephew can stand in for a son.

Asakir. But in this case the son's alive. It's his duty before anybody else, to avenge the shedding of his father's blood. He's alive, Alive. He's about amongst the living.

Simeida. Just try to tell yourself that he's dead.

Asakir. I wish he had really died, drowned in the sluice of the water-wheel when he was a child. We would then never have had to wait all those years, writhing and roasting on the live coals of our pent-up anger, waiting to no purpose. I wish he had truly died. We would have been able to live honorably then, and not be wearing our garment of shame. But he is alive, and it has been broadcast in the market places and in the whole neighborhood that he is alive. Oh, the shame. The ignominy. The disgrace!

Simeida. Aunt, don't be so upset.

Asakir. It's impossible not to be upset by a disgrace like this. Carrying such a shame, life will be impossible. How can I go on living in this village now that people know that I have a son like this. How many a mouth will spit whenever his name is mentioned. From all directions the cry will be heard: "Cursed be the womb that brought him forth!" Yes, this womb (*Striking her belly hard and wildly*). A curse on this womb. All the women of the village will mock it: even the ugly, the dim-witted, the barren. This womb... this womb... this womb.

Simeida (*tries to stop her*). Aunt Asakir, don't punish yourself so!

Asakir. Fetch the knife, Simeida, fetch the knife, and rip it open.

Simeida. Have you gone mad?

Asakir (*screams*). Simeida: are you a man?

Simeida (*looks at her intently*). What is it you want?

Asakir. Stop your cousin's disgrace.

Simeida. Ilwan's?

Asakir. And his mother's, your Aunt Asakir's. Prevent her shame.

Simeida. How?

Asakir (*takes the knife from the saddle bag*). Kill him with this knife.

Simeida. Kill who?

Asakir. Ilwan. Dig this knife into his heart.

Simeida. I kill Ilwan? Your son?

Asakir. Yes. Kill him. Send him to join the dead.

Simeida. Pull yourself together, aunt.

Asakir. Do this, Simeida...for my sake and for his!

Simeida. For his sake!

Asakir. Yes. Better for him and better for me that it should be said he was killed, than for folk to say that he fled from his duty of avenging his father's murder.

Simeida. My own cousin!

Asakir. If you're a man, Simeida, you must never let him bring shame upon the Azizes. Never again will you be able to carry yourself like a man. Men will whisper and laugh behind their hands at you and point at you in the marketplace, and say: "There goes no more than a woman and one who's given shelter to another mere woman, at that."

Simeida (*to himself*). A woman!

Asakir. If the Tahawis had such a son they'd never have let him live for an hour.

Simeida (*to himself*). A woman—giving shelter to another woman!

Asakir. Yes, that's so; that'll be you if you allow him to behave as he means to.

Simeida (stretches out his hand resolutely). Give me the knife.

Asakir (hands him the knife). Here it is. But wait till I wash the dried blood and the rust off its blade.

Simeida (impatiently). Give it to me, before he slips away by the evening train.

Asakir (gives him the knife eagerly and forcefully). Take it. Let his blood wash away the blood of his father that's dried upon the blade.

Simeida (goes off with the knife). If I manage to kill him, you'll hear my voice raised in song at the outskirts of the village, aunt.

(Exit quickly. Asakir remains alone, fixed to the spot like a statue, gazing motionless and absently. After a while, Mabruka appears, carrying a water pitcher on her head)

Mabruka (puts down the pitcher). I've brought some dried fish for Sheikh Ilwan.

Asakir (turns to her slowly). May your life be longer than his, Mabruka.

Mabruka. Who are you talking about?

Asakir. Ilwan.

Mabruka. Your son?

Asakir. He's no longer mine; he belongs to the dust.

Mabruka. What are you saying, Asakir? I left him with you only a moment ago. Where is he?

Asakir. Gone to the station on his way back to where he came from. Giving his back to the duty of avenging his father's murder.

Mabruka (her head bowed down). Just as my heart has been telling me.

Asakir. Your prophecy has come true, Mabruka.

Mabruka. If only he had never come.

Asakir. Seventeen years we've been waiting.

Mabruka. Every year you used to say, "He's growing." You measured him by the handspan as if he were a shoot of maize. But then, when he grew tall and his cob was ripe, you stripped him, only to find that there was no grain on the cob.

Asakir. It wouldn't have been such a disaster if he were no more than a bare cob. We never expected any material gain through him. We expected him to give us back our dignity—that was all. How proud I was of him, Mabruka, how often I boasted about him to you. I thought I'd brought forth the son who'd cleanse the stain off the honor of the family. And how has he turned out now? The very son I've given birth to, the son I took great care to hide like a treasure in a crock of clay—he's no more than a stain on our tree, like a blight overtaking a cotton plant. God's mercy be on your soul, my husband:

they spilt your blood and it has not been avenged. I've given you a son who brings comfort to your enemies and makes them gloat.

Mabruka. Oh shame. Shame on the Azizes!

Asakir. If he stays alive. But before long he'll be buried in the earth.

Mabruka (turns round suddenly). Where's Simeida?

(The whistling of a train is heard)

Asakir (listening intently). Hush! There's the evening train entering the station.

Mabruka. Asakir, where's Simeida?

Asakir (still listening intently). Be quiet. Now, at this instant, at this very instant.

Mabruka (astonished). What happens at this instant?

Asakir (as if to herself). Do you think the train has carried him off? Or has he been carried off by—

Mabruka. If he's gone to the station, as you say, he must have got on the train. All these curses you are heaping on his head will do no good.

Asakir. Do you really think he has got on the train?

Mabruka. What could have stopped him?

Asakir (slipping out the answer). Simeida!

Mabruka. Simeida? Did he go after him to stop him leaving?

Asakir. Yes.

Mabruka. When did he go?

Asakir. A short while before you came.

Mabruka. I shouldn't think he could have overtaken him.

Asakir (sighs in relief). Do you really think so?

Mabruka. Unless he ran very fast.

(The train whistle is heard again)

Asakir (listens intently). There, the train is leaving the station.

Mabruka (stares at her). What's wrong with you, Asakir? Why have you gone so pale?

Asakir. What does your heart tell you, Mabruka?

Mabruka. It tells me that he has gone.

Asakir. Gone. Gone—where?

Mabruka. Where he came from.

Asakir. What do you mean?

Mabruka (watches her). Why is your breast heaving like that?

Asakir (in a whisper, her eyes wandering). Gone where he came from!

Mabruka. Do you still hope for some good from him?

Asakir. No.

Mabruka. You must think of him as if he'd never been.

Asakir (*as if to herself*). Yes. His death is less shameful than his life.

Mabruka. And thank God that he's far away.

Asakir (*to herself*). Is he on the train now?

Mabruka. Who knows? Perhaps Simeida was able to catch him up and persuade him not to go: perhaps he'll bring him back now.

Asakir (*as if dreaming*). Bring him back now?

Mabruka. Why not? If Simeida ran really fast he wouldn't have missed the train.

Asakir (*whispers*)...Was able to catch him up...

Mabruka. And it may not be long before we see them coming back again together.

Asakir (*to herself*). No. This time Simeida will be coming alone.

Mabruka (*watches her anxiously*). Your face, it fills me with terror.

Asakir (*listens intently*). Hush! Listen! Listen! Can't you hear anything?

Mabruka. No. What do you want me to hear?

Asakir. Singing.

Mabruka. No, I cannot hear any singing.

Asakir (*with relief*). Nor can I.

Mabruka. Did Simeida tell you he was going to sing?

Asakir (*to herself, anxiously*). Perhaps he hasn't reached the edge of the village yet.

Mabruka. I should imagine he has, by now.

Asakir (*breathing more freely*). And he is not singing!

Mabruka. Now the blood has come back to your cheeks.

Asakir (*whispers*). He hasn't caught him up.

Mabruka. You'd rather he didn't come back, Asakir, wouldn't you? You'd rather the train carried him away from this village. So would I. I'd much rather he returned to his Cairo, to his preachers and the other students. He doesn't belong to us, nor we to him. He's done well to leave us so soon, before the people of the village could meet him and get to know what we know about him. (*Asakir listens to a distant sound*) You're not listening to me, Asakir. Don't you think I'm right?

Asakir (*in a rough, alarmed voice*). No, no, I can't hear anything!

Mabruka (*listens*). It is Simeida singing. (*Turns, alarmed, to Asakir, whose eyes have glazed over*). Asakir! Asakir! What's wrong? You scare me!

Simeida (*outside, sings*).

O my dear one,
Your bitter voice accuses:
Repentance and excuses
Were all I ever gave
You reproached me then the more,
And out of grief my clothes
To shreds I tore.
When they told me of your father,
It was my silent shame
Which set unmanly cheeks aflame,
Where eyes ran dry
And made a desert of my face.

Asakir (pulls herself together, to stop herself from collapsing, but lets slip a faint choking cry like a death rattle). My son!

CURTAIN

Translated by Mustafa Badawi[23]

Part VIII

MODERN ARABIC LITERATURE

Abu al-Qasim al-Shabi

I do not weep for thee,
My yesterday,
That fate hath plundered me
Of gorgeous majesty
And glorious sway:
I care not for life's dream
And glory's gleam.

Nor that my little tale
Of days is spent,
Resistless to prevail
When fortune did assail
The battlement;
Lo, yet my youth is bright
With morning light.

Nay, it is not for this
I weep, and sigh,
The longed-for goal of bliss
My ardent heart must miss
And let go by;
Men have of life such fill
As God may will

It is for love they flow,
My bitter tears,
Love's glory, that doth glow
O'er all the world I go
Through all the years,
Each gleaming morn.

Where songbirds warble, there
Love echoeth;
Such fragrance soft and rare
As scenteth all the air
Is love's sweet breath;
Love stirreth in its hour
The fluttering flower.

Love's beauty ruleth, king
O'er heav'n supreme,
Magic embroidering
Each live and living thing
In beauty's dream;
My heart, in dawn's embrace,
Knows the god's grace.

TO THE TYRANT

Imperious despot, insolent in strife,
Lover of ruin, enemy of life!
You mock the anguish of an impotent land
Whose people's blood has stained your tyrant hand,
And desecrate the magic of this earth,
Sowing your thorns, to bring despair to birth.

Patience! Let not the Spring delude you now,
The morning light, the skies' unclouded brow;
Fear gathers in the broad horizon's murk
Where winds are rising, and deep thunders lurk;
When the weak weeps, receive him not with scum.
Who soweth thorns, shall not his flesh be torn?

Wait! Where you thought to reap the lives of men,
The flowers of hope, never to bloom again,
Where you have soaked the furrows' heart with blood,
Drenched them with tears, until they overflowed,
A gale of flame shall suddenly consume,
A bloody torrent sweep you to your doom!

Translated by A. J. Arberry[1]

Naguib Mahfouz

AN UNNERVING SOUND

He sat there in his usual morning seat at the Tree Casino sipping coffee and smoking a cigarette. He was either looking at the still waters of the Nile or else upwards at the clear July sky, the color of which faded in the intense sunshine. He had some uneasy thoughts, closed his eyes to concentrate, and then opened them again. He noticed his notebook open at a white page and his pencil thrown across it at his beck and call. Looking around the rest of the of the café, he saw two people here and two others there, but they were the only ones. Even the waiter was sitting on the wall overlooking the Nile having a sort of holiday. He

was the only one who came to this place to do any work; he had come on this stubborn recalcitrant July day to look for some inspiration for a new topic to fill his column *Yesterday and Today* in his weekly magazine. And this topic had to be something new week after week, and so it went on forever. His whole happiness depended on his success in this work, his nice apartment, his wife, his baby who was almost two years old, his Opel car, not to mention his bachelor place in the East building which was available for unforeseen requirements.

"Heavens, be generous with your ideas...."

He looked through his glasses at a palace on the other bank of the river directly opposite where he was sitting. The windows and doors were locked, and the walls gleamed brightly in the sunlight, but there was no movement anywhere; even the trees were still and looked as solid as statues.

"Oh, to live in a palace! No bother about earning a living, no worries except just thinking!"

He looked at the dregs in the bottom of his coffee cup. "I have ideas and projects," he told himself with a sigh, "but I waste my entire life recording various observations and proposing familiar solutions to familiar problems. Ugh...."

"Professor Adham," said a gentle voice from behind which startled him, "good morning...."

He turned round with a smile so as to hide the shock he felt and then released himself from his thoughts. "Nadra," he said, "how nice to see you."

They shook hands, and she sat down opposite him, putting her handbag on top of the white page. "I saw your back from the road," she said, "and recognised you."

"When will you recognise me from the front as well as from the back?"

"Your face is imprinted in my heart," she replied jokingly.

All the time, he was looking at her svelte figure and face which gleamed with a spirit of youth. Even though childhood and adolescence were still close together in her life, she had make-up on her face, her eyes, eyelids, brows and lashes and nails.

"Were you on your way to or from an appointment?" he asked without bothering about her little joke.

"I don't like morning appointments. I was dithering around in the car with no particular purpose in mind."

No purpose! Infectious terminology! But you're thirty-five and she's seventeen. She is free enough to arouse the interest of any married man with a bachelor place of his own. She reads a lot and is very fond of Françoise Sagan. She had certainly surprised him on the night when he had first met her along

with a group of friends in *Sans Souci*. She could comment on life in an extraordinary way and, when necessary, did not mind cracking a dirty joke. She had been studying scenario since abandoning her university studies; maybe she was striving for the stars. She had written several artistic pieces but, in spite of her beauty, she had failed to get them published in magazines or broadcasts. When they had last met, she had declared in the presence of some friends how much she admired atheist existentialism.

"What can I order for you?" he asked, and then carried on in a semi-serious tone, "or would you prefer us to postpone that till we go to my private apartment?"

"Order some coffee and stop dreaming...."

He offered her a cigarette and lit it for her. She started drinking the coffee without bothering about the way he was staring at her.

"How's the existential anxiety?!" he eventually asked jokingly.

"Fine. But I only slept for two hours yesterday."

"Thought and philosophy?"

"A row with Mother and Father as you can imagine."

With a start he remembered the topic he was looking into seriously.

"Finish your education," she continued, imitating her parents' tone of voice. "Get married...don't play around as young men do..."

A typical recording, but the girl was beautiful and the session was proving inspiring. Who knows?! However, he had to finish today's topic even if it meant cancelling his evening appointments. "How do you expect them to understand a little philosopher like you?" he asked.

A frown warned him against proceeding any farther with that kind of joking.

"No one's prepared to admit," she said, "that I'm struggling to create myself, but I'm living with the People of the Cave!"

He remembered that her father had ideas more than once on television. "But your father is a man of the times," he said.

"Man of the times!"

"Compared with my father at least."

"Compared with the Stone Age perhaps?" she replied suppressing a laugh.

He looked into the distance as though he were dreaming.

"The Stone Age!" he said with fascination. "If only we could go back to that period just for an hour, I would carry you off on my shoulder, with no one to stop me and take you to my cave in the East Building!"

"I told you to stop dreaming," she said. "Let me tell you why I've come...."

"Oh! So we didn't meet by chance then?"

"You know that I know that you spend every morning here writing."

"Then let's go to the East Building," he said in mock seriousness, "so that we can find a suitable place to talk seriously!"

"Can't you see I'm not joking?" she said, lighting one cigarette with another. She fixed him with her piercing eyes as pure as honey. "You promised me once," she continued, "that you'd introduce me to Mr Ali al-Kabir."

"Are you serious?" he asked anxiously

"Absolutely."

"No doubt, you admire him as an actor!"

"Of course..."

They looked at each other.

"He's forty-five!" he said.

"I know. Have you heard about the magic of time?"

"No. But I've heard a lot about the tragedy of time."

"You set yourself up as some kind of moral counselor in *Yesterday and Today*. But here..."

"What's my part in the story?"

"You're his best friend."

"He has a daughter your age."

"That's right. I think she's at law school..."

"Tell me what's on your mind," he said after thinking for a while. "Are you thinking for example of destroying his family life and then marrying him?"

"I'm not thinking of any such thing," she replied letting out a laugh.

"Just love then?"

She shrugged her shoulders without saying anything.

"A quick way to a screen part?" he asked.

"I'm not an opportunist," she replied disdainfully.

"Well then?!"

"You must keep your promise."

Suddenly he had an idea. "You've given me the inspiration for a topic!" he shouted.

"What is it?"

"Free love, yesterday and today," he replied after a moment's thought.

"Tell me more."

He felt himself impelled by an urge which he made no attempt to dislodge. "Take an example on the subject," he said. "In olden times, when a girl went wrong, she was said to be a fallen woman; whereas now they say it's anxiety caused by civilization or else philosophical anxiety."

"You're antediluvian," she said angrily, "even though you pretend to be

forward-looking."

"What do you expect from someone whose ancestors lived in the Stone Age?"

"Can't you look at me as a human being who's like you in every way?"

"If you were narcissistic, yes."

"There you are making fun of me, and my father yells at me."

"What about you?"

"I'm still asking you to keep your promise."

"Let me give you some idea about him first. He's a great artist; in many people's view, he's the foremost film actor. He has a familiar policy which he never changes. If he's introduced to a girl like you, he takes her straightaway to his private house near the Pyramid, and then begins where other people leave off."

"I'm grateful for your kind of advice."

"You still want to meet him?"

"Certainly...?"

"Fine," he said provocatively. "But I must ask for the cost in advance!"

She moved her head to show that she did not understand. That dislodged a strand of black hair curled in a circle over her eyebrow.

"I'd like you to pay me a visit at the East Building."

She smiled without saying anything or indeed believing he was serious.

"Agreed?"

"I'm sure your mind is cleaner than that."

"I'm afflicted by the anxiety of the age!"

"No, no. Don't mix jokes and serious discussion. I've wasted your valuable time," she said apologetically.

She lit a third cigarette, and they looked at each other for a long while. They smiled together. He started thinking about his topic again. The atmosphere had been totally cleared of any misunderstanding, and an oppressive feeling of heat and humidity had returned.

"You're a reactionary in trendy clothing!" she said jokingly.

"No, I'm not! You're not being frank with yourself. But you're really delightful, and your jokes are fun. I'll arrange the meeting in my office at the magazine; drop in—quite by accident—on Wednesday evening at nine."

"Thanks."

"I owe you my thanks for next week's article."

"I'll see how you deal with it."

"When I'm writing, I become a totally different personality!"

"You stick to some preordained pattern or other which has to be followed, even if it means going against what you really feel."

"Perhaps. The truth is that the best of me hasn't expressed itself yet."

When she noticed him looking at the notebook, she stopped arguing with him and put her handbag on an empty chair. He looked once more at the sleepy palace deep in its cloistered magnificence. He liked the balcony adjoining the garden and admired even more the balcony on the higher floor resting on pillars which looked like obelisks. How nice it would be to sit on that balcony in the moonlight, he thought, and be free to think without being bound by appointments and conventions; or to own a yacht and travel round on the ocean meeting people and seeing other countries with no boundaries and on condition that your wife stayed in Cairo; to play with roses in Hawaii and forget about the topics for *Yesterday and Today* and all the other problems like poverty, ignorance, and disease. You have a certain amount of doubt about your own talents, but these sudden outbursts keep obscuring your doubt. They are strange, staggering outbursts which ignore any idea of responsibility, unintelligible, unquestionable and uncontrollable, but commentators from taverns and *hasish* rings keep volunteering to explain them.

"Nadra, what do you think of the absurd?" he asked.

"Very rational!" she replied enthusiastically.

"It's toying with me like a dream."

"I'm thinking of writing a theatre-of-the-absurd play for the puppet theatre," she said and then added with a sorrowful sigh, "if it weren't for my father, I would have written a crazy story about my experiences..."

"I wish you'd include me in those experiences!" he replied, not able to control his jocularity.

"Stop joking and think of the success they deserve."

A delightful period of contemplation ensued, and they both lost themselves in a long period of silence.

Suddenly a sharp noise rang out which made them both start at the same time, a human voice shouting, "Ho!" They saw a man tying up a boat with folded sails. It looked as though he were standing stock still, or else moving so very slowly and heavily as to be almost standing still. He was almost touching the outside of the wall just two metres away from where they were sitting and dragged the boat along with a long rope wrapped round his shoulders. Throwing himself forward, he flexed his muscles for all they were worth with great determination. The boat was moving slower than a turtle on the stagnant water in the still atmosphere. An old man wearing a *gallabiyya* and turban was standing in the bow and watching the other man struggle with a languid and sympathetic stare. The two of them sitting at the table no longer felt worried; anger had taken the place of anxiety, but neither of them said a word.

The man carried on putting all his energy into his exhausting job till he was level with the spot where they were sitting. He was a young man in his twenties, dark-skinned, with swarthy features; he had nothing on his head or feet and was wearing a colorless *gallabiyya* with the top torn part open. The strain brought out all the varicose veins on his legs. His eyes bulged, his lips were taut, and he kept his back bent so as to avoid the scorching sun. Every time he felt exhausted, he would stop for a minute to take a deep breath.

"Heave ho!" the old man would yell.

"Ho!" he would yell in his turn.

His cruel struggle continued. In the minutes when he was alongside them, they could smell the stench of his body which reeked of sweat and mud. Their faces flinched, and Nadra put her delicate nose into a handkerchief impregnated with a beautiful scent. They both tried to pretend they were not disgusted and shocked as they watched the painful ordeal going on. They watched him move step by step till eventually this sharing in his task wore them both out. They turned away and looked at each other. With smiles of sympathy, each of them lit a cigarette.

Translated by Akef Abadir and Roger Allen[2]

Jabra Ibrahim Jabra

A STRANGER AT THE FOUNTAIN

A blade of grass split a stone:
is it a cock's crow that resounded,
pierced the darkness, dragged the sun from his hair, and proclaimed
the sovereignty of day?
It is the miracle of thunder to the waste land,
to the parched lips which turned
wide open to the sky, and rain poured!
Take the soul, take the body,
take the mind, take, take
O fingers that have planted their nails
as rose bushes in my blood.
Your beloved carries the night and the sun together between his palms
and from the inside of the earth he comes

like a blade of grass splitting a stone
winged bedewed, he sprinkles
the deserts of your eyes, your hands,
O fingers that plant their nails
as fountains of love in my blood.

The breeze of the road surging at night with eyes,
sheltering strangers and prophets
in love with long sidewalks,
the breeze of the road that is heedless and roaring
descending from the house to the cave and the fountain,
ascending from the house to Golgotha,
from the bed of dreams to the Cross—
the breeze of the road, carrying the smell of dung and jasmine
of panting, death and the last laugh from beginning
and end, comes
in anger as smooth as a sleeping snake, as a
maiden of twenty kissing in the dark
a man for the first time, as a virgin with heated
breasts seeking pleasure and resisting it
swerving inveigling,
touching whispering burning
with the frenzy of flesh and blood,
uttering words that embody the spirit and drip with
fragrance on the tongue and the lips.

It is the spirit which causes ecstasy and pain. Like a mad man it
hits the corridors of the brains and the heart with its hoofs.
It is the inevitable lie, the lie whose
truth proceeds from the road beloved by prophets and
fugitives. The spirit is the road, the breeze is its whisper.
the touch of the loving breasts in the long heat of night.

The end of the trip is its beginning,
let the clocks of the city strike in vain!
Neither night now possesses its bats
nor morning threatens with coming death.
On the mountain, where the threatening Piece of Wood was set up,
the rock of water has exploded in cataracts

and the wild horses of night neighed
at the edge of the cool fountain.
A stranger in whose face are two dimples, in
whose hair is the taste of threshing-floors,
and in whose mouth is the summer of vineyards,
began dipping his feet in the flood
shouting: whose are these horses of night?
whose except the Stranger's who turned time into circles
and kissed the crown of thorns until
the horses, the night and all the docks of the city went mad.

Translated by Issa J. Boullata[3]

Khalil Hawi

THE BRIDGE

It suffices me that I have the children of my contemporaries,
That of their love I have wine and bread.
It suffices me that from the harvest of the field
The harvest feast is enough for me.
And that I have many feasts
Whenever a new lamp is lit in the village,
But I have not carried roses to the dead
And have not cared for the wedding of slaves.
For their child is born an aged bat.
One who annihilates, revives, restores,
Undertakes to create a new child,
To wash him in oil and sulfur
From the stink of pus,
One who annihilates, revives, restores,
Undertakes to create the offspring of the eagle
Is different from the descendants of slaves.
The child does not recognize his father and mother
He does not bear the slightest resemblance to them.

Why is it that our house is split in twain
And the sea is divided between old and new?
A cry, wombs torn and veins cut
How do we remain under one roof
While seas—an obdurate wall—separate us?
When will we rise, become strong and build
Our new free home with our own hands?

They cross the bridge blithely in the morning
My ribs are stretched out as a firm bridge for them
From the caves of the East, from the swamps of the East
To the New East
My ribs are stretched out as a firm bridge for them.
"They will go and you will remain
Empty-handed, crucified, lonely
In the snowy nights while the horizon is ashes
Of fire, and the bread is dust;
You will remain with frozen tears in a sleepless night
The mail will come to you with the morning:
The news page...how often you ruminate its contents,
Scrutinize it...reread it!
They will go and you will remain
Empty-handed, crucified, lonely."

Shut up, O owl that knocks at my chest.
What does the owl of History want of me?
I have inexhaustible treasures in my coffers:
The joy of the hands that gave,
Faith and memory.
I have embers and wine,
I have the children of my contemporaries
And of their love I have wine and bread
It suffices me that from the harvest of the field
The harvest feast is enough for me,
I am not afraid of you, O snowy resurrection day
I have embers and wine for resurrection day.

Translated by Issa J. Boullata[4]

'Abd al-Wahhab al-Bayati

APOLOGY FOR A SHORT SPEECH

Ladies and Gentlemen:
My speech was short
Because I hate that words take my time,
And my tongue
Is not a wooden sword
My words, Ladies, are of gold
My words, Gentlemen, were grapes of wrath
I am not drunk but I am tired
The candles are put out
The nights are cold
And I carry my heart in a suitcase
Like a dead child who drenched his cross with tears
Over thousands of treacheries and thousands of mean lies.
My speech was short
I am not drunk but I am mocking
My suffering
I am not Caesar:
Rome is burning
My soul is choking
Among thousands of treacheries and thousands of mean lies
So farewell
Ladies and Gentlemen.

Translated by Issa J. Boullata[5]

Salah 'Abd al-Sabur

THE TATARS ATTACKED

The Tatars attacked
The Tatars attacked
And played havoc with our ancient city
Our battalions returned torn in the heat of day
The black flag, the wounded, the dead caravan
The hollow drum, the humiliated footsteps, turning not backwards
A soldier's hand knocking on the wood
A tune of hunger
The trumpet sounding, out of breath
The ground burning like fire
The horizon choked with dust
A smashed cart rolling on the road
The horses looking with defeat
Noses dripping with defeat
Eyes tearful with defeat
The ears pricked by dust
The soldiers' arms hanging down near their feet
Their shirts wrinkled and stained with blood spots

Mothers fled behind the dark hill, horrified by the fire
By the crumbling cracks
By the Tatars' hateful eyes staring them in the face
And their hands lustfully stretched towards their flesh
Destruction and defeat marched
Oh my city! The Tatars attacked

In the far isolated prison of the captives
The night, the wires, the guards armed to the teeth
The stupid darkness, the wounded, the odor of pus
The jest of drunken Tatar soldiers
Smacking their lips with victory
The end of a happy trip
While I embrace my defeat, sink my feet in the sand
And remember—O Mother—our long blissful evenings

And weep—O Mother—for a memory like a breeze
And old words like clouds
Mother! While you were at the foot of that hill among the runners-away

While night knotted terror under the eyelids of the
little ones. While hunger, raggy garments
The deaf, the demons and the dark squatted in the caves
Did you weep because our village is rubble?
Because memorable days are gone and will not return?
Oh Mother! We shall not perish
I hear a friend here from our good old neighborhood
I hear the cough of a crippled defeated man
And a mouth muttering threats from afar
And I, and all our comrades, Mother, swore by hatred at the close of day
That we shall cry out in the forenoon for the Tatars' blood.
Mother! Say to the little ones:
"O little ones
We shall rummage among our dark homes when day breaks
And we shall build up what the Tatars destroyed."

Translated by Issa J. Boullata[6]

Mahmoud Darwish

PRIDE AND FURY

O Homeland! O eagle,
Plunging through the bars of my cell,
Your fiery beak in my eyes!
All I possess in the presence of death
Is pride and fury.
I have willed that my heart be planted as a tree,
That my forehead become an abode for skylarks.
O eagle!
I am unworthy of your lofty wing,
I prefer a crown of flame.
O homeland!
We were born and raised in your wound,
And at the fruit of your trees,
To witness the birth of your daybreak.
O eagle unjustly languishing in chains,
O legendary death which once was sought,
Your fiery beak is still plunged in my eye,
Like a sword of flame.
Unworthy of your lofty wing,
All I possess in the presence of death
Is pride and fury.

Translated by Mounah A. Khouri and Hamid Algar[7]

PROMISES FROM THE STORM

So let it be.
I have to refuse death,
To burn the tears of the bleeding songs,
To denude the olive trees
Of all fake branches.
If I am singing to joy
Beyond the eyelids of frightened eyes
That is because the Storm
Promised me wine,
New toasts
And rainbows;
And because the Storm
Swept away the song of stupid birds
And artificial branches
From the trunks of standing trees.
So let it be.
I have to be proud
Of you, O wound of the city,
O tableau of lightning
In our sad nights.
The street frowns at my face
But you protect me from the shadow and grudging looks.
I shall sing to joy
Beyond the eyelids of frightened yes,
Since the Storm has blown in my homeland
And promised me wine and rainbows.

Translated by Issa J. Boullata[8]

Adonis

IRAM THE MANY-COLUMNED

Our city fled
So I ran to see its roads
I looked—I saw nothing but the horizon
I saw that the fugitives tomorrow
And those returning tomorrow
Were a body that I tore on my paper.

And I saw—the clouds were a throat
The water was walls of flame
I saw a yellow sticky thread
A thread of history hanging on to me
With which a hand that inherited
The race of puppets and the dynasty of rags
Was pulling at my days, knotting them and undoing them.

I entered the ritual of creation
In the womb of water and the virginity of trees
I saw trees trying to seduce me
Among their branches I saw rooms
Beds and windows resisting me,
I saw children to whom I read
My sand; I read to them
The chapters of "The Clouds" and the verse of "The Stone";
I saw how they traveled with me
I saw how behind them shone
The ponds of tears and the corpse of rain.

Our city fled
What am I? An ear of corn
Weeping for a skylark
That died behind the snow and the hail
And did not reveal its letters
About me and did not write to anybody
I asked it as I saw its corpse

Lying at the edge of Time
And I shouted, "O icy silence
I am a homeland to its estrangement
I am a stranger and its tomb is my homeland."

Our city fled
So, I saw how my foot changed into a river roaming in blood
And boats going far and growing larger
I saw that my banks were a drowning
Which tempted, and that my waves were wind and swans.

Our city fled
Rejection is a broken pearl
Whose remains settle on my ships
Rejection is a woodcutter living
On my face—gathering me and kindling me
Rejection is distances that distract me
So that I see my blood and beyond my blood.
My death talking to me and following me.

Our city fled
So I saw how my shroud shone on me
And saw—I wish death would grant me a respite.

Translated by Issa J. Boullata[9]

BEGINNING SPEECH

That child I was
Came to me once
An unfamiliar face
He said nothing—we walked
Each glancing in silence at each other
One step
An alien river
 Flowing.

Our common origins
 Brought us together
And we separated
A forest written by the earth
And told by the seasons

Child that I once was, advance,
What now brings us together?
And what have we to say to each other?

Translated by Lena Jayyusi and John Heath-Stubb[10]

Badr Shakir al-Sayyab

A CITY WITHOUT RAIN

A fire with no flames keeps our City awake at night,
Its lanes and houses have fever. When the fever goes
And sunset colors it with all the clouds it carried,
A spark is about to fly, its dead are about to rise:
"Tammuz has awakened from his muddy sleep under the grape bowers,
Tammuz has awakened, returned to green Babel to care for it."
The drums of Babel are about to beat, but through its castles
The wind's whistle and the moan of its sick predominate
In the chambers of Astarte
The earthenware censers remain empty with no fire.
Invocation rises as if all the throats of the reeds
In the swamps were crying:
 "Panting with exhaustion,
The goddess of blood returns, the bread of Babel, the sun of March.
We roam aimlessly like strangers from house to house,
Asking for her gifts.
Hungry are we. Alas! Her hands are empty,
Her eyes are harsh
And cold as gold.
We spent year after year after year watching
Thunderous, lightning clouds with no rain

And winds like storms which neither pass as a storm
Nor lie quiet—we sleep and wake up in fear of them.
O gods looking with no compassion:
Your eyes are stones which we feel out in the dark
Pelting us with no grudge,
Turning like slow millstones chewing our eyelids until we are inured to them.
Your eyes are stones as if they were the bricks of a wall
That we built with our hands, with what hands do not
build. Our virgins are sad and listless around Astarte
As water dries up bit by bit in—her face,
And branch after branch the vine withers.
Slow is our death inching its way between light and darkness,
What a lion it is, woe to it, from whose wide jaws we suffer.
Is there lightning fire or a temple flame in its eyes?
Are there two censers kindled for Astarte in its eyes?
Or are they two windows of the kingdom of the Dark World
Where yearly the saviour bears his burning wound,
The wound of the rotating world,
And yearly returns to redeem it and brings flowers
And rain—his hand awakening us with a wound?
But years have passed, so many we have not counted them,
With no rain—not even a drop,
With no flowers—not even one flower.
With no fruits: as if our barren palms were idols we erected
So that we might wither and die under them.
 Our lord has forsaken us
 Ah, for his tomb!
Is there not in your muddy bottom one jar
In which there are remains of the lord's blood, or a seed?
His little gardens we ate yesterday when we hungered;
We stole from the ants' homes, from their granaries, millet and oats
And impurities which we had sowed.
We kept our vow—but he did not."
The little ones of Babel walked carrying cactus baskets
And fruits of earthenware as offerings for Astarte.
Like a shadow of water, plant and fire
A shimmer of lightning lights
Their little round faces as they pray for rain
A field of blossoms is about to open up as they shine.

And like a thousand butterflies scattered on the horizon,
Their little hymn rises softly:
 "Our brothers' tombs call us.
Our hands are groping for You.
For fear fills our hearts, the winds of March
Rock our cradles and scare us. The voices call us.
Hungry are we, trembling in the darkness,
Looking in the night for a hand that will feed us and cover us,
To whose bare arm our searching eyes can firmly cling.
In the darkness we look for You, for two breasts, for a nipple.
O You whose bosom is the great horizon and whose breast is the cloud:
You have heard our sob and seen how we die—give us then to drink!
We are dying while You—alas—are hard and merciless.
O fathers of ours, who will redeem us? Who will revive us?
Who will die, who will offer his flesh as a banquet to us?"
The sky lit up with lightning as if a lily of fire
Was opening itself up over Babel. Our valley shone,
And incandescence penetrated the bottom of our land and bared it
With all its seeds, its roots and its dead:
Beyond the walls that Babel built around its fever
And its thirsty earth, beyond its pillars and its ramparts,
Clouds burst in rain which would have satiated it, but for these walls.
In an eternity of listening between one thunder and the next,
We heard—not the rustle of palms under torrential rains
Or the whispers of winds under wet trees—
But the sound of footsteps and hands,
A chuckle and an "Ah!" of a little girl who with her right hand
Caught a moon fluttering about like a butterfly, or seized a star,
A gift from the cloud,
A shiver of water, a drop which a breeze whispered
So that we know that Babel will be cleansed of its sins.

Translated by Issa J. Boullata[11]

RAIN SONG

Your eyes are two palm tree forests in early light
Or two balconies from which the moonlight recedes.
When they smile, your eyes, the vines put forth their leaves,
And lights dance... like moons in a river
Rippled by the blade of an oar at the break of day;
As if stars were throbbing in the depths of them...

And they drown in a mist of sorrow translucent
Like the sea stroked by the hand of nightfall;
The warmth of winter is in it, the shudder of autumn,
And death and birth, darkness and light;
A sobbing flares up to tremble in my soul
And a savage elation embracing the sky,
Frenzy of a child frightened by the moon.

It is as if archways of mist drank the clouds
And drop by drop dissolved in the rain...
As if children snickered in the vineyard bowers,
The song of the rain
Rippled the silence of birds in the trees...
Drop, drop, the rain...
Drip...
Drop...the rain...

Evening yawned, from low clouds
Heavy tears are streaming still.
It is as if a child before sleep were rambling on
About his mother (a year ago he went to wake her, did not find her,
Then was told, for he kept asking,
"after tomorrow, she'll come back again...")
that she must come back again,
yet his playmates whisper that she is there
in the hillside, sleeping her death for ever,
eating the earth around her, drinking the rain;
as if a forlorn fisherman gathering nets
cursed the waters and fate
and scattered a song at moonset,

drip, drop, the rain...
drip, drop, the rain...

Do you know what sorrow the rain can inspire?
Do you know how gutters weep when it pours down?
Do you know how lost a solitary person feels in the rain?
Endless, like spilt blood, like hungry people, like love,
Like children, like the dead, endless the rain.
Your two eyes take me wandering with the rain,
Lightnings from across the Gulf sweep the shores of Iraq
With stars and shells,
As if a dawn were about to break from them,
But night pulls over them a coverlet of blood.
I cry out to the Gulf: "O Gulf,
Giver of pearls, shells and death!"
And the echo replies,
As if lamenting:
"O Gulf,
giver of shells and death..."

I can almost hear Iraq husbanding the thunder,
Storing lightning in the mountains and plains,
So that if the seal were broken by men
The winds would leave in the valley not a trace of Thamud.
Hear the villages moaning and emigrants
With oar and sail fighting the Gulf
Winds of storm and thunder, singing
"Rain...rain...
drip, drop, the rain..."

and there is hunger in Iraq,
the harvest time scatters the grain in it,
that crows and locusts may gobble their fill,
granaries and stones grind on and on,
mills turn in the fields, with them men turning...
drip, drop, the rain...
drip...
drop...

when came the night for leaving, how many tears we shed,
we made the rain a pretext, not wishing to be blamed
drip, drop, the rain...
drip, drop, the rain...
since we had been children, the sky
would be clouded in wintertime,
and down would pour the rain,
and every year when earth turned green the hunger struck us.
Not a year has passed without hunger in Iraq.
Rain...
Drip, drop, the rain...
Drip, drop...

In every drop of rain
A red or yellow color buds from the seeds of flowers,
Every tear wept by the hungry and naked people,
Every spilt drop of slaves' blood,
Is a smile aimed at a new dawn,
A nipple turning rosy in an infant's lips,
In the young world of tomorrow, bringer of life.
Drip, drop, the rain...
Drip...
Drop...the rain...
Iraq will blossom one day in the rain.

I cry out to the Gulf: "O Gulf,
Giver of pearls, shells and death!"
The echo replies
As if lamenting:
"O Gulf,
Giver of shells and death."
And across the sands from among its lavish gifts
The Gulf scatters fuming froth and shells
And the skeletons of miserable drowned emigrants
Who drank death forever
From the depths of the Gulf, from the ground of its silence,
And in Iraq a thousand serpents drink the nectar
From a flower the Euphrates has nourished with dew.
I hear the echo

Ringing in the Gulf:
"Rain...
Drip, drop, the rain...
Drip, drop."
In every drop of rain
A red or yellow color buds from the seeds of flowers.
Every tear wept by the hungry and naked people
And every spilt drop of slaves' blood
Is a smile aimed at a new dawn,
A nipple turning rosy in an infant's lips
In the young world of tomorrow, bringer of life.

And still the rain pours down.

Translated by Lena Jayyusi and Christopher Middleton[12]

Yusuf al-Khal

THE DESERTED WELL

I knew Ibrahim, my dear neighbor, for
A long time. He was a well whose water overflowed
But people
Passed by and did not drink from it, nor did they
Throw even a stone in it.

"If I could spread my brow
On the mast of light again,"
Says Ibrahim on a small piece of paper
Stained with his unavenged blood, "will the brook,
I wonder, divert its course? Will the boughs bud
Or the fruits form in autumn,
Will plants grow on the rocks?

"If I could,
If I could die and live
Again, will the sky soften its face
So that eagles do not tear the long train

Of victims in the desert? Will factories laugh,
With smoke? Will noise stop in the fields,
In great boulevards? Will the poor man eat
His daily bread by the sweat of his brow,
By the sweat of his brow not the tears of humiliation?

"If I could spread my brow
On the mast of light,
If I could live for ever,
Will Ulysses return, I wonder?
Will the prodigal son, will the Lamb?
Will the sinner stricken with blindness
So that he can see the Way?"

When the enemy aimed the cannon of death
And soldiers charged under a shower
Of bullets and death,
Someone shouted at them, "Retreat, Retreat.
In the shelter at the rear there is a place
Safe from bullets and death."

But Ibrahim kept advancing,
Onwards advancing,
His little chest filling space.
"Retreat. Retreat.
In the shelter at the rear there is a place
Safe from bullets and death."
But Ibrahim kept advancing
As if he heard no echo.

Some said it was madness.
Perhaps madness it was.
But I knew my dear neighbor for a long time,
I knew him since childhood
A well whose water overflowed,
But people
Passed by and did not drink from it, nor did they
Throw even a stone in it.

Translated by Issa J. Boullata[13]

Muhammad al-Fayturi

TO TWO UNKNOWN EYES

Mistress
Should these enamored words chance to meet your eyes
Or pass between your lips
Then forgive me; it was your eyes
In whose shade one evening I leaned resting
And snatched brief slumber
In their repose I caressed the stars and moon
I wove a boat of fancy out of petals
And laid down my tired soul
Gave to drink my thirsty lip
Quenched my eye's desire

Mistress
When we met by chance as strangers meet
My sorrow too was walking on the road,
Bare, unveiled
With heavy tread
You were my sorrow
Sadness and loss
Silence and regret
Were embracing a poet consumed by struggle
For poetry, mistress, is a stranger in my land
Killed by emptiness and void
My spirit trembled when I saw you
I felt suddenly as if a dagger delved into my blood
Cleansed my heart, my mouth
Prostrated me with soiled brow and supplicating hands
In the shade of your sweet eyes

Mistress
If suddenly we meet
If my eyes see those your eyes
High-set, green, drowned in mist and rain
If on the road by another chance we meet

And what is chance but fate?
Then would I kiss the road, kiss it twice

Translated by Mounah A. Khouri and Hamid Algar[14]

SORROW OF THE BLACK CITY

When the night sets up its trellis of twigs
On the city streets
And sprinkles its deep sorrow on them,
You see them quietly resigned
Staring at the cracks
And so you think they are submissive
But—they are on fire!

When the dark builds up
On the city streets
Its marble statues
Which it ungratefully destroys,
And when its spiral stairs
Take creatures downwards
To a deep remote past,
And when its amber shores
Are drowned in memories
Almost never to awake,
And when in every soul rises a wall
Of clay, diamonds, and desires
And the night becomes sleepy
And a day rises as lamps in array
Are set against the darkness,
The blood of tranquility becomes
As dry as tombs
And the heart of the city becomes
Like a despicable thing
Like a stove in midday heat
Like a lamp in a blind man's way
Like Africa in the dark ages:
An old woman shrouded in incense

A pit for a bonfire
An owl's beak
A beast's horn
An amulet with an ancient prayer
A night with many mirrors
A dance of naked blacks
Singing in black joy
In absence of sins
Worried by their master's lust
And by ships laden with comely slave-girls,
Musk, ivory, saffron,
Gifts without festivities
Driven by the wind at every moment
To the white man of this age
Master of every age.
A plantation extends in the world of imagination
Clothing the naked, undressing the nude
Its gloom running in the veins of life
Coloring the waters
Dyeing the face of God
Its sorrows being a laugh on the lips
Growing even tyrants
Even slaves
Even iron
Even fetters
Growing something new every day.

But when the dark builds up
On the city streets
Barriers of black stone
They stretch out their hands in silence
To the balconies of the morrow
Their cries imprisoned
Their land imprisoned
Their days being wounded memories
Of a wounded land
Their faces, like their hands, sad
You see them quietly resigned
Staring at the cracks

And so you think they are submissive
But—they are on fire!

Translated by Issa J. Boullata[15]

Nazik al-Mala'ika

WHO AM I?

The night asks who am I?
 I am its secret—anxious, black, profound
 I am its rebellious silence
 I have veiled my nature, with silence,
 wrapped my heart in doubt
 and, solemn, remained here
 gazing, while the ages ask me,
 who am I?

The wind asks who am I?
 I am its confused spirit, whom time has disowned
 I, like it, never resting
 continue to travel without end
 continue to pass without pause
 Should we reach a bend
 we would think it the end of our suffering
 and then—void

Time asks who am I?
 I, like it, am a giant, embracing centuries
 I return and grant them resurrection
 I create the distant past
 From the charm of pleasant hope
 And I return to bury it
 to fashion for myself a new yesterday
 whose tomorrow is ice.

The self asks who am I?

I, like it, am bewildered, gazing into shadows
Nothing gives me peace
I continue asking—and the answer
will remain veiled by a mirage
I will keep thinking it has come close
but when I reach it—it has dissolved,
 died, disappeared.

Translated by Mounah A. Khouri and Hamid Algar[16]

FIVE HYMNS TO PAIN

I

It gives our nights sorrow and pain;
It fills our eyes with sleeplessness.
We found in it our way,
One rainy morning
And gave it, out of love,
A stroke of pity and a little corner
In our throbbing heart.

It never left or vanished from our way,
Stalking us to the corners of the world.
If only we gave it no drop to drink,
That sad morning!
It gives our night sorrow and pain;
It fills our eyes with sleeplessness.

2

Why does this pain come to us?
Where does it come from?
From old it has dwelled in our dreams
And nurtured our rhymes.
For we are a thirsting mouth
By which, thriving, we are satisfied.

At last, we dragged it to the lake,
Shattered it and scattered it to the waves,
Leaving neither a sigh nor a tear,
Thinking it would no longer afflict our smiles with grief
Or hide the bitter wails behind our songs.

Then we received a lovely scented rose,
Sent by loved ones from across the seas
What were we expecting from it?
Joy and happy contentment.
But it shook and began to flow with tears
Over our sad tuned fingers.
O pain, we love you!

Why does this pain come to us?
Where does it come from?
From old it has dwelled in our dreams
And nurtured our rhymes.
For we are a thirsting mouth
By which, thriving, we are satisfied.

3

Can we not conquer pain,
postpone it to another day,
keep it busy one evening,
divert it with a game, a song,
a forgotten ancient tale?

What can it be, this pain?
A tender, little child with searching eyes,
Quietened by a gentle, kind touch
And put to sleep with a smile and a lullaby.

O you who gave us our regrets and tears,
Who else but you closed his heart to our grief
Then came to us in tears, asking for refuge,
Who but you bestowed the wounds with smiles?

Child, most innocent of tyrants,
Loving foe or mortal friend,
A stab asking us to offer our cheeks,
Without a qualm and without a pang of pain.

Child, we have forgiven that hand and mouth
That dig trenches for tears in our eyes
And reopen the wound...
Yes, we have forgiven the sin, the damage, long ago.

4

How do we forget pain,
How do we forget pain?
Who will light for us
The night of its memory?

We shall eat it, we shall drink it,
We shall pursue it with songs,
And if we sleep, its shape
Will be the last thing we see.

And in the morning, its face
will be the first thing we discern,
and we shall bear it with us
wherever our desires and wounds take us.

We shall allow it to raise walls
Between our longing and the moon
Our anguish and the cooling stream,
Our eyes and our sight.

We shall allow it to afflict our eyes
with sorrow and distress,
and we shall shelter it
among the ribs of our joyful songs.

At last, it will be swept down the river,

and will be buried under the cactus,
and the forgetfulness will descend on our valley.
Good evening, sadness!

We shall forget pain,
we shall forget it,
having nurtured it with satisfaction.

Beloved pain,
we deified you in the drowsiness of dawn
bowed our heads at your silvery altar
burned the seeds of sesame and flax
offered sacrifices
sang verses to Babylonian tunes.

We built for you a temple with strange walls
And anointed the ground with oil, pure wine,
And burning tears.
We burned for you fires with leaves of palm
And stalks of wheat and our grief,
With closed lips, on a long night.

We sang and called and made our offerings:
dates from intoxicated Babylon
and bread and wine
and cheerful roses.
Then we prayed to your eyes
And offered a sacrifice,
And we gathered the bitter teardrops
And made a rosary.

O you who bestow on us our music and our songs,
O tears that lead to wisdom,
O fountain of all thought, fertile abundance,
O cruel tenderness, merciful punishment,
We have hidden you in our dreams,
In every note of our sad songs.

Stay as you are, a secret world

Not such thing as a soul discerns
Spinner of poems, the last muse
In a world whose mirrors are dimmed
What song did not flow with honey
If you were to smile your praise upon it?

Why do we fear words?
Some words are secret bells, the echoes
of their tone announce the start of a magic
And abundant time
Steeped in feeling and life,
So why should we fear words?

Translated by Nathalie Handal[17]

Mona Fayad

WHISPER

A whisper is a sibilant thing
Sliding from the throat
Straight to the ear
An intimate thing
I'd say to a sister.
A whisper provides
An access into
Boundless caverns
Echoing myself.
A whisper breaks
Narcissus' reflection
Of himself. A whisper
Is Echo's words.
This time, they are heard.

Translated by Nathalie Handal[18]

Salma al-Khadra al-Jayyusi

WITHOUT ROOTS

I

The ringing burst loud and frightening
Then that voice persistent and sad:
"Send your aid eastwards
All your uncles have become refugees."
I heaved a deep sigh and grieved sorely over them
Then I sent my uncles clothes
Which I had piled up for beggars
Raisins which if had but we would not eat
Sticky piasters with no bright sheen or ringing jingle
And tears and tears and tears and a groan.

Since that day I gave my piasters to no beggar
For my cousins had become refugees.

II

My uncle hungered and we lamented his hunger
Then we fed him for a month as a guest
And rested from the pangs of conscience
We then gave him up to the great wide world
And got absorbed in our own worlds.
"Many a dove calling in the forenoon" stirred our sadness
And we remembered him and plunged in tears
And rested from the pangs of conscience.
Who frightened away the white-legged horses from their hills?
Who toppled down their riders?
Who feeds them in their nakedness?
Who knows the green summits?
A strong noble people was living there then...went astray

III

Then we met—my cousin and I
I shouted to him, "My cousin, 'the apple of my eye,'
O noble man, I am still loyal to the fond memories
How much we loved each other as youngsters
and competed with the near star.
And wandered up green summits, and in the fertile meadow
(We had no idea how fertile it was)
We were sad at the sun's escape behind the horizon
Before we finished all we had to say.
A fragrance still clings to my heart of the fig leaves that shaded us.
You were a world of bloom: the sun and heaps of wishes
Were your sweet hope, your faith, your yearning and I...
Do tell me something new about you and I will
tell you something about my life
About my dream, my ambition, my thoughts and travels
Hey, what? Why are you turning away from me, distracted
Impatient? Are you not my cousin, O noble man?"
He said to me with indifference, "No, a stranger" and he disappeared.
Memories died at his heels...and we vanished
 Farewell, stranger.
In spite of death, he was my cousin
We had lived together on our land
My cousin was the prime
Of all the young men of our town
What made him freeze?
He was no dead man, I know him
For we set up our wishes together
And worshipped the birth of fire in us
We opened up our selves to a great desire
We grew up knowing the bitter hatred as of custom
We held fingers together
We demonstrated with the large crowds
And shouted with the fullness of the heart's faith
With the fullness of echoing expanse
"O Britain, do not overdo it
Do not say: 'Conquest is pleasant'
Nights will come to you

Whose lights are shining spears."
"O Britain? Those who died are dead. Lie down, O Spears."
Olive trees did not bear oil and fire
The color of their leaves faded
The morning breeze did not convey to us a desire, a stimulus
It embraced the strangers with its yearning

IV

I asked the land and the sea about them
The paleness of dawn, the sad night.
A star with an extinguished eye led me to them
And the traces of boxthorn carried from their valleys.
For they feared to die in their homeland
In order to live as refugees.
I came to the old man to quench my eagerness
He used to cherish me, babble to me, sing to me as a child
"My town is high...on the top of a hill
O my dear little girl...O jasmine bud."
He taught me old poetry,
The principles of religion (Ah for his despair!) and the Qur'an.
He used to protect me from my angry father
From my own unruliness.
Who can touch the jasmine while the old man is around!
A little girl with her grandfather can never have enough of his love.
She leans her head against his gentle chest
And he gives her the warmth of his heart.

I said, "Grandfather, peace and guidance."
I said, "Grandfather, we seek your satisfaction."
I said, "Grandfather, don't you know my voice?
Has it not made an echo while remembering you?"
My grandfather said, "Get up and leave us.
Our ears are heavy with deafness
The echo is a wound in the depths of the heart
I would have returned your bitter call
If I could speak. Get up and leave us
You do not understand the meaning of silence in a broken heart."

He used to cherish me, to babble to me, to sing to me
as a child My town is high...on the top of a hill
My town is high...on the top of a hill
My town is...The echo is a wound in the depth of the heart
My town...is high...on the top...of a hill
The call to prayer rose high
But my grandfather's heart is distracted and cannot hear it
A baby cried and cried too much
Having lost her who kissed his tears dry.
My uncle shouted, "Silence that sick baby
Ask our neighbor to suckle him
His pregnant mother nursed him little and he is lean
I shall not burn my days for him."

O my sweet one, my dear...O jasmine bud
Silence that sick baby!
O my sweet one, my dear...O jasmine...bud.

 V

Pale lips do not approach prayer at dawn
Pale lips do not know the purity of kisses
They do not kiss today except their lust
And though their feverish passion bears fruit
Pale lips do not kiss naked children
Born without roots, without a morrow,
From a passion that has no love;

O sons of the dead, are you dead like them
Or are you orphans? Or the scar of a wound in a sad people?
We are all that...
A word of a hoarse discordant tone united us "Refugees".

Translated by Issa J. Boullata[19]

IN THE CASBAH

I thought the war was...
Here we died, Mai and I,
Flattened by armored wheels
While you were fooling around
 In the Casbah...

I found my children's broken bodies
Lying in the streets and picked them up,
I swam over my head in nightmare,
Then yanked off my skin,
Hung it over the flame to dry
And once more I almost dreamed
 In their dream.

I flew, crawled, hid—
I heard the wind crying:
 "Salma...Salma
they've bought and sold you"
thousand snakes—a blazing coil
 around my heart.
And you were fooling around
 In the Casbah,
 Weren't you,
When our nation became
War's killing ground?

Translated by Charles Doria [20]

SCRAPPING LIMITS

Did I do it
 Step over the line?
 Yes
 Do my lovers know
 How I prayed God

 I would
 Stretching
 Beyond Sky
 To shatter wall
After wall
 In my way?

Scrapping limits
 I crossed to a world
 Where lovers never sleep
 They are so far gone
 Into each other
 Leaping fences
 I abandoned my sleepy fountain
 Where I loved and drowsed
 Completely
 Quiet and content.
I found fire's seed and entered
 Watching the innocence in my dreams
 Die
 Hipocritic standing guard
 Eager to become my tyrant

High noon sun blaze
 I pass the impassable
 Desire ending my journey
 Deserting the twilit world herded
 Gulled by the shadows
 Even moss casts
 On the walls that hem me in

Spotlight I can't get out of
 I won't strip for you
 Reveal myself
 I love dark corners
 With their wrap-around night
 I love staying home nights
 With one I love
 To be strange

The stranger at the crowd's heart

No Salma there's no turning back
 Harden now your tired heart
 And push on
 You completely the creature
 Of noon-day sun

Where you were before is chasm now
 Column of salt, body nailed to the gibbet
 Going bare discloses
 Loving heart's courage
Eyes ahead go on the way you came
 Humble road's steepest
 Walking up the stairs of hell

When you're there
 At your feet a spring
 Gushes free of the rock

APRIL WOMAN

Poem to my son

I am an April woman:
December ash that consumes itself
 Frightens me
My son, hide me while you rocket to the stars
Spreading over the earth like grass
Winter thunderstorm will drink down
My river flowing with love's secrets,
Muffling that music in whose echoes
 You were born

But you shrug your shoulders:
 "this woman is planted in time

she bridges the air like a dove
a thousand years old.
She is a willow, I know her:
Bend her—she springs back
She is a palm tree, I know her
Pick her fruit—she makes more
Honey and dates
She is a cypress tree, I know her
She never loses her leaves
What do December storms mean to her?"

Yet the winter winds do howl, my son,
Night and day I yearn for you
For your sweet sarcastic voice
Your voice wise and cruel, innocent and selfish.

Night and day I miss you
We both live in space, in the wind and the rain
Each of us drinks his own wine
Each of us is poured in his own glass
For you were made of my elements.

I gave you:
My impetuous soul
My constant disappearance
Flitting far away across the world
My chronic elusiveness
A will like rock, loyal
As true stars
In the sky's valleys.
And I gave you:
Love's ecstasy
The will to conquer
Passionate devotion
And the enchantment of the spirit
In the presence of holy fire.
Should I blame you?

And you gave me:

 A promise and a pledge
 Security forever delayed
 Love that's here and is never here
Should you blame me?
 I am a wild gazelle
 You are a rock
 My head is bloodied.

Translated by Charles Doria[21]

Fudwa Tuqan

A PRAYER TO THE NEW YEAR

In our hands is a fresh yearning for you,
In our eyes songs of praise and unique melodies,
Into your hand as choral offerings we will thrust them.
O you who emerge as a sweet fountain of hope,
O you who are rich with promise and desire.
What is in store for us that you hold?
What have you got?
~

give us love, for with love the treasures of bounty within us burst forth...
with love our songs will grow green and will flower
and will spring with gifts
riches
fertility.
~

give us love, so we may build the collapsed universe within us
anew
and restore
the joy of fertility to our barren world.
~

give us wings to open the horizons of ascent,
to break free from our confined cavern, the solitude
 of iron walls.
Give us light, to pierce the deepest darkness

And with the strength of its brilliant flow
We will push our steps to a precipice
From which to reap life's victories.

Translated by Lena Jayyusi and Naomi Shihab Nye[22]

ELEGY

The nightingale mourned in the glade for his mate,
And his grief wrung tears from the blossoms' eyes;
Sorrow surging importunate
Chosed his bosom with burning sighs.
Who hushed the singer, and wrapped him round
In silence, the silence of the tomb?
What runed his rapture to gloom profound,
That he shuns the nest, and the birds in the bloom?

When his brother dear he no longer viewed,
And no more captured his warbled note,
On a tender thorn-twig the mourner stood
And stretched to the skies his supple throat;
His yearning anthem throbbed in the dell,
And the boughs of the thorn-bush shook with pain
As forlornly he bade the mead farewell,
And the singer he would not find again.

In the still of night, and a world at rest,
Save the traveler glad in the stars' pale shine,
Grieving my heart for thee made quest,
Searching, and finding never a sign:
Yet with echoing grief, and refrain of sighs,
Weeping I make my poesy
Of the beat of my heart, and my tear-bright eyes,
Till the riders of death shall silence me.

Translated by A.J. Arberry[23]

IN THE FLUX

That evening
Faces faded around us
The room was drowned in fog
Nothing lived
But the shining blue of your eyes
And the call in the shining blue
Where my heart
Sailed, a ship
Driven by the tide
 The tide carried
 Us onto a sea
 Without shores
 Stretching
 Limitless current
 And flow
 Waves telling the endless
 Story of life
 Now abridged in one glance
 And the earth drowned in the rushing
 Flood of winds and rain

That evening
My garden awoke
The fingers of the wind
Unhinged its fences
Grasses swayed, flowers bursting,
Fruits ripening
In the blissful dance of wind and rain
Faces faded, all else was a fog
That evening
Nothing existed
But the blue shining light in your eyes
And the call in the shining blue
Where my heart sailed
Like a ship driven by the tide.

Translated by Patricia Alanah Byrne[24]

Mai Sayigh

DEPARTURE

In this the moment of departure,
Point your red arrows,
Disarm the lightening, and open wide
The gate to my exile.
Close the sky's open face, and ride away.
I long so deeply that the shores unfold their seas
And horses bolt!
Hooves have trampled my heart a thousand times,
A thousand waves have broken over it!
Now I'll carry the roads and palm trees in my suitcase,
I'll lock my tears in the evening's copybooks
And seal the seasons.

Let's begin our song: here is Beirut *wearing* you
 Like her own clothes.
You must sit well on the surface of her glory
Abandoning tears
In her blue froth
She contains you like eternity
Like the sense of beginning that comes with certainty

—How can you be dead, yet so absolutely present?

Let the rivers abandon their sources,
The winds abandon their skies,
And the seas dry out!
Everything in the universe has an end
Except my spilled blood...
Each time I think of it
You remain as large as your death.
The war planes choose you, discover you, plant
Their blackness in you.
From all those clouded last visions,
How will you begin the story of harvest?

War planes select you,
At the start of your sleep,
At the end of your sleep.
How often did the sky explode over you
 With hatred?
How often were you taken aside?
How many massacres did you survive?
Now you collect all the wounds, taking refuge with
 Death,
Wearing dreams as wings.

Translated by Lena Jayyusi and Naomi Shihab Nye[25]

Nizar Qabbani

BREAD, HASHISH AND MOONLIGHT

When the full moon is born in the East
And the white rooftops go to sleep,
Beneath waves of light that are deep...
People leave their shops and in throngs move forth
To meet the moon
And to the mountaintops carry bread...a radio...
and their opiates.
There they sell and buy fantasies of the mind
And images,
And they die when the moon comes to life.
What does a disc full of light do
To my land?
The land of prophets
The land of simple folk,
Those who chew tobacco and are drug merchants
What does the moon do to us,
That we lose our pride
And live to beg from heaven?
What can heaven offer
The lazy and the weak?

Those who turn into dead corpses when the moon comes to life
And shake the tombs of saints
In the hope that these tombs may bestow upon them some rice, some children
Their beautiful and elegant carpets they spread out
And console themselves with an opium that we call Fate and Destiny
In my land, the land of simple folk.
How weakness and dissolution
Afflicts us when the light shines forth!
The carpets and the thousand baskets,
Glasses of Tea and Children all over the hills.
In my land,
Where the naïve weep
And live in the light they do not see;
In my land
Where people live without eyes
Where the naïve weep
And pray
And fornicate,
And in resignation continue to survive,
As they always have lived in resignation,
Calling on the crescent moon:
"O Crescent Moon!
O Fountainhead gushing forth, raining diamonds,
Hashish and drowsiness!
O suspended God of marble!
O Incredible object!
For the East, for me, you have always remained
A cluster of diamonds,
For the many millions who have been rendered senseless."

In those nights in the East when
The full moon shines forth
The East relinquishes all honour
And ability to defend itself
For the millions who run barefoot
Who believe in having four wives,
And in the day of judgement.
The millions who find their bread
Only in their dreams;

The millions that spend the night in houses
Built of coughs
Who have never known what medicine is
And fall down dead beneath the light.
In my land,
Where the stupid shed tears
And perish weeping,
Whenever they see the crescent moon
Their weeping intensifies
Whenever a lowly lute touches their hearts...
or they hear the song "of the Night"
Which in the East we call
Songs "of the Night"
In my land
In the land of simple folk
Where we ruminate endlessly the night songs
A form of consumption decimating the East;
Our East that ruminates its own history,
Its languid dreams,
Its hollow legends;
Our East that seeks to discover every heroic deed
In some fanciful tale of Abu Zayd al-Hilali.

Translated by Suheil Bushrui [26]

POEMS

Between us
Twenty years of age
Between your lips and my lips
When they meet and stay
The years collapse
The glass of a whole life shatters.
The day I met you I tore up
All my maps
All my prophecies
Like an Arab stallion I smelled the rain
Of you

Before it wet me
Heard the pulse of your voice
Before you spoke
Undid your hair with my hands
Before you had braided it

There is nothing I can do
Nothing you can do
What can the wound do
With the knife on the way to it?

Your eyes are like a night of rain
In which ships are sinking
And all I wrote is forgotten
In mirrors there is no memory.

God how is it that we surrender
To love giving it the keys to our city
Carrying candles to it and incense
Falling down at its feet asking
To be forgiven
Why do we look for it and endure
All that it does to us
All that it does to us?

Woman in whose voice
Silver and wine mingle
In the rains
From the mirrors of your knees
The day begins its journey
Life puts out to sea

I knew when I said
I love you
There was no inventing a new alphabet
For a city where no one could read
That I was saying my poems
In an empty theater
And pouring my wine

For those who could not taste it.

When God gave you to me
I felt that he had loaded
Everything my way
And unsaid all His sacred books.

Who are you
Woman entering my life like a dagger
Mild as the eyes of a rabbit
Soft as the skin of a plum
Pure as strings of jasmine
Innocent as children's bibs
And devouring like words?

Your love threw me down
In a land of wonder
It ambushed me like the scent
Of a woman stepping into an elevator
It surprised me
In a coffee bar
Sitting over a poem
I forgot the poem
It surprised me
Reading the lines in my palm
I forgot my palm
It dropped on me like a blind deaf wildfowl
Its feathers became tangled with mine
Its cries were twisted with mine
It surprised me
As I sat on my suitcase
Waiting for the train of days
I forgot the dates
I traveled with you
To the land of wonder

Your image is engraved
On the face of my watch
It is engraved on each of the hands

It is etched on the weeks
Months years
My time is no longer time
It is you

Translated by Lena Jayyusi and W.S. Merwin

LANGUAGE

When a man is in love
How can he use old words?
Should a woman
Desiring a lover
Lie down with
Grammarians and linguist?

I said nothing
To the woman I loved
But gathered
Love's adjectives into a suitcase
And fled from all languages.

Translated by Diana Der Hovanessian and Lena Jayyusi

May Rihani

THE WEDDING OF MY CITY

I remember...growing up and her streets of light
I remember...staying up with her all night
I remember...she was the beloved of the poets
I remember...how they thronged around her!

My city—
They said the celebration would not last
Your marriage feast was interrupted
Your wedding dress stained with blood

But you stood firm
Your youthful form filled with vigor
Rage entered all the houses
Bursting out from blood-shot eyes
And showers of lead lashed and scourged us

After long, long years
The bouquet of flowers still remains
In the hands of the bride wearing the stained dress

And still—

Blazing fires are etched against the Beirut sky
Ominous rumbling fills her head
Fear lurks in her silent streets
Children draw bomb shelters on the sky of their notebooks

And a tear trickles down the face of God.

Translated by Suheil Bushrui [29]

PALM TREES

Do you think Palm trees dream?
What resides in their minds?
Do you think the Palms of Texas yearn for the Palms of Baghdad?
Which ones departed? Which migrated?
Are they twins, carrying between them a long mirror
Reflecting the character of the West, reflecting the face of the East;
Searching for a magical thread that links the far corners with each other?

Do you think the Palm chants in solemn Silence
Words about the similarities in the mirror?
Do you think they whisper to the Earth in solemn Silence
Do not lose Hope?

Perhaps this is what makes the Earth a bead in the rosary of a dervish
that is eternally spinning,
Spinning invisible threads that link the caravans of humanity.

Translated by Z. al-Faqih [30]

Antoine Raad

A POET'S TREASURE

All I possess in my shattered
Days of exile:
Are gifts of patience and ashes of love;
Fragments of old tales and dreams aborted;
Withered aspirations, and ferocious longing gnawing at my heart
Daily at eventide.
These are my treasures, O my foreign friends—
Treasures to be rifled or stolen,
All laid out at the edge of time in summer or winter.
None is there to guard my treasures,
None is there to steal them.
I wonder then, my impoverished friends,
Who would be tempted to steal from a poet's treasure?

Translated by Suheil Bushrui[31]

Henri Zoghaib

THIS IS THE NOW

This is the now "I am"! Forgive who I was before I met you.
Do not lash me with a past you were not in
I began to be and was born the day we met
It was a promising future that led me to you!
Sustain it then, and mould me anew.

You have been the reward of life…My life deserved
To be rewarded since you came into it.
Wrapped in your contentment and from it I receive
My bliss in full sufficiency.

Many a life has passed until you learnt

To love me so tenderly
With a mother's contentment you embrace my fate
And with a new breath flows my utterance.

You are what you are! Tempestuous! Defiant!
Madly in love, turbulent! Shaking all my being and scared away
But the burden of your absence weighs heavily in my heart
Touches me like a storm and when I meet you
I am overcome by timidity.

Translated by Suheil Bushrui[32]

NOTES

Part I – The Pre-Islamic Period

1 "Ode of Imru al-Qais", translated by Sir William Jones, ed. W. A. Clouston, *Arabian Poetry for English Readers*, London, Darf Publishers, 1986.

2 "The Ode of Labid", translated by Lady Anne Blunt & William S. Blunt, *The Seven Golden Odes of Pagan Arabia*, Chiswick Press, London 1903.

3 Ka'b Bin Zuhair, "Su'ád is gone...", translated by Reynold A. Nicholson, ed. W. A. Clouston, *Arabian Poetry for English Readers*, London, Darf Publishers, 1986.

4 al-Aswad Bin Yafur, "Ode from the Mufaddaliyat", translated by Charles J. Lyall, *The Mufaddaliyat*, New York, Clorendon Press, 1930.

5 al-Khansa, "Lament for My Brother", translated by Omar Pound, *Arabic and Persian Poems*, Cambridge, Fulcrum Press, 1970.

6 al-Tirimmah, "In the Heart of the Desert", translated by Omar Pound, *Arabic and Persian Poems*, Cambridge, Fulcrum Press, 1970.

7 Jamil, "Oh, That Youth's Flower Anew Might Lift its Head", translated by R. A. Nicholson, *Translations of Eastern Poetry and Prose*, London, Cambridge University Press, 1922.

8 Katari of Mazin, "To His Own Soul", translated by C. J. Lyall, *Translations of Ancient Arabian Poetry, Chiefly Pre-Islamic*, New York, Williams & Norgate, 1930.

9 Umar Ibn Abi Rabi'ah, "Blame Me No More, O Comrades!", translated by R. A. Nicholson, *Translations of Eastern Poetry and Prose*, London, Cambridge University Press, 1922.

Part II – The Islamic Age

1 Muhammad Asad, *The Message of the Qur'an*, Dubai, Oriental Press, 2008.

2 *Hadith: Selected Sayings,* translated by S. B. Bushrui.

3 "Selected Sayings", translated by Ezzedin Ibrahim & Denys Johnson-Davies, *al-Nawawi's Forty Hadith*, Damascus, Islamic Texts Society, 1976.

4 "Islamic Law of Nations", translated and introduced by Majid Khadduri, *The Islamic Law of Nations: Shaybani's Siyar*, Baltimore, Johns Hopkins University Press, 1966.

Part III – The Ummayad Dynasty

1 al-Akhtal, "Youth departed but often I enjoyed it...", translated by Arthur Wormhoudt, *Diwan al-Akhtal Abu Malik Giyath ibn Gauth al Taghibi*, Oskaloosa, Iowa, William Penn College Press, 1974.

2 al-Farazdaq, "Let all weep for al-Hajjáj...", translated by R. A. Nicholson, *A Literary History of the Arabs*, Cambridge, Cambridge University Press, 1930.

3 Jarir, "al-Farazdaq Visited the Folk of Hijaz", translated by Arthur Wormhoudt, Diwan al-Akhtal Abu Malik Giyath ibn Gauth al Taghibi, Oskaloosa, Iowa, William Penn College Press, 1974.

4 Abd al-Hamid al-Katib, "The Art of Secretaryship", translated by Franz Rosenthal.

5 Ibn al-Muqaffa, "The Rabbit and the Elephant", translated by Herbert Howarth & Ibrahim Shukrullah, I*mages from the Arab World: Fragments of Arab Literature*, London, The Pilot Press Ltd, 1944.

6 Ibn Ishaq, "The Prophet's Mission", translated by Alfred Guillaume, *The Life of Muhammed*, London, Oxford University Press, 1955.

7 Bashshar Ibn Burd, "Will No Emissary Be Found", translated by Hilda Kasanina, *Arabic Literature*, Moscow, Nauka Publishing House, 1966.

Part IV – The Abbasid Dynasty

1 Rabia al-Adawiya, "O My Joy and My Desire and My Refuge", translated by Margaret Smith, *Rabia the Mystic and her Fellow Saints in Islam*, Cambridge, Cambridge University Press, 1928.

2 Ibn al-Ahnaf, "Love", translated by Omar Pound, *Arabic and Persian Poems*, Cambridge, Fulcrum Press, 1970.

3 Abu Nuwas, "Four Things" and "Thou Scolder of Grape and Me" translated by R. A. Nicholson, *Love Songs of Asia*, New York, Alfred Knopf, 1946.

4 Abu Nuwas, "The Great Offence", translated by Powys Mathers, *Love Songs of Asia*, New York, Alfred Knopf, 1946.

5 Abu Nuwas, "Hurry, for the Beergardens are Blooming", translated by Herbert Howarth & Ibrahim Shakrullah, *Images from the Arab World*, London, The Pilot Press Ltd, 1944.

6 Abu Nuwas, "Thus by the Camel He Loves", translated by Arthur Wormhoudt, *The Diwan of Abu Nuwas al-Hasan ibn Hani al Hakami*, Oskoloosa Iowa, William Penn College Press, 1971.

7 Abu'l Atahiya, "Vanity: To Harun al-Rashid", translated by James Kritzeck, *Anthology of Islamic Literature*, London, Penguin Books, 1964.

8 Abu'l Atahiya, "Surely Shall Fate Disjoint the Proudest Nose", translated by R. A. Nicholson, *Translations of Eastern Poetry and Prose*, Cambridge University Press, 1922.

9 Abu'l Atahiya, "Virtue Cast an Eye at Me Coming", translated by Herbert Howarth & Ibrahim Shakrullah, *Images from the Arab World*, London, The Pilot Press Ltd, 1944.

10 Dibil, "I Recall the Campsite at Arafah", translated by Leon Zolondek, *Di'bil bin Ali: The Life and Writings of an Early Abbasid Poet*, Kentucky, University of Kentucky Press, 1961.

11 al-Jahiz, *The Book of Proof: Concerning Ascetism*, translated by R. A. Nicholson, Cambridge, Cambridge University Press, 1922.

12 Abu Tammam, "In Praise of the Caliph Mu'tasim", translated by Herbert Howarth & Ibrahim Shakrullah, *Images from the Arab World*, London, The Pilot Press Ltd, 1944.

13 al-Buhturi, "Bodies of Water Like Horses", translated by Herbert Howarth & Ibrahim Shakrullah, *Images from the Arab World*, London, The Pilot Press Ltd, 1944.

14 Ibn Qutayba, extracts from *Uyun al-Akhbar*, translated by Josef Horovitz, *An Introduction to Classical Arabic Literature*, New York, Twayne, 1974.

15 Ibn al-Rumi, "The Chess Champion", translated by Herbert Howarth & Ibrahim Shakrullah, *Images from the Arab World*, London, The Pilot Press Ltd, 1944.

16 Ibn al-Rumi, "The Compromise", translated by Omar Pound, *Arabic and Persian Poems*, Cambridge, Fulcrum Press, 1970.

17 Ibn al-Rumi, "He Defends Himself", translated by Henry Baerlein, *The Singing Caravan*, London, John Murray, 1910.

18 al-Tabari, "The Battle of Badr", translated by Herbert Howarth & Ibrahim Shakrullah, *Images from the Arab World*, London, The Pilot Press Ltd, 1944.

19 al-Junayd, "The Book of the Cure of Souls", translated by A. J. Arberry, *Journal of the Royal Asiatic Society*, London, Royal Asiatic Society, 1937.

20 al-Hallaj, "Three Qasidas", translated by Herbert Mason, *An Introduction to Classical Arabic Literature*, New York, Twayne, 1974.

21 Ibn al-Mu'tazz, "In Praise of Chess", translated by N. Bland, ed. S. Hillelson, *Weekend Caravan*, London, William Hodges, 1937.

22 Ibn al-Mu'tazz, "Night", translated by Henry Baerlein, *The Singing Caravan*, London, John Murray, 1910.

23 Ibn al-Mu'tazz, "We Shouted for Servants, but all Slept", translated by Herbert Howarth & Ibrahim Shukrullah, *Images from the Arab World*, London, The Pilot Press Ltd, 1944.

24 al-Razi, "The Repelling of Grief", Translated by A. J. Arberry, *The Spiritual Physick of Rhazes*, London, John Murray, 1950.

25 al-Farabi, "The City and the Household", translated by D. M. Dunlop, *Aphorisms of the Statesman*, Cambridge, Cambridge University Press, 1961.

26 al-Mas'udi, "Pearl Fishing" and "Character of the Caliph Muhtadi", translated by R. A. Nicholson, *Translations of Eastern Poetry and Prose*, London,

Cambridge University Press, 1922.

27 al-Mutannabi, "Parting Has Just Taught Our Eyelids Separation", translated by R. A. Nicholson, *Poems of al-Mutanabbi*, Cambridge University Press, Cambridge, 1967.

28 al-Mutannabi, "Shame Kept My Tears Away", translated by Omar Pound, *Arabic and Persian Poems*, Cambridge, Fulcrum Press, 1970.

29 al-Mutannabi, "Couplet", translated by Henry Baerlein, *The Singing Caravan*, London, John Murray, 1910.

30 al-Mutanabbi, "How Glows Mine Heart" and "Naught Kills the Noble like Forgiveness", translated by R. A. Nicholson, *A Literary History of the Arabs*, Cambridge, Cambridge University Press, 1930.

31 al-Mutannabi, "My Songs Gave Eyes to the Blind, Ears to the Deaf", "An Induction", and "Here is the Final Stretch", translated by Herbert Howarth & Ibrahim Shakrullah, *Images from the Arab World*, London, The Pilot Press Ltd, 1944.

32 Abu Firas al-Hamdani, "Thy Fiercest Foe is One Thou Dost Not Fight", and "Grief Amasses, Patience Scatters", translated by D. S. Margoliouth, *The Table-Talk of a Mesopotamian Judge*, London, Royal Asiatic Society, 1922.

33 al-Tawhidi, "Arabs and Non-Arabs", translated by John Dumis, *An Introduction to Classical Arabic Literature*, New York, Twayne, 1974.

34 al-Tanukhi, "Table Talk", translated by D. S. Margoliouth, *The Table-Talk of a Mesopotamian Judge*, London, Oriental Translation Fund, 1922.

35 al-Kalabadhi, "The Sufi Doctrine of Vision", translated by A. J. Arberry, *The Doctrine of the Sufis*, Cambridge, Cambridge University Press, 1935.

36 al-Hamadhani, "The Assembly of Qazwin", translated by W. J. Prendergast, *The Maqamat of Badi al-Zaman al-Hamadhani*, London, Curzon Press, 1973.

37 al-Biruni, "Determination of the Length of Ramadan", translated by E. Sachau, *The Chronology of Ancient Nations*, London, W. H. Allen, 1879.

38 al-Ma'arri, "The Epistle of Forgiveness", translated by G. Brackenbury, *The Poetry of the Jinns*, Cairo, Cairo University Press, 1947.

39 al-Ma'arri, "Letter to Abu Ahmad 'Abd al-Salam ibn al-Husain", translated by D. S. Margoliouth, *The Letters of Abu al-'Ala*, Cairo, Cairo University Press, 1898.

40 al-Ma'arri, from the "Diwan", translated by Henry Baerlein, *The Diwan of Abu-Ala*, London, John Murray, 1908.

41 al-Ma'arri, from the "Lazumiyat", translated by Ameen Rihani, *The Quatrains of Abu'l-Ala*, London, Grant Richards, 1904.

42 al-Ma'arri, "'Tis said that spirits remove by transmigration...", "In the Casket of the Hours" and "Thou Art Diseased in Understanding and Religion", translated by R.A. Nicholson, *Eastern Poetry and Prose*, Cambridge, Cambridge University Press, 1922.

43 Ibn Sina (Avicenna), "Concerning the Temporal Origin of the Soul", translated by F. Rahman, *Avicenna's Pyschology*, Oxford, Oxford University Press, 1952.

44 Ibn Sina (Avicenna), "Epistle of the Soul", translated by E. G. Browne, *A Literary History of Persia*, Cambridge, Cambridge University Press, 1924.

45 Ibn Sina (Avicenna), "On Prophecy", translated by A.J. Arberry, *Avicenna on Theology*, London, John Murray, 1951.

46 al-Hariri, "The Assembly of Hajr", translated by F. Steingass, *The Assemblies of al-Hariri*, London, Williams & Norgate, 1867.

47 al-Hariri, "The Assembly of Damascus", translated by R.A. Nicholson, *Translations of Eastern Poetry and Prose*, London, Cambridge University Press, 1922.

48 al-Ghazzali, "The Beginning of Guidance", translated by W. Montgomery Watt, *The Faith and Practice of al-Ghazzali*, London, Allen & Unwin, 1953.

49 al-Ghazzali, "The First Duty of Brotherhood", translated by Muhtar Holland, *al-Ghazzali on the Duties of Brotherhood in Islam*, Leicester, Islamic Foundation, 1983.

50 al-Ghazzali, "The Physcial Sciences", translated by S. A. Kamali, *The Incoherence of the Philosophers*, Karachi, Pakistan Philosophical Congress, 1958.

51 Ibn Rushd (Averroes), "The Law Makes Philosophic Studies Obligatory", translated by G. F. Hourani, *Averroes on the Harmony of Religion and Philosophy*, Luzac & Co., London, 1961.

52 Usama, "The Protection of Allah", translated by G. R. Potter, *The Autobiography of Ousama*, London, Routledge, Kegan & Paul, 1929.

53 Ibn Tufayl, "Hayy Admires the Work of the Creator", translated by Paul Brönnle, *The Awakening of the Soul*, London, John Murray, 1910.

54 Ibn Tufayl, "Playing with Fire", translated by George Ashwell from the Latin rendering by Edward Pocock, *The History of Eb'n Tockdan, an Indian Prince*, London, privately published, 1686.

55 Ibn Jubayr, "A Description of the Mosque of the Apostle of God and of His Sacred Rawdah", translated by R. J. C. Broadhurst, *The Travels of Ibn Jubayr*, London, Jonathan Cape, 1952.

56 Ibn Arabi, "The Wisdom of Virtue in the Word of Luqman", translated by R. W. J. Austin, *The Bezels of Wisdom*, London, SPCK, 1980.

57 Ibn Arabi, "Whoso Knoweth Himself...", translated by T. H. Weir, *Whoso Knoweth Himself*, London, Beshara Publications, 1976.

58 Ibn Arabi, "The Tarjuman al-Ashwaq", translated by Reynold A. Nicholson, *A Collection of Mystical Odes*, London, Royal Asiatic Society, 1978.

59 Ibnu'l Farid, "The Meeting", translated by Powys Mathers, *Love Songs of Asia*, New York, Alfred Knopf, 1946.

60 Ibnu'l Farid, "Where Eyes Encounter Souls in Battle-Fray" and "Lo, From

Behind the Veil Mysterious", translated by R. A. Nicholson, *Translations of Eastern Poetry and Prose*, London, Cambridge University Press, 1922.

61 Ibn Khallikan, "How the Game of Chess was Invented", translated by Macguckin de Slaine, *Ibn Khallikan's Biographical Dictionary*, London & Paris, Oriental Translation Fund, 1842–1871.

62 Ibn Khallikan, "Ja'far and al-Rashid", translated by Herbert Howarth & Ibrahim Shukrullah, *Images from the Arab World*, London, The Pilot Press Ltd, 1944.

63 al-Busiri, "The Prophet", translated by Herbert Howarth & Ibrahim Shukrullah, *Images from the Arab World*, London, The Pilot Press Ltd, 1944.

Part V – Al-Andalus, Arab Spain

1 Ibn Hazm, "Of Fidelity" and "Of Betrayal", translated by A. J. Arberry, *The Ring of the Dove*, London, Luzac Oriental, 1994.

2 Ibn Hazm, "Anxiety", translated by James Kritzeck, *Anthology of Islamic Literature*, London, Penguin Books, 1964.

3 Ibn Hazm, "Twice Times Then is Now", translated by Omar Pound, *Arabic and Persian Poems*, Cambridge, Fulcrum Press, 1970.

4 Ibn 'Abd Rabbihi, "Modest Blush", translated by A. J. Arberry, *Moorish Poetry: A Translation of The Pennants*, an anthology compiled in 1243 by the Andalusian Ibn Said, London, Cambridge University Press, 1953.

5 Ibn Zaydun, "Poem to Wallada", translated by R. A. Nicholson, *A Literary History of the Arabs*, Cambridge, Cambridge University Press, 1930.

6 al-Mutamid, "The Moon, the Stars, and a King", translated by Harold Morland, *Arabic-Andalusian Casidas*, London, Phoenix Press, 1949.

7 Abu'l Hasan Ali ibn Hisn, "The Pigeon", translated by Harold Morland, *Arabic-Andalusian Casidas*, London, Phoenix Press, 1949.

8 Ibn Hamdis, "The Andalusian Fountains", translated by Herbert Howarth & Ibrahim Shakrullah, *Images from the Arab World*, London, The Pilot Press Ltd, 1944.

9 Ibn Hamdis, "Flowing Stream", translated by A. J. Arberry, *Moorish Poetry: A Translation of The Pennants*, an Anthology compiled in 1243 by the Andalusian Ibn Said, London, Cambridge University Press, 1953.

10 Abus Salt, "The Incense Burner" and Ibn Quzman, "The Radish", translated by A. J. Arberry, *Moorish Poetry: A Translation of The Pennants*, an anthology compiled in 1243 by the Andalusian Ibn Said, London, Cambridge University Press, 1953.

11 Ibn Hayyun, "The Girl with the Beauty-Spots" and Ibn Sa'ad al-Khair, "The Draw-Well", translated by Harold Morland, *Arabic-Andalusian Casidas*, London, Phoenix Press, 1949.

12 Ibn al-Faras, "Moon of Beauty" and Ibn Said, "The Guardians", translated by

A. J. Arberry, *Moorish Poetry: A Translation of The Pennants*, an anthology compiled in 1243 by the Andalusian Ibn Said, London, Cambridge University Press, 1953.

13 Ibn Maimon (Moses Maimonides), *Guide for the Perplexed*, translated by Michael Friedlander, New York, Dover Publications Inc., 1954.

14 Saadia Gaon, "Concerning How it is Most Proper for Man to Conduct Himself in this World", translated by Samuel Rosenblatt, *The Book of Beliefs and Opinions*, New Haven, Yale University Press, 1948.

15 Solomon ibn Gabirol, "The Ethics of Solomon Gabirol", translated by Stephen S. Wise, *The Improvement of Moral Qualities*, New York, AMS Press Inc., 1966.

Part VI – The Age of Depression

1 Ibn Battuta, "Across North Africa", translated by H. A. R. Gibb, *Travels in Asia and Africa*, London, Routledge, 1929.

2 Ibn al-Khatib, "Time of Meeting", translated by Herbert Howarth & Ibrahim Shakrullah, *Images from the Arab World*, London, The Pilot Press Ltd, 1944.

3 Ibn Khaldun, Five Extracts from *Muqaddimah*, translated by R. A. Nicholson, *Translations of Eastern Poetry and Prose*, London, Cambridge University Press, 1922.

4 Ibn Khaldun, "A Sign of Royal Authority", translated by Franz Rosenthal, *The Muqaddimah: an Introduction to History*, London, Routledge & Kegan Paul, 1958.

5 Antar, "Antar Goes to Mecca", *The Romance of Antar*, translated by Terrick Hamilton, *Antar: A Bedoueen Romance*, London, John Murray, 1819.

6 Antar, "'Abla's Treasures Restored", translated by Diana Richmond, *Antar and Abla: A Bedouin Romance*, London, Quartet Books, 1978.

7 "The Tale of the Birds and Beasts and the Carpenter", *The Arabian Nights*, translated by Richard F. Burton, *The Book of the Thousand Nights and One Night*, London, H.S. Nichols, 1894.

8 "The Story of the Envier and the Envied", *The Arabian Nights*, translated by Edward William Lane, *The Arabian Nights Entertainment*, London, East-West Publications, 1981.

9 "Men in the Judgment of their Wives", *The Arabian Nights*, translated by Powys Mathers, *The Book of the Thousand Nights and One Night*, London, Routledge, Kegan & Paul, 1982.

10 "Adventure of the Caliph Haroon al-Rasheed", *The Arabian Nights*, translated by Jonathan Scott, *The Arabian Nights Entertainment*, London, Nimmo & Bain, 1883.

Part VII – Al-Nahda

1 Abd al-Rahman al-Kawakibi, *The Virtues of the Arabs*, translated by Sylvia G. Haim, *Arab Nationalism: An Anthology*, Berkeley, CA, University of California Press, 1952.

2 Ahmad Shawqi, from Act I of *Majnun Layla*, translated by A. J. Arberry, *Majnun Layla*, Cairo, privately published, 1933.

3 Ahmad Shawqi, "To a Late Composer", translated by Herbert Howarth & Ibrahim Shakrullah, *Images from the Arab World*, London, The Pilot Press Ltd, 1944.

4 Ahmad Shawqi, *The Feast of Time*, translated by S. B. Bushrui, *al-Shawqiyyat*, collected poems of Ahmad Shawqi.

5 Ahmad Shawqi, "An Andalusian Exile", translated by M. Mustafa Badawi & John Heath-Stubbs, *Modern Arabic Poetry: An Anthology*, New York, Columbia University Press, 1987.

6 Hafiz Ibrahim, "Elegy to Mustafa Kamil", translated by John A. Haywood, *Modern Arabic Literature 1800–1970*, London, Lund Humphries, 1971.

7 Khalil Mutran, "The Arab Awakening", translated by A. J. Arberry, *Modern Arabic Poetry: An Anthology with English Verse Translations*, London, Taylors Foreign Press, 1950.

8 Ma'ruf al-Rusafi, "Fairest", translated by A. J. Arberry, *Modern Arabic Poetry: An Anthology with English Verse Translations*, London, Taylors Foreign Press, 1950.

9 Ilya Abu Madi, "Envoi" and "Life and Love", translated by A. J. Arberry, *Modern Arabic Poetry: An Anthology with English Verse Translations*, London, Taylors Foreign Press, 1950.

10 Ilya Abu Madi, "The Phoenix", translated by Issa Boullata and Naomi Shihab Nye, *Modern Arabic Poetry: An Anthology*, New York, Columbia University Press, 1987.

11 Gibran Kahlil Gibran, "The Poet", translated by S. B. Bushrui, *Jubran Khalil Jubran: Mukhtarat wa-dirasat*, Dar al-Mashriq, 1970.

12 Gibran Kahlil Gibran, "From a Speech by Khalil the Heretic", translated by S. B. Bushrui, *Jubran Khalil Jubran: Mukhtarat wa-dirasat*, Dar al-Mashriq, 1970.

13 Ameen Rihani, "Light", translated by Mounah H. Khouri & Hamid Algar, *Anthology of Modern Arabic Poetry*, Berkeley, CA, University of California Press, 1974.

14 Ameen Rihani, "Supplication: A Prayer", translated by S. B. Bushrui, "Najwa", *Hutaf al-Awdiya*, Beirut, Rihani Publishing House, 1955.

15 Mikhail Naimy, "A New Year", translated by J. R. Perry, *A New Year*, Leiden, E. J. Brill, 1974.

16 Mikhail Naimy, "Comrade", translated by A. J. Arberry, *Modern Arabic*

Poetry: An Anthology with English Verse Translations, London, Taylors Foreign Press, 1950.

17 Taha Hussein, "An Egyptian Childhood", translated by E. H. Paxton, *An Egyptian Childhood*, AUC Press, Cairo, Egypt, 1992.

18 Taha Hussein, from *The Stream of Days*, translated by Hilary Wayment, *The Stream of Days*, London, Longmans Green, 1948.

19 Abbas al-Aqqad, "Drinking Song" and "Double Trouble", translated by A. J. Arberry, *Modern Arabic Poetry: An Anthology with English Verse Translations*, London, Taylors Foreign Press, 1950.

20 May Ziadah, "Rejoice", translated by S. B. Bushrui, *Literature and the Art of Creation: Essays and Poems in Honour of A. Norman Jeffries*, Colin Smythe, 1988.

21 Ahmad al-Safi al-Najafi, "To a Clock", translated by A. J. Arberry, *Modern Arabic Poetry: An Anthology with English Verse Translations*, London, Taylors Foreign Press, 1950.

22 Mahmud Taymur, "The Fare", translated by John A. Haywood, *Modern Arabic Literature, 1800–1970*, London, Lund Humphries, 1971.

23 Tewfiq al-Hakim, "Song of Death", translated by Mustafa Badawi, ed. Mahmud Manzalaoui, *Arabic Writing Today: Drama*, Cairo, AUC Press, 1977.

Part VIII – Modern Arabic Literature

1 Abu al-Qasim al-Shabi, "I Weep for Love" and "To the Tyrant", translated by A. J. Arberry, *Modern Arabic Poetry: An Anthology with English Verse Translations*, London, Taylors Foreign Press, 1950.

2 Naguib Mahfouz, "An Unnerving Sound", translated by Akef Abadir & Roger Allen, *God's World*, Minneapolis, Biblioteca Islamic, 1973.

3 Jabra Ibrahim Jabra, "A Stranger at the Fountain", translated by Issa J. Boullata, *Modern Arab Poets: 1950–1975*, Washington, DC, Three Continents Press, 1976.

4 Khalil Hawi, "The Bridge", translated by Issa J. Boullata, *Modern Arab Poets: 1950–1975*, Washington, DC, Three Continents Press, 1976.

5 'Abd al-Wahhab al-Bayati, "Apology for a Short Speech", translated by Issa J. Boullata, *Modern Arab Poets: 1950–1975*, Washington, DC, Three Continents Press, 1976.

6 Salah 'Abd al-Sabur, "The Tatars Attacked", translated by Issa J. Boullata, *Modern Arab Poets: 1950–1975*, Washington, DC, Three Continents Press, 1976.

7 Mahmud Darwish, "Pride and Fury", translated by Mounah A. Khouri & Hamid Algar, *Anthology of Modern Arabic Poetry*, Berkeley, CA, University of California Press, 1974.

8 Mahmoud Darwish, "Promises from the Storm", translated by Issa J. Boullata, *Modern Arab Poets: 1950–1975*, Washington, DC, Three Continents Press, 1976.

9 Adonis, *Iram the Many-Columned*, translated by Issa J. Boullata, *Modern Arab Poets: 1950–1975*, Washington, DC, Three Continents Press, 1976.

10 Adonis, "Beginning Speech", translated by Lena Jayyusi & John Heath-Stubb, *Modern Arabic Poetry: An Anthology*, New York, Columbia University Press, 1987.

11 Badr Shakir al-Sayyab, "A City without Rain", translated by Issa J. Boullata, *Modern Arab Poets: 1950–1975*, Washington, DC, Three Continents Press, 1976.

12 Badr Shakir al-Sayyab, "Rain Song", translated by Lena Jayyusi and Christopher Middleton, *Modern Arabic Poetry: An Anthology*, New York, Columbia University Press, 1987.

13 Yusuf al-Khal, "The Deserted Well, Translated by Issa J Boullata, Modern Arab Poets: 1950-1975, Washington, DC, Three Continents Press, 1976.

14 Muhammad al-Fayturi, "To Two Unknown Eyes", translated by Mounah A. Khouri & Hamid Algar, *Anthology of Modern Arabic Poetry*, Berkeley, CA, University of California Press, 1974.

15 Muhammad al-Fayturi, "Sorrow of the Black City", translated by Issa J. Boullata, *Modern Arab Poets: 1950–1975*, Washington, DC, Three Continents Press, 1976.

16 Nazik al-Mala'ika, "Who Am I?", translated by Mounah A. Khouri & Hamid Algar, *Anthology of Modern Arabic Poetry*, Berkeley, CA, University of California Press, 1974.

17 Nazik al-Mala'ika, "Five Hymns to Pain", translated by Nathalie Handal, *The Poetry of Arab Women: A Contemporary Anthology*, Northampton, MA, Interlink Books, 2001.

18 Mona Fayad, "Whisper", translated by Nathalie Handal, *The Poetry of Arab Women: A Contemporary Anthology*, Northampton, MA, Interlink Books, 2001.

19 Salma al-Khadra al-Jayyusi, "Without Roots", translated by Issa J. Boullata, *Modern Arab Poets: 1950–1975*, Washington, DC, Three Continents Press, 1976.

20 Salma Khadra Jayyusi, "In the Casbah", translated by Charles Doria, *The Poetry of Arab Women: A Contemporary Anthology*, Northampton, MA, Interlink Books, 2001.

21 Salma Khadra Jayyusi, "Scrapping Limits" and "April Woman", translated by Charles Doria, *Modern Arabic Poetry: An Anthology*, New York, Columbia University Press, 1987.

22 Fudwa Tuqan, "A Prayer to the New Year", translated by Lena Jayyusi & Naomi Shihab Nye, *The Poetry of Arab Women: A Contemporary Anthology*,

Northampton, MA, Interlink Books, 2001.

23 Fudwa Tuqan, "Elegy", translated by A. J. Arberry, *Modern Arabic Poetry: An Anthology with English Verse Translations*, London, Taylors Foreign Press, 1950.

24 Fudwa Tuqan, "In the Flux", translated by Patricia Alanah Byrne with the help of the editor, and Naomi Shihab Nye, *Modern Arabic Poetry: An Anthology*, New York, Columbia University Press, 1987.

25 Mai Sayigh, "Departure", translated by Lena Jayyusi & Naomi Shihab Nye, *The Poetry of Arab Women: A Contemporary Anthology*, Northampton, MA, Interlink Books, 2001.

26 Nizar Qabbani, "Bread, Hashish and Moonlight", translated by S. B. Bushrui, *al-A'mal al-Shi'ryyah al- Kamila*, Mansurat Nizar Qabbani, Beirut, 1967.

27 Nizar Qabbani, "Poems", translated by Lena Jayyusi and W.S. Merwin, *Modern Arabic Poetry: An Anthology*, New York, Columbia University Press, 1987.

28 Nizar Qabbani, "Language", translated by Diana Der Hovanessian and Lena Jayyusi (first translator), *Modern Arabic Poetry: An Anthology*, New York, Columbia University Press, 1987.

29 May Rihani, "The Wedding of My City", translated by S. B. Bushrui, *Yaliffu Khasr al-Ar*, Washington DC, Blackform International, 1992.

30 May Rihani, "Palm Trees", translated by Z. al-Faqih, *Yaliffu Khasr al-Ar*, Washington DC, Blackform International, 1992.

31 Antoine Raad, "A Poet's Treasure", translated by S. B. Bushrui, author's own manuscript, 1999.

32 Henri Zoghaib, "This is the Now", translated by S. B. Bushrui, author's own manuscript, 2008.

NOTES ON AUTHORS

RABIA AL-ADAWIYA (717–801)
Mystical poet, one of the earliest Sufi writers and saints. Her writings and sayings are widely revered in the Muslim world.

ADONIS (1930–)
Real name 'Ali Ahmad Sa'id
A prolific Syrian-born poet who is considered one of the most influential 20th-century poets in the Arab world. Politically active his entire life, his verse is primarily concerned with social and intellectual concerns.

AL-AKHTAL (c. 640–710)
Real name Ghiyath Ibn Gawth Ibn al-Salt
Considered one of the leading poets and panegyrists of the early Ummayad period. He was later overshadowed by his contemporaries, al-Farazdaq, whom he supported, and Jarir, whom he despised. Born a Christian he converted to Islam.

ABU TAMMAM (c. 805–845)
Abu Tammam Habib Ibn Aws
Born in Syria he was a self-educated poet of the Abbasid period. He became famous chiefly for his collection of pre-Islamic poems under the title of *Hamasa*. It is one of the few records of pre-Islamic oral poetry and is considered the most important compilation of its kind after the *Mu'allaqat* and the *Mufaddaliyat*.

ILYA ABU MADI (1890–1957)
Lebanese poet who started writing poetry in Egypt but later settled in America in the early part of the 20th century along with his fellow mahjar poets, Gibran Khalil Gibran and Mikhail Naimy. He wrote mainly in Arabic and his poetry is widely read in the Arab world.

ABU'L ATAHIYA(748–828)
Real name Abu Ishaq Ismail Ibn al-Qasim Ibn Suwaid Ibn Qaisan
Abbasid poet who was known by his nickname, meaning "Father of Craziness". He pioneered Arabic religious poetry in stark contrast to the bucolic verse of his contemporary, Abu Nuwas. He was among the first poets to break with the traditions of the past qasida form of poetry which relied heavily on desert imagery and themes and had become obsolete in the bustling urban society of the Abbasid Caliphate.

ABU'L HASAN ALI IBN HISN (11th century)
Andalusian poet and politician from Seville.

ABBAS AL-AQQAD (1889–1964)
Abbas Mahmud al-Aqqad
Born in Upper Egypt he was renowned for his poems, critiques, and essays. His didactic verse had a great influence on his contemporaries and the burgeoning reform movements in Egypt. He also founded al-Diwan, a school for poets with some of his contemporaries.

ABD AL-WAHHAB AL-BAYATI (1926–1999)
Iraqi-born poet exiled from his homeland as a young man, principally because of his Communist views. He was a prolific writer of socialist realist poetry, mostly in verse form.

BASHSHAR IBN BURD (715–783)
Abu Mu'adh Bashshar Ibn Burd
The first major non-Arab poet to write in Arabic. Born blind and of Iranian extraction, he was nicknamed "al-Mura'ath" which means "the wattled". He is considered the first Abbasid poet to rebel against the archaic styles – thus he is a forerunner of the great poets, Abu Nuwas and Abu'l Atahiya. He was eventually sentenced to death by the Caliph for his often irreverent poetry, which bordered on heresy.

Al-BIRUNI (973–1048)
Abu'l-Raihan Muhammad Ibn Ahmad al-Biruni
Considered one of the greatest Arab scholars, scientists and polymaths in the fields of mathematics, geography and astronomy, he travelled throughout the Abassid empire conducting his studies. His writing was noted for its originality, detail, and objectivity.

AL-BUHTURI (820–897)
Al-Walid Ibn Ubayd Allah al-Buhturi
Arab poet born in Syria between Aleppo and the Euphrates. In Baghdad he wrote verses in praise of the Caliph al-Mutawakkil and of the members of his court. He devoted much of his poetry to the praise of Aleppo and much of his love-poetry in dedication to Aiwa, a maiden of that city.

AL-BUSIRI (1211–1294)
Sharaf al-Din Muhammad Ibn Sa'id Ibn Hammam Ibn Muhsin al-Busiri
Considered the most important Mamluk poet, owing entirely to his splendid

Qasidat al-Burda (Mantle Ode). This work was written in praise of the Prophet after the poet's miraculous recovery from paralysis.

MAHMOUD DARWISH (1942–2008)
Considered the Palestinian national poet, his work symbolized and portrayed the struggles, sufferings, hopes and dreams of the Palestinian people. His entire life and work was devoted to achieving a just peace between Palestinians and Israelis.

DIBIL (765–861)
Real name Abu 'Ali Muhammad ibn Ali ibn Razin al-Khuzai
An Abbasid poet. Most of his verse displays hostility towards everything held sacred by his contemporaries.

AL-FARABI (c. 870–950)
Muhammad Ibn Muhammad Ibn Tarkan Abu Nasr al-Farabi
One of the greatest Muslim thinkers and a precursor of Ibn Sina. He wrote widely on music and medicine as well as on philosophy, which he strove to reconcile with Islam.

AL-FARAZDAQ (c. 640–728)
Real name Hammam Ibn Ghabib Ibn Sa'sa'a
Principle Ummayad poet, who bore the nickname "the Lump of Dough". A dissolute, gifted composer of lampoons and panegyrics, he was famed for his slanging matches with his contemporary, Jarir.

MONA FAYAD (1950–)
Lebanese–Shiite poet and writer, she frequently contributes to *an-Nahar* magazine. Dr Fayad is also a Professor of Psychology at the Lebanese University of Beirut.

MUHAMMAD AL-FAYTURI (1930–)
Sudanese poet who has strongly espoused the cause of Black African Liberation. He has lived his entire life in Egypt where he studied at al-Azhar University. He has also travelled in the Arab world as a journalist.

SOLOMON IBN GABIROL (1021–1058)
Andalusian Jewish philosopher and poet who had a lasting effect on the philosophers of his community and beyond.

SAADIA GAON (882/892–942)
Famous rabbi and first of his age to write about Jewish theological matters in Arabic. He travelled extensively through the Muslim Empire.

AL-GHAZZALI (1059–1111)
Real name Abu Hamid Muhammad Ibn Muhammad al-Tusi al-Shafi
Considered the great Arab mystical philosopher. He is regarded as the pre-eminent figure in Muslim religious thought. Later in life he increasingly turned to Sufism and became highly critical of his fellow philosophers. His most important work is his monumental *Ihya ulum al-Din* (The Revivification of the Religious Sciences).

GIBRAN KAHLIL GIBRAN (1883–1931)
Lebanese poet and philosopher who spent most of his life in America. He became the pre-eminent Arab writer in English. His finest work, *The Prophet*, is among the world's bestsellers. A Christian strongly influenced by Sufism, Gibran's literary work reconciled Eastern and Western Philosophy.

TEWFIQ AL-HAKIM (1898–1987)
The most important playwright in the Arabic language, he was also a novelist, essayist and short-story writer of distinction. His plays are focused mostly on social and intellectual themes.

AL-HALLAJ (858–922)
Real name Abu'l-Mugith al-Husain Ibn Mansour Ibn Mahamma al-Baidawi
An early Sufi poet. His unswerving devotion to mystical doctrine brought him a violent martyrdom at the hands of a weakening Baghdad government.

AL-HAMADAHANI (967–1007)
Abu'l Fadl Ahmad Ibn al-Husain Ibn Yahya Ibn Said Ibn Bishr al-Hamadhani
Earliest exponent of the maqama, later perfected by al-Hariri, he was held in great esteem by his contemporaries who dubbed him "Badi al-Zaman" (Wonder of the Age).

ABU FIRAS AL-HAMDANI (932–968)
Real name al-Harith Ibn Abi'l-'ala' Sa'id ibn Hamdan al-Taghlibi
This Syrian poet who was a near contemporary of al-Mutanabbi. He was particularly esteemed for his war poetry which stemmed from his own considerable experience in battle.

AL-HARIRI (1054–1122)
Abu Muhammad al-Qasim Ibn Ali Ibn Muhammad Ibn al-Bishr al-Hariri
Arab philologist whose Maqamat, despite their very bawdy content, are
regarded as second only to the Qur'an in eminence among Arab literary works.
His command of language was considerable, and his works contains some of
the finest rhymed prose in any language.

KHALIL HAWI (1919–1982)
Lebanese poet trained at Cambridge and Professor of Arabic Literature at the
American University of Beirut. He wrote mainly philosophical verse that dealt
with the upheavals in the Arab world, the travails of Arab nationalism and the
tortuous unrest within his homeland.

TAHA HUSSEIN (1889–1973)
One of the giants of 20th century Arabic literature. His fame rests above all on
his "stream of consciousness" autobiographical novel, al-Ayyam (The Days),
one of the most original and influential works to have been written by an Arab
in the previous century.

IBNU'L FARID (1181–1235)
Real name 'Umar Ali al-Misri al-Sadi
Foremost Arab mystical poet. He wrote a relatively small number of odes, all of
them highly impressive in their stylistic individuality.

IMRU AL-QAIS (c. 501–544)
Imru al-Qais Ibn Hujr
The most eminent of the pre-Islamic poets and author of one of the seven odes
known collectively as the Mu'allaqat. He was reviled by early Muslim puritans
but subsequently revered as the outstanding exponent of the early Qasidah.

IBN ISHAQ (c. 704–768)
Abu 'Abd Allah Muhammad Ibn Ishaq
The earliest and most reliable biographer of the Prophet Muhammad who
wrote Sirat Rasul Allah (Life of God's Messenger); he invented the style of
interpolating poems into narrative text.

JAMIL (c. 660–701 AD)
Jamil Ibn 'Abd Allah Ibn Ma'mar al-Udhari
Notable Ummayad poet regarded as one of the greatest love poets of Arabic
literature. He composed popular verses, many with a folk-song flavour. His
poem "Jamil Buthayna" is on a par with Majnun Layla.

JARIR (650–728)
Jarir Ibn 'Atiyya Ibn al-Katafa Ibn Badr
Considered along with al-Farazdaq as one of the two most important Ummayad poets. Pre-eminent as a satirist with a biting tongue, often at the expense of al-Farazdaq, he also wrote eulogies and panegyrics.

KATARI OF MAZIN (c. 697)
Poet of the Orthodox Caliphate and Ummayad periods.

LABID (c. 560–660)
Abu 'Aqil Labid Ibn Rabia
The most important pre-Islamic poet (one of the seven poets of the *Mu'allaqat*) to survive beyond the time of the Islamic dispensation and to convert to the new Faith.

IBN MAIMON (1135–1204)
Musa (Moses) Ibn Maimon
Known also by his Greek name Maimonides, Ibn Maimon is one of the most famous Jewish philosophers who wrote in the Arabic language. His works greatly advanced the philosophical thought of his age and continued to exert influence on modern Jewish theological study.

IBN AL-MUQAFFA (d. 757)
Abu'l Bashar Ibn al-Muqaffa
Zoroastrian convert to Islam and a skilled translator, he produced the first literary version of *Kalila wa Dimna*, which he translated from the Persian rendering of the original Sanskrit.

ABU NUWAS (747–810)
Abu Nuwas al-Hasan Ibn Hani' al-Hakami
Immortalized in *The Arabian Nights* as the dissolute boon companion of Caliph Harun al-Rashid, Abu Nuwas was one of the most influential poets in Arab and Islamic history. His verses are among the treasures of Arabic literature, notwithstanding their obsession with the twin glories of love and wine. He became famous for his masterful poetry on themes considered taboo in Islamic culture.

IBN 'ABD RABBIHI (860–940)
Ahmad Ibn Muhammad Abu 'Umar Ibn 'Abd Rabbihi
Andalusian poet laureate and litterateur from Cordova. He was the author of a twenty-five-volume anthology entitled *al-Iqd al-Farid* (The Unique Necklace). Each of the volumes is named after a jewel in the necklace.

IBN AL-RUMI (836–896)
Ali Ibn al-Abbas Ibn Jurayj Ibn al-Rumi
Gifted Abbasid poet who made many enemies through his outspokenness –
not to be confused with the great Persian mystic Jalal al-Din Rumi.

IBN AL-AHNAF (750–809)
al-Abbas ibn al-Ahnaf Abu'l Fadl
Contemporary of Abu Nuwas and Caliph Harun al-Rashid. His poems are
almost all simple love lyrics in the ghazal form which he pioneered.

IBN ARABI (1165–1240)
Abu Bakr Muhammad Ibn 'Ali, Muhyi'l-Din, al-Hatami Alta'i al-Andalusi Ibn
Arabi
Celebrated Muslim mystic who was born in Murcia, Spain. He exerted a great
influence on religious philosophy – both Muslim and Christian – for centuries
after his death. He was an outstanding writer of both prose and poetry.

IBN BATTUTA (1304–1368)
Muhammad Ibn Abd Allah Ibn Muhammad Ibn Ibrahim Abu 'Abd Allah,
al-Latawi al-Tanji Ibn Battuta
One of the two great Muslim travelogue writers, Ibn Battuta was born in
Tangiers and spent most of his life as a peripatetic. He wrote vividly and enter-
tainingly at a time when Arabic was going into decline as a literary language.

IBN AL-FARAS (1130–1200)
Andalusian poet and lawyer from Granada – not to be confused with Ibn Faris,
the 10th-century philologist and grammarian.

IBN HAMDIS (1056–1133)
The most distinguished Arab poet to originate from Sicily, Ibn Hamdis
wrote most of his verse at the court of al-Mutamid, King of Seville. He has
been compared to Wordsworth. He travelled the Western Mediterranean and
composed for several Muslim royal courts.

IBN HAYYUN (12th century)
Andalusian poet from Seville, but not to be confused with Ibn Hayyan, the
11th-century historian from Cordoba.

IBN HAZM (994–1064)
Abu Muhammad 'Ali Ibn Ahmed Ibn Sa'id Ibn Hazm
One of the greatest of the Andalusian scholars. He was more successful as a

prose-writer than as a poet. His book on chivalrous love, *Tauq al-Hamama* (The Dove's Neck-Ring) is a classic of its kind. He was also an important and controversial theologian.

IBN JUBAYR (1145–1217)
Abu'l Husain Muhammad Ibn Ahmad al-Qanini Ibn Jubayr
Along with Ibn Battuta, he was one of the greatest Arab travel writers and geographers. Born in Valencia, Spain, he was especially noted for his account of a pilgrimage to Mecca from Granada.

IBN KHALDUN (1332–1406)
Wali al-Din 'Abd al-Rahman Ibn Khaldun
Great Arab philosopher-historian who was born in Tunis of Andalusian descent. His *Muqaddimah* (Prologomenon) is one of the most important treatises on history ever written. He held the posts of both ambassador and judge.

IBN KHALLIKAN (1211–1282)
Ahmad Ibn Muhammad Ibn Ibrahim Ibn Khallikan Shams al-Din Abu'l Abbas al-Barmaqi al-Irbili al-Shafi'i
Outstanding Arab biographer famed for his *Wafayatu'l A'yan* (Obituaries of Eminent Men), which remains the standard source of information of the first six centuries of Islam. This work contains entertaining anecdotes as well as comprehensive biographical information.

IBN AL-MU'TAZZ (861–908)
Abu'l Abbas Ibn al-Mu'tazz 'Abd Allah
Abbasid court poet and son of the Caliph al-Mu'tazz, he was noted for his learning and good taste. After being drawn into a conspiracy that led to his ascending the throne for one day, he was put to death.

IBN QUTAYBA (828–889)
Abu 'Abd Allah Muhammad Ibn Muslim al-Qufi Almarwazi al-Dinawari Ibn Qutayba
Versatile essayist, historian and an influential philologist, he did much to establish correct usage of the Arabic language. His wide knowledge was reflected in his literary thesaurus, *Uyun al-Akhbar* (Choice Histories).

IBN QUZMAN (c. 1078–1160)
Abu Bakr Muhammad Ibn 'Isa Ibn 'Abd al-Malik Ibn Quzman
Troubadour poet born in Cordoba, Spain, he was one of the most famous of the Andalusian poets. He was celebrated chiefly as the leading composer of the *zajal* or popular ballad form of verse.

IBN RUSHD (AVERROES) (1126–1198)

Abu'l-Walid Muhammad Ibn Ahmad Ibn Muhammad Ibn Rushd

One of the most important Arab philosophers. He was well known in the West for his study of Aristotle. He refuted al-Ghazali's *Tahufat al-Falasifa* (The Incoherence of the Philosophers) in his other major work, *Tahufut al-Tahufut* (The Incoherence of the Incoherence).

IBN SA'AD AL-KHAIR (12th century)

Andalusian poet and lawyer from Valencia.

IBN SAID (1213–1286)

Andalusian poet from Alcala la Real who compiled an anthology of Andalusian poetry entitled *The Pennants*. He is not to be confused with his namesake and contemporary.

IBN SINA (AVICENNA) (980–1037)

Abu Ali al-Husain Ibn 'Abd Allah Ibn Sina.

The leading philosopher of his age. He also wrote important works on medicine, astronomy and the natural sciences as well as some poetry. He wrote in both Persian and Arabic, and exerted a great influence in both the East and the West.

IBN TUFAYL (c. 1105–1186)

Abu Bakr Muhammad Ibn 'Abd al-Malik Ibn Muhammad Ibn Muhammad Ibn Tufayl al-Qaisi

He was a philosopher famed almost solely for his revision of a tale of Avicenna entitled *Hayy Ibn Yaqzan* (Live, Son of the Awake), which describes the awakening to religion of an infant raised entirely by animals.

IBN ZAYDUN (1003–1071)

Abu'l Walid Ahmad Ibn 'Abd Allah Ibn Ahmad Ibn Ghalib Ibn Zaydun

Considered by many to be the most illustrious of all Andalusian poets, he lost favour at the court of Cordova after romancing the Caliph's daughter but was later honoured by al-Mutamid, poet-King of Seville.

HAFIZ IBRAHIM (1872–1932)

After his contemporary, Ahmad Shawqi, he is the most important poet of the late 19th-century Arab literary renaissance. He is best known for his elegies as well as his use of classical poetic form and metre to discuss modern issues and portray modern realities.

JABRA IBRAHIM JABRA (1919–1994)

Christian Palestinian writer from Bethlehem, who was regarded as one of the leading contemporary Arab poets and critics. After the events of 1948 he settled in Iraq. He was also a distinguished novelist.

AL-JAHIZ (781–868)

Abu 'Uthman 'Amr Ibn Bahr al-Fuqaimi al-Basri al-Jahiz

An early free-thinker and prose-writer from Basra noted for his great learning and wit. His most important works are *Kitab al-Bayan* (The Book of Proof) and *Kitab al-Hayawan* (The Book of Animals).

SALMA AL-KHADRA AL-JAYYUSI (c. 1922–)

Palestinian poetess and one of the leading contemporary woman writers in the Arab world. She is one of the preeminent translators, critics, editors and authors of contemporary Arabic Literature.

AL-JUNAYD (830–910)

Abu'l-Qasim Ibn Muhammad Ibn al-Junayed al-Khazzaz al-Kawariri al-Nihawandi

Celebrated sufi from Baghdad. He was influenced by al-Hallaj and laid the foundations for later Sufism. His greatest work is *Risa'il*, which consists of letters to private persons and tractates on mystical themes.

AL-KALABADHI (c. 990 AD)

Abu Bakr Muhammad Ibn Ishaq al-Kalabadhi

Sufi writer heavily influenced by al-Hallaj and in some ways the forerunner of al-Ghazzali. He was a very precise and meticulous writer.

ABD AL-HAMID AL-KATIB (d. 750)

Real name Abd al-Hamid Ibn Yayha ibn Sa'd

Nicknamed "The Scribe" (al-Katib), he worked as the secretary to the last Ummayad Caliph. In this position, he pioneered the art of Arabic prose writing and letter writing. His fame spread for his six stylized "epistles", one of which described the function of his own office.

ABD AL-RAHMAN AL-KAWAKIBI (1855–1902)

Abd al-Rahman Ibn Ahmad Ibn Mas'ud al-Kawakibi

Syrian champion of the Arab nationalist movement, which fought against Ottoman oppression. His fervent nationalism finds eloquent expression in his *Umm al-Qura* (Mother of Communities).

YUSUF AL-KHAL (1917–1987)

Lebanese poet, journalist and teacher. In Beirut, he founded *Shi'ir* magazine, one of the most influential poetry magazines of its time. He was also a long serving editor for *an-Nahar* newspaper.

AL-KHANSA (590–644)

Real name Tumadir Bint 'Amr

The greatest female Arab poet, nicknamed "The Snub-Nosed". A near contemporary of the Prophet, she wrote particularly fine elegies. Upon meeting the Prophet she converted to Islam along with her children all of whom would later die in the Battle of Qadisiyah.

IBN AL-KHATIB (1313–1375)

Lisan al-Din Abu 'Abd Allah Muhammad Ibn 'Abd Allah Ibn Sa'id Dhu'l Wizaritain, Ibn 'Ali Ibn Ahmad al-Salmani Ibn al-Khatib

Andalusian statesman, poet and prose writer who wrote on many subjects including history and geography. He spent most of his life writing in the Sultan's court in Granada. He was the last great composer of the *muwashshah* style of verse.

AL-MA'ARRI (973–1057)

Abu'l-'Ala Ahmad Ibn 'Abd Allah Ibn Sulaiman al-Ma'arri

Blind poet from Northern Syria, pre-eminent among free-thinkers in Arabic verse. He was a harsh critic of hypocrisy and superstition, a champion of justice, and a distinguished teacher of poetics and diction.

NAGUIB MAHFOUZ (1911–2006)

The leading novelist in the Arab world. Progressed from mainly historical novels to graphic portrayals of contemporary life such as *Zuqaq al-Midaq* (Midaq Alley). His most important work is his *Trilogy*, which has been compared to *The Forsyte Saga*.

NAZIK AL-MALA'IKA (1922–2007)

Born in Baghdad. She studied comparative literature in the United States. Upon completion of her studies she returned to Iraq to teach and write. She was one of the first Arab poets to achieve success with free verse.

AL-MASU'DI (c. 896–956)

Abu'l Hasan 'Ali Ibn al-Husain al-Masu'di

Well-travelled, eminent historian and geographer, precursor of Ibn Khaldun. Revered especially for his highly entertaining anecdotal style as well as for his philosophical approach.

AL-MUTAMID (1040–1095)
Abu'l-Abbas Ahmad Ibn Jafar al-Mutamid 'Ala 'llah
Third and last King of Seville in the Abbasid Dynasty who waged a series of
wars to control Cordoba. He was also a very gifted poet in his own right and a
munificent patron of the arts.

AL-MUTANABBI (915–965)
Real name Abu'l Taiyib Ahmad Ibn al-Husain al-Jufi
Regarded as the "Arab Shakespeare" and nicknamed "He who professes to be a
prophet". He is considered by many to be the greatest of Arab poets. He wrote
very complex verse which is difficult to translate. Assassinated in an ambush
near his home in Baghdad.

KHALIL MUTRAN (1872–1949)
Christian poet and journalist from Lebanon who settled in Egypt after fleeing
from the Ottomans. He exerted great influence on modernizing poets in the Arab
world through use of his publications and his translations of European literature.

MIKHAIL NAIMY (1889–1988)
Poet and thinker who formed *al-Arrabitah* (Pen-bond) in the USA with his
fellow Lebanese Christian *Mahjar* writers, Gibran and Rihani. He wrote in
both Arabic and English, and is best known for his work *The Book of Mirdad*.

AHMAD AL-SAFI AL-NAJAFI (1894–1978)
Iraqi poet who spent most of his life in Syria and Lebanon. His simple and
traditional verse focused on the social ills of society as well as the simple life of
his communities.

NIZAR QABBANI (1923–1998)
Influential modern poet born in the Syrian capital, Damascus. He specialized
in powerful love poetry but also wrote and published on a variety of topics
including feminism, Arab Nationalism and religion.

AL-RAZI (864–925)
Abu Baker Muhammad Ibn Zakariyya al-Razi
The greatest of Muslim physicians, known to the West as "Rhazes". He was also
a noted philosophical writer and sceptic. He compiled an important medical
encyclopedia entitled *al-Hawi* (The Comprehensive Book).

ANTOINE RAAD (1940–)
One of Lebanon's foremost creators of children's literature. He is a poet, a

writer and an educator. Former President of the Lebanese Teacher's Union and Winner of the Louise El-Hawa Prize for Moral Literature for Children, Raad lived in exile in London during the civil war in Lebanon (1975–1990) where he also served as President of the Arab Club. In 2005 he published *al-Sinbad* which was translated into English and French, illustrated and set to music.

'UMAR IBN ABI RABI'AH (644–719)

Earliest known Arab composer of love lyrics who provided a sharp contrast with the Bedouin poetry that preceded him. He continued to write love poetry at court during the time of the Prophet, which many pious Muslims opposed.

AMEEN RIHANI (1876–1945)

Lebanese essayist and poet who wrote in both Arabic and English. He was a well-travelled scholar who spent much time in America, as one of the three great *mahjar* writers. He became an unofficial ambassador for his country.

MAY RIHANI (1964–)

Born in Beirut, Lebanon, she is the niece of her country's famed writer and thinker, Ameen Rihani. She continues his work of promoting global dialogue and understanding through her efforts as an international education and gender equality specialist. In addition to papers and books on innovative approaches to education, she has published three collections of Arabic poetry. She presently resides in Washington, DC.

MA'RUF AL-RUSAFI (1875–1945)

The most important poet of the literary renaissance in Iraq. Focused on the ills of society in the Arab world of his time, he was also highly critical of the ongoing British involvement in Iraq.

SALAH 'ABD AL-SABUR (1931–1981)

Leading modern Egyptian poet and playwright who was inspired by modernist movements in European poetry such as socialist realism and existentialism. He also wrote both romantic and metaphysical poetry dealing with the search for new values and the longing for youth and rural life.

ABUS SALT (1067–1134)

Abus Salt Ummaya Ibn 'Abd al-'Aziz Ibn Abi'l-Salt al-Andalusi

Andalusian poet and litterateur, who was born in the Near East, but is more associated with Seville. He made his fame as a scholar who also wrote on logic, astronomy and the sciences.

MAI SAYIGH (1940–)

A Palestinian poet who writes about life as a refugee and the lives and perspectives of women. She studied in Cairo and continues to publish from Paris, where she now lives.

BADR SHAKIR AL-SAYYAB (1926–1964)

An Iraqi poet who forsook communism for the cause of Arab nationalism. He was renowned as a pioneer of free verse in Arabic, merging modern Arab themes and imagery with the new European form and structure.

ABU AL-QASIM AL-SHABI (1909–1934)

Born in Tunisia, al-Shabi was one of the most outstanding modern poets of North Africa. His poetry is mainly romantic and bears the influence of the mahjar poets. He died of an incurable illness at the age of 25.

AHMAD SHAWQI (1868–1932)

The most eminent poet and writer of verse drama in the modern Arab world, he was dubbed the "Prince of Poets" by his contemporaries. He wrote many poems on political themes, but his shorter narrative poems are more accessible and successful.

AL-SHAYBANI (749–805)

Muhammad Ibn al-Hasan al-Shaybani
An Arab jurist of the early Abbasid period. He authored the *Kitab al-Siyar* (Islamic Law of Nations), one of the most important works on Islamic jurisprudence. He was one of the disciples of Abu Hanifa, the founder of the Hanafi School of Islamic Jurisprudence.

AL-TABARI (839–923)

Abu Jafar Muhammad Ibn Jarir al-Tabari
Great Arab historian who wrote a much-needed commentary on the Qur'an called the Tafsir. His monumental and largely reliable universal history, covering the first three centuries of Islam and before, provided valuable material for subsequent historians.

AL-TIRRIMAH (660–725)

al-Tirrimah Ibn Hakim al-Ta'i
Syrian poet of the Ummayad period and a champion of Islam. Noted for his resolute opposition to the unorthodox, especially as expressed in the poetry of his contemporaries.

AL-TANUKHI (938–994)
Abu 'Ali al-Muhassin al-Tanukhi
Much read author of belles-lettres which are principally anecdotal in form, drawing heavily on oral sources and having a strong social content. He was a judge in Baghdad during the Ummayad Dynasty.

AL-TAWHIDI (c. 923–1023)
al Ibn Muhammad al-Tawhidi
Eminent Arab prose-writer noted especially for the splendid characterization evident in *Kitab al-Wazirayan* (The Two Viziers) and *Kitab al-Imta wa'l Mu'anasa* (The Book of Enjoyment and Good Company).

MAHMUD TAYMUR (1894–1974)
Egyptian writer who pioneered the art of short-story writing in Arabic. Strength of characterization and humor are notable features of his stories and plays.

FUDWA TUQAN (1917–2003)
Born and raised in Nablus, the Palestinian poet changed her focus from her early works of love poetry to poetry of resistance. She described the suffering and the ongoing struggle that her homeland witnessed.

USAMA (1095–1188)
Usama Ibn Murshid Ibn Ali Ibn Muqallad Ibn Nasr Ibn Munkidh al-Shaizari al-Qinani
Writer of autobiography which is the most important document about the Crusades from an Arab standpoint. He lived to a remarkable old age.

AL-ASWAD BIN YAFUR (c. 500)
Abnu'l-Jarrah al-Aswad Ibn Yafur Ibn 'Abd al-Aswad al-Tamimi
Pre-Islamic poet, two of whose odes are contained in the collection known as *Mufaddaliyat*.

MAY ZIADAH (1886–1941)
Lebanese poet and essayist who settled in Egypt and contributed much to the emancipation of Middle Eastern women and the promotion of the nascent Arab feminist movement. She maintained a close friendship with her fellow Lebanese poet Gibran Khalil Gibran. She wrote in Arabic, French and English.

HENRI ZOGHAIB (1948–)

Lebanese poet and writer with many poetry and prose books to his credit. Co-chairman of the International Association for the Study of Life and Works of Kahlil Gibran, for Lebanon and the Arab world (since 1999), he founded the Center for Lebanese Heritage at the Lebanese American University in 2002 which he still directs. His last book *Kahlil Gibran, People and Places* sheds new light on Gibran's life and literary achievement.

KA'B BIN ZUHAIR (6th/7th Century)

Son of one of the seven poets of the *Mu'allaqat*. He wrote a famous panegyric to the Prophet Muhammad entitled *Banat Su'ad* (Suad is Gone), which is the only surviving description by a contemporary poet of the beginnings of Islam.

ACKNOWLEDGEMENTS

We are grateful to the following copyright holders who have given us permission to reprint the selections included in this anthology:

AMS PRESS INC.
"The Ethics of Solomon Gabirol" by Ibn Gabirol, translated by Stephen S. Wise, *The Improvement of Moral Qualities*, New York, AMS Press Inc., 1966. Reprinted by permission of AMS Press Inc.

AMERICAN UNIVERSITY OF CAIRO PRESS
"Song of Death" by Tewfiq al-Hakim, translated by M. M. Badawi, ed. by Mahmud Manzalaoui, *Arabic Writing Today: Drama*, Cairo, AUC Press, 1977. "An Egyptian Childhood" by Taha Hussein, translated by E. H. Paxton, *An Egyptian Childhood*, AUC Press, Cairo, Egypt, 1992. Reprinted by permission of AUC Press.

BESHARA PUBLICATIONS
Whoso Knoweth Himself... by Ibn Arabi, translated by T. H. Weir, London, Beshara Publications, 1976. Reprinted by permission of Beshara Publications.

BIBLIOTECA ISLAMICA
"An Unnerving Sound" by Naguib Mahfouz, translated by Akef Abadir and Roger Allen, *God's World*, Minneapolis, Biblioteca Islamic, 1973. Reprinted by permission of Biblioteca Islamica.

CAMBRIDGE UNIVERSITY PRESS
"The City and the Household" by al-Farabi, translated by D. M. Dunlop, *Aphorisms of the Statesman*, Cambridge, Cambridge University Press, 1961. "Parting Has Just Taught Our Eyelids Separation" by al-Mutanabbi, translated by R. A. Nicholson, *Poems of Al-Mutanabbi*, Cambridge University Press, Cambridge, 1967. Reprinted by permission of Cambridge University Press.

CENGAGE LEARNING
"Arabs and Non-Arabs" by al-Tawhidi, translated by John Dumis, *An Introduction to Classical Arabic Literature*, New York, Twayne, 1974. Extracts from "Uyun al-Akhbar" by Ibn Qutayba, translated by Josef Horovitz,

An Introduction to Classical Arabic Literature, New York, Twayne, 1974
"Three Qasidas" by al-Hallaj, translated by Herbert Mason, *An Introduction to Classical Arabic Literature*, New York, Twayne, 1974. Reprinted by permission of Cengage Learning.

COLIN SMYTHE
"Rejoice" by May Ziadah from Thulumat wa Ashi'ah, translated by S. B. Bushrui, *Literature and the Art of Creation: Essays and Poems in Honour of A. Norman Jeffries*, Colin Smythe, 1988. Reprinted by permission of S. B. Bushrui.

COLUMBIA UNIVERSITY PRESS
"Veiled Land" by Gibran Kahlil Gibran, *Modern Arabic Poetry: An Anthology*, translated by Adnan Haydar and Michael Beard, New York, Columbia University Press, 1987
"The Seven Stages" by Gibran Kahlil Gibran, *Modern Arabic Poetry: An Anthology*, translated by Adnan Haydar and Michael Beard, New York, Columbia University Press, 1987.
"The Pleasures of Darkness" by Ahmad al-Safi al-Najafi, *Modern Arabic Poetry: An Anthology*, translated by Salma Khadra Jayyusi and John Heath-Stubbs, New York, Columbia University Press, 1987.
"al-Maqalih, Two Telegrams of Tenderness for San'aa", translated by Lena Jayyusi, *Modern Arabic Poetry: An Anthology*, New York, Columbia University Press, 1987.
"Scrapping Limits" by Salma Khadra Jayyusi, translated by Charles Doria, *Modern Arabic Poetry: An Anthology*, New York, Columbia University Press, 1987.
"April Woman" by Salma Khadra Jayyusi, translated by Charles Doria, *Modern Arabic Poetry: An Anthology*, New York, Columbia University Press, 1987.

DAR AL-MASHRIQ
"The Poet", by Gibran Khalil Gibran, translated by S. B. Bushrui, *Jubran Khalil Jubran: Mukhtarat wa-dirasat*, Dar al-Mashriq, 1970.
From a Speech by Khalil the Heretic by Gibran Khalil Gibran, translated by S. B. Bushrui, *Jubran Khalil Jubran: Mukhtarat wa-dirasat*, Dar al-Mashriq, 1970. Reprinted by permission of S. B. Bushrui.

DARF PUBLISHERS
"Ode of Imru al-Qais", translated by Sir William Jones, ed. W. A. Clouston, *Arabian Poetry for English Readers*, London, Darf Publishers, 1986.

"Su'ád is gone..." by Ka'b Bin Zuhair, translated by Reynold A. Nicholson, ed. W. A. Clouston, *Arabian Poetry for English Readers*, London, Darf Publishers, 1986. Reprinted by permission of Darf Publishers.

E.J. BRILL
"A New Year" by Mikhail Naimy, translated by J. R. Perry, *A New Year*, Leiden, E. J. Brill, 1974. Reprinted by permission of E. J. Brill.

EAST-WEST PUBLICATIONS
"The Story of the Envier and the Envied", *The Arabian Nights*, translated by Edward William Lane, *The Arabian Nights Entertainment*, London, East-West Publications, 1981. Reprinted by East-West Publications.

FULCRUM PRESS
"Twice Times Then is Now" by Ibn Hazm, translated by Omar Pound, *Arabic and Persian Poems*, Cambridge, Fulcrum Press, 1970. Reprinted by permission of Fulcrum Press.
 "Shame kept my tears away" by al-Mutannabi, translated by Omar Pound, *Arabic and Persian Poems*, Cambridge, Fulcrum Press, 1970.
"Lament for My Brother" by al-Khansa, translated by Omar Pound, *Arabic and Persian Poems, Cambridge*, Fulcrum Press, 1970.
"In the Heart of the Desert" by al-Tirrimah, translated by Omar Pound, *Arabic and Persian Poems*, Cambridge, Fulcrum Press, 1970.
"Love" by Ibn al-Ahnaf, translated by Omar Pound, *Arabic and Persian Poems*, Cambridge, Fulcrum Press, 1970.
"The Compromise" by Ibn al-Rumi, translated by Omar Pound, *Arabic and Persian Poems*, Cambridge, Fulcrum Press, 1970.
"Shame kept my tears away" by al-Mutannabi, translated by Omar Pound, *Arabic and Persian Poems*, Cambridge, Fulcrum Press, 1970. Reprinted by permission of Fulcrum Press.

HOLT, RINEHART AND WINSTON
"Anxiety" by Ibn Hazm, translated by James Kritzeck, *Anthology of Islamic Literature*, London, Penguin Books, 1964. Reprinted by permission of Holt, Rinehart and Winston.
"Vanity: To Harun al-Rashid" by Abu'l Atahiya, translated by James Kritzeck, *Anthology of Islamic Literature*, London, Penguin Books, 1964. Reprinted by permission of Holt, Rinehart and Winston.

INTERLINK BOOKS

"Five Hymns to Pain" by Nazik al-Mala'ika, translated by Nathalie Handal, *The Poetry of Arab Women: A Contemporary Anthology*, Northampton MA, Interlink Books, 2001.

"Whisper" by Mona Fayad, translated by Nathalie Handal, *The Poetry of Arab Women: A Contemporary Anthology*, Northampton MA, Interlink Books, 2001.

"In the Casbah" by Salma al-Khadra al-Jayyusi, translated by Charles Doria, *The Poetry of Arab Women: A Contemporary Anthology*, Northampton MA, Interlink Books, 2001.

"A Prayer to the New Year" by Fudwa Tuqan, translated by Samira Kawar, *The Poetry of Arab Women: A Contemporary Anthology*, Northampton MA, Interlink Books, 2001.

"Departure" by Mai Sayigh, translated by Lena Jayyusi and Naomi Shihab Nye, *The Poetry of Arab Women: A Contemporary Anthology*, Northampton MA, Interlink Books, 2001. Reprinted by permission of Interlink Books.

ISLAMIC FOUNDATION

"The First Duty of Brotherhood" by al-Ghazzali, translated by Muhtar Holland, *Al-Ghazzali on the Duties of Brotherhood in Islam*, Leicester, Islamic Foundation, 1983. Reprinted by permission of Islamic Foundation.

ISLAMIC TEXTS SOCIETY

"Selected Sayings", translated by Ezzedin Ibrahim and Denys Johnson Davies, *Al-Nawawi's Forty Hadith*, Damascus, Islamic Texts Society, 1976. Reprinted by permission of Islamic Texts society.

ISSA J. BOULLATA

"A Stranger at the Fountain" by Jabra Ibrahim Jabra, translated by Issa J. Boullata, *Modern Arab Poets: 1950-1975*, Washington, D.C., Three Continents Press, 1976.

"Without Roots" by Salma al-Khadra al-Jayyusi, translated by Issa J. Boullata, *Modern Arab Poets: 1950-1975*, Washington, D.C., Three Continents Press, 1976.

"The Bridge" by Khalil Hawi, translated by Issa J. Boullata, *Modern Arab Poets: 1950-1975*, Washington, D.C., Three Continents Press, 1976.

"Apology for a Short Speech" by al-Bayati, translated by Issa J. Boullata, *Modern Arab Poets: 1950-1975*, Washington, D.C., Three Continents Press, 1976.

"The Tartars Attacked" by 'Abd al-Sabur, translated by Issa J. Boullata, *Modern*

Arab Poets: 1950-1975, Washington, D.C., Three Continents Press, 1976.

"Promises from the Storm" by Mahmoud Darwish, translated by Issa J. Boullata, *Modern Arab Poets: 1950-1975*, Washington, D.C., Three Continents Press, 1976.

"Iram the Many-columned" (fragment) by Adonis, translated by Issa J. Boullata, *Modern Arab Poets: 1950-1975*, Washington, D.C., Three Continents Press, 1976.

"A City Without Rain" by Badr Shakir al-Sayyab, translated by Issa J. Boullata, *Modern Arab Poets: 1950-1975*, Washington, D.C., Three Continents Press, 1976.

"The Deserted Well" by Yusuf al-Khal, translated by Issa J. Boullata, *Modern Arab Poets: 1950-1975*, Washington, D.C., Three Continents Press, 1976.

"Sorrow of the Black City" by Muhammad al-Fayturi, translated by Issa J. Boullata, *Modern Arab Poets: 1950-1975*, Washington, D.C., Three Continents Press, 1976.

Reprinted by permission of Issa J. Boullata.

JOHNS HOPKINS UNIVERSITY PRESS
"Islamic Law of Nation" by al-Shaybani, translated and introduced by Majid Khadduri, *The Islamic Law of Nations: Shaybani's Siyar*, Baltimore, Johns Hopkins University Press, 1966. Reprinted by permission of Johns Hopkins University Press.

LUND HUMPHRIES
"Elegy to Mustafa Kamil" by Hafiz Ibrahim, translated by John A. Haywood, *Modern Arabic Literature 1800-1970*, London, Lund Humphries, 1971.

"The Fare" by Mahmud Taymur, translated by John A. Haywood, *Modern Arabic Literature, 1800-1970*, London, Lund Humphries, 1971. Reprinted by permission of Lund Humphries.

LUZAC ORIENTAL
"Of Fidelity and of Betrayal" by Ibn Hazm, translated by A. J. Arberry, *The Ring of the Dove*, London, Luzac Oriental, 1994. Reprinted by permission of Luzac Oriental.

"The Law Makes Philosophic Studies Obligatory from Kitab Fasl al-Maqal" by Ibn Rushd (Averroes), translated by G. F. Hourani, *Averroes on the Harmony of Religion and Philosophy*, Luzac & Co., London, 1961. Reprinted by permission of Luzac Oriental.

NAIM ATTALA
"Abla's Treasures Restored" by Antar, translated by Diana Richmond, *Antar and Abla: A Bedouin Romance*, London, Quartet Books, 1978. Reprinted by permission of Naim Attala.

NAUKA PUBLISHING HOUSE
"Will no emissary be found" by Bashshar Ibn Burd, translated by Hilda Kasanina, *Arabic Literature*, Moscow, Nauka Publishing House, 1966. Reprinted by permission of Nauka Publishing House.

ORIENTAL PRESS
The Message of the Qur'an, translated by Muhammad Asad, Dubai, Oriental Press, 2008. Reprinted by permission of Oriental Press.

PAULIST PRESS
"The Wisdom of Virtue in the Word of Luqman" by Ibn Arabi, translated by R. W. J. Austin, *The Bezels of Wisdom*, London, SPCK, 1980. Reprinted by permission of Paulist Press.

TAYLOR AND FRANCIS BOOKS UK
"Men in the Judgment of their Wives", *The Arabian Nights*, translated by Powys Mathers, *The Book of the Thousand Nights and One Night*, London, Routledge & Kegan Paul, 1982. Reprinted by permission of Taylor and Francis Books UK.
"The Assembly of Qazvin" by al-Hamadhani, translated by W. J. Prendergast, *The Maqamat of Badi al-Zaman al-Hamadhani*, London, Curzon Press, 1973. Reprinted by permission of Taylor and Francis Books UK.

THEOSOPHICAL PUBLISHING HOUSE
"The Tarjuman al-Ashwaq" by Ibn Arabi, *A Collection of Mystical Odes,* translated by Reynold A. Nicholson, London, Theosophical Publishing House, 1911. Reprinted by permission of Theosophical Publishing House.

UNIVERSITY OF CALIFORNIA PRESS
"Pride and Fury" by Mahmoud Darwish, translated by Mounah A. Khouri and Hamid Algar, *Anthology of Modern Arabic Poetry*, Berkeley, CA., University of California Press, 1974.
"To Two Unknown Eyes" by al-Fayturi, translated by Mounah A. Khouri and Hamid Algar, *Anthology of Modern Arabic Poetry*, Berkeley, CA., University of California Press, 1974.

"Who Am I?" by Nazik al-Mala'ika, translated by Mounah A. Khouri and Hamid Algar, *Anthology of Modern Arabic Poetry*, Berkeley, CA., University of California Press, 1974.

"Light" by Ameen Rihani, translated by Mounah H. Khouri and Hamid Algar, *Anthology of Modern Arabic Poetry*, Berkeley, CA., University of California Press, 1974. Reprinted by permission of University of California Press.

UNIVERSITY OF KENTUCKY PRESS

"I Recall the Camps at Arafah" by Dibil, translated by Leon Zolondek, *Di'bil bin Ali: The Life and Writings of an Early Abbasid Poet*, Kentucky, University of Kentucky Press, 1961. Reprinted by permission of University of Kentucky Press.

WILLIAM PENN COLLEGE PRESS

"Thus by the camel he loves" by Abu Nuwas, translated by Arthur Wormhoudt, *The Diwan of Abu Nuwas al-Hasan ibn Hani al Hakami*, Oskoloosa Iowa, William Penn College Press, 1971.

"Youth departed but often I enjoyed it..." by al-Akhtal, translated by Arthur Wormhondt, *Diwan al-Akhtal Abu Malik Giyath ibn Gauth al Taghibi*, Oskaloosa, Iowa, William Penn College press, 1974.

"Al Farazdaq visited the folk of Hijaz" by Jarir, translated by Arthur Wormhoudt, *Diwan al-Akhtal Abu Malik Giyath ibn Gauth al Taghibi*, Oskaloosa, Iowa, William Penn College press, 1974. Reprinted by permission of William Penn College Press.

NOTES ON EDITORS

SUHEIL BUSHRUI is a distinguished author, poet, critic, translator, recipient of many international awards, and particularly revered as an authority on the works of W.B. Yeats and Kahlil Gibran. A university professor for the last 56 years, Bushrui has taught at universities in Europe, the Middle East, Africa, and North America. Currently, Bushrui is the professor and first incumbent of the George and Lisa Zakhem Kahlil Gibran Chair for Values and Peace at the University of Maryland, where he is also a Senior Scholar of Peace with the Center for International Development and Conflict Management. A Fellow of the Temenos Academy, Professor Bushrui's publications are extensive in both English and Arabic. His most recent works include *The Spiritual Heritage of the Human Race* (2010), and its translation into Arabic under the title *Turathuna al-Ruh: Min Bedayat al-Tarikh ila al-Adyan al-Mu'aserah* (2011). In 2006, Professor Bushrui and David Cadman edited the *Selected Speeches and Articles of His Royal Highness the Prince of Wales* (2006), which was then translated to Arabic under the title *Sahib al Samou al Malaki Al-Amir Charles Yatahaddath* (2010).

JAMES M. MALARKEY is a specialist on Middle Eastern and North African affairs. The Chair of Humanities and General Education at Antioch University McGregor, Malarkey has taught Anthropology at Antioch College, Cultural Studies at the American University of Beirut, Linguistics at the University of Constantine, Algeria, as well as World Classics at Antioch University McGregor.